Joseph O'Connor

was born in Dublin in 1963. His debut novel, *Cowboys and Indians* was shortlisted for the Whitbread Prize, and his first collection of short stories, *True Believers*, received widespread critical acclaim. In addition, he has written film and television scripts, journalism and a biography of the Irish poet Charles Donnelly, *Even the Olives are Bleeding*. His work has received a number of prizes, including the Hennessy New Irish Writer of the Year Award, the *Time Out* Magazine Travel Writing Prize and the 1993 Macaulay Fellowship of the Irish Arts Council.

From the reviews of *Desperadoes*:

'*Desperadoes* is a swift-moving, richly eventful account. This is a very entertaining novel. It is also a generously humane one.'
Sunday Times

'O'Connor is unusual in being a novelist of deeply serious intentions who makes a virtue of accessibility. He interleaves his Nicaraguan scenes with a sequence of flashbacks which describe, in tender and regretful detail, the complete progress of Frank and Eleanor's courtship, marriage and slow decline. *Desperadoes* is generous and episodic.'
London Review of Books

'O'Connor writes each scene like a film script with a great sound track.'
The Times

'O'Connor's achievement is to incorporate sex, guns and rock 'n' roll into the Conrad tradition without losing fluency or conviction.'
Arena

'O'Connor writes with aplomb and experience . . . you'll laugh and cry at the same time, but you won't be able to put it down.'
Elle

Further reviews overleaf

'O'Connor's portrait of culture at cross-purposes is hilarious, the stuff of gentle farce, and his eye for the absurdities is splendid. There is more to the book than broad humour . . . O'Connor has a rare sensitivity. His is a sympathy that never fails to move.'
Mail on Sunday

'O'Connor is a marvellous writer and *Desperadoes* is a beautifully crafted novel . . . A strong, sensitive book filled with huge energy.'
Good Housekeeping

'An enjoyable adventure into the chaotic heart of Nicaragua, filtered through an Irish mist.'
Observer

ALSO BY JOSEPH O'CONNOR

Fiction

Cowboys and Indians
True Believers
The Salesman

Non-Fiction

Even the Olives are Bleeding
The Secret World of the Irish Male
The Irish Male at Home and Abroad
Sweet Liberty: Travels in Irish America

Drama

Red Roses and Petrol
The Weeping of Angels

Screenplays

A Stone of the Heart
The Way Home
Ailsa

JOSEPH O'CONNOR

Desperadoes

Flamingo
An Imprint of HarperCollins*Publishers*

Flamingo
An Imprint of HarperCollins*Publishers*
77–85 Fulham Palace Road,
Hammersmith, London W6 8JB

Published by Flamingo 1995
9 8 7 6 5

First published in Great Britain by
Flamingo an Imprint of HarperCollins*Publishers* 1994

Author photograph by Jerry Bauer

ISBN 0 00 654697 8

Set in Linotron Bembo

Printed and bound in Great Britain by
Omnia Books Ltd, Glasgow

Grateful acknowledgement is made to Sean O'Connor,
Kevin Holohan and to the Tyrone Guthrie Centre at Annaghmakerrig,
County Monaghan, Ireland, where part of this novel was written.

For Marie

1

Managua, Nicaragua, July 1, 1985

WHEN THE DARKNESS came down on the third night Frank Little began to get scared again.

Scared of robbers and vicious insects, of food poisoning, of ghosts. Scared of not being able to speak to the natives. Scared of looking like an outsider to the men with guns at the street corner by the Cine Dorado. Scared of diarrhoea and water rationing and scorpions. Scared of the street map and of knowing nothing. Scared of having a heart attack. Scared of being fat and breathless and tired. Scared of being alone and middle-aged. Scared, above all, of sleep.

Not that you could have called it sleep. When the night oozed down over Managua the darkness seemed to hum, and all Frank could do was lie on the bunk in his *pensión*, hot, naked, smeared in mosquito cream, feeling like a grease-basted bird in an oven, praying, swigging mouthfuls of warm duty free gin, inhaling the smell of his sweat, waiting for the light that would eventually return and make things seem almost comprehensible again.

For three nights he had sweated in his tiny room, wishing to Christ for the sound of the rain, for the splash and smack of rain on the corrugated iron roof. He had tried to read the newspapers, and tried to write letters. He had waited for the blood-coloured sun to rise out of the sludge of Lake Managua. Only then had he slept. Only when the room was bright with pink light had he closed his eyes and surrendered to the nightmares which he knew would be waiting for him.

On the fourth morning he had woken early, disturbed by the insistent rhythms of drills and hammers, pickaxes and saws. Waking up in Managua, he thought, was like waking up in the

9

fucking ark. He lay very still, listening to the noises of building, trying to remain calm although he wanted to open his mouth and scream. These people got up too damn early. You just couldn't trust them at all.

He got up. He washed himself quickly and shaved with the cold yellow water. He put on shorts and a sports shirt. The *Señora* brought him coffee in the courtyard. It was bitter and black. He smoked two cigarettes and then went up to the plaza.

By eight o'clock the heat was already beginning to rise. He bought a week-old *International Herald Tribune* and sat down outside one of the *cantinas*. He sipped his Fanta orange and stared across the granite swelter of the Plaza Carlos Fonseca. He hated this town, the way most people can only hate another human being. He loathed it, from the Aeroflot office all the way down to the Barrio Monseñor Lescano, from the *Ministerio del Interior* across to the ruined cathedral with the tattered red and black flag dangling from the steeple. This town was shitsville, Frank Little thought. It was one of God's out-takes.

By the time the church clock struck nine the white stone floor of the plaza was sucking the heat into itself. He opened his guidebook, slapping away the zizzing mosquitos. He tried to read a page but could not concentrate. The light of the day was silver, dazzlingly painful. A skinny black dog lay panting on its back by the fountain. The water babbled against the stone.

A gang of blond teenagers came strolling into the plaza, some of them carrying guitars, all of them wearing identical T-shirts. They sat down in a ragged circle by the *gaseosa* stand. '¡VIVA LA REVOLUCION!' the T-shirts said, '¡OBREROS Y CAMPESINOS AL PODER!' Frank had seen these T-shirts before. You could buy them almost anywhere in the city. They cost five dollars.

The kids were drinking Cokes and singing '*La Bamba*', alternating the Spanish words with the lyrics of 'Twist and Shout'. They laughed and whistled, then one by one they stood up and began to dance, hugging each other, whooping, throwing their hats in the air. Americans, he thought. You could spot Americans anywhere.

The plaza was alive with sound now; the surge of laughter and frantic conversation, the clank and stutter of tape-recorded salsa, the calls of the Indians selling cheap cigarettes and Taiwanese watches, above it all, the stomach-churning buzz of pneumatic drills and jackhammers.

The heat was burning his face, stinging his forehead and the crown of his bald scalp. He opened a tube of sunblock and smeared some over his wet flesh. His fingers were soaked with sweat. His shirt was already sticking to his back. Fuck, fuck, *fuck*, thought Frank Little. What the fuck am I doing here?

He closed his eyes and wished that Smokes would show up. He thought, just for a moment, about the face of his dead son. He said the words, under his breath. 'My son is dead,' he whispered. He said the words to check that they were true.

'American?' said the voice. 'You want cigarettes today?'

When he opened his eyes the light blazed. A tall, middle-aged Indian with a downturned mouth was standing in front of him, holding a wooden tray. The tray was stacked with beaded bracelets, fluffy toy animals, faded postcards, packets of cigarettes.

'*¿Yanqui, sí?*'

'Irish,' Frank said.

'*¿Dónde?*'

'Ireland. You know, Ireland? Near England?'

The Indian wrinkled his nose. He picked up a pack of Marlboro Lights and offered it.

'Three dollars,' he murmured.

'No,' Frank said, 'I'll pay you in *córdobas*.'

The Indian sighed and looked disappointed. He reached into his poncho and pulled out a pocket calculator, holding it in front of himself and beginning to tap at the buttons.

'*Mil novecientas córdobas*,' he said, then. He took a pencil from behind his ear and wrote '1900' on the paper tablecloth.

'They were only fifteen hundred on Tuesday,' Frank said.

The Indian shrugged and looked away. '*Mira, hombre*,' he said, 'this revolution is a motherfucker for money.' Frank took a stack of *córdoba* bills from his wallet. The Indian smiled as he pocketed them. He pointed to his own face.

'*Hermano*, you are lucky here,' he said, 'in the eyes.'

Frank allowed himself a laugh. 'Appearances don't count for much,' he said, but the Indian didn't seem to understand. 'Yes' – the Indian grinned – 'very lucky in the eyes.' He saluted, then walked quickly away, weaving around the tables, hooting and whistling at the passing *turistas*.

Another hour went by with no sign of Smokes. Frank felt himself beginning to panic. Jesus, he thought, if the kid's been in an accident or something. He knew nobody else in this shitty town, nobody at all except this one friend of his dead son. His sunglasses slipped off his moist face and fell on the table. He picked them up and opened his guidebook again.

'Managua,' it announced, 'is a place without a heart.' That was certainly true. In 1972, the introduction said, an earthquake had devastated the centre of the city. An earthquake with very good taste, as far as Frank was concerned. There was nothing here now, just a flattened, ruined sprawl of shanty towns and shacks and crushed office blocks with crumbled facades, laying bare the crippled metal skeletons beneath. The only buildings breaking into the skyline were the cathedral, the Imperial Hotel and the Bank of America. That told you something, Frank reckoned. It told you whose side God was on when the chips were down.

Every single person in this nasty little rash of a town was so much wiser than him. That was what hurt the most. He knew it, knew there was nothing he could do about it, but the knowledge still drove him crazy with frustrated anger. The taxi drivers cruising the Gringolandia highway, the old women pleading to buy dollars outside the empty supermarkets, the teenage girls tramping up and down outside the Imperial Hotel in miniskirts and thigh boots, every single one of them was on to a score. Everyone in this town had a price, and that really did get to him. They all knew something that he didn't know. You could see it in their eyes, if you had eyes to see these things. You could see it, he thought, in the way that people looked at you.

He ordered an ice cream and took a runny mouthful. It was good. He held the steel bowl against his aching forehead and called for another Fanta. He closed his eyes again and tried to locate some part of his mind that felt controlled. Hold it in, he thought, hold it *in*. Whatever you do, just hold it all in.

When his drink came, he plucked an ice cube from the glass and swallowed it whole. Smokes had warned him not to do this. Smokes had told him the water contained weird little octopus-shaped microbes that would corkscrew into your gut and kick seven shades of shit out of your enzymes. But just at that moment Frank did not care. He swallowed three Lomotils and a couple of malaria tablets, took another ice cube and dropped it with a delicious shudder down his back. He lit a cigarette. Things seemed almost tolerable now. He didn't have to like this town, after all. That was something to be grateful for and these days you couldn't afford to be particular.

It was Monday morning. It was a week to the day since the telephone call had come. The morning had been fine and he had been in the garden, smoking a cigarette. Veronica had come to the kitchen door and beckoned him inside to take a telephone call. A woman's voice, a soft Cork accent. He had written down her number and called her straight back. He'd been sure it was some kind of horrible sick joke. But the woman had answered the telephone after just one ring. 'I'm afraid it's true, Mr Little,' she said, 'your son has been killed over there. We don't know what happened yet. It seems they have some kind of war going on. It's really a matter for Foreign Affairs now.'

Now it was Monday morning again. Eleanor would arrive on tomorrow's Aeroflot from Shannon. She would be calm. She would be composed and efficient. And she would be talkative, in the same way that had irritated him so much when they had been married. She would have changed, of course, in the couple of years since he had seen her, but she would still be the kind of woman to whom talk comes easily. They would be polite to each other. They would not waste time on anything else. They would go to the hospital and identify the body. They would look at the dead body of their only son, and they would identify it. Then the authorities would sign the papers, and Frank and Eleanor would bring their son's body home to Ireland. The funeral would be on Wednesday week in Dublin. It would be small. There would be beer and sandwiches afterwards. Eleanor would look after the sandwiches. She was the kind of woman who talked a lot, and the kind of woman who could be trusted to look after sandwiches.

He had no time to mourn and no time to get upset. These were not options. The time would come for these things, but the time was not right now. He had no time to think about what had happened to his only son, whatever weird madness he had got caught up in, no time to worry about seeing his wife again.

Making sense of things could come later. Just now he had to hold things in, pray to Christ not to lose control. It was not pleasant, but he could put up with it. Sometimes in life you had to accept things. Sometimes you had to be a man. There were times, he thought, when you owed at least that to people.

Suddenly he saw Smokes Morrison approach from the side of the Cine Dorado. Smokes loped across the white stone plaza in blue jeans and a black vest, swinging his long arms as if he couldn't care less, bounding along with the breathtaking confidence possessed only by Americans in other people's countries. He stopped at the fountain and ducked his head into the bowl, right under the water, coming up with a splutter and a shake of his long dirty blond hair. The Indians pointed and laughed at him. One of them tapped his forehead and pulled a crazy face. But Smokes Morrison didn't even look. He just kept walking, swinging those lanky arms, pushing his wet hair back behind his ears, oblivious to anything that might have bothered somebody else.

'Yo, Franklin,' Smokes said, '¿qué pasa?'

'You're two hours late,' Frank said, 'and I told you not to call me that.'

Smokes had pale skin, a slightly upturned nose, wide childish eyes that were a little too large for his face. He lifted the chair, turned it, sat down, his tattooed arms crossed on the backrest.

'Just been rapping with Nuñez's man, Franklin,' he said. 'He got back down from the war zone last night.'

'And how is his majesty?' Frank murmured. 'Is he going to grant me an audience?'

Smokes sighed. 'The guy's gotta revolution to run, Frank. He ain't a social worker.'

'Yeah, surprise me. Do you want a beer or what?'

Smokes nodded. He slicked back his hair, pulled a pair of mirrored blue sunglasses from his hip pocket and slipped them on. Then he began to laugh.

'The *guerrilleros* attacked again while he was up there. Man, he was out of the joint faster than a hot snot from a headbanger's nose.'

'I bet,' Frank said. 'These penpushers never have any balls.'

Smokes leaned forward, looking serious.

'He says he got to talk to a few of the brass up there. For the enquiry, you know? Johnny shouldna been up there, Franklin. *Extranjeros* ain't supposed to be in the war zone. Nuñez's homeboy says the *Commandante* is real pissed about it.'

'Oh dear,' Frank said, 'stop the bloody world.'

The waiter brought two beers to the table. He looked at Smokes as if he wouldn't exactly want his daughter to marry him. He plucked an opener from his waistcoat pocket and briskly uncapped the bottles, poured the beers, emptied the ashtray on to the ground and silently took the banknotes from the saucer where Frank had placed them.

'Eleanor's definitely gonna bring the dental records, right?' Smokes said. 'Nuñez told his man that'd be important.'

'Yes, yes.' Frank sighed. 'I don't see why these penpushers have to invent problems.'

Smokes took off his sunglasses. He peered at Frank with questioning eyes.

'Well, God,' Frank said, 'he was our son, Smokes. We should know what he looks like, shouldn't we?'

Smokes swallowed hard and tried to smile. 'It's just formal shit, Franklin,' he muttered. 'You got a lot of formal shit when you're talking about a place like this.'

They sat at the table, not talking at all for some minutes. Frank thought of Eleanor's voice on the telephone, when he had called to tell her the news. It was a steady voice. It was relaxed. It was the kind of voice that could sell ice cream to the Eskimos.

He had told her what the man from Foreign Affairs had said. The body would not be allowed to leave Nicaraguan territory until it had been formally identified by a member of the family. That was the rule, apparently, and it was just not up for discussion. Were there any brothers or sisters? No? Well, in that case, one of the parents would have to make the journey.

They had argued about this, of course. Eleanor had wanted to go. She'd suggested that Frank stay behind and make the arrangements, but Frank had insisted this was ridiculous, that these Third World places were not safe for a middle-aged woman on her own. These Third World places were full of people who'd slit your throat for a five dollar bill and not think twice about doing it. 'Do you never read a paper?' he asked her. 'It's shagging chaos over there. They're crazier than a barrel of monkeys over there.'

Then Eleanor had said she was perfectly well able to look after herself, and if he was going to use that kind of language there was nothing else to be said on the subject.

'Don't start your nonsense,' he told her. 'I'm going, and I want no palaver about it.'

'You're not,' she said. 'Frank Little, *I'm* going, and if you try to stop me, there'll be trouble.'

In the Plaza Carlos Fonseca, Smokes looked up and sighed. 'There was no need for you both to come.'

'Well, I wouldn't let her come on her own,' Frank snapped. 'No matter about anything else, it wouldn't be right, a woman on her own in a God-forsaken awful dump like this.'

'We would've taken care of her, man. Cherry and me.'

'He was my son too,' Frank said. 'Some people seem to forget that.'

'I know, Franklin. I didn't mean it that way, babes.'

Frank tried to swallow his anger. 'A lump of fucking meat.' He nodded. 'That's all he is to these people.' He raised his glass and drained it, then lit a cigarette and sucked hard. Smokes smiled at him sadly.

'I'm just feeling a bit tense.' Frank shrugged. 'It's just the heat, son. It's nothing personal.'

Smokes stared into his empty glass. He picked it up and waved it gently from side to side in a way that Frank found strangely irritating. Smokes caught his eye again. He put his glass down and his fingers drummed lightly on the rim.

Frank looked at his watch. 'I should phone Veronica,' he said. 'She'll be fretting.'

Smokes shook his head. 'Lines to Europe are still down, Franklin. I checked again this morning.'

'Fuck sake.' Frank sighed. 'Some kip this is. You can't even make a call.'

'It's the war, man. It ain't their fault. The Contras blew the exchange in Matagalpa.'

Frank said nothing. He felt his heart thud against his ribs. A dull ache flowered in the pit of his stomach. His eyes scanned the plaza. A young man and woman were standing by the fountain kissing, pressing their bodies hard against each other. The man was holding the young woman's hands behind her back. Frank

watched them, and the heat made his eyes smart. His head was already beginning to pound.

'You feel like a drive, man?' Smokes said brightly. 'It's cooler outside the city. Come on. I got Claudette parked down by the Telcor. Let's just split for a few hours.'

'What's there to see?' Frank said. 'The countryside is the bloody countryside, no matter where you are.'

Smokes stood up and stretched.

'Geography is everything, Franklin,' he said. 'I mean, it ain't exactly Vegas, but it does have its moments.'

The music had started up again now. In the far corner of the plaza the American kids were jiving with each other. Someone was playing a flute. Someone else was playing a bongo drum. The kids danced over to the fountain and formed a ring around it, all of them laughing and singing.

> Para bailar la Bamba,
> Para bailar la Bamba,
> Se necesita una poca de gracia,
> Una poca de gracia para mí, para tí,
> Ay arriba, arriba,
> Arriba iré, por tí seré . . .

And then, with a sudden jolt, the chugging roar of the pneumatic drills burst out again. The table vibrated. The empty glasses danced. The waiter threw down his tray and stuck his fingers in his ears. Frank put his hands to his hot wet face.

'Let's go then,' he shouted. 'Let's go for this drive before I just die of fucking laughter.'

2

Dublin

AFTER SHE HAD SCRUBBED the kitchen floor, Eleanor Little did the ironing and watered the Mother-in-Law's Tongue. Then she made a pot of tea, put her feet up and switched on 'Coffee Time' on the BBC. She liked Philip and Sally, the handsome young couple who presented 'Coffee Time'. She felt oddly close to them. They were married to each other, in real life, as they sometimes put it. Philip had been married before, to another woman, but now he was married to Sally and they seemed very happy together. Sometimes they talked about their children. They had twins. But this morning they did not talk about the twins. This morning they talked about hysterectomies.

She turned off the television and telephoned the church again. The arrangements were coming along nicely, Father Rogan said. He assured her that everything was in hand, wished her God speed with the journey, told her that he would be remembering her at Mass every morning until she returned next week with poor Johnny. He sounded nice, as he always did, but he seemed to be in a hurry to get off the phone.

'I won't keep you now, love,' he said. 'You'll have a million things to do, I'm sure. God bless now.'

After she got out of the bath she found herself wandering around the house in her dressing gown. The house was clean now. The carpets were hoovered and the windows were absolutely spotless. It was a good house when it was bright, she thought. If anything happened while she was away, and if the neighbours had to come in, they wouldn't find anything out of place. Would the woman come in by herself, she wondered, or would she send in her husband, that little man with the toothbrush moustache who always sang Gilbert and Sullivan at parties? She did not like the little man with the moustache. He was far too delighted with himself. She did not like the way he went on. Perhaps, she mused, they might both come in together, if anything went wrong. Perhaps they would root around the place and open drawers and make love in her bed? But of course not. She blushed. This was the south side, after all. This was not Sean O'Casey. There were certain things you could just take for granted.

The Mass cards were lined up along the mantelpiece, all black borders and saintly smiles. She had the bottles in already, for afterwards. People would expect to be asked back to the house. There were two bottles of whisky and three crates of beer. There was gin and mineral water, tonic and soda, Coca-Cola for the nephews and the niece. There was sherry and port, and a litre bottle of Australian Chardonnay which had been on special offer in the Merrion Centre branch of Quinnsworth. There were peanuts and crisps, boxes of sweets, bars of chocolate. There was a joint of beef in the freezer, with packets of frozen peas and a family-size carton of cauliflower cheese. There was a side of salmon. People would want to come back to the house. You could not just give people a sandwich.

There was the question of Frank, of course. Would he expect to be let bring that woman back with him? Would he even want to come himself? Well, she would not dwell on that now. She would wait, and she would think about the right way to approach things.

She unlocked the door of the back bedroom and went in. Her son's room smelt of nicotine and aftershave. Some of his posters were still up on the walls. One said 'SEX PISTOLS' in black letters that looked as if they had been cut out of newspaper headlines. Another showed a group of surly-looking fellows in leather jackets. 'THE CLASH' it said. 'SANDINISTA'. A third poster showed a sneering young woman with blue lipstick and too much mascara. When she opened his drawer she found a pair of underpants and a coffee cup full of green and orange mould. His books were stacked in heaps on the floor. His paint-stained dungarees lay folded over the radiator. A dollar bill was glued to the wall over his bed. There were clean squares on the walls where his posters and photographs had been. There were strips of sellotape and buds of Blu-Tack around the edges of the squares.

She took his grey suit out of the wardrobe. In the breast pocket she found a beer mat with a telephone number scribbled on it, and a name that she could not read. She wondered whether to take the suit with her. It wouldn't be right, she thought, to bury a handsome young man in a big brown shroud. But then there was the nature of the injuries to consider. The man from Foreign Affairs had told her to be prepared for the worst. Disfigurement had come into it, apparently, burns of various kinds. And in that heat, too, over there in Nicaragua. Perhaps an open coffin would not be on the cards. People's feelings had to be taken into account. She looked at herself in the wardrobe mirror. She held the suit close to her body, just for a moment, then put it carefully back in the wardrobe.

In the front room she checked that the windows were closed and locked, that the heat was off, that the alarm was on. She noticed the bottle of Bailey's Irish Cream on top of the piano. One of her students had given it to her for Christmas, but she had never opened it. She looked hard at the bottle. It would have been so nice to have a drink. For an instant she was tempted, she had to admit it. But then she closed her eyes and said her prayer and the surge of temptation simply faded away.

She sat down at the piano and played a few bars of a Chopin Polonaise. Chopin had written it in the monastery at Valdemosa, in Mallorca, when he was dying. She and Frank had been there once, after things had got so bad between them. She could not remember much about the way it had looked. But she could remember the smell of the oranges coming down from the orchards on the hills. It was a heavy smell and it lingered like cheap perfume. She let the sound of the sad minor chords sweep through the room. She enjoyed the magic of them, their drama and promise. But her fingers were aching from scrubbing the kitchen floor, and, anyway, it was too sturdy a piece to be wholly melancholic.

In the kitchen she boiled the kettle, but she really didn't feel like drinking more tea. She scooped the leftover chicken casserole from the pot on the cooker and into a Tupperware box. She put the box into the freezer.

She found herself thinking about Frank's voice on the telephone, on the Monday morning when he had called to tell her the news. How very strong he had sounded, she remembered. She had not been able to bring herself to cry because she was afraid of what he would say to her. Frank had always hated tears. She knew that. But imagine, after all these years, still being afraid of what he would think of her. The authorities over there had said one of the parents would have to come to their country and identify the corpse – 'corpse', they had called him – before Johnny could be brought back to Ireland. When Frank had told her that he would go, they'd had a bit of a row. Well, it was ridiculous, a man of Frank's age in a country like that by himself. And with his heart too. Typical man, she thought, not an ounce of bloody sense, just wants to play the hero.

She peered through the lace curtain. When she was sure that the neighbours were watching, Eleanor Little picked up her suitcase, left her house, locked the front door, walked very calmly to the gate and waited for the taxi to come.

It was one of Frank's taxis. It was late. Of course.

3

Claudette

CLAUDETTE WAS MAYBE fifteen feet long, with a cracked windscreen, a second-hand radio, and an engine held together with elastic bands and optimism. 'A camper van,' Smokes cackled, 'and hey, Franklin, they don't come camper than Claudette.'

Now that Smokes had hosed her down and scrubbed off the grime, Frank could see what he'd meant. Claudette's sides were painted with elongated silver and gold spirals, rising blue suns, huge surfboards, electric guitars, red and black Sandinista flags, psychedelic Che Guevaras and multicoloured peace symbols. A purple and green shooting star trailed a comet of sparks all across the back doors. The tyres were bright red and yellow and the hubcaps were daubed with black bolts of lightning. Two surfboards were strapped to the roof rack. One was electric blue, the other white, with a bikini-clad Vargas girl draped languidly along it. Across the bonnet were some fat golden words. *LOS DESPERADOS DE AMOR: THE LAST REBELS OF ROCK AND ROLL.* Underneath these were some smaller words, also in gold: *WEDDINGS, BAR MITZVAHS, RIOTS: TEL SMOKES, MANAGUA 2147.*

'Sweet Jesus Christ on a bike, son.' Frank laughed. 'I've seen better motors in scrapyards.'

Claudette backfired dramatically as they rumbled across the Plaza Diecinueve du Julio. Hearing the bang, the young sentry on duty outside the Palacio yanked out his pistol and stepped forward into firing position. Smokes hit the horn hard and laughed, slamming his foot down on the accelerator. Claudette creaked and moaned like a battered old ship in a storm. When she turned left she rattled. When she straightened up again she churned her gears and coughed.

'Fuck me,' Frank said, 'I don't know how you'd drive a bone-shaker like this.'

Smokes shook his head. 'Trouble with you, Franklin' – he grinned – 'you got no individuality, babes.'

'Don't call me Franklin.'

Claudette's engine gave a sudden squeak and started to vibrate. Smokes jammed on the brakes, reversed ten feet, then started up again. 'You gotta do that sometimes,' he explained. 'She gets temperamental.'

Frank grabbed hold of the dashboard. He said Claudette was the worst pile of sawdust and cinders he'd ever seen. 'And I've been in the taxi game for thirty years.' He chuckled. 'Believe me, son, I've seen a few first-rate bangers in my time.'

'You're a cab driver, Franklin?'

Frank nodded. 'Well, I own the company now, so I don't do that much driving. I have heart problems. There's talk of a by-pass.'

'So what's that like, Franklin? Cab driving?'

Frank shrugged. 'Ah, it's a mug's game now. I don't know how a young man would do it. Costs you maybe forty grand to cover a plate. Then you have your overheads, and you're working with a bad element. Drunks, bloody prostitutes, you name it.'

'Like being a priest.' Smokes laughed. 'People tell you their problems, right?'

'Oh, I don't know about that. Some priest I'd make.'

They drove on, picking up a little speed.

'And you, Smokes?' Frank said. 'How do you knock it out? Do you make anything from the music?'

Smokes chortled as he lit up a cigarette. 'What are you, man, crazy?'

'So what do you do for a crust then?'

Smokes shrugged. 'I guess I just manage. Sometimes I do stuff for magazines back home in the States. You know, interviews, stuff like that.'

'So the band's just for the crack?'

Smokes nodded. 'Yeah, Franklin. Strictly for hysterics. And we're in a real mess now Johnny's gone. Lorenzo's been doing the vocals, but he just can't cut it.'

When they pulled up at a corner, a young boy clambered on to Claudette's bonnet to wash the windscreen. The boy was wearing shorts and a Michael Jackson T-shirt. He was very thin. Smokes said something to him in Spanish and gave him a thousand *córdoba* note. They drove on.

'So what was he like?' Frank asked. 'As a singer, I mean.'

'What? Johnny? He was good, man. I mean, no Elvis or nothing, but he had his *momentitos*.'

'Not like me so,' Frank smiled. 'Put the crows to shame.'

'Yeah, Franklin? I thought Johnny told me you were a crooner.'

'Oh, I hadn't a bad voice when I was younger.' He held up a cigarette. 'Then I took up these coffin nails.'

'And you were a drummer too, right Franklin? I thought Johnny told me his old man was a drummer.'

Frank felt his face flush. 'No, no,' he said, 'that was years ago, when I was just a kid.'

Smokes raised his eyebrows. 'I think you're being *modesto, hombre*.'

'Not at all. Well, I was in this little skiffle group, you know, just me and some fellows on the street. Skiffle was the thing then. Lonnie Donegan. People like that.'

'I never heard of Lonnie Donegan, Franklin.'

'No,' Frank said. 'Well, he was going years ago.'

They drove on in silence until the town began to fade and the suburbs came into view. There were long lines of opulent houses, with dogs and armed guards in uniform outside their steel gates. Most of the houses had swimming pools. Some had sleek European cars in their driveways. Claudette crossed the *periferico*, and Managua began to give way to the open country. The fields were a mosaic of vivid colours; yellow and blue, deep red and gold. Twisted olive trees marked out their boundaries; maize plants and yucca and low, broad coffee bushes filled the spaces in between.

'And I was a drummer,' Frank said, 'he really told you that?'

'He really did, yeah.'

'Well, the clown.' Frank laughed. 'That was neither today nor yesterday.'

The road forked and Smokes took the right-hand track. Clouds of fine dust billowed into the air. A huge hand-painted sign announced the '*COOPERATIVA RIGOBERTO LOPEZ PEREZ*'.

Smokes slowed Claudette down and began to explain the colours of the fields to Frank. Gold was for wheat. Black and red was for coffee, yellow for corn. A large white ranch house stood in the middle of the largest field. A red and black flag was flying from the balcony and on the rooftop an old-fashioned black cannon jutted out in the direction of the city. Women were working in the fields around the house, bent double, or on their knees, rifles strapped across their backs.

When they saw Claudette, the women in the fields began to laugh and wave. Smokes honked the horn and let out his high-pitched girlish giggle.

'God help them,' Frank said, 'working in that heat.'

Smokes selected a cassette from the dashboard and rammed it into the stereo. 'Don't be such a *gringo*, man,' he said. 'These people are tough as shit.'

The brattish chirp of Eddie Cochran singing 'Summertime Blues' came whooping out of the speakers. Smokes turned up the volume.

'My God.' Frank laughed. 'Is that stuff still in?'

'So far in, Franklin, it's comin' out the other side.'

Smokes began to sing along with the music, thumping the steering wheel as he sang. Frank stared out at the unrolling countryside. The small stone walls reminded him of the west of Ireland. He said this to Smokes, but Smokes just kept on singing, shaking his head from side to side, doowopping frantically when he didn't know the words. Smokes was an absolutely dreadful singer. His voice was a tuneless and drab monotone. He sounded like Bob Dylan after a bad night on the town.

'Jesus,' Frank said, 'I'd stick to the drums if I was you, son.'

'Yeah.' Smokes grinned. 'Tell you the truth, man, I don't even like rock and roll so much. I want to play salsa, you know, but Lorenzo and Guapo never let me.'

Frank looked at Smokes's long thin hands, as they clapped against the fur-covered steering wheel. He felt the air rush in through the open window against his hot moist face. For the first time in four days he felt the knot in his stomach begin to unravel.

'And he told you I was a drummer?' he said. 'God, now, that's a good one. I'll never see those days again.'

'He said you were hot, man. He said Ringo Starr fucked Charlie Watts in an airplane rest-room and you, Franklin, were their love child.'

Frank slapped his arm.

'Go away out of that, you tinker. A whole lot of water's been passed since then, and that's the bloody truth.'

The flight to London was pleasant enough. She got the coach from Gatwick Airport into the city. It was a very cold day for the first of July. A light drizzle was falling over the stern greyness of Kensington. The taxi driver didn't know where the Nicaraguan Embassy was, but he said he was sure he could find it.

As they drove through the grey streets she found herself remembering her honeymoon. That was the first time she had ever been to London. It was the first time she had been out of Ireland. She remembered the nights they had gone dancing, the long, cold afternoons sitting in coffee bars in Soho, holding hands. She smiled as she thought back to the old days. They had been so happy together during those ten cold days in London. There had been signs up all over the city with the words 'Take Courage' written on them. She and Frank had thought these signs were something to do with religion, but they were actually advertisements for beer. They had laughed about it when they had found out the truth. She remembered that, for some odd reason. She remembered the way he used to laugh.

When the taxi turned on to Kensington Gore the driver stopped to ask a policeman for directions. The policeman took off his cap and scratched his head. He switched on his radio and spoke into it, but he couldn't help them, he said. He had never come across an embassy for Nicaragua. They drove around for a while, and after a time the taxi driver began to curse with impatience.

When they eventually found the embassy, a beautiful dark-eyed woman in her early twenties opened the door. She was wearing jeans and a black T-shirt. She had a thin purple scar across her forehead. She spoke English with an American accent. She examined Eleanor's passport very carefully. Then she gave her a visa, a map of Managua, and a pamphlet about the historic achievements of the Nicaraguan revolution.

'*Vaya con Dios*,' the young woman said. 'Go with God.'

'Oh, thank you, dear,' Eleanor replied. 'Go with God, yourself.'

By the time she got out to Heathrow they were calling her name over the intercom.

They parked Claudette by the side of the track and walked slowly down towards the lake. The sand was very fine, the colour of milky tea. Their feet crunched on tiny brittle shells as they walked. The sun had burned the morning haze out of the sky and the day was blazingly hot now. Smokes pulled off his T-shirt and wiped his face with it. He had a small tattoo on his chest, a scarlet heart with the words 'Forever A Rebel' underneath.

'Where is this?' Frank asked him. 'Where are we now?'

Smokes pulled a bottle of water from his bag, took a slurp and gasped. 'This is Xiloa, Franklin. This is, you know, where people come at the weekend?'

Long lines of straw umbrellas spiralled around a two-storey mock Greek building in marble. There were empty stalls in front of the building, and there was a line of portable public toilets. A tattered bandstand with no floorboards stood down by the lake's edge. Two men were working in the bandstand, submerged in the foundations so that only their heads were visible. They had a radio playing loud salsa music; the sound echoed against the water.

'See all this, Franklin,' Smokes said, making a sweep with his hand. 'Everything here, two hundred acres. All the General's personal patch before the revolution. The whole shooting gallery.'

Frank sighed. 'Don't start all that again, Smokes, for Jesus' sake.'

Smokes grinned smugly. 'Just clueing you in, babes. Just clueing you in, that's all.'

They walked on, trudging over the shells and bracken. The water was light green, but very clear and still. A fat red fish jumped with a splash, gobbled at a firefly and plunged again. They walked for half an hour, saying nothing at all, around the edge of the lake to where the eucalyptus trees stood in the shade of the mountain. They went deeper into the woods then, pushing through webs of fern and ivy, enjoying the shadows and the foddery smell of vegetation. They stopped at a tiny inlet to stare at a rusted burnt-out Cadillac which lay with its fender submerged in the glossy water. They both lit cigarettes and gazed at the shattered car, listening to the sound of the larks.

'So Frank,' Smokes said suddenly, 'I guess I should ask you what Eleanor's like?'

A blush heated Frank's neck. 'Oh well, we don't see much of each other these days. Haven't for a few years. We fell out, you see.'

Smokes nodded. 'Yeah, Johnny told me.'

'Did he now? What did he say?'

Smokes sat down on a fallen spruce trunk and began to pick at the bark with his fingers. 'Not much I guess.' He shrugged. 'Just, you know, it wasn't exactly Bogie and Bacall.'

'No,' Frank said. 'No, it certainly wasn't.'

'He told me you guys fought, Franklin. He told me you hadn't spoken in a while. I guess he was upset about it.'

'I wasn't mad about it myself.'

'No, Franklin. I'm sure, man.'

'Sometimes people seem to bloody forget that. It was no picnic for me either.'

A gentle breeze rolled in from the lake, making the leaves fidget in the trees around them.

'She gives piano lessons anyway,' Frank said, not looking at him. 'That's where the real music comes from in our family.'

Smokes nodded. 'And you're married again now, right?'

He felt himself become more uneasy. 'Well,' he said, 'I'm with Veronica, but we're not officially married. You can't in Ireland. There isn't divorce. I suppose he told you that too.'

'Yeah, I heard that. But, hey, it's just a piece of paper, right?'

'Well, no son, it's not. But the law of the land is the law, you know?'

Smokes laughed. 'It's like I told you, Franklin. Geography is every damn thing.'

They walked on, emerging from the woods and into the warm yellow light. A young woman was swimming in the lake now, with solid, rhythmic strokes. A trail of white water formed behind her as she moved steadily towards the tiny island, which was overgrown with thick-leafed trees. On the far shore the two workmen were sitting on the edge of the bandstand, eating their lunch and watching her.

'So,' Frank said, 'and what about you and this Cherry one?'

'Oh, it's fine, I guess.' Smokes shrugged. He stopped walking and smiled. 'She'd like it to be an opera by Puccini, you know, Franklin? She'd like it to be love, love, love. But it ain't too serious really.'

They sat on a long wooden bench and stared out over the lake. Squealing grey birds whirled around in the air, swooping down at the water and soaring back into the trees with wriggling fish in their beaks. The young woman had reached the island now. She got out of the water and stretched her arms. She was naked. Smokes giggled.

'Hey, you feel like a swim today, Franklin?'

'I've no togs.'

'She don't either, man. Take a dip. I won't look if you're feeling bashful.'

Frank shook his head. He sat down on a rock and lit a cigarette, laughing to himself.

'I never learnt to swim until Johnny did,' he said. 'There was a swimming pool in his school, you see, and this little knacker pushed him in one day. Bob Brady, the kid's name was. Well, I went down to the school, you know, to complain, and the PE teacher turned out to be a decent skin; he used to play rugby for Ireland, actually. We got nattering and he said they were having lessons for parents. So I started to go down then. It was just one of the nights during the week. Johnny would come down with me, you see. He used to laugh at me, because the chlorine would be making my eyes stream. I had this big stupid float thing. Pink, it was. He used to give me an awful slagging over it.'

The water was smooth and the light a little softer now, with butter-coloured clouds moving across the sky. Frank turned.

'Did he ever say anything good about us, son? About his mother and me?'

Smokes pursed his lips. He stared into the distance as though he had heard some strange sound that he was trying to locate. He sat very still and then, after a moment, he spoke.

'Yeah, Frank, course he did, man. I'll fill you in sometime. But my head's just shot to pieces right now.'

Frank nodded. 'Yes,' he said. 'Well, I just wondered. That's all.'

★   ★   ★

On the plane she sat beside a nice young Swedish woman. Eleanor could tell she was Swedish because she was wearing a baseball cap with I ♥ SWEDEN on it. Well, that alone wasn't enough, of course. She could have bought it on holiday in Sweden. Or maybe she had never been to Sweden in her life. Maybe she had a handsome lover who lived in Sweden and maybe he had sent her that baseball cap as a present. Yes. But, then again, Eleanor was sure she was Swedish. She looked so clean and healthy. She looked European anyway. She had European teeth. She just had that air of the Continental about her.

The nice young Swedish woman was skimming through a fat paperback edition of *War and Peace*. But she was turning the pages so quickly that Eleanor thought she could not have been reading it at all. Not taking it in, at any rate.

She looked at the computer screen on the wall of the aeroplane. It showed a map of the world with a white line that marked the position of the plane. There were some words too, but the words were written in Russian script, so she could not understand them. But they were halfway across the Atlantic Ocean now. She could see that. If the plane were to crash, Eleanor thought, *we would all be drowned*. They would have to get divers. The sharks might eat us. It would be on the news, and people would think it a terrible tragedy. Father Rogan would probably be interviewed about it by that nice David Hanley on the 'Morning Ireland' radio programme. He would say that it was dreadfully sad, this fine Christian woman, on her way to a far-off country to collect her son's body. Or would he? What on earth would he say about her?

'That book was a film,' she said, 'wasn't it?'

'Yes.' The Swedish woman smiled. 'Audrey Hepburn and Henry Fonda. But I do not know if Tolstoy will have approved.'

'Yes,' Eleanor said. 'People say my father used to look like him.'

'Who?' said the woman. 'Tolstoy?'

'Oh no, Henry Fonda.'

The woman nodded. Eleanor sipped her Coca-Cola and tried to think of something else to say. The hostess passed in the aisle, pushing a trolley stacked with shrink-wrapped sandwiches and vodka miniatures and tiny white plastic busts of Lenin. She smiled at Eleanor, the way only an Aeroflot employee can smile.

'You're off on holiday, is it?' Eleanor asked.

The Swedish woman laughed. She closed her book and stuffed it into the magazine pocket. Nicaragua, she said, was not the kind of place you would go for a holiday. It was too hot and too dangerous, and there was the war to think about too. She told Eleanor all about this war. It was between the government and the Contras, she said. The Contras were rebels. The Americans were on the side of the rebels and everyone else was on the side of the government. She herself was a dentist.

'I am going to pull the teeth. Of the peasants in the mountains.'

'Oh,' Eleanor said, 'that's nice for you.'

The Swedish woman pulled an ugly face and made a sudden twisting motion with her hand.

'But not so nice I think for them.' She grinned, and then she laughed out loud as though what she had said was hilarious. Her breasts moved when she laughed. They were quite small breasts, Eleanor thought, for a Swede.

'And why do *you* go to Nicaragua?' the woman asked.

Eleanor leaned towards her and whispered.

'My son died,' she said. 'Those guerrillas you were telling me about. They attacked or something. I'm not sure of the politics of it.'

'Oh no,' the Swedish woman said. Her blue eyes were suddenly very wide. She took off her glasses and gaped at Eleanor. 'Oh no. This is terrible.'

Eleanor felt almost proud, because the nice young Swedish woman seemed to be so impressed. She felt her face flush.

'Oh yes, he was there for two years. I don't really know why he went. To pick the coffee, I believe. Now, why these people can't pick their own coffee is another story, of course.'

'That's awful,' the Swedish woman said, 'that really is awful.'

'Yes, it is. But I suppose there's nothing I can do.'

Tears began to prick her eyes, but she wiped them away. 'Maybe it's God's will,' she sniffed, 'I don't know. I have to go and identify him, you know.'

'And your husband? He is coming also?'

'Frank's there already. My former husband he is. We're separated now.'

'Oh,' the Swedish woman said, 'I am sorry.'

'Yes, well, I couldn't let him come on his own all the same. I mean, you know what men are like.'

The woman smiled. She touched Eleanor's hand very gently.

'You are a brave woman,' she said.

'Oh no,' Eleanor replied. 'Oh no, dear. If I was really brave, I wouldn't have come at all.'

Night was falling again over the city.

When Smokes had dropped him back at the *pensión* and gone home, Frank felt suddenly very lonely. He drank a cup of coffee and tried to read a few pages of Frederick Forsyth. Then he changed his shirt and went out to walk in the streets for a while. It was against Smokes's advice, but he could feel another headache coming on, and he needed to be out of that tiny room with its bitter odour of dirty sheets and disinfectant. He needed to feel the air on his face. He needed to find a way of seeing things clearly, with some definition.

He walked past little shacks made of corrugated iron and cardboard, past adobe houses, their rooms suffused with the blue light of television screens. President Ortega was making another of his speeches and the people were in their houses listening to him, sometimes shouting '*Sí*' or '*No, no*' or '*Claro*' or '*Puta*'. From some houses he heard the sounds of men and women fighting; from one, he thought he heard the soft sighs of a couple making love. Old men sat on their cabin steps reading *Barricada* by the moth-filled light of the streetlamps. Strangers nodded warily when they caught his curious eye.

The air was cooler as he walked down the Gringo highway and slowly through the Barrio Martha Quezada. He turned up the steep hill that climbed towards the Prisión. Far in the distance he saw the mountain, with the huge letters FSLN picked out in white stone and seeming to shimmer in the yellow floodlights. The sight almost made him smile, because it made him think of the HOLLYWOOD sign that he had on a postcard in his office. The S stood for Sandino, that little man in the cowboy hat whose silhouette was stencilled on walls all over the city. Smokes had told him this. The FSLN used to be the bandits, but they were the government now. That was sometimes the way things went. That was the way things had been in Ireland once. He remembered his grandfather telling him about the old days. In 1916, Eamon de Valera had been condemned to death as a terrorist, but then, years later, he'd ended up being President. Frank remembered thinking how odd that was. And he remembered standing on the flyover bridge outside Belfield on the day de Valera died, looking down with his son, as President de Valera's coffin, covered in the green, white and orange flag of Ireland, was driven slowly underneath the bridge and down the dual carriageway. The cortege had moved along so slowly that the army motorcycle outriders had to keep stopping and putting their feet down on the ground to steady themselves. People around him on the bridge had been crying. Some of them had been holding little tricolour flags. It was some time in the seventies. He couldn't remember the year. It was some time before Eleanor had gone away.

At the top of the hill a group of young soldiers stood guarding the entrance to the Prisión. Most of them looked very tired. They had M-16s and Akas slung over their backs. Their olive green uniforms were ruffled and untidy. One of the soldiers was sharing around a polythene bag of apples. Another had a transistor radio which was turned up very loud. They were not listening to the President's speech. They were listening to some kind of sporting event; the frantic voice of the commentator was crackling out into the street. It was a football match perhaps, or a baseball game, but Frank did not know. It was just something else not to be sure about. He nodded at the soldiers, but they said nothing. He walked on.

He stared down over the white marble pomposity of the Imperial Hotel. It was the ugliest building he had ever seen, a vast white pyramid with fake trellises and too many windows. It was like a tinker's wedding cake. Coloured disco lights were flickering on the top floor and people were dancing. He could see them moving in the distance. He listened to the sound that the crickets made. A beautiful sound. Trilling? Was that the word? Just like the sound in the cowboy films. He walked past the Café Yerbabuena, where all the lefty tourists hung out, strumming their bloody balalaikas and singing about Joseph bloody Stalin. The Sandalistas, Smokes called them. The bleeding hearts.

Crossing the Plaza de Los Héroes y Mártires, he tried to find another memory of his son. Summer days. The tinkling sound of an ice cream van. The warm feel of sun on skin. The salt smell of beaches in Connemara, fat jellyfish oozing in the shallows. The spark and spit of dodgem cars. The sting of iodine on bloodied knees. He felt confused. Was he remembering his son's childhood or his own?

He looked at the purple sky. Eleanor was up there now. Her plane was somewhere up there, thousands of miles up in the black clouds. She would be here soon. She would be coming soon, to collect her son and to take him home.

Alone in the hot room of his *pensión*, Frank sat down on the bed. He poured some gin into a cup and drank it. He took off his trousers and his underpants. Out in the hallway, the *Señora* and her daughter were singing a sad Spanish song.

> *Nicaragua, Nicaraguita*
> *La flor más linda de mi querer*
> *Abonada con la bendita*
> *Nicaraguita, Nicaraguita*
> *Sangre de Diringen*

He held his penis in his hand, feeling it harden. Tears came into his eyes. He lay down on his side and wrapped the sheet tight around his body. He listened to the sound of his breath, to the sound of the *Señora* singing outside with her daughter.

He lay very still, waiting for the night to fall.

4

The Augusto Cesar Sandino
Memorial Airport

THE AUGUSTO CESAR SANDINO Memorial Airport consisted of
a steel scaffolding radar tower with two long wooden prefabs
in the middle of a vast flattened maize field. Dark green tanks
had been dug in at regular intervals along the edge of the lumpy
runway, and a monstrous-looking anti-aircraft gun was mounted
on top of the Departures Terminal. There were soldiers everywhere.

As Eleanor stepped through the doors of the airplane the heat
washed over her like a wave. She gasped at its touch. It was only
ten in the morning, but the heat was almost overwhelming. She
had never felt anything like it before. This was the kind of
heat that has a smell. As she crossed the tarmac she could feel it
throbbing through the soles of her shoes.

Loud orchestral music was booming from a bank of loudspeakers on top of one of the buildings. She noticed two long
wooden flagpoles. One had a blue and white flag with a blue
volcano in the centre. The other had a flag that was black and
red. She saw a long line of scarlet words painted on a hoarding.
¡REAGAN SE VA! ¡LA REVOLUCION SE QUEDA!

When she came through the Arrivals gate she felt almost carefree. It was exciting to be arriving in this strange hot place. It was
almost like being on holiday. 'Wouldn't the heat just kill you?'
she said to Ulla with a smile. A spectacularly ugly young soldier
winked and clicked his tongue as they passed. Ulla said something
in Spanish and the soldier grinned. Eleanor's heart started to
pound.

She picked him out of the crowd almost immediately. He

35

looked very tired and he had put on a little weight. His hair was thinning too, but he was still quite handsome, even in a shocking yellow sports shirt that did not really suit him at all. For some moments, he seemed not to see her. He glared at his watch and then said something to the lanky, long-haired youth who was standing beside him. He put his hands on his hips and stared impatiently around the building.

'Frank?' she called out.

Their glances met, but he did not smile. As she walked quickly towards him she noticed the way his weary eyes moved over her face, up and down her body. She felt like touching his hand, or his arm, but for some reason she did not do this. He nodded, vaguely, but did not say hello. He turned his eyes away from her. He did not seem to want to look at her face.

'This is Smokes Morrison,' he said. 'A friend of Johnny's. Smokes, this is Johnny's mother.'

'Eleanor,' she smiled, and shook the young man's hand. 'Smokes, is it? That's a queer one.'

'Yes, Mam,' Smokes mumbled. 'I'm real sorry about everything, Eleanor. We were real good friends, Johnny and me.'

She felt Frank's eyes on her again as she swallowed her tears and squeezed Smokes's hand very tightly. It was a thin expressive hand. More like a girl's hand really.

'Smokes was in this group with himself,' Frank explained. 'Himself was the singer, if you don't mind.'

'Are you an American, Smokes?' she asked.

Smokes beamed. 'As American as apple pie and Texas chain saws. I'm from New York City.'

The Swedish woman laughed, by Eleanor's side.

'Oh,' Eleanor said, 'I was neglecting my manners. This is Ulla. She's a dentist. From Sweden.'

'A dentist from Sweden,' Smokes said. 'Man, don't some people just get all the damn luck.'

Ulla laughed out loud. She liked Smokes, Eleanor could see it. And Smokes liked her too. Eleanor had an eye for these things. She knew that she was not physically beautiful herself, and this did not bother her any more. But she could recognize the expression on Smokes's face. She knew that a man can look like a simpering schoolboy if a beautiful woman is near. She recognized the look on his face. It was a look that nobody had ever given her. Nobody except Frank Little, and that had been a very long time ago.

She allowed the two young people to drift ahead while she and Frank waited by the baggage carousel. Passengers manoeuvred themselves closer to it, sweating and red-faced. For several minutes she and Frank stood saying nothing at all, like strangers in a bad television advertisement. He lit a cigarette and stared at the ceiling. She took a bottle of *eau de toilette* from her handbag and squirted her neck and the backs of her wrists.

'The heat would kill you,' she said.

He nodded and sucked hard on his cigarette.

'I don't know how the people must function,' she said, 'in this heat.'

He stared down at his shoes. Her bags were among the last to appear on the carousel. They wound their way slowly around.

'Here we are now,' she said. 'I didn't know how much to bring.'

Still he said nothing. She stepped forward and dragged her cases from the revolving track. They were heavy. When she glanced up, he was staring at his watch.

'I'm to carry my own things, I suppose,' she muttered.

He sighed as he picked up her cases. They began to walk across the Arrivals building, towards where Smokes and Ulla were standing. Smokes and Ulla were laughing together now. They looked like old friends.

'Your flight was alright?' Frank asked suddenly.

'A little rough,' she answered, blushing. 'But you have to expect that at this time of year. It's the trade winds apparently. The captain came on to the radio and explained it all.'

'Ready to rock and roll?' Smokes grinned.

Frank nodded. 'Yes,' Eleanor said, 'he had a beautiful speaking voice. And very good English too. For a Communist I mean.'

At lunch she was unusually quiet. And it was so strange to see her face again, especially here, especially now, that he could think of very little to say himself. It was still a lovely face. It was a face that was utterly lacking in guile, and her mouth was still beautiful. Her hair was almost completely grey and her eyes had thin lines at the sides. But her hair looked thick and soft and her nervous

37

eyes were full of light. She was wearing a little make-up. Her fingernails had been painted pink. She was still wearing her wedding ring.

Smokes had dropped them back at the Pensión Dorado and then gone off with Ulla, who had promised to show him her life-size set of polyurethane molars. There had been no fuss. Frank had booked a single room for Eleanor, across the corridor, just down from his own room. It was as they had discussed. She had not complained about the tiny room with its sticky linoleum floor, its scrawny mattress and its wire mesh window. She had just put her handbag down on the bed and slipped off her jacket.

'This looks fine, Frank,' she'd said. 'Absolutely fine.'

'Well, they've no proper hotels here,' he'd told her, 'except the Imperial, and they've some bloody conference on there, so it's all booked out.'

'Not at all,' she'd said. 'Sure, this is grand. And isn't it only for the two nights anyhow?'

He told her about the electricity rationing. The water might go off too, for hours at a time. When it was on it was rarely hot. When it was cold, you couldn't drink it unless you put a couple of Halzones in first. You had to be very careful with the heat and the food. You had to wear a hat all the time. You could not eat red meat or fish or raw fruit. Anything unfamiliar was risky, with the food and with everything else. There was a dollar shop on the Carretera Massaya out in the suburbs and you could get things like soap and powder there. 'Women's things,' he'd said.

You could not go out walking at night. There were no streets as such, since the earthquake, so it was easy to get lost. You needed to carry your passport and visa with you at all times. The official exchange rate was twenty-seven *córdobas* to the dollar. On the black market you could get six hundred, and the figure was rising every day. There was no shortage of money here, there was just nothing to spend it on. If she needed currency, she was to ask him. He had booked lunch at the Churrasco. She was to bring diarrhoea pills.

'Oh,' she said, 'it's that kind of place, is it?'

He told her he wasn't in the humour for jokes.

The Churrasco stank of heat and stewed meat and over-ripe fruit. Three large fans dangled from the ceiling, but they were not working, the waiter explained, because of the war. They sat at a table in a quiet corner and she left the business of ordering to Frank. He called the waiter back and pointed out what they wanted from the menu.

'Will you take a beer, Eleanor?' he asked.

'No, I'll have an orange or something.'

'The beer's only water.'

'No,' she said firmly. 'A mineral, please.'

He ordered a *cerveza Victoria* and a Fanta orange and the waiter smiled and went away. Frank lit a cigarette.

'You're still puffing away on those fags?' she asked with a smile. 'You'll make yourself sick, Frank, if you're not careful.'

He nodded. 'Everyone needs something.'

'So,' she said, 'and how's Veronica?'

'Fine.'

'I sometimes see her at the unislim down in Monkstown, but she never says hello. Always in a big rush.'

He nodded again. 'She can be quiet. It wouldn't be meant as anything.'

The waiter brought the drinks and poured them out. He took a vase of carnations from a trolley and placed it with a theatrical flourish on their table.

'*Oh, gracias,*' Eleanor said.

'*De nada, Señora,*' the waiter replied, flicking at her side plate with his glasses cloth.

'I didn't know you spoke the lingo,' Frank said.

'Oh, I went to this extra-mural in UCD last year,' she told him. 'I went with Maura Regan. It was either Spanish or the pre-Socratic philosophers, you see, on a Monday night, so we plumped for the Spanish. But I only know the basics.'

When the waiter left there was silence between them again. He sipped at his beer and flicked his cigarette ash on the floor.

'Good God,' she sighed, fanning her face with a menu. 'This heat.'

'Eleanor,' he said, 'do you mind if we talk about something more important than the bloody heat?'

She looked at him. 'No, Frank,' she answered quietly. 'But there's no law against politeness, after all.'

'There's a man here,' Frank continued, 'Nuñez his name is,

fucking penpusher. He's at the Ministry of the Interior if you don't mind. Well, this eejit is looking after things at this end. I haven't met him yet. Smokes has. He says he's too busy to meet me.'

'God,' she said. 'How can that be, Frank?'

'It's this war, apparently. That's the excuse for everything.'

'I see,' she said. 'God.'

'Yes. He had a fellow up in the north, you know, where the whole business happened. They'll be bringing himself down tonight. We're to go to the hospital tomorrow morning. I went the day I got over, but there was a mistake.'

'A mistake?'

'Yes. They phoned to say he'd arrived.' Frank mopped his face with his tie. 'But he hadn't arrived. It was a mistake.'

'Oh dear.'

'Oh dear is right. There seem to be an awful lot of fucking mistakes here, if you ask me.'

With a sudden gushing sound, the fans on the ceiling whirred into movement. The customers murmured their appreciation. The waiter joined his hands and beamed with the intensity of a medieval martyr.

'About fucking time too,' Frank said, running his finger around the inside of his shirt collar.

'And you?' she said. 'I mean, how are you, Frank?'

He did not return her strained smile. 'How do you think I am, Eleanor?'

'I don't know, Frank. That's why I'm asking you.'

A fat man at the next table gaped at them.

'I've been a lot bloody better in my time,' Frank said.

She pursed her lips and looked away. 'Well, there's no call for that tone, Frank. That tone will help nobody at all.'

'Well, I'm sorry then. I suppose I'm just feeling a little down. I mean that's allowed I suppose?'

'Of course, Frank,' she said. 'I didn't say it wasn't, did I?'

The salad came, two lettuce leaves, three shrivelled tomatoes, a thick dollop of a grey pasty-looking substance. Eleanor peered at her plate.

'It's the war,' Frank explained. 'It's affected the food some way.'

'It's grand,' she said sharply. 'I'm only peckish anyhow. I was picking away at things on the plane.'

She looked at her husband as he began to eat. She felt a little sorry for him now. It was something to do with the size of his hands. Frank's hands had always made her feel sorry for him. They were too big for the rest of his body. They were too awkward. She reached out for a bread roll and crumbled it over her plate.

'I'm sorry, Frank,' she said, 'will we start again?'

He nodded. 'Yes. I'm sorry too, Eleanor. It's the awful heat. It makes you throw the head.'

She put down her knife and fork. 'It's just,' she said, 'well, it's just that I'll miss him an awful lot.'

He dried his lips with his napkin. 'He was close to you,' he murmured. 'We all know that.'

'I never heard him say a bad word against you, Frank. I think you got that all wrong.'

He shrugged, as though he did not care about what she was saying. He ate for a few moments, sawing his tomato into halves, and then into quarters. From time to time he glanced up at the clicking fans.

'And you're bearing up yourself?' he asked suddenly, staring at his plate.

'Oh yes,' she said, 'I'm making out. I have two new girls coming to me now, for the academy exams. And I'm thinking of having the bathroom done.'

'I mean about the news,' he said.

She looked away. 'I'm soldiering on.' She tried to smile again. 'But I find' – she raised her napkin to her face – 'but I find I'm still at the weepy stage.'

Frank put down his cutlery and chewed hard at his food. He discovered his fingers twisting the edges of his napkin while he listened to her voice. She was speaking slowly now, with great deliberation.

'If there had just been time to say goodbye,' she said, and her voice trailed off into a gentle sob. She began to breathe hard, and she raised the napkin to her forehead once more. When she looked up at him again, her eyes were spilling over with tears. She swallowed and gaped around the room, a look of incomprehension on her face. Her shoulders trembled as she sobbed.

'Oh, I'm sorry Frank, I promised myself not to make a holy show.'

'It's only natural. It's not a bloody crime.'

'Oh, but in front of people,' she whispered, her voice shaking. 'Really and truly.'

'Fuck them all. We're paying good money to be here, aren't we?'

She excused herself and went to the ladies' room.

After lunch they took a taxi back to the Pensión Dorado. The taxi was a battered and rattling little Fiat with a long crack down the windscreen and the letters 'TV' in bright tape across the bonnet. A magnetic medal of Saint Christopher and a creased photograph of Marilyn Monroe with no clothes on were stuck to the dashboard. The driver was a fat happy-looking man who spoke a little English. When Frank told him that he too was a taxi driver, the fat man seemed even happier. He told Frank that business was very good these days, with all the *extranjeros* – he pointed at Frank and Eleanor – in town. But spare parts and petrol were a problem. '*Por la guerra*,' he explained dolefully. 'Don't tell me,' Frank said. 'Because of the shagging war.'

When they pulled up at the *pensión* the driver jumped out and opened the back door. Frank offered him a ten thousand *córdoba* note, but the driver raised his hands and shook his head. He insisted that he would take no money. When he came to Ireland one day, he said with a smile, Frank would owe him a free trip.

'Don't be silly,' Eleanor said. 'You've a living to make.'

'No, no,' the driver insisted, 'not for my *amigos* from Ireland.'

Frank shrugged and pocketed the money. The driver clapped him hard on the back. '*Vivan los taxistas*.' He laughed. Then they shook hands, and the fat, happy man stepped back into his taxi. He rolled down his window and made a thumbs-up sign.

'*Viva* Bobby Sands,' he shouted, 'and fuck off to Maggie Thatcher.' He revved up his engine and rattled away down the Calle Camillo Ortega.

Eleanor was tired now. She said she wanted to sleep off the jet lag. Frank led her down the corridor and told her to get a good rest. He would be in his own room if she needed anything.

If there was a piano in the room she would have played

Rachmaninov. She would have liked to sink her fingers into the low keys and hear something dramatic. She would have given anything for this, but, of course, there was no piano.

She opened a case and unpacked some of her clothes. She ran her finger through the dust on the surface of the mirror, carving a sweeping spiral. Then she pulled off her damp blouse and wiped the mirror clean with it.

She was not afraid now. That surprised her. She was a very long way from home, but she was not afraid. Frank was in his room, just across the corridor, just down the way. The knowledge of his presence was comforting. It made her feel as capable as anyone could be in this situation. It made her feel she was safe.

She unzipped her skirt and stepped out of it, then pulled off her tights and her pants. She left her bra on as she looked at herself in the mirror. She put her fingers on the folds of flesh around her abdomen and lifted the flesh in her hands.

'You look old now, Eleanor Little,' she told herself. 'If I were to see you in some magazine, I'd say who does that old trout think she is.'

She washed herself at the sink, put on a pair of pyjamas and lay down on the bed, wiping the fresh sweat from her arms with the sheet. She wondered what Smokes and Ulla were doing right at that moment. She heard children out on the street singing a skipping song. She wondered if the house was alright, and if she had really checked that all the windows were properly closed. She was a very long way from home. She was further from home than she had ever been in her life.

The smell of cooking took her back to her grandmother's house in Galway. She remembered sleeping there as a young girl on humid summer nights. Her whole body felt hot and tired. Her feet pulsed with heat. If she were to put them into a basin of cold water, she thought, fat clouds of steam would fizzle from them. Eleanor closed her eyes. Outside the children were still singing.

She lay very still, blessed herself and joined her hands.

'Sweet Jesus,' she whispered, 'bless me, your child. Bless Frank. Have mercy on the souls of my mother and father, on the soul of Catherine Little, on the soul of my son, Johnny, and on all the souls of the faithful departed, that they may rest in peace, Amen.'

She dreamed of her grandmother's house. She dreamed the smell of mothballs and turf and fresh-baked cake. She dreamed of a tiny white coffin, frozen into a block of yellow ice.

At eight o'clock that evening he knocked on the door of her room. When there was no answer he turned the handle and crept in as quietly as he could. She was asleep, lying on her back in a pair of pyjamas, breathing very deeply. Her left arm was hanging over the edge of the bed. Her hand was resting on the floor. He lifted it and placed it across her chest.

He went back to his own room and scribbled a note. A sudden bolt of pain throbbed through his gut, making him wince. He took a bundle of banknotes from his holdall bag and stuffed them into his wallet. Then he left his room again and pushed the note under Eleanor's door. The note told her not to worry. He was going to have a drink up at the bar in the Imperial. He would be back in an hour. She was not, under any circumstances, to go out. He underlined the word 'not' three times.

He stepped out into the night. The air was warm and moist and smelt of bougainvillaea. Children were kicking a soccer ball against the *pensión* wall. He decided to walk down to Smokes's house in the Barrio Monseñor Lescano. He turned down the Calle Williams Romero and headed in the direction of the lake. Crossing by the Museo del Ruinas de la Gran Hotel, he was stopped and searched by a tiny policeman who scrutinized his passport very closely and wrote down some details in a notebook. By the time he got to the house Smokes was gone. The front door was locked and there was no sign of Claudette.

Beside the police station, on the corner of the block, was a single-storey concrete building with a glass front and bright fluorescent light inside. Frank had never noticed this building before. Inside he could see six or seven lines of unvarnished wooden benches. The benches were full of middle-aged women; there was not one man among the group. At the far end of the little room was a small stage, with a table, a chair and a red velvet curtain at the back. A large box-shaped object sat on top of the table. A black and gold cloth covered the box.

He crossed the street of caked mud and broken brickwork and went up close to the glass. It felt oddly cool to the touch. He

44

leaned his forehead against it. Inside, the lights suddenly went out. The women began to clap and cheer.

A man in a shabby evening suit walked on to the stage. He held up his hands to stop the applause. He was wearing white gloves. He bowed very low and said some words in Spanish. With a sudden and ostentatious wave he whipped the cloth from the top of the box. The women began to stamp their feet. The box was made of glass and was full of little coloured balls. The man in the evening suit pressed a switch. Suddenly the balls started to dance up and down. Frank laughed. A neon sign on the wall began to flash. GRINGO BINGO. GRINGO BINGO. $$$$$. GRINGO BINGO. $$$$$.

A clanking blue taxi pulled up in the street behind him. The driver yelled out, 'Hey buddy, ya wanna ride?' Frank jumped in and told the driver to take him up to the Imperial Hotel. The driver was a young Indian in sunglasses and a studded leather jacket. Frank tried to talk to him about carburettors and brake pads and spark plugs, but the words 'Hey buddy, ya wanna ride' turned out to be the only English the driver knew.

Claudette was parked in front of the Imperial, surrounded by giggling children and drunken beggars. Frank went in through the side door. The air in the crowded lobby was shockingly cold. Waiters scurried around in white tuxedos and red bow ties. Over by the souvenir shop, photographers were taking pictures of a handsome black man in a fawn-coloured military uniform. The mix of people seemed odd to Frank. There were opulent-looking couples standing around sipping wine, the men in light silk jackets, the women in lace and taffeta. And there were weary-looking American students in T-shirts, cycling shorts and odd socks sitting on top of bulging rucksacks. Frank made his way down to the Bar Casablanca. Smokes was perched on a high stool with his arm around Ulla. He looked very drunk. He was talking to a middle-aged man who was standing beside him, a short, portly man in a dark pinstripe suit that looked vaguely inappropriate. The man in the suit was sweating heavily, mopping his forehead with a paper towel and rocking backwards and forwards on his heels. He and Smokes seemed to be having an argument. Ulla's head was slumped forward and resting on the bar. She looked far too drunk to care. Smokes gaped up.

'Yo, Franklin Delano Little,' he slurred, wiping his lips with the back of his fingers, 'hey, what's shaking, *hombre*? Here, have a *cerveza*.'

'Don't call me Franklin,' Frank said.

The middle-aged man turned, looking surprised. He held out his hand.

'Hollis Clarke, sir,' he said. 'I'm with the *Washington Times* bureau down here.'

Hollis Clarke had a sunburnt puffy face and sad eyes. His head was slightly too small for his body. His thin hair was grey and damp-looking, combed back hard across his scalp. He smiled as Frank introduced himself. He looked like a man who might have once been handsome.

'Oh yes, Mr Little.' He nodded. 'I know who you are.'

Frank sat down on a bar stool. 'You do?' he said. 'And how would that be?'

Clarke cleared his throat. 'Well, the thing of it is, sir, we've heard about your situation in the bureau here. Your boy and so on. It's a very tragic story.'

Frank looked him in the eye. 'It isn't a story, Mr Clarke.'

Clarke grinned nervously. 'Oh, Hollis, please. No. It isn't a story, sir. I didn't mean that. But I mean, if you wanted . . .'

Clarke's voice trailed off. Smokes plonked another round of *cervezas* on to the counter. He nudged Ulla, who looked up, smiled blearily at Frank, then put her head back down on the bar.

'What were you saying, Clarke?' Frank asked.

'Well, I absolutely don't mean to offend you, Mr Little. But the thing of it is, the guys in the bureau here just think what happened to your boy is a damn disgrace. And we just think it goes to show these people down here couldn't run a damn chicken farm, never mind a country.'

He lifted his glass and peered into it. 'I'm just a newspaper man.' He shrugged. 'I just thought it would make a good story. If I'm out of line, I'm sorry.'

Smokes stood up, looking drunk and angry. 'Now why don't you hang ten and fuck yourself, Hollis?' he snapped.

Clarke grinned at Frank. 'My friend here should be working for *Newsweek*,' he said. 'Such a wonderful command of English.'

Smokes tottered and clutched at the bar. 'And who are you working for, Hollis? You're so far up the CIA's ass you're coming out Bill Casey's eyeballs.'

Clarke sighed, 'Oh cut it out, Smokes.'

'Yes, hold on now,' Frank said. 'Just hold your horses, for Jesus' sake.'

'Who pays your wages, Hollis?' Smokes snapped. 'Why don't you tell us all that?'

Clarke snuffled with laughter. 'Not my girlfriend's trust fund anyway, Sport.'

Smokes stepped closer. 'You little fuck,' he said. 'You gonna go kiss the ambassador's ass on Thursday?'

Clarke looked at Frank and smiled. 'The embassy people are having a little garden party Thursday, sir, for the fourth of July, you know. I figure Smokes is jealous actually, seeing as how he's not invited.'

'Hollis,' Smokes said, 'you say that again, you're cruisin' for a bruisin'.'

Clarke looked at him, raising his brows in a silent question.

'Aw, put your eyes back in your head, Smokes,' he chuckled. 'I'm just having a conversation with the man, OK?'

Smokes sat down sulking. Clarke straightened his tie, slicked back his hair and took another sip of beer.

'I'm sorry, Mr Little.' He nodded. 'This isn't the time to talk about this. I'm sorry.'

'No,' Frank said. 'I don't like the set-up here any more than you do, but there's a time and a place.'

Smokes stood up again. 'Jeez, Franklin, I mean, what's so wrong with the fucking set-up, man? I mean, people have stuff to eat now, you know? Little luxuries like that?'

Clarke shook his head. 'Good Lord,' he sniggered. 'It's just like summer camp for you people, isn't it? I mean, down here on your trust funds, down to the bar-stool Bolshevik Disneyland, before you go running back to Greenwich Village to put on coffee mornings for Jesse Jackson.'

Smokes poked him in the chest. 'This is a free fucking country now,' he hissed. 'That's what pisses you fascists off so much.'

'Oh, beautiful, Smokes. A free country? OK, so when's the election?'

'What about the one last year, deadhead? If you ever stuck your fat butt outside this bar, you mighta noticed it.'

'Come on, Smokes. That farce was more stacked than Madonna's chest.'

'Hey, Carlos,' Smokes called out to the barman, jerking his thumb in Clarke's direction. 'Hey, man, I thought you guys outlawed prostitution in this hotel.'

The barman laughed and continued cleaning the glasses.

'Now, Smokes,' Frank said, 'just calm down. I mean, the man does have a point. Nothing works here. The telephones, the lifts. I mean, nothing *works*.'

'Yeah, Franklin, that's because there's a fucking war, man. The Contras ain't Sergeant Bilko, man. That's because people like this peckerhead are bankrolling a fucking *war* against these people.'

'Calm down, Smokes,' Frank said.

Smokes started to yell. 'Like, where do you guys get off with this shit?' he raged. 'I mean, just what is your fucking point, Hollis?'

'My point, Smokes,' Clarke murmured. 'My point is that people like his son get killed.'

Smokes stepped off the bar stool and grabbed Clarke by the lapels. 'You slimy little Nixon-fucking Nazi,' he roared. 'I'm gonna send you back to Texas in a Tupperware lunchbox.'

'Alright,' Frank snapped. 'That's enough now.'

Two of the barmen grabbed Smokes and held him back. Frank took Clarke by the elbow and propelled him towards the door of the bar, pushing him firmly out into the corridor. Clarke staggered and tripped over an armchair. People laughed. Somebody took a photograph. Frank rushed out and tried to help him to his feet.

'I'm sorry, Clarke,' Frank said. 'Are you alright?'

Clarke stood up looking shocked and frightened, his nose bleeding. Frank took a handkerchief from his pocket and gave it to him. Clarke clamped it against his face and threw back his head. His fingers and cuffs were spattered with blood.

'Jesus, I'm sorry, Clarke,' Frank said again.

Clarke shook his head. 'No, it's OK,' he said. 'It's fine, Frank.'

In the doorway of the bar, Smokes was still on his feet, pulling against the barmen, stabbing the air with his finger.

'I'll kick your balls, man. You come back in here, man, I'll spread your *cojones* on fucking French toast.'

Clarke dusted off his suit and began to walk down the corridor, limping slowly, handkerchief still clasped to his nose. His trousers were torn at the right knee and he had lost one shoe.

When Frank came back into the bar, Smokes was sitting down again, giggling into his beer. Frank stared at him.

'So,' he said. 'And that was socialism, was it?'

Smokes ignored him.

'That's some kind of lovely behaviour now. That fellow is old enough to be your father.'

Smokes slapped his hands on the counter. 'Don't get righteous with me, man. Jesus, don't start. You remind me of Johnny when you get like that.'

Frank sat down. 'And what's that supposed to mean?'

Smokes looked away and lit a cigarette. 'Nothing,' he said.

'No. Tell me, Smokes.'

Smokes tried to smile, but his fingers were shaking.

'It's nothing. It's nothing, OK? He could just be a righteous mother at times, that's all. I'm saying he could be very fucking judgemental, Frank.'

He picked up a beer mat and crumpled it. 'I mean, fuck it, Frank, you wouldn't know what side the guy was on sometimes.'

'And is that so bad?'

Smokes nodded. 'Yeah, it is, man,' he said bitterly. 'Sometimes you take sides, you dig? Some stuff is right and some stuff is wrong, OK?'

'Yes, Smokes. And sometimes you have to figure out the bloody difference for yourself.'

Smokes whipped around to face him. 'Frank, the guy was my best friend. I loved the guy. But we didn't see eye to eye on every damn thing, OK? He could be a royal pain in the ass sometimes, you know what I'm saying?'

Frank laughed. 'Jesus now, Smokes. I'm his father. You don't have to tell me what he was like.'

'Oh yeah? Don't I?'

'No, son. No, you don't.'

Smokes turned away. They sat at the bar for a while, saying nothing at all. Smokes kept running his fingers through his hair, cursing under his breath. Ulla woke up and stared around as though she didn't know where she was. Frank drained his glass, looked at his watch and stood up.

'Well, I'll slip on,' he said. 'I'll leave you to it.'

'Buy you a beer, Franklin?' Smokes asked. 'One for the road?'

'I've had enough, thanks.'

'Hey, come on, babes.' Smokes grinned. 'Don't be a party poop. Don't be evil with me now, OK?'

Frank sighed. 'Well, alright, son. I'll have a parting glass. I'll have a short if that's alright.'

He sat back down. Smokes ordered a large Irish. They drank until the bar closed, and then Ulla threw up in the swimming pool.

When he got back to the *pensión* she was sitting with her eyes closed in the middle of the courtyard, an opened book resting against her abdomen. She was wearing a light blue dressing gown, and her hair was tied in a thick blue band. She was barefoot.

The silver and orange light from the streetlamps washed down over the yard. A light breeze rustled the curtains, making shadows dance in the corners. Out in the street the dogs were yowling as distant music came drifting up from the *parque*. Eleanor's head was leaning far back. Her fingers were intertwined, and her skin looked very pale.

He stood in the gateway and watched her for a moment, frightened by her delicacy, by the rawness of the memories it aroused. He felt a little drunk. It came into his mind that somewhere up in the hills young men were killing each other and dying. But he did not care. That was the odd thing. Right at that moment he did not care about this.

'Here I am,' he said.

She opened her eyes, looking startled. Her fingers went to the neck of her gown and she held it closed. She smiled at him.

'Frank,' she said. 'God, I must have nodded off.'

'You're alright. You must be jacked after the journey.'

She looked up sleepily at the sky.

'I came out to look at the stars. They've the loveliest stars here, Frank. Shooting stars and everything.'

He laughed. 'Aren't they only the same stars you see in Ireland?'

'Not at all, Frank. The world turns, you know.'

She held up her hand and swivelled her wrist, gazing at him. 'It turns,' she said. 'It's to do with gravity.'

'Stars are stars,' he shrugged.

She looked up again, intensely now, as though strange music was coming from the clouds.

'They're all dead, Frank, did you know that? It takes that long for the light to get here. It takes millions of years, you know, and we only see the light after the stars have died. It's sad in a way, isn't it, Frank? It would make you think.'

'You're gas,' he said.

She rolled her eyes, then yawned and tapped her watch. 'I thought you were only going to be an hour.'

'Yes. Well, I met Smokes you see. I bumped into him up there. He's an awful man for the juice. He'd suck it out of a dishcloth.'

'Oh, now,' she said. 'He's after a fashion.'

He cleared his throat, and when he began to speak again his voice came hoarsely.

'I was just thinking, Eleanor, how healthy you're looking. You know, you look very well.'

His hand moved towards his face.

'Here,' he said. 'You look well rested or something.'

'Get away, Frank Little,' she laughed. 'You're just trying to get on my soft side.'

He felt awkward now, clumsy and out of place. He could think of nothing else to say to her.

'Well' – he nodded – 'I suppose I'll hit the hay.'

'Yes,' she said. 'Goodnight then, Frank. Sweet dreams.'

He went into his room and lay on the bed, his stomach beginning to cramp up again.

5

Francis Street

FRANK LITTLE WAS BORN IN 1938, over a butcher's shop in
Francis Street, in the oldest part of Dublin, the Liberties. The
Liberties were outside the ancient walls of the city, and the people
who lived there thought of themselves as rebels. Frank Little's
grandparents had owned the butcher's shop, but when his grandfather had died, Frank's mother had taken over the running of it.
Now Frank's grandmother had a little upstairs room in a house
across the street, and she had been dying in that room for as long
as he could remember.

Every afternoon, after school, Frank went to visit his grandmother, to do errands for her and sit by her bedside. Sometimes she would talk to him in Irish, but when she did this
he could not understand her. Except when she called him by
his Irish name, *Proinsias*. He understood *Proinsias*, but that was
almost all.

She had bad lungs and a weak heart, and by the time he was
seven, Frank's grandmother was completely bed-ridden. He
would hear her rasping breath and hacking cough as he walked
up the dark stairs to see her. He was afraid of this old woman,
afraid of her thin bony hands and her quaking body, of the colour
of the phlegm that she coughed into the metal bowl on her bedside
table. When his grandfather had died, the undertaker had made a
mistake with the spelling of his name on the headstone, and the
old lady had kept the stone, leaning up against the wall of her
dark little bedroom, its carved letters leering out like the eyes of
a skull. Frank was afraid of that too.

One day in the very cold winter just after the war, she sat
straight up in bed and looked at Frank with her yellow eyes.

'*Proinsias?*' she whispered to him. 'Do you want to see a leprechaun?'

Her thin fingers scrabbled under her pillow and took out a matchbox, thrusting it into his hands. He opened it, and inside, wrapped up in a wad of cotton wool, was a shrivelled grey mushroom, shaped precisely like a tiny man in a floppy hat. It was the most extraordinary thing Frank had ever seen.

There were two chemist shops in Francis Street, Mushatt's and Rickaby's. Frank went to the chemist shops for his grandmother's medicine, and sometimes he went to buy saltpetre. His mother would add the saltpetre to cold water, then take a big syringe and inject the mixture into the slabs of meat in the stockroom. It was a way of preserving meat, the kind of meat on which poor people lived. But then one day the government banned the sale of saltpetre, and his mother had to buy a fridge. The IRA had discovered that you could make bombs with saltpetre, so the government said it could not be sold any more. His mother didn't know what to do. The fridge would cost an arm and a leg, she told her son. The IRA were going to put her out of business.

'Ireland's freedom, my bloody hat,' she said to him. 'That fridge is going to be English if I can help it.'

'Brother Gorman in school says the English are bad. He says they came over here to put us out.'

'That fellow is an awful craw-thumper,' she said. 'The English are the best people you could ever meet. Isn't Mrs Rickaby in the chemist's English?'

'I don't know. Is she?'

'Of course she is, Frank. That fellow would give you a pain now, where you never had a window. The ordinary English people are lovely. Not like some of them going about over here these days. The fellows who talk the most about the Irish bloody Republic are the ones who'd put you out of business.'

'But can you not get rid of the shop, Mam,' he asked her. 'It's very hard for you. Couldn't you not get a job somewhere else?'

'We don't work for other people in this family,' she said. 'You remember that, Frank, son. You'll never get on if you're punching a clock. I'm always telling your father, but he won't be said by me. If you've an ounce of wit you'll have a shop too, when you're big. It's a great life.'

He began to think about this. He wondered what kind of shop he would like to have when he was big. He thought about all the other shops in Francis Street. There was the Boylan Brothers, where they had sacks of rice, dried figs, nuts, flour, barrels of oats and glass jars full of coloured sweets. There was O'Hora's drapery, and Johnny Fox's barber shop. There was a shop where they repaired musical instruments. There was a cooper's forge, where they made cartwheels and barrels for the Guinness brewery up in Thomas Street. And there was Johnny Rea's Ice Cream Parlour.

Johnny Rea's smelt of sugar and peppermint and strong coffee. It had a solid mahogany counter and black and white tiles up and down the walls. There was an Italian cappuccino machine and a jukebox with Frank Sinatra and Dean Martin tunes. There were paintings of faraway places behind the bar, Italy and Greece, Egypt and New York. There was a glass tank full of fat goldfish. There was a crystal chandelier. It was a place that felt magical.

Johnny Rea loved to talk. He would stand behind the counter, flicking at the air with his yellow duster, and he would talk to whoever would listen. Frank could hardly ever understand him, but he was fascinated by everything Johnny Rea had to say. One day he heard him say there was a man in the government who was a Communist. His name was Doctor Browne and he was a bad lot. He was against God and the Church, Johnny Rea said, and people like him were bad for Ireland.

At night Frank thought about this man, Browne. He lay in his bed and thought about him. How could he be a bad man if he was a doctor? Why was he bad for Ireland? What *was* Ireland? What was a Communist? He asked his father about these things. His father shook his head and said a Communist was a cunning fellow who wanted to slither his way in with the working man and destroy his faith and his principles. A Communist was a sleeveen who said there was no God. There were Communists in Russia, and they had shot the poor little Tsarina, and Our Lady had appeared in Lourdes and said everyone would have to pray for Russia, to get rid of the Communists.

'But is God really there?' Frank asked his father. 'Is it not just a story?'

His father turned and glared, an angry expression on his face. He put his hand on Frank's shoulder and pointed at him.

'There was this fellow I knew once,' he said. 'Oh, he was smart as you please. And at half past eight one night he said there was no God. Do you know what happened to him?'

'No,' Frank said. 'What?'

His father leaned in close, eyes wide. 'At nine o'clock he was dead,' he said. 'That's what happens to smart fellows who say there's no God.'

One day in March 1950, when he was twelve years old, Frank walked into Johnny Rea's ice cream shop and Eleanor Hamilton was sitting there, laughing with her school friends. He had seen her once before, at Mass in Saint Michael's church. He knew she had a cousin in Francis Street, and he knew that she lived out in one of the new houses in Drimnagh. He watched as she played jacks with her friends on the marble table top. He watched the way she moved, the way she tossed back her long black hair. He listened to the sound of her laugh and felt himself melt like the ice cream in his glass.

He watched her for almost half an hour, quaking with nervousness. Then he stood up, breathed in deeply and walked straight over to her table, clutching his matchbox in his hand. 'Do you want to see a leprechaun?' he said. It was the bravest thing he had ever done.

Her friends burst into laughter. Eleanor Hamilton glared at him as though he had vomited on the floor. She pushed her dark hair out of her face. 'Would you go away, you little scut,' she winced. 'You're only a bloody leprechaun yourself.'

He did not speak to her for two years after that.

6

The Hospital Karl Marx

WHEN SMOKES WOKE UP he had the kind of stabbing, stomach-blending headache that makes you clench your teeth and feel guilty, even if you haven't done anything worth feeling guilty about. It was almost eight thirty and the Swedish woman had already left. On the bedroom window she'd scrawled the words 'CIAO BAMBINO' in lipstick. When Smokes saw this, he was relieved that she'd gone. You just couldn't get involved with a woman who'd actually do something like that.

As his face loomed up at him in the bathroom mirror, he tried to piece the night back together. They'd stayed up until it was bright, drinking duty free rum and singing the choruses of Abba songs. Then, halfway through 'Can You Hear the Drums, Fernando?', they'd decided to do it in the shower.

'Do you want me sexually?' she'd asked, in that reticent Scandinavian way.

'Do I want you?' he'd replied. 'Honey, is this a trick question?'

Sex in the shower hadn't worked out. Sex anywhere else hadn't worked out either. They'd had a brief and – in Smokes's view – unnecessarily frank discussion about the detumescent effect of a bellyful of *chilli con carne* and *Cuba libre*. Then they'd slept in each other's arms, mumbling, snorting, snivelling, belching, waking up and groping each other every few minutes until the noise of the traffic and the road repair men had begun to fill the street outside.

Cherry would be back today, but he'd already made up his mind not to tell her anything. In Smokes's book, infidelity was not a thing to be lightly confessed. It was cruel to do that. It was just looking for forgiveness. In this situation it was morally preferable to lie, every time. Smokes would lie, and he would protect Cherry's feelings. This scenario would have the added advantage of allowing Smokes to continue life with both testicles still attached to his body.

He looked at himself in the mirror. Jesus, man, he thought, your face looks like the map of Managua. He laughed out loud and thought about the Swedish woman. He just couldn't wait to tell Johnny about her. It was only then that he remembered.

He drove to the *pensión* and got there by nine, his head hammering in the early morning heat.

Eleanor and Frank were sitting at a table in the courtyard, eating bananas and white bread. Frank had a copy of *La Prensa* propped up against the water jug and was avidly pretending to read, a sulky look on his face.

Eleanor was wearing sunglasses and a white shirt. She waved at Smokes as he walked unsteadily into the yard. She looked relieved to see him. Chickens scattered as he moved towards the table. He wondered how they'd been getting along. They weren't as bad as Johnny'd made them out to be. OK, so the conversation wasn't exactly flowing like the United Nations, but at least they weren't throwing the furniture at each other. Not yet, anyway.

He remembered the night he and Johnny had got drunk in the Bar Casablanca, the night Johnny had told him how much his parents despised each other. He remembered the terrified look on his friend's face as he had spoken. He remembered all the stories. How Johnny had once broken a musical statue of the Virgin Mary that was in his bedroom and how the sound of his mother running up the stairs had made him vomit with fear at what she was going to do to him. He remembered how Frank Little had once been taken away by the police for beating his wife. He looked at them both now. He looked at Frank and Eleanor and wondered how these things could possibly have happened.

'S'up?' he asked, sitting down at the table.

'Nothing, dear,' Eleanor replied in a firm voice. 'We're just getting ready to go.'

Smokes grinned uneasily. 'You OK, Franklin?' Frank nodded, without looking up from his newspaper.

'We're just in a bit of a mood,' Eleanor explained.

'Eleanor, please.'

'We just got out the wrong side of the bed today.'

'Eleanor, I'm just trying to be sensible,' Frank hissed. 'It's you I'm thinking about.'

'Well, you needn't bother,' she said.

There was silence then. Frank rustled his newspaper maliciously, and Smokes began to feel uncomfortable. He poured himself a cup of coffee and waited for somebody to speak.

'Hey, guys' – he giggled – 'you give me five bucks, I could go to the movies.'

'I'm trying to get her to see reason, Smokes,' Frank said. 'Of course, I should have known I'd be wasting my time.'

'No, Smokes,' she interrupted, 'he's trying to stop me coming to the hospital with you.'

Frank lowered his voice and leaned across the table. 'For Jesus' sake, I've seen the pictures in the papers, Eleanor. These people don't mess around when they bump you off.'

'Frank Little,' she warned, 'I've come halfway around the world. We've had enough now.'

He looked across the table at Smokes, raising his eyebrows in a silent plea.

'Well, you know, Eleanor,' Smokes began, 'old Franklin may have a point here. He may not be a pretty sight.'

Frank started to get excited again. 'Yes. Tell her, Smokes. Maybe she'll listen to you.'

'Who's *she*?' Eleanor snapped. 'The cat's mother, is it?'

She took off her glasses and looked him in the eye. Her finger tapped against the table as she spoke.

'He's my son,' she said quietly. 'I brought him into this world. You mark my words, Frank Little, I'll see him out of it too.'

It was not a tone of voice to be argued with. She stood up and said she was going to the bathroom.

'We'll set off when I come back. And there'll be no more bloody nonsense about it.'

Frank sighed and began to clean his fingernails with a match, shaking his head and slapping the mosquitos away. After a minute, he looked up.

'Women!' He shrugged, blushing.

'Hey, tell me about 'em, Franklin. What the fuck are you gonna do with them?'

The *Señora* came out of the house carrying a bucket of feed. She squinted in the glare and began to scatter the grain across the stones, laughing to herself as the chickens flapped and squabbled.

'*Mis hijos.*' She chuckled. '*Mis hijos.*'

'*Sí, sí,*' simpered Smokes. Through gritted teeth, he hissed at Frank. 'Hey, smile, man. The broad is crazy. She's saying the chickens are her babies, man.'

Frank rolled his eyes and opened his newspaper. Smokes watched as the scrawny *pensión* dog staggered to its feet and began to wander towards them. Its mouth was open wide and its drooling tongue was hanging out. It sidled up to Frank and began to rub its belly and its soft pink penis against his leg, growling softly with pleasure.

'Fuck off out of that,' Frank said, slapping the dog away with the newspaper. The dog leapt forward again, clamping its legs around Frank's knee, thrusting its pelvis wildly back and forth, panting.

'Hey, Franklin' – Smokes chuckled – 'you've made an *amigo*. He wants to do the *samba y caramba* with you.'

'Would you listen to the moans out of it?' Frank laughed, still smacking the dog away. 'It's like a fucking Christian.'

He shook his leg, but the dog clung on hard, an expression of ecstatic happiness in its one yellow eye.

'Jesus, Smokes,' Frank said, 'what'll I do?'

'I dunno, Franklin. I'd fake an orgasm, and quick.'

The *Señora* came out of the house, looking aghast. '*Madre de Dios,*' she gasped. She rushed over and roared at the dog. It released Frank and slunk away, looking dejected, its long red tongue hanging out of its dribbling mouth.

'Oh, *Señor,*' she whispered. '*Lo siento, Señor.*' She knelt down and began to run her dishcloth gingerly up and down Frank's trouser leg.

'Hey, Franklin,' Smokes said, 'you're doing OK this morning.'

'And you. You did well enough last night. Oh, look at the holy innocent. I'm talking about that Swedish bird.'

Frank tapped the side of his nose. 'Mum's the word.' He winked. Smokes laughed back, but he suddenly felt uncomfortable again. The occasion felt too light. They were going to see the dead body of his friend, in the morgue of the city hospital. They were going to see a thing no parent should ever have to see. They were going to sign forms. They should not have been laughing together.

'Here I am, so,' Eleanor said.

When they turned she was standing in the gateway, wearing a black hat with a black lace scarf around her neck. She looked uneasy under their gaze. Her eyes darted around the little stone yard.

'What's that fellow called anyway?' she asked, nodding at the dog.

'¿Cómo se llama el perro?' Smokes asked the Señora.

'Fidel Castro,' the Señora said. And she laughed so much that her false teeth fell out of her mouth and into her hand.

The traffic was absolutely terrible. A raucous chorus of car horns and police sirens blared all the way up to the Plaza de España, where the mains water pipe had burst, spraying dirty brown water high into the air and down into the frantic streets.

The heat blazed as they inched their way through the middle of the ruined city. Claudette's chugging interior felt like a sauna. They stopped by a huge black tank, dug into a pit at the entrance gate to the Parque del Poder Popular. The tank had yellow Arabic script stencilled on its side and its long barrel protruded in a way that made Eleanor think it looked stupid. A gang of shoeless young boys and girls danced around it in an untidy ring, holding hands, screeching at each other, chanting a rhythmical song. Just as Claudette began to move again, one of the boys broke out of the ring. He jumped up and grabbed the gun barrel, swinging from it, kicking his scrawny legs. It tilted slowly downwards under his weight. A little girl stood on tiptoes and stared into the mouth of the gun, laughing out loud with nervous joy. 'Boom,' she shouted, 'Booma-Booma-*Boom*.'

They were driving through the poorest part of the city now. The rough streets gave way to tracks of hard mud and shattered masonry, between long rows of polythene tents and tottering scrap metal shacks. Wherever a ragged wall still stood, every inch of peeling white plaster had been splashed with graffiti – FSLN, PLI, PCN, silhouettes of guns and enormous love hearts, Sandino's cowboy hat, crucifixes, cartoon penises, quotations from the bible, political slogans – *¡VIVA CHRISTO TRABA-JADOR! – ¡OBREROS AL PODER!* – skulls and crossbones, red and blue targets, hammers and sickles, clenched fists, bloodstained American flags with large black Xs slashed through them, huge red Rolling Stones lips.

'*Muerte a los yanquis,*' Eleanor pronounced slowly.

'Oh, yes,' Frank said, 'they want to kill all the Americans. It's called socialism apparently.'

'We don't know the situation, Frank. Let's leave all that alone.'

'Bloody kip,' he muttered. 'No mistake about it.'

Smokes turned the music up even louder.

Outside the Hospital Karl Marx sat a row of dirty green armoured cars. Young soldiers, men and women, slouched in the hot sunshine, playing cards and talking. They watched Frank and Eleanor climb out of Claudette. One of the soldiers had a small silver statue of the Virgin Mary dangling from his belt. He gazed at Claudette as though he had never seen anything like her in his life. Another soldier was drinking Coke out of a clear plastic bag, sucking at a tiny hole that he'd gnawed in the corner, the way a child would suck at its mother's breast. There was a shortage of bottles, Smokes explained to Eleanor, so if you bought a Coke from a street trader, he'd just pour it into a bag of ice for you. This was because of the war, Smokes said. The war was affecting every damn thing.

The soldiers were wearing Kalashnikov assault rifles, small pistols and eighteen-inch bayonets in belted scabbards. Many of them had red and black kerchiefs around their throats. One or two wore military medals. They frisked Eleanor and Frank very thoroughly. They were polite but not friendly. They looked sulky, like bored schoolchildren, and very nervous. Smokes, in denim shorts and vest, they allowed to pass without searching.

Eleanor looked up at the white building. Slogans had been painted in long blue letters all along the facade. *¡LUCHAMOS PARA VENCER! ¡NO PASARAN! ¡SEGUIMOS AL FRENTE CON EL FRENTE SANDINISTA! ¡HASTA LA VICTORIA SIEMPRE!* This was the place which contained the body of her only child.

Inside, the reception area was clean and bright. Martial music was playing from somewhere. Smokes said a few words to the middle-aged man behind the desk. The man glanced at Eleanor and Frank, then picked up his telephone and dialled a number, turning away from them as he spoke.

After a minute, a thin and tired-looking young woman in a white coat came quickly across the reception area. She had olive-coloured skin and a beautiful mouth. She nodded efficiently at Frank and Eleanor, reaching out to shake their hands.

'I am Doctor Perez,' she said. 'You must be the boy's family?'

'And this is a friend,' Eleanor answered. 'Smokes Morrison.'

Doctor Perez nodded.

'We met before.' Smokes grinned. 'How goes the revolution, Doc?'

Doctor Perez glared at him. 'We are not interested in revolution here,' she said sharply. 'We leave that to others.'

Smokes shrugged and put his hands in his pockets. The doctor looked at her watch.

'I am very sorry. This is a shock for you both.' She glanced at her watch again. 'Now perhaps, if we are all prepared?'

Eleanor nodded. Doctor Perez told them to follow.

They walked down a long wide corridor lined with murals of handsome young men with bandages on their heads. The young men were brandishing rifles and laughing.

They turned into another corridor and climbed some steep stairs, then crossed the floor of a large room which was obviously a gymnasium. The air smelt of rubber and liniment and stale sweat. A huge portrait of President Ortega hung from the rafters above the climbing ropes. He had a pleasant, shy face, Eleanor thought; he looked a little uncomfortable. There were more murals of young men and women in uniforms, but these were not as big as the picture of President Ortega. The young people in these paintings had all been injured in various ways; they wore bandages, slings, patches over their eyes. Some of them had crutches and others were sitting in wheelchairs. One was waving a spanner. Another was holding up a book of poetry. A third was swinging a reaping hook in the air. All of them were laughing, beautiful, young. All of them looked happy.

They passed without speaking into a larger room with no windows. The walls had been painted with vivid flowers, dark green trees, a silver blue lake. The room was lined with white park benches and white plastic garden seats. Young men sat on the benches, their heads and limbs wrapped in blue bandages. One of the men was holding his head in his hands, rocking a little and moaning. A handsome priest in a cream linen suit was moving among the men, distributing Communion wafers from a wooden chalice. Jaunty march music came bouncing out of speakers on the walls. There was a very large *PROHIBIDO FUMAR* sign on the wall, but almost everyone in the room was smoking. Some of the young men stared at Frank and Eleanor as they moved quickly across the floor.

Just outside this room was another staircase. It was steep and very dark and it led down towards the basement of the building. Doctor Perez stopped. She pushed her hair out of her eyes. She bowed her head.

'We're down there?' Frank asked. She nodded.

Eleanor wrapped her arms around herself as though she was suddenly very cold. The doctor turned to look at her.

'Eleanor,' Frank said softly. 'Please now, pet. There's no need for us both.'

'I'm ready now,' she said, in a trembling voice. 'I'm ready to see my son.'

Doctor Perez took Eleanor by the hand. Very slowly, she began to lead her down the dark stairs. Frank followed with Smokes. Halfway down they stopped, just for a moment. In the dull green glow of the emergency light, Frank could see that Smokes was crying now, sobbing gently, his right wrist over his face.

'Don't upset yourself, son,' he whispered, clasping Smokes by the hand.

The doctor pushed open a door. Bright colourless light flooded their eyes.

With her husband and her son's friend, Eleanor Little walked into the long narrow room. Everything was white or steel grey. Giant steel drawers ran up and down the walls. The air was so very cold that it turned their breath to vapour, and for a moment it was almost pleasant to be there. The walls were hung with clean and glittering instruments, scalpels, files, saws, large steel bowls. In the middle of the floor stood a squat white table made of enamel. It looked like an altar, Eleanor thought. There was a plughole in the middle of the table. A sucking sound came from the plughole.

At the far end of the room two men in white uniforms were playing chess on an upturned steel barrel. When they saw Eleanor and Frank they jumped up and took off their caps. The younger man looked a little frightened. His eyes were bright and pale. Doctor Perez approached the men and whispered something to them. The older man put his cap back on. He went to a desk and took out a notebook. He looked in the notebook, then walked to the vertical row of huge steel drawers.

He found the drawer he was looking for and his fingers touched the handle. He glanced at Eleanor again. He made the sign of the Cross, swallowed hard and pulled open the steel drawer, then stepped back very quickly, turning his head away, as though he was ashamed of what he had just done.

The body was naked, except for a pair of black running shorts. The hair on the head was matted and greasy. The back of the head was resting on a folded white towel. Part of the back of the skull and part of the right cheek were missing. An ugly gangrenous-looking wound was slashed across the forehead, from the hairline to the right eyebrow. The jaw was twisted out of shape, making the face leer stupidly. The lips were white. A dirty white bandage had been wrapped tightly across the eyes. Blood had seeped through the bandage, leaving dull brown stains on the cloth. The flesh on the face was yellow and purple. Around the mouth and underneath the eyes the flesh had decayed to the consistency of soft cheese, revealing the yellowed bone beneath.

The boy's chest was hairless and scrawny, criss-crossed with purple welts and black bruises. A large triangular bruise covered the abdomen. A thin line of hair ran from the hem of the shorts up to the boy's navel. The right hand was clenched. The tip of the left thumb was missing. The right knee was bandaged. The left knee and the soles of both feet were scarred. The toenails on each foot were very long.

Eleanor felt the tears begin to smoulder in her eyes. She gripped on to the rims of the steel drawer and tried to weep silently, with some pretence of control. She felt her husband's hand on her shoulder and she heard Smokes's voice saying 'My God, my God, my God' over and over.

Through blurred eyes she saw that her husband's face was the colour of milk now. His eyes looked wild with fear. He had one hand on the drawer, as if to support himself. He was trembling. She watched him take a tissue from his pocket and wipe his lips. He handed the tissue to her, and she held it to her hot eyes.

'We shouldn't stay here,' he croaked, 'this isn't something we need to see.'

'But, Frank,' she whispered.

He put his hand to the side of his head and closed his eyes.

'No,' he said. 'I don't want to. Please.'

'But, Frank. You don't understand.'

Eleanor felt the pulse throb in her neck. She turned to Doctor Perez, hearing her voice quake as she tried to speak calmly. And even though laughter felt wrong, she laughed, because she could not help herself any more.

'You see, dear,' she said, 'there's been a mistake.'

'What mistake?'

Eleanor looked into the doctor's eyes. 'Well,' she said, 'that poor boy there is not my son.'

'What?'

And for some reason Eleanor let the tears come then. She hung her head and clutched her hands together and began to sob, silently at first, then wildly. She opened her mouth wide and wept with pain. She moved her fingers through her hair. 'It's not him,' she cried out, 'it's not him.'

'Eleanor, please,' Frank said. 'Please, love.'

'It's not him,' she moaned. 'That's not my son in there.'

Eleanor was staring into the steel drawer again. She gazed at the young man's ripped hands, at his smashed face, at the light blue veins that meandered up his naked legs like the tributaries of a river on a map.

'I am sorry, *Señora*,' Doctor Perez said gently. 'These things are always a shock, I know.'

'That's enough now, El,' Frank said. 'Come on now and we'll go home. Maybe the doctor can give you something to settle you.'

He put his big hands firmly on her shoulders, but she shook them off and closed her eyes.

'Frank Little,' she breathed. 'For Christ's sake can't you listen to me, for just once in your life?'

And now he felt that he was going to cry too. He took her fingers and squeezed them. 'Eleanor, please,' he whispered. 'Please don't say that, pet.'

She moved her hands to her head. 'Would you please, *please*, listen to me,' she repeated. 'That is not my son.'

She grabbed Frank's wrist and stared into his face, beginning to speak excitedly, rapidly.

'Remember when he broke his ankle, Frank? That time he was playing chasing up in the field with the Duignan boy? Don't you remember, Frank?'

'Yes,' he said. 'Of course.'

'Well, where's the scar from the stitches? That's not him. It couldn't be.'

Frank felt his mouth go dry. 'Good Christ,' he said.

'And his feet,' she said. 'They're not his feet. He had size eleven feet, like yours, and your father's. Those are like a woman's feet.'

'*Señora*, please?' sighed Doctor Perez. 'I think perhaps we should all get some air.'

She pushed the doctor away. 'No, I don't need air. Take those shorts off him.'

'That's enough, *Señora*. Calm yourself.'

'That poor boy's pants,' she said. 'Would you mind taking them off please.'

'*Señora* . . .'

With a sudden movement Eleanor reached out and grabbed the hem of the boy's shorts. She heard the loud babble of Spanish words. She felt the doctor's hands on her own. One of the attendants began to shout. The other looked absolutely terrified. Roughly, she pulled the shorts down around the dead boy's thighs.

'*Madre de Dios*,' the doctor said.

Eleanor knelt down dizzily on the cold floor. She felt the sensation of falling slowly through air. Her tongue seemed like a stone in her mouth and she was so cold now that she could feel her heart pumping heat into the rest of her body. She could feel her heart moving, trying to keep her alive.

'He was circumcised,' she whispered, as the room began to melt into whiteness. 'My son was circumcised when he was born. The doctor told us it was the thing to do.'

When she woke up she was lying on a bench in the corridor. Doctor Perez, a male doctor and a nurse were all standing over her, slapping her cheeks and trying to pour water between her lips. Smokes was pacing up and down, tears streaming down his face. And Frank was kneeling by her side, clutching her hands, breathing very hard, loudly threatening to sue the living daylights out of somebody if there wasn't a fucking good explanation for all this.

'It's not him,' Eleanor said. 'Jesus help his poor mother, but that poor boy is not my son.'

In her book-lined office, with a portrait of Augusto Cesar Sandino smiling sadly down over the desk, Doctor Honoria Perez was trying very hard to remain polite.

'I assure you, *Señor*, my information is that this is the body of your son. I am very sorry, but that is the fact.'

'Don't you assure me, darling,' Frank scoffed. 'I don't want any assurances from you.'

'*Señor* . . .'

'Listen, pet, I don't know how familiar you are with the male anatomy. But a circumcision isn't a bloody haircut. The fucking thing doesn't grow back, now does it?'

Doctor Perez looked at this hot, angry, overweight man on the other side of her desk. She felt that he should really go on a diet, but perhaps this was not the time to suggest it.

'That boy,' she said, calmly, 'he had your son's passport in his pocket when they brought him in here.'

'So?' Frank said. 'Big deal. You can buy a passport down in the Barrio Lescano any night of the week.'

'But you yourself thought it was him.'

He pointed his finger. 'I did not say that. I didn't get a decent look at him.'

She put her hands to her face. '*Señor*,' she sighed, 'shock is very common in these situations. That is what happened to your wife.'

'Don't you tell me about my wife,' he warned. 'Just don't you dare tell me about my own wife.'

The office door opened, and a man in a white coat entered the room. He came to Doctor Perez's desk and said something before handing her a piece of paper. She glanced at it. The fluorescent light buzzed. She pulled open her drawer and lit a cigarette, took a pull and cleared her throat. This was not going to be easy.

'*Señor* Little.' She nodded. 'It seems there *has* been a mistake. I am sorry. The dental records show that this is not your son.'

He stood up slowly, feeling hot and light-headed.

'You see?' he said. 'I can't even recognize my own flesh and blood, no?'

She shook her head. 'It is a matter for the *Policia* now. You must go to the Missing Persons office at the *Ministerio*.'

She held out an envelope, and he took it from her hand.

'I am sorry,' she shrugged. 'Mistakes happen in war.'

He glared at her. 'You're some doctor alright.'

'*Señor*,' she snapped, 'if people like your son stayed at home, perhaps I would have time to be a better doctor.'

'You people,' he said. 'And you wonder why your country's in a state.'

'We are trying to run things differently now.'

'You people could not run water, darling.'

Outside in the car park, Smokes and Eleanor were sitting on a bench, drinking Coca-Cola, surrounded by worried-looking soldiers. Eleanor was holding a red and black bandanna to her forehead. Smokes looked as if he might throw up at any moment.

Eleanor looked up with fear in her eyes. He gazed at her upturned vulnerable face and he walked slowly towards her through the heat. She held out her hand. He wanted to take her in his arms and hold her very tightly, but he did not do this. Instead, he clasped her hand between his own hands and sat down beside her on the bench.

'It's not him,' he said quietly. 'He's alive. He's alive some-where.'

Smokes jumped up and threw his arms around a soldier. The soldier clapped him on the back. '*Está vivo*,' Smokes yelled, and all the soldiers whooped and cheered.

'Thanks be to God,' Eleanor cried. 'Oh, Frank, thanks be to God.'

Frank lit a cigarette. 'My fucking heart is rattling,' he said. 'That gentleman will be thanking God alright, when I get my shagging mitts on him.'

7

Cherry Balducci

THEY SAT AT A WHITE tin table in the Plaza de España, drinking cold beer and grapefruit juice, trying to remain calm enough to discuss things. This was difficult. Smokes kept standing up and yelling '*fuckin' A*' with his head in his hands, until a couple of Germans at the next table got upset and asked him to stop.

Frank wanted to telephone the Irish consulate in Mexico, see if they'd send somebody down straight away. He wanted to telephone the newspapers back home. He wanted to send faxes and emergency telegrams.

Smokes said none of this was a good idea. Not for the moment anyway. Better to see if they couldn't sort things out themselves. They'd go over to the *Ministerio* in a while and chain Nuñez to a chair until he wised them up.

'Well, now,' Frank said, 'I just think a few bloody phone calls. Just to put the skids under these penpushers.'

Smokes shook his head. 'These people are real *sensitivo*, Franklin. Too much pressure, they can be jerks.'

'But I know this chap in the Taoiseach's department, you see, back in Dublin, Billy Spain his name is, and now, I've done Billy a favour or two in my time, and . . .'

'Frank,' Eleanor interrupted, 'Smokes knows the situation here. We'd be as well to listen to his advice.'

Frank nodded. He sipped his juice. 'Yes. You're right, of course. Yes. We wouldn't want to do anything stupid.'

The midday sun screamed down into the plaza. There was no trace of haze left in the sky. People were sitting under trees and umbrellas, not moving at all, just waiting for the afternoon to arrive before they stirred again.

'You'll be wanting to let Veronica know, of course,' Eleanor said quietly. 'She'll be worrying.'

When he looked up at her she seemed to be searching her handbag for something.

'Gimme a fax number, Franklin,' Smokes said. 'I'll try and get a message to her from the *Ministerio*.'

Frank lit a cigarette. He clenched his fist and put it against his forehead. He bit his lip and tried to keep calm. He felt Smokes's fingers on his wrist.

'Yes,' Frank mumbled. 'Yes. Thank you, Smokes.'

Very suddenly, Frank hung his head. He covered his eyes with his hands and ran his fingers through his hair, trying not to cry. He dug his fingernails into his palms until they hurt.

'Oh, Johnny,' he whispered. 'Oh, Johnny, son.'

Smokes glanced at Eleanor. She was gnawing her lip and looking out over the plaza. 'We'll find him, Franklin,' Smokes said. 'Chill out, man. We'll find him.'

'Of course we will,' Eleanor said, and she put her hand on the back of Frank's wrist, very lightly, and just for a second.

'I'll tan his bloody backside for him,' Frank said.

Smokes laughed. 'The little mother's just gone AWOL. Sure wouldn't be the first time.'

Frank took out a tissue and blew his nose. 'What?'

'Just Johnny.' Smokes shrugged. 'This shit just used to happen with the guy. Man, he was one weird puppy. He used to just take off for days at a time, tell nobody.'

'What?'

'Oh yeah,' Smokes said. 'Johnny Little? You kidding me?'

'He used to disappear?'

'Well, he used to go away, yeah.'

'Where to?'

'I dunno, Franklin. All over, I guess.'

'All over where, Smokes?'

Smokes chuckled. 'Well, tell you the truth, it was usually to see some broad. There was one in Chinandega. Another one, she lived up in the north. Up near Corinto, I think. You know, near where the attack was? He used to go see these broads sometimes, I guess. For weekends, you know?'

'And what's this girl's name? The one in the north.'

Smokes scratched his head. 'I think it's Maria something. Or Pilar, maybe. I'm not sure. He had lots of babes.'

'You're not sure?'

'Jeez, she's some chick who works in an ice cream bar in Corinto, Franklin. It was nothing serious.'

'I can't believe you didn't tell us.'

'Frank, man'.– Smokes laughed – 'don't get uptight here. It was nothing. Don't you think I'd know if it was serious, Frank? Johnny had lots of girls, man, all over. There was some chick down in Rivas. Another one in Matagalpa. The guy was popular, you know? He used to go off sometimes by himself, that's all I'm saying.'

'But for Jesus' sake, Smokes. Why didn't you tell us that before, son?'

Smokes looked uncomfortable. 'Frank, I guess they never found his body before.'

'Now,' Eleanor said, 'I think we should all calm down.'

Frank began to sulk. 'Look,' Smokes said. 'We're playing the Revolution Day show up there next week, man. It makes you feel better, I'll go check out this chick, OK?'

'I thought you said it wasn't bloody serious. Why would you go and see her?'

'Franklin, it wasn't. I'm just saying, man, we're booked to do a show up in Corinto, you know. I'll look her up.'

'So you know where she lives?'

'Well, no, Frank,' Smokes said. 'I don't.'

'Jesus Christ, son. For his best friend you don't know much, do you?'

'Stop it now, Frank,' Eleanor said. 'There's no need for an atmosphere.'

'Jesus H, Franklin,' Smokes said quietly. 'The guy played his cards close sometimes. What can I tell you?'

A very pretty young woman with long red hair came wandering across the plaza, weaving through the metal tables. She had a long straight back and a thin face. She wore black jeans with slashes at the knees, black loafers, an open tartan shirt tied under her midriff and a black bra. She approached their table and stood behind Smokes. She looked at Frank and Eleanor, winked and put her finger over her lips.

'¿Amor?' she said. Smokes grinned. He stood up and turned.

'Cherry, baby. You're back in the land of the living.'

They hugged each other and kissed. Smokes bit her neck, and she squirmed as he slid his hand up the back of her shirt. Frank rolled his eyes and folded his arms. Eleanor coughed diplomatically.

'Honey pie,' Smokes said, 'this is Frank and Eleanor, Johnny's folks.'

Cherry Balducci's face saddened. She shook hands with Frank and Eleanor and sat down at the table.

'I'm real sorry about what happened,' she said.

'No' – Smokes laughed – 'You don't understand. *Jesus*, babes, have we got some news for you, man.'

As Smokes told the story, Cherry began to look absolutely stunned. 'No way,' she kept saying. 'Get out of here, Smokes.' She put her hand to her chest and opened her eyes wide. 'Oh my God. Gag me with a spoon.'

'No, it's true.' Smokes giggled. 'It really wasn't him.'

Eleanor began to laugh too, and Smokes stood up and yelled '*fuckin' A*' again. The Germans glowered, but he didn't even look at them. The waiter came over and asked him to cool it. Smokes sat down and drained his glass of beer.

'It wasn't him.' He beamed.

'Course,' Cherry said, 'it still don't mean he's alive.'

There was a silence. Smokes gaped at her.

'And what's that supposed to mean?' Frank said.

She looked around the table, blushing. 'Well, it's just . . .' Her fingers began to twist the edges of the tablecloth. 'I mean, it don't *mean* anything, Mr Little. We know he was up in San Juan the night the Contras came. The night he disappeared? I mean, just because they ain't found the body . . .'

Frank snapped the napkin from his lap and threw it on to the table.

'Well, that's a beautiful attitude now,' he said.

'I'm sorry, Mr Little,' Cherry murmured. 'I didn't think.'

He shook his head from side to side and slapped at the flies.

'She's right, Frank,' Eleanor said. 'She's right, you know. I didn't think of things that way.'

Smokes clapped his hands. 'You know, I think we should go see Nuñez right now. We'll insist, Franklin. Get the old posse together and go kick some butt. What do you say, man?'

Frank said nothing.

'He's probably just hiding out somewhere, Franklin. He probably doesn't even know he's causing all this shit.'

Frank still said nothing. His mouth hung open and he stared at the table with wide eyes. Cherry looked worried. She turned to Eleanor and asked if she'd brought a photograph of Johnny with her. When Eleanor said no, she hadn't, Frank looked up and glared.

'Well, what would I bring a photo for, Frank?' She laughed. 'I mean, God, I didn't think about that.' He kept staring, refusing to speak, looking sternly into her eyes.

'I'm real sorry, Mr Little,' Cherry pleaded. 'I just didn't think, I guess.'

Frank stood up so sharply that he knocked over his glass. Pink juice dribbled across the tablecloth. He scraped his seat away from the table, grabbed his holdall and walked off very quickly across the plaza, hands thrust into his pockets, scattering birds into the air all around him. After a moment, Smokes sighed, hauled himself out of his seat and began to follow.

'I'm so sorry, Mrs Little,' Cherry said.

'Don't worry, dear. Tell me, when was the last time you saw him?'

'The end of May, I guess. A month ago. He told me he was going up to San Juan on his motorbike. He said he was just going up there to kick around for a while. It's a little town near Corinto. He called me just before the end of May.'

'And how did you hear what happened?'

'Nuñez's guy called Smokes to say there'd been an attack and they'd found this body. Our number was in the dead guy's wallet. He told us the dead guy's passport said his name was Johnny Little, so Smokes told him to call you and Frank.'

Cherry looked as if she was going to cry now. She pursed her lips and blinked hard.

'I'm sorry, Mrs Little,' she said. 'Me and my mouth.'

'Never mind, dear,' Eleanor said. 'Tell me now, did you have a good trip? Back home, were you?'

'Yeah,' she said. 'My mom's real sick. She has breast cancer. She's in the hospital down in Baton Rouge.'

'Oh dear. And here we are thinking about our own troubles.'

Cherry bit her red fingernails and stared across at Frank and Smokes.

'Tell me now, Cherry, love,' Eleanor said, 'you're Smokes's girlfriend, are you?'

Cherry nodded, looking worried. 'He don't like me to say that, but I guess it's what I am.'

She smiled at Eleanor. 'He says we're not having a relationship, we've just had three hundred and forty consecutive one-night stands.'

'Oh, men,' Eleanor sighed. 'They're funny, aren't they?'

'Really. Go figure 'em.'

They looked over at Frank and Smokes, who were standing by the fountain now, not speaking to each other. Smokes was trying to shoo away a drunken beggar who was playing an accordion and staggering up and down the steps.

'And did you know my son well?' Eleanor asked. 'I mean, *do* you. I suppose we shouldn't be talking about him in the past tense.'

'I guess, yeah. He was in the band, you know? He *is* in the band. He helped me out of a real jam one time.'

'What was that?'

She smiled again, a beautiful broad smile. 'Oh, I'll tell you some other time. You know, it's the weirdest thing, but you look exactly like him.'

'Oh, God help the poor devil.'

'No. He's real nice looking. Cute, you know?'

'You're not in love with him?'

'Oh, yeah.' Cherry beamed. 'At least fifty per cent. I mean, everyone is. He was that type I guess. He was a real ten.' She paused. 'He *is* a real ten, I mean.'

'Do you know this girl he had up in the north?'

Cherry lit a cigarette. 'You mean the one who works in the bar? No, I don't, Mrs Little. Why?'

Eleanor shrugged. 'Wondering,' she said.

'I think her name's Eneyda,' Cherry said. 'I ain't too sure.'

Cherry looked across the plaza again. Frank was still standing by the fountain, holding on to the stone rim now, looking as though he might jump in at any minute. Smokes had his hand on Frank's shoulder. He was speaking very rapidly.

'Jeez, Mrs Little,' Cherry sighed. 'I really am sorry about this. I got a mouth like the Panama Canal.'

Eleanor clasped Cherry's hand. 'Don't upset yourself, love. It's as well to be prepared for the worst, after all. And call me Eleanor, for heaven's sake. You make me feel old with your Missus Little.'

'Johnny always says that,' Cherry said. 'It's smart to expect the worst. So if bad stuff happens, you're not upset about it, and if it don't, you're ahead on points.'

'Oh, he gets that from you know who,' Eleanor laughed, nodding in Frank's direction. 'Practical.'

'If that's the word,' Cherry said, and she laughed too.

Frank and Smokes began to walk back over to the table. Frank still had his hands in his pockets, and a cigarette hung from his lower lip. Smokes looked happier now, holding his head up high. He grabbed Frank's hand and started to swing it up and down until Frank slapped him away.

'I'm real sorry, Mr Little,' Cherry said. 'You gonna forgive me?'

'Forget it, pet. It's just this heat. Makes you lose the fucking rag.'

'Good God, Frank,' Eleanor sighed. 'Language, really.'

'Yeah, yeah. You know what I mean all the same.'

He looked at Cherry then. She grinned at him, pushing her hair out of her eyes. She really was very beautiful, he thought, with that lovely smooth skin and that wonderful hair, so red and long. He smiled back at her and sat down.

He coughed. 'Well now,' he said, 'if I'd known that gentleman had such pretty-looking friends, I'd've been over here myself long ago.'

'Oh, would you listen to the charm of it,' Eleanor said.

'Hey, Mr Little' – Cherry laughed – 'I think you must've kissed the Blarney Stone.'

'He swallowed it, dear,' said Eleanor.

He was feeling better now. He was feeling almost happy in fact. He reached for the jug, poured himself a large glass of beer and drained it in two gulps.

8

The Quiet Man

FRANK LITTLE LEFT SCHOOL at the age of fourteen and got a job making the tea in a taxi office on Thomas Street. The office was in the basement of a dark old Georgian house and the boss was a man named Johnny Doyle, who had lost a finger fighting for the old IRA in the Black and Tan war and then run off to join the merchant navy. Whenever a sailor died at sea, it had been Johnny Doyle's job to perform the ceremony. Johnny Doyle loved the words of the burial rite, and he loved to quote them to the taxi drivers whenever he was feeling bored and restless.

'Oh, we have not here a lasting city,' Johnny Doyle would sigh, shaking his head glumly, when business was bad and there was not enough work to be done. Johnny Doyle liked Frank Little. He told him stories about the people he had met in Africa. He showed him how to work the radio. One day he taught him a song about a young woman who had run off to sea with a band of desperate pirates.

> Well it's of a handsome female, as you may understand
> Her mind being bent on rambling to some far distant land
> She dressed herself in men's attire or so it would appear
> And she joined those hairy buccaneers
> To serve them for a year.

Just before Easter 1953, Frank went to a party at his cousin Michael Houlihan's house and Eleanor Hamilton was there. She played the piano and sang 'The Star of the County Down' and 'Kevin Barry' and 'Glory Oh, Glory Oh, to the Bold Fenian Men' and afterwards all the young boys in the room wanted to talk to her.

They hovered around her, telling her jokes, offering to get her drinks and sandwiches. She was the centre of everything, but she scoffed at them all. They were bits of kids, she told them. She was fifteen years old herself.

When she left the party to go home, he ran out into Bride Street and called after her. She turned and put her hands on her hips. He asked her to go to the pictures with him and, to his great surprise, she said yes. He went back in to the party and sat in a corner by himself, watching the quadrille dancing and thinking about her. He did not sleep at all that night.

They went to see a film called *The Quiet Man*, starring John Wayne and Maureen O'Hara. The film had been made in Ireland and this was fantastically exciting. Nobody could remember an American film ever being made in Ireland before. One of Johnny Doyle's taxi drivers claimed he had picked up John Wayne outside the Gresham Hotel one night, with Hilton Edwards and Micheál Mac Liammóir. He had got John Wayne's autograph on the back of an old envelope, and he kept it in the glove box of his car to impress the skulls. A skull was a passenger. Frank told Eleanor, and she laughed then. He liked it when she laughed. As they sat in the cinema waiting for the film to begin, he told her about all the men in the office, about James McLoughlin, who could play the guitar and sing country songs, and about Oliver O'Connor, who went running and won medals nearly every week, and she listened to him very carefully, laughing, watching his eyes as he spoke. When the lights went down and the newsreel film started he reached out gently in the darkness and took her hand. He felt her close her fingers around his. Her eyes never left the screen once.

The newsreel said that twenty-four thousand people had left Ireland that year. There were flickering pictures of men and women standing on the Pier at the North Wall, waving shyly at the camera. Frank closed his eyes and tried to imagine what twenty-four thousand people would look like.

When the film was over they went up to Johnny Rea's to have ice creams and coffee. They sat at a table in the window and talked about *The Quiet Man*. There had been a scene where Sean Thornton and Mary Kate Danagher had got married, and a big double bed had to be taken into their cottage by the embarrassed locals. When Frank laughed about that she blushed and told him to stop.

Some of the boys from the street came into the shop. When they saw Frank and Eleanor they began to whistle and hoot. They put romantic songs on the jukebox. They blew kisses. They sniggered and jeered. But Frank did not care. He was absolutely thrilled that his friends had seen them together.

He walked her all the way home to her house in Drimnagh. She talked about her family on the way. She had four brothers and two sisters. Her father was in Guinness's brewery and her mother was from Galway. Whenever there was a silence between them, she started to talk about her family again. She had a brother who was going to Chicago. Her sisters worked in the handbag factory in Wicklow Street. She had an uncle in the guards. She had a cousin who had once come second in a beauty pageant.

'You'd come first,' he told her.

'Stop, you' – she laughed – 'I would not.'

Outside the house he asked if he could see her again. She smiled at him, and said yes, she thought that would be alright.

9

Captain Nuñez

THEY SAT IN THE HALL at the *Ministerio del Interior* reading the old copies of *Time* and *Revista Cultural* which were stacked in piles on the tables, waiting for Nuñez's clerk to come back from his meeting. He was almost an hour late, and when eventually he bustled through the doors and across the lobby he looked very hot and irritated.

Cherry jumped up and approached him straight away. They exchanged a few words in Spanish and the clerk started to shout. He was a short fat man, completely bald, and he was so angry now that the sweat on his scalp was turning to steam. It looked as if smoke was pouring from the top of his bullet-shaped head. He ran his hand between his neck and his collar, grunting and puffing, his face bright purple with rage.

'He says the Doc called him,' Cherry told them. 'He's pissed now. He says it ain't his responsibility.'

'Fucking little gom,' Frank muttered. 'Tell the little wanker we'll have him sent to Siberia.'

'Don't,' Smokes said. He stood up, went to the counter and began speaking to the clerk in a calm, placatory tone.

The clerk scoffed. He put one hand between his legs and clutched at his testicles, making a squeezing gesture with the other. '*Me cago en la madre que le parió,*' he sneered.

Smokes turned around. 'Well' — he flushed – 'I guess he's not in a real good mood today.'

'What did he say to you?' Frank asked.

Smokes glanced over at Eleanor. 'Some other time, Franklin,' he said. 'It's, you know, just something they say around here.'

A sudden flurry of activity filled the lobby behind them. When they turned, a tall slender man in a captain's uniform was striding across the white floor carrying a briefcase. A young soldier was with him, rifle clamped over his shoulder, and another man was chasing across the lobby, waving a notebook and shouting. 'Oh, bueno,' called the man. 'Por favor, un momento de su tiempo.' Frank recognized him. It was Hollis Clarke of the *Washington Times*. The Captain suddenly stopped walking. He whirled around to face Clarke and began to speak, counting off points on his long fingers. Clarke listened hard, scribbling notes.

'Go on, Smokes,' Cherry urged.

'I can't,' Smokes hissed. 'Look, the guy is busy, man.'

'Jesus, Smokes. He's only talking to Hollis. You want me to do it?'

Smokes got up and began to walk towards the men. The clerk barked at him, but he paid no attention. The clerk grabbed a telephone, jabbed a few numbers and slammed the phone back on the receiver. '*Que le den por culo,*' he spat.

'Who's that?' Eleanor asked.

'It's Nuñez,' Cherry said. 'He's the guy you need to see.'

Smokes was talking to Nuñez now, and Nuñez was nodding impatiently, looking very serious, trying to ignore Hollis Clarke completely. Smokes took a step back and pointed towards Frank and Eleanor. Nuñez looked very sullen as he nodded and listened. Clarke sighed and put his notebook away. Nuñez peered at his watch. He stood with his hands behind his back, talking insistently to Clarke, while Smokes hurried back towards them.

'Franklin, Eleanor, come on' – he beckoned – 'Nuñez is going to see you. Cherry, you wait here, OK?'

'I wish to Christ he wouldn't call me that,' Frank sighed.

They crossed the lobby with Smokes. Close up Nuñez looked younger, thirty at most. He had deep brown eyes and a thin moustache. He was speaking very angrily to Hollis Clarke.

'Eleanor, Frank,' Smokes interrupted, 'this is Captain Nuñez. *Compañero, le quiero presentera dos amigos irlandeses.*'

Nuñez's handshake was strong and warm. '*Mucho gusto,*' he said, bowing slightly to them. Clarke recognized Frank. They shook hands and Frank introduced him to Eleanor. Nuñez coughed and tapped the face of his watch.

'*Vámonos,*' he said briskly, pointing towards the ceiling.

They walked through a hatch in the counter and then through a large X-ray frame. A woman sentry scanned their bodies with a bleeping electronic gun. She took Eleanor's handbag and Frank's holdall and put them into cardboard boxes, saying they could collect them on the way out.

The large room behind the counter was full of filing cabinets and wooden packing cases. Metal pieces from some sort of machine were spread out all over the floor and a young soldier was trying to assemble them with the help of a manual. Nuñez shouted at him, and the soldier stood wearily to his feet and saluted.

There were two lift doors in the wall. The soldier led them to the door on the right. He pressed the button a few times but the door refused to open. After a moment, Nuñez said something sharp and they all went towards the other lift. The soldier motioned for them to enter.

Inside, the doors closed with a squeal. The lift began to move, then suddenly stopped between floors with a dull grinding sound. Nuñez clicked his tongue and began to rock back and forth on his heels. The lift shuddered and started to move again.

Suddenly Frank felt his stomach rumble. He clutched his abdomen and belched softly. The soldier sniggered.

'Frank Little,' Eleanor gasped. 'For the love of God.'

'Well, I can't help it,' he whispered. 'It's the awful grub in this place.'

Nuñez turned to look at him.

'You are correct, *Señor* Little,' he said briskly. 'The food and the water are poor. Very bad for the digestive tract. The revenge of the General, we call it.'

The sentry chuckled again. 'You speak English?' Frank said, astonished.

Nuñez held up his hands. '*Sólo un poco*. A little only.'

'Captain Nuñez is being real modest,' Smokes said. 'Captain Nuñez writes *poetry* in English.'

Nuñez shook his head. 'I make only a very poor effort, whenever I have the time. But *Comandante* Borge writes beautiful poetry.'

The lift jolted again. Nuñez muttered angrily. For a minute, nobody spoke. Then the whine and growl of the cable trailed its way down the shaft and they started to move upwards once more.

Suddenly Nuñez raised a finger. 'One day,' he announced, 'I shall write him a poem, as cold and passionate as the dawn.'

Frank gaped at him. 'Beg pardon?'

'William Yeats,' Nuñez said. 'One of the truly great writers of Ireland, no?'

'Oh, absolutely,' Frank said. 'We have him on the twenty pound note at home.'

'And our country has very great writers also. Have you heard about Rubén Darío?'

'No. I must admit now, I haven't.'

Nuñez pursed his lips and nodded.

'*Bueno*, Rubén Darío is a great favourite of our people. Also of *Comandante* Borge, my superior. The *compañero Comandante* is a very great lover of poetry.'

'Good for him,' Frank said.

'Yes,' Nuñez agreed, 'good for him. *Verdad.*'

Nuñez's office was small and shabby and it looked down on the ruins of the city, right over the Barrio Monterrey and the roof of the shattered cathedral. In the distance the yellow sun glimmered on Lake Managua and a creamy haze wrapped itself around the peaks of the volcanoes.

The office contained four filing cabinets, a few wooden chairs, a long narrow table and a vast wooden desk. The desk was scratched and lopsided; a thick book had been wedged underneath its short leg. A huge map of Nicaragua was spread out on the table, with tiny flags stuck into it. Some of the flags were red and black. The others were green or blue. A bicycle leaned against one of the filing cabinets, looking awkward and out of place.

The back wall of Nuñez's office was completely covered with crucifixes. Many were vivid and garish, made of coloured glass and bright stones. Naive Christs beamed down over the office, grinning like babies, rays of light streaming from their open hands. There were Christs crucified in the ermine robes of emperors and kings. There were female Christs, black Christs, yellow Christs with oriental eyes. Some were battered or broken, with limbs and heads missing, ancient twisted bodies agonizing in oak and black ash. There were blue and red Russian icons.

There was an abstract white steel cross in a black steel circle, and there was a Christ in jeans and T-shirt with syringes jabbed into his palms and feet.

'Well, you must be a very holy fellow, Captain,' Eleanor said. 'You must never be off your knees.'

He shook his head. 'I am not a believer. I merely collect them as artifacts. My first wife used to like them. She had an eye for them, I think you would say in English.'

'They're very beautiful,' Eleanor said.

'Yes, of course. The *compañero* Minister for Culture, Father Cardenal, he is very hopeful that they will convert me, but I do not think so.'

'Oh, well, one day?' – she smiled – 'You never know.'

'No,' he said. 'I do know.'

Nuñez sat down at his desk. His movements were very precise. He opened his jacket, unbuckled his holster and put his pistol carefully on top of a book. The soldier sat down by the door and lit a cigarette. Nuñez said something to him and the soldier mashed the cigarette out on the floor.

'You will begin now, please,' Nuñez said. 'There is not much time.'

As Frank and Eleanor told their story he listened patiently, showing no emotion at all until they told him about the body in the morgue. '*Santa María*,' he sighed then, but not a single muscle in his face moved. After a few minutes he began to take notes, leaning his hand on his notebook and writing very quickly in large black letters. He asked them to repeat some things. Others he understood immediately.

When they had finished speaking he folded his hands and peered at them.

'And your son,' he said quietly. 'He had no permission to be in the zone of war.'

'I wouldn't know about that,' Frank said, glancing surreptitiously at Smokes. 'I'm not too sure about that.'

Nuñez tapped his pen on the desk and stared at Frank. He said nothing for a moment. The air conditioning chugged. He put his pen down and sighed.

'*Señor*, if you waste my time I cannot help you. Your son was illegal in the *zona*. Do you dispute this with me?'

'No. No, I don't.'

'And this is very serious. You are aware of how extremely serious this is, of course?'

'Yes, Captain. We're aware of that.'

'*Bueno*,' Nuñez said. 'That is very important. Your son has broken the law and that is very important. If I go to your country and if I break your law in Ireland, is it important?'

'Yes.'

'Yes, *Señor*. I think it is.'

Nuñez muttered to himself. He leaned over his desk and wrote something down. He asked them some more questions, then got up and looked at the map on his table. After a moment, he went back to his desk, opened a drawer and took out a book. He licked his fingers and turned a few pages, looking into the book, then scribbling on the fly-leaf. He came back across the room and leaned his hands on the table, staring hard at the map for a while, then moving some of the tiny flags around. He seemed to be whispering to himself. He glanced at his watch. He went back to his desk, sat down again and wrote for another five minutes, peering into the book from time to time.

'And what do you think of our country?' he asked suddenly.

'Oh, we like it very much,' Frank said. 'We're finding it very educational. Aren't we, Eleanor?'

'It's dreadfully hot,' she said.

Nuñez nodded. '*Sí*. It is too hot now, even for us *Nicas*. It is bad for the crops.'

'And nothing seems to work,' she continued. 'I mean, I'm not being funny now, but everything seems to be out of order.'

'Yes,' Nuñez said. 'Since the counter-revolutionary economic war against us, this too is a problem.'

Frank coughed nervously. 'But I mean, the people, Eleanor. I must say, they're terribly friendly, after all.'

'Our people can be a little suspicious of foreigners,' Nuñez said.

'Oh,' said Eleanor, 'but you can't blame the poor dears. They've had an awful time from foreigners over the years.'

'In the past, yes. But now the people are taking charge of their own affairs, through the revolutionary structures and the mass organizations.'

'And now,' Smokes said, 'lots of foreigners come here to help, don't they, Captain? To help the revolution?'

Nuñez glared at him. 'You think?'

'Well,' Smokes grinned, 'I mean people like Johnny.'

'Ah, *sí*.' Nuñez nodded. 'You think your friend is a help to our revolution, *compañero*? You think it is helpful to come here and disobey our laws? You think we have laws for no reason perhaps? You think we have laws for our own amusement?'

Smokes hung his head and said nothing.

'Our people have had this kind of help before,' Nuñez said. 'We have had many *gringos* come here and break our laws before. This is not the kind of help our people need.'

The door opened. A young woman brought in a jug of coffee. The soldier came to the desk and poured it into cups. He passed a plate of hard-looking biscuits to Frank and Eleanor. Nuñez did not drink his coffee. He sat very still, with his arms folded, watching everybody. And then suddenly he began to speak again.

'We have never been to your country. But the *compañero Comandante* Borge will be visiting with your Prime Minister FitzGerald in the winter, and so we are all very jealous.' He paused.

'We are green,' he said. '*¿Verdad?* We are green with envy?'

Frank and Eleanor laughed dutifully. Then there was silence again. Nuñez got up from his desk and walked to the window. He stared down over Managua for what seemed like a long time.

Eleanor and Frank glanced at each other. She nodded briskly towards the door.

'Well now, Captain,' Frank said, 'I know you'll do everything to help us.'

Nuñez bowed his head without turning.

'*Claro*,' he said. 'But I can make no promises, *Señor*.'

He kept touching the glass and then taking his hand away, examining the trace of his handprint. He did this for some moments, then reached slowly into his pocket, pulled out a handkerchief and wiped the glass clean.

'We really appreciate what you people are doing here,' Frank said. 'You know, our son used to tell us about it. Whenever he wrote.'

'It is not an easy time for our country,' Nuñez said, still without turning from the window. 'The people are suffering greatly. This is an agony to us all. The *Comandante* especially, of course. The *Comandante* has a very great love for the people.'

'Well, I've written to my member of parliament back home, to say he should do something about it.'

Nuñez came back to his desk, sat down and sipped his coffee. 'Very kind.' He nodded. 'The solidarity of the non-aligned countries is invaluable to our people.'

'Those Americans,' Frank scoffed. 'They think they own the world. I meet a lot of them in my line. Loudmouths. Ewe-nited States, you know. They think they own you.'

Nuñez peered up at him. 'We have no quarrel with the people of North America. We have good friends there. There will be a demonstration, in fact, in Washington tomorrow. It is the fourth of July. The famous actor Martin Sheen will speak.'

Frank paused. 'Well, yes,' he said. 'Obviously. But that Reagan fellow, right? Who the blazes does he think he is?'

'Is that the time?' Smokes said quickly. 'I guess we better split.'

Nuñez looked at the floor. 'Where are you staying, sir?'

'Oh, we're at the El Dorado. Little place, you wouldn't know it.'

Nuñez took a biro from his breast pocket and began to stir his coffee with it. 'You will move to the Imperial,' he said. 'It will be more comfortable for your wife. They have the air conditioning there.'

'Well now,' Eleanor laughed. 'It's a bit on the pricey side.'

'It's not that,' Frank said. 'They're full, you see. They've some conference on.'

Nuñez shook his head. 'If the *Comandante* wishes it, they will find room. And forgive me, *Señora*, I meant as guests of the people, of course.'

'Oh,' she said. 'Do you own it now?'

Nuñez pursed his lips. 'The people own it now. The people need hard currency.'

'But we couldn't do that,' Frank said firmly. 'We're grand where we are.'

'*Señor* Little,' Nuñez said, '*Comandante* Borge would wish you

87

to be comfortable. I presume you do not wish to offend *Comandante* Borge?'

Eleanor glanced at Frank. He shook his head.

'It *would* be nice, Frank,' she whispered. 'It's a lovely place, and you'd sleep better with the air conditioning.'

She looked at Nuñez. 'It's hard to get any sleep,' she said. 'Frank really feels the heat, you see.'

'Eleanor, please,' Frank hissed. 'Captain Nuñez doesn't want to know about that.'

'*Compañero*,' said Nuñez to Smokes, 'you can move our guests and their belongings?'

Smokes nodded. 'Sure thing, man.'

Nuñez wrote in his book again. 'I will make a call,' he said, 'I think you will be more comfortable.'

'Well, thank you, Captain,' Frank said. 'We're embarrassed by your generosity.'

Nuñez nodded. 'The generosity of the Nicaraguan people is well known.'

He stood up and turned his back to them. He lit a cigarette, picked up his telephone and dialled a number. He spoke very quietly for several minutes and when he put the phone down he made another note in his book before turning.

'It is done,' he said. 'I have spoken with the *Comandante*. He has instructed me to convey his best wishes. He has authorized me to arrange everything.'

'Captain,' Eleanor said, 'do you think we could meet the *Comandante*? To explain things to him personally?'

Nuñez shook his head in astonishment. 'Impossible,' he said. '*Comandante* Borge is very busy. I shall keep him informed of all developments.'

'Oh yes, he'd be very busy, Eleanor,' Frank said. 'The Captain will do what he can for us.'

'Oh,' she said. 'Well, I know.'

Nuñez looked at her and nodded, stubbing out his cigarette.

'I am like one of your saints, *Señora*. I am authorized to intercede with those greater than myself.'

Frank laughed nervously. 'Well now, that fellow of ours,' he said, 'I'll tan that messer's hide for him.'

Nuñez stared. 'You will explain, please?'

'Tan his hide,' Frank explained. 'I'll give him a good bloody talking to.'

Nuñez looked at his watch. 'Young men make mistakes,' he said. 'That is what they are young for, yes?'

'Well, yes,' said Frank. 'You're right there. They get these big ideas.'

Nuñez nodded. 'And old men, *Señor*. Sometimes they get big ideas also. ¿*Verdad?*'

Frank looked at him, unsure of what to say.

'Well, I suppose so, yes. Sometimes.'

'*Bueno*,' Nuñez said. 'And now we must go. We have an urgent meeting of the agriculture committee.'

He got up and put on his cap. The soldier stood to attention. Nuñez began to shuffle through the papers on his desk.

'Hey, Captain,' Smokes tittered. 'I bet you never thought you'd end up having dullsville meetings about the coffee harvest? When you were up in the mountains, fighting?'

Nuñez looked up, his face expressionless. Smokes began to stutter.

'I just meant, you know, you must sometimes wish you were back up there. Back up in the mountains.'

Nuñez went back to the papers on his desk. When he had finished gathering them, he took a cigarette from his pocket and lit it. He took a deep drag, exhaled and pointed the cigarette at Smokes.

'*Compañero*,' he said, 'if you had ever fought in a revolution yourself, you would know how wrong you were to say that.'

'I think we'll head on now,' Eleanor said.

'I didn't mean anything.' Smokes grinned. 'I was just thinking, man.'

Nuñez nodded. 'And you must give me the great benefit of your thoughts some other time. In the meantime, as you say, I must attend a very dull meeting about the coffee harvest. A very dull meeting about the economic survival of our revolution.'

'I know, man. I didn't mean that.'

Nuñez pointed to the door of his office, and the soldier opened it. Smokes glanced at Eleanor. Frank went over to Nuñez and held out his hand.

'It was a great pleasure to meet you, Captain.'

Nuñez shook hands very quickly.

'Thank you,' he said. 'You will go now, please. We are very busy.'

They walked out into the corridor and down towards the lift.

'Frank Little,' Eleanor said, 'I hope you're ashamed. Telling those lies about writing to people.'

'Oh, put a sock in it, you. And how do you know I didn't?'

'I know well enough. You'd say night was day if you were let.'

She shook her head and walked on ahead, into the lift.

Frank turned to Smokes and laughed. 'He put you back in your box anyway.'

Smokes looked him in the eye. 'Fuck off, Frank,' he said. 'OK?'

Outside the Imperial Hotel, three clowns were dancing around the car park on stilts. A swarm of photographers followed them, clicking and flashing as the clowns swayed from side to side, yelling, whooping, threatening to fall.

Frank and Eleanor walked through the smoothly gliding electronic doors. The lobby was buzzing with people. Piles of suitcases were stacked by the counter, and uniformed bellboys were lugging them into the lifts. Framed reproductions of famous paintings decorated the length of the hallway. A vast tapestry of *The Laughing Cavalier* hung over the reception desk. The pillars in the lobby were shaped like naked women, hands over their heads, in mock classical white plaster. Gilt-covered armchairs were arranged around coffee tables with fat, sturdy sofas. Each table had a little red and black flag stuck into a bowl of fruit. The lilt of Muzak oozed through the building. There were plants everywhere, and the gurgling sound of water trickling into fountains. The figure in the biggest fountain was in the shape of a huge golden swan, water spouting from its beak. A man was leaning in over the pond, on tiptoe, polishing the swan's wing with the back of his cuff. He turned out to be the manager.

He was a dapper little man in a blue polka-dot bow tie and a black suit, with white cuffs protruding from the ends of his sleeves. His hair was smooth, slicked back and glossy. He introduced himself and shook hands.

Eleanor looked around and sighed. It was a lovely place, she told the manager. Were they very busy just now?

'Oh yes, Madame.' He nodded. 'We have the peace conference of the socialist heads of state. This is why you see so many people with guns in the building.'

Eleanor tittered, unsure whether this was a joke. But the manager did not look too happy.

One of the clowns wandered past, holding hands with a miserable-looking monkey. The monkey was wearing a top hat with a stars and stripes pattern around the rim.

'And the National Circus,' the manager continued. 'We are also privileged to have the National Circus of the Soviet Union. For one week.'

Eleanor nodded. She looked at the monkey as it loped across the lobby, trailing its horny hand along the shaggy black carpet. It was not very hygienic, she thought, to allow a wild animal into a hotel, but she decided to say nothing about it.

The manager said they would have the very best rooms in the house. He clicked his fingers and a bellboy in a white uniform rushed over.

'You are on the twenty-fifth floor' – the manager beamed – 'in the suite.' He leaned close and whispered, '*Señor* Howard Hughes stayed there, you know, in the old days. He was a very good friend of the General.'

'The General?' Frank said.

The manager nodded. 'The General,' he repeated, his face the picture of inscrutability.

'Well, thank you very much for your help,' Eleanor said.

The manager bowed. '*De nada*,' he said, looking her in the eye. 'Any friend of the revolution is a friend of our establishment.'

The enormous bedroom was cool and bright. It smelt of fresh flowers and clean linen. There were paintings of volcanoes and lakes on the walls. There was a four-poster bed with a scarlet canopy. The bedroom door led to a vast lounge with a sofa and two overstuffed armchairs. The wallpaper was red and silky. There was a glass chandelier. There was a television set and an enormous stereo, and just off the lounge a small kitchen full of gleaming pots and pans. There was a bathroom full of fluffy white towels, scented soaps and shampoo in plastic bottles, and, sunk in its floor, a black marble jacuzzi.

'Oh, Frank,' Eleanor said. 'God, I feel guilty just being here. And would you look down there at the view.'

'Yes, this is grand. You'll be set up here.'

Eleanor said she would take a shower and then meet him in the bar for a drink. 'You do that,' he said. 'I'll go find my room and get myself organized.'

The trouble started when he asked for his own room. The bellboy seemed very confused. He did not seem to understand what Frank was saying to him.

'My room,' Frank insisted, 'where is my room?'

The bellboy looked around. '¿Aquí?' he said. 'This is your room, sir?'

'No,' Frank said. He thought for a moment.

'This the room of my *wife*,' he said, loudly. The bellboy smiled and nodded.

'You know,' Frank said. '¿*Muchacha?*'

'¿*Muchacha? ¿Una mujer?*'

Frank traced an hourglass figure in the air. 'This is *Señorita*'s room,' he shouted. '*Señorita*. And where is *my* room?'

'Ah, *sí*.' The bellboy grinned. He came close to Frank and whispered, 'Fifty dollars, *Señor*.'

'What?'

'You want a girl to come. Fifty dollars.'

'No, no,' Frank snapped. 'My room. I just want my room.'

'But *this* is your room, *Señor*.'

'No, look,' he said, raising his voice again, but speaking more slowly. '*My* room. Where is *my* room?'

'Here, *Señor*?'

'No, listen, son, listen to me, alright? . . .'

'*Sí. ¿Qué quiere, Señor?*'

Frank gazed blankly at the bellboy. 'Oh, get out,' he sighed, 'go on, vamoose, you little melt.'

The bellboy shrugged and left. Frank picked up the bedside telephone and called the manager. There was some kind of misunderstanding, he said. He and his wife would be needing separate rooms. The manager apologized, but he said there was absolutely nothing he could do. Every room was taken, and the hotel was completely full. They'd only got that suite because the

Yugoslavian Minister for Education had been taken to hospital with a severe case of food poisoning.

Eleanor stood in the doorway, her wet hair dripping on to the shoulders of her dressing gown.

'What's the matter, Frank?' she asked.

He sat down on the bed. 'You'll never believe it. These incapable bloody penpushers have booked us both in here. I'll have to phone that Nuñez fellow myself if they don't sort it out.'

'Frank' — she laughed – 'for heaven's sake, don't be making such a fuss.'

'I'm telling you. I'll phone that bucko myself and I'll let him know who he's damn well dealing with.'

She rubbed her soapy eyes. 'You have the bedroom,' she sighed. 'I'll take the couch in there.'

He shook his head. 'It wouldn't be right,' he said.

'Frank, for heaven's sake. What difference would it make?'

He got up and walked to the window. He looked out at the mountains in the distance. They were tall and pink in the light, dotted with green patches of forest and field.

'It's ridiculous,' she said. 'I suppose it's Veronica you're worried about?'

'Of course it's not. Don't be bloody dense.'

'Well, I'm not going to jump on you in the middle of the night, Frank. You needn't worry.'

'Eleanor, for God's sake,' he said, his face purpling with embarrassment.

She came into the bedroom and unplugged the hair dryer. Then she stood for a moment, watching him.

'I'm trying to be practical, Frank. I thought you'd understand that much.'

He stared out of the window. Two of the clowns were still lurching and dancing on their stilts.

'Well,' he said quietly, 'I wouldn't put you out of your bed. I'll take the sofa inside.'

'Fine then. Just let's not have any more silliness.'

She took her handbag from the bedside table and disappeared back into the bathroom.

10

Endearing Young Charms

AFTER THEY HAD BEEN to the pictures three times, Frank Little began to dream about Eleanor Hamilton. He would wake up shaking and anxious, with the sound of her gorgeous laugh still ringing in his ears. At work, he thought about her all day. He was distracted. He was distraught with desire. He was sixteen years old and he was in love.

He stopped seeing her for a while, because she reduced him to such a frazzle of inarticulate nervousness. He read a book on how to talk to girls. He read his sister's magazines. Johnny Doyle said women were stranger than anything he had ever encountered on the seven seas. You could never be sure where you stood with a woman, he told him. Some of the drivers said you had to do certain things to keep a woman keen. They would laugh together then, but Frank would not understand what they were laughing about. One day he asked his mother what to do. 'Well, try to get to know her as a person,' she told him. 'That's what your father did with me. He asked me questions about myself. It's hard not to fall for someone if they ask you a lot of questions. You just be yourself and show her a bit of consideration.'

'The fellows in work say you have to pretend you don't give a damn.'

'Don't mind those poor eejits,' she said. 'There isn't one of them would know what to do with a woman, if their life depended on it. All any girl wants is a bit of gentleness, Frank. Don't you mind what anyone else tells you.'

'But she's always on about film stars, Ma. She's always on about how gorgeous film stars are.'

His mother laughed. 'And what's wrong with a young girl

94

saying that?' she said. 'You could make a bit more of yourself, Frank. You're not the worst-looking fellow, but you don't make enough of an effort. That might be what she's trying to tell you.'

He bought a second-hand suit. He bought two ties. He saw her a few more times and they went to see Cary Grant and Spencer Tracy films. She left school that summer and got a job in Harry Gaffney's handbag factory, where her sisters worked. He stopped seeing her again, but he could not stop thinking about her, no matter how hard he tried.

One day in November 1953, when he had not seen her for nearly a month, he hung around outside the handbag factory until she appeared from her work. He called out her name and waved from a shop doorway. She whispered to her girlfriends and they laughed and walked on. She ran across the street and smiled at him.

'Hello, stranger,' she said. 'I thought you were dead.'

'No,' he said. 'I was just busy.'

'Oh,' she said. 'Busy? And what had you so busy?'

'Work, just. They get very busy sometimes.'

'Poor you,' she said.

They went for coffee in Bewley's Café on Grafton Street. She told him she was playing the piano now for a dancing teacher who gave lessons out in Harold's Cross. And she liked working in the factory, she said. Some of the girls were very nice. He asked her as many questions as he could remember and then she said she had to go. Outside, shoppers were bustling through the busy street and a choir was singing Christmas carols.

'Well, I suppose I won't see you for ten years now,' she said. 'And you so busy.'

'Some of the fellows in work got tickets for a concert,' he told her. 'It's at the Olympia.'

'Good for them,' she said, buttoning her collar against the cold.

'Well, it's a couples thing.'

She laughed. 'Is that what we are?' she said. 'A couple?'

'I don't know,' he said. 'I'm fond of you.'

She linked his arm and laughed again. 'Don't be embarrassing me,' she said. He walked her all the way home, around the Green, up Harcourt Street, through Rathmines, down the canal, and

95

across Dolphin's Barn Bridge, to Drimnagh. He felt a little easier with her now.

On the night of the concert, she was waiting outside the theatre when he arrived with his friends. She was wearing a blue dress, blue shoes, a white hat and gloves. The golden yellow light glowed out from the lobby and when she turned to look at him the light made her seem almost like an angel. He told her that she looked absolutely beautiful. 'Would you stop it?' she said. 'Have you the tickets?'

There was a red-haired girl who played the harp and sang Percy French songs. There was a fat little Cockney comedian who told bad jokes that made the audience groan. 'We were so poor in our house,' he said, 'we thought knives and forks were jewellery.' Then the Italian tenor came on. He sang 'Che faro che Euridice' and 'Che gelida manina' and then 'E lucevan le stelle' from *Tosca*, making a great show of breaking down in tears at the end. When the crowd roared and cheered for more, he came back on and bowed. He told them that he had wanted to perform an Irish song but his pianist hadn't known the music. Some of the crowd shouted out for him to sing it anyway. People clapped. The tenor laughed and bowed again. He walked to the very front of the stage, held out his arms and began to sing

> O believe me if all those endearing young charms
> Which I gaze on so fondly today
> Were to change by tomorrow and fleet in my arms
> Like fairy gifts fading away
> Thou wouldst still be adored
> As this moment thou art
> Let thy loveliness fade as it will
> All around the dear ruin each wish of my heart
> Would entwine itself verdantly still.

When he finished the song there was a standing ovation.

After the concert, they all walked up Grafton Street and around the Green to the Shelbourne Hotel. Rose Tynan was performing in the ballroom. The band played 'Here In My Heart' and 'I Believe' and 'Outside of Heaven'. Frank and Eleanor danced for a while and then the band slowed the music down to a country waltz.

He moved towards her and held her in his arms. She refused to look into his eyes. The mirror ball threw flecks of light around the large scarlet room. Her hands rested on his shoulders. They circled slowly and she looked around the hall, smiling. He tried in vain to think of something to ask her.

'You're a great dancer,' she said. 'You know all the steps.'

'I like dancing,' he told her.

'I have two left feet,' she laughed.

The band picked up the tempo again. 'Let's sit this one out and have a mineral,' she said. They went upstairs to the bar. He had a bottle of beer and she had lemonade. Her fingers tapped on the side of the bottle as the music played.

Afterwards, they walked home through the cold dark streets of Dublin. Light snow was falling into Stephen's Green. There were Christmas trees in the windows of some of the houses. They walked along the silent banks of the canal and he recited a Shakespeare sonnet to her. She listened and linked his arm, humming to herself as they strolled through the crisp new snow.

They stood outside her doorway. She told Frank that she'd had a very nice evening. He felt suddenly breathless with nerves.

'Well, I better go on in,' she said. 'They'll be wondering.'

'You looked really beautiful,' he blurted.

'Go away.' She laughed. 'I looked a sight. Some of the girls there were lovely.'

'You were nicer than any of them.'

She looked up at the dark blue clouds and said nothing.

'I'm very fond of you, Eleanor.'

'I know you are,' she said quietly. 'You show me that.'

She held out her gloved hand. He took her fingers and raised them to his lips.

'You're an awful messer, Frank Little,' she said.

He stepped into her arms. Her lips were very cold against his face. He touched her hair. He put his arm around her waist and pulled her close to him. They kissed. Then she stepped quickly away from him into her house, closing the door behind her.

On the way back to his house, he was so happy he felt he could have reached out his hand to stir the stars around in the sky.

11

Principles

FOR TWO LONG DAYS there was no news at all. Eleanor slept late in the air-conditioned room, then soaked and prayed in baths full of foam. In the hot afternoons she sat by the pool, reading a Spanish textbook and drinking mineral water.

A young Norwegian priest came to see her. He was wearing an earring and a denim jacket with the sleeves cut off. That seemed odd to her. He was a long way from Father Rogan, the parish priest in Dun Laoghaire. The young priest had heard about Eleanor and Frank from a journalist he knew. He hoped she didn't mind the intrusion, he said, he had just wanted to offer any help he could. He held her hand in the bedroom. They knelt down on the floor, saying the rosary together, and then he gave her Holy Communion. She felt better then. She ordered lemon tea and asked him all about Norway. It was a very beautiful country, he told her, but very cold and very expensive.

'For instance' – he smiled – 'one beer is six dollars there.'

'Good heavens. That must keep you all sober.'

'Yes.' He nodded. 'You would need to be a millionaire to be an alcoholic in Norway.'

On Friday afternoon Smokes and Cherry turned up with Guapo Gomez. Guapo was the bass player with the Desperados de Amor and they wanted to introduce him to Frank and Eleanor. He had a face like Tony Curtis, twinkling brown eyes and a mop of shiny black hair. He wore very tight black trousers and a clinging white shirt which was slightly ruffled. He was ludicrously attractive, Eleanor thought, the most handsome man she had ever seen.

'My God almighty,' she whispered to Cherry. 'That fellow is only gorgeous.'

'Yeah, he is, but boy does he really know it.'

Guapo spoke hardly any English at all, but he still managed to flirt. He plucked an orange flower from the Imperial Hotel garden and presented it with a warm and mischievous smile to Eleanor. He was absolutely delighted that she could understand a little Spanish. The flower was a *malinche*, he told her. Cortéz had named it after one of his lovers. He put the flower into Eleanor's button-hole, then took hold of her hand and kissed it.

'Jesus, Guapo,' Smokes sighed. '*Por favor.*'

Guapo pulled a face at him. 'Guapo, *por favor*,' he sniggered, imitating Smokes's accent. He kissed Eleanor's other hand and told her she was beautiful.

'Jesus,' Smokes said, 'make him cut that out, Cherry, willya?'

'What, Smokes?' She laughed. 'He's fine.'

'God, he's grand,' Eleanor said. 'I've no complaints anyway.'

'Well, I just think it's really sexist actually,' Smokes said. 'He's slobbering all over Eleanor.'

'Don't be such a putz, Smokes,' Cherry sighed.

'I'm not. Jesus, every time a guy stands up for his principles around here he gets it in the damn neck.'

'Don't make me laugh, baby. You think principles is an album by Fleetwood Mac.'

Guapo came up close to face Smokes. He turned down the corners of his mouth and began to pretend to cry, tracing tears down his cheeks with his fingers. 'Oh, Marilyn,' Guapo sobbed mockingly. '*Pobrecita* Marilyn.'

Cherry put her hand to her mouth and snorted with laughter.

'Just fuck off, Guapo,' Smokes said.

'What's he saying now?' Frank asked.

'He calls him Marilyn,' Cherry said. 'It's because Smokes is blond. It really bugs the hell out of him.'

'It does not,' Smokes said. 'I just think it's really childish actually, that's all.'

'They think blond guys are unmanly,' Cherry said.

'It's pathetic,' Smokes said. 'It really sucks.'

'Oh, Marilyn, Marilyn, *mi amor*,' Guapo said, blowing Smokes a kiss. 'Marilyn *amorcita*,' he cooed.

'Macho shit,' Smokes said.

Guapo told Eleanor he had been a soldier in the Sandinista army.

He had fought with the rebels when they were illegal and he'd joined the army immediately after the revolution. But he'd hated being in the army, he told her. It wasn't the same as being a *guerrillero*. It was a hard life, and he had lost his stomach for the fight when his best friend went crazy and had to be locked away. One day shortly after that, Guapo had got shot in the hand in a skirmish near Jinotega, and he had woken up in hospital with his left little finger missing. He had learnt to play the bass guitar in hospital. Some rich American rock star had sent down a plane load of musical instruments and Guapo had picked the bass guitar, he told her, because it was shaped just like an old girlfriend, Estela Suarez, who had run off to Miami with one of the local butcher boys.

He had met Cherry and some English guy in a *cantina* one night. They'd been singing rock and roll songs and throwing popcorn into each other's mouths. Cherry had been very drunk, and she'd started an argument with Guapo about whether the Beatles were better than the Rolling Stones. After a while the English guy had got bored and gone home, and the argument had ended with Cherry and Guapo wandering the streets of Managua at two in the morning, singing 'Angie' and 'I Can't Get No Satisfaction'. They'd come to a statue of General Somoza on his horse, and Guapo had climbed up on to it to sing his unique version of 'Jumpin' Jack Flash'. The local people had called the police, and Cherry and Guapo had spent the night cooling off in the jail. From then on, they'd been the best of friends. He'd joined up with the Desperados de Amor and never regretted it. And if that damn horse had only been faster, he said to Eleanor, the police never would have caught him.

'And you met Smokes then?' Eleanor laughed. 'When you joined the group?'

Guapo rolled his eyes. 'Oh, Marilyn,' he sighed. '*Sí*.'

'Douchebag,' Smokes said.

Eleanor chuckled guiltily, then she asked Guapo how he had met her son.

Guapo told her he'd got to know Johnny just after he'd arrived from Ireland nearly two years ago. He and Smokes had just bumped into him down in the *parque* one afternoon, sitting under a tree, strumming a guitar and eating a bag of oranges. He'd just looked up at Guapo and Smokes and invited them over to join him. There was a very beautiful woman with him, Guapo said, but he'd never seen her again. But he had liked Johnny straight away. He was funny. He was loyal. He was *simpático*.

'*Fue como un hermano para mí*,' he whispered, shaking his head.

'Like a brother,' Eleanor said. 'Isn't that lovely now, Frank?'

Smokes began to chuckle. 'Guapo always exaggerates. They didn't know each other that well.'

'They did too, Smokes,' Cherry said. 'What are you talking about?'

'Well, I don't think they did. Not really.'

Cherry turned away and ignored him.

'You guys must meet Lorenzo too,' she said. 'Our guitar player. He was crazy about Johnny. Johnny used to crease him up and Lorenzo's a pretty serious guy.'

'Really?' Frank said. 'I never thought of him as funny now. Did you, Eleanor?'

Smokes laughed out loud.

'Who? Johnny? Jeez, Franklin, the guy was crazy as a coot when he got going. He was wild, really. These stories he used to tell when we'd be on the road. You know, you get bored at night. And Johnny and me would start up with these crazy stories. Oh yeah, Johnny was just hilarious, man.'

Smokes giggled into his drink. Cherry glared at him.

'Well,' Eleanor said, 'please God now, he'll have a good story for us when we find him.'

'I really miss him,' Smokes said. 'We had some wild times.'

'I never knew that about him,' said Frank. 'That's a fact. I never heard him crack a joke in his whole bloody life.'

'I'd rather people stopped using the past tense,' Eleanor said. 'It's only a small thing, but I really would rather it.'

On Friday night Smokes and Cherry went away with the band to play a concert at the Matagalpa summer fiesta. It surprised Eleanor how much she missed them. Eleanor liked Cherry a lot. She liked the way she laughed a little too loudly. She had a frightened quality which reminded Eleanor of herself when she was younger.

In public, she sometimes needled Smokes mercilessly. In private conversation, it was obvious that she absolutely adored him, even though Eleanor sometimes wondered why.

'He's a good guy,' Cherry had told her. 'He's got a good heart under all the garbage. I know he's a retard sometimes, but hey, who the hell's looking for a rocket scientist?'

Eleanor tried to write in her diary, but she found that she could not manage anything more than a few lines. She lay by the pool scribbling spirals and mazes on the pages. She sketched the ruined skyline of the city, with black biro for the buildings and red biro for the burning sun.

By Saturday, there was still no news from Nuñez's office. She began to worry about Frank. He seemed totally unable to relax now. He was practically chain-smoking, not eating nearly enough, drinking rum until very late down in the Bar Casablanca. Every night he had woken her, stumbling through the bedroom on his way to the couch, knocking into the furniture, breathing very heavily as though he was in pain. He kept losing his temper and complaining to the manager about the slightest thing. And he was spending a lot of time with that Hollis Clarke, a man she did not like the look of at all.

She had seen them sitting in the breakfast room, talking very intensely to each other. When he'd noticed her coming, Clarke had whipped out a pack of playing cards and begun to shuffle and deal. She knew that the topic of conversation had been changed as soon as she'd sat down at the table. She could tell. Eleanor had an instinct for these things.

'Well, Mam,' Clarke had said with a grin, 'I hope you won't mind me saying you look pretty as a picture this morning.' She'd wanted to drag him out to the bathroom and give him a good bloody wash, scrub that bloody grin off his slippery mouth.

'And haven't you the life of Riley, Mr Clarke,' she'd said. 'Playing cards at this hour of the morning.'

When Clarke's bleeper had sounded, he had jumped up and run out to the lobby. She tried to speak to Frank then, but he had very little to say. His face looked very red. There were thick black lines around his eyes and when he reached out for the bread she noticed that his fingers were trembling.

She knew that he had finally managed to get through on the

telephone to Veronica. She suspected that they'd had an argument of some kind. She recognized the symptoms, of course, but there was a limit to what she was prepared to ask.

That night Eleanor went to Mass in the Barrio Monterrey. Behind the altar there was a huge mural of Christ in the uniform of a Sandinista soldier. In the clouds above the crucifixion, podgy angels unfurled red and black banners. When she got back to the Imperial, Frank was in the bar with Hollis Clarke again. She went straight up to bed. At five o'clock in the morning he came shambling into the room, muttering and cursing under his breath, stinking of drink and stale smoke.

Next day was Sunday and he did not get up until lunchtime. And then he did not speak to her at all. He swam up and down the pool for an hour and then sat on a deck chair, sulking in the sunshine and pouring himself *Cuba libres* from a huge jug. 'Nothing, nothing, nothing,' he said whenever she asked him what was wrong. At four o'clock, he looked at his watch, stood up and told her he was going out for a while.

'Where to?' she asked him.

'Just out,' he said. 'Don't bother me with your questions.'

When he got outside the Imperial, Hollis Clarke was under a palm tree by the taxi rank, wearing a white sunhat and smoking a cigar, and talking furtively to two scrawny soldiers.

'Well, Sport,' he said when he saw Frank. 'What's new?'

Frank glanced over his shoulder. A mosquito flew at his face and he smacked at it, cursing and stumbling.

'Watch those babies.' Clarke laughed. 'They'll have you for lunch, Frank.'

He looked down at Clarke and nodded.

'Are you going to your office now?'

'In two shakes, Sport. Why?'

'I've thought it over, that's all. I'm going to give you your story.'

Clarke's bleary eyes widened with delight.

'Now, you won't regret it, Frank.' He beamed. 'You just watch what happens. I'll have that piece in first thing tomorrow and they'll find your boy pretty damn pronto.'

Clarke reached into his bag and took out two cartons of

Marlboro and a bottle of Jack Daniels. He handed these to the soldiers and said, '*Hasta luego*.' The soldiers walked quickly away.

A black limousine pulled slowly up to the taxi rank, catching the sunlight in its mirrored windows. The driver honked the horn three times.

Clarke held up his hand and picked out invisible words. 'Unarmed college kids wander round the war zone.' He grinned. 'I can see the headline now.' He took Frank by the arm and began to lead him towards the purring car.

'These commies, Frank,' he said, 'see, they can't stand being embarrassed. It's the only way to get anything done. I put your story in the paper, you're gonna see some action, believe me.'

'I hope so,' Frank said. 'I'm worn out waiting.'

'You're doing the right thing, Sport. They'll turn this damn country upside down and shake it out till they find him.'

They stepped into the back of the car and Clarke told the driver not to spare the horses.

That night Frank and Eleanor went to dinner at Los Antojitos, twenty miles out of the city on the Carretera Norte. Frank was in a better mood. He told Eleanor how well she was looking, and he sat back in his chair, sipping a large gin and tonic, listening to the *mariachis* strumming their guitars.

'You're out of that fierce humour anyway,' she said.

'How's your mother?' he asked. 'I meant to ask you before. I ran into Liam Doyle and he told me about her op. I sent flowers.'

'Yes,' she said quietly, 'that was much appreciated, Frank. I meant to get in touch.'

He shrugged and tucked into his salad. She continued to speak.

'She's happy as a lark with Trevor and Sheila, of course. Loves having the kiddies around. But she still misses Daddy I think.'

'Mine were lucky,' he said, 'to go so close together.'

Eleanor sighed. 'Mammy keeps talking about cremation. That's the latest. Afraid of waking up in the coffin.'

'Bloody right too. I think she's right.'

'I think I'd like to be fed to the lions, Frank. Up in the zoo. I'd like to go into the food chain fairly high up.'

'Plain old cremation will be good enough for me. Not that I'll know anything about it.'

'I have this friend' – she giggled – 'and he says he wants to be just left on a mountain somewhere and eaten by the eagles. And the funny thing is, he has this big nose. I mean, he looks a bit like an eagle himself.'

Frank reached for a bread roll. 'Who's that?' he said.

'Oh, just this friend of mine. James, his name is. We go to concerts sometimes.'

The *mariachis* strolled over towards the table and began to play a slow waltz.

'Do you go out much?' he asked. 'This James and you?'

'We went to see Rostropovich at the concert hall. He was very good of course, but the people there bugged me a bit. All decked out in their finery. I thought they only wanted to be seen.'

'And this James character? How did you start knocking about with him?'

'Frank Little!' She laughed. 'That's for me to know and you to find out.'

He felt himself blush. 'A woman has to be careful these days,' he said. 'There's some queer types knocking about. You want to hear the stories my drivers come in with.'

'Yes,' she said. 'Well, he's seventy-four, Frank. I think my honour is safe enough.'

He tried to make his voice sound casual.

'And he's musical is he? This James?'

'He used to play the trumpet in the RTE orchestra. I met him at one of my meetings, you know. At AA.'

'You're still at that?'

'Yes, Frank. I find it a help.'

He speared a lettuce leaf with his fork.

'Well' – he shrugged – 'I don't understand music any more. Why anyone would have nothing better to do than play music.'

'Oh, Frank,' she said. 'You're such an actor. Sometimes it really makes me smile.'

They called a taxi to take them back to the Imperial. From a distance Managua managed to look almost glamorous, a wide matrix of sequinned light below the vast dark green hulk of the mountain. White searchlights swept up and across the cloudless sky, picking out landmarks, the leaning steeple of the cathedral, the giant green *cerveza* bottle winking in neon over the Ciudad

Plástica, the twisted skeleton of the ruined television steeple in Barrio Sandino.

Back at the hotel they made tea and sat on the balcony listening to a classical concert on the radio. The orchestra played extracts from Beethoven and Brahms and a couple of Schubert songs. The night air felt warm and liquid. After a few minutes Eleanor closed her eyes and began to breathe deeply. Frank was going to wake her up, but she looked so content that he decided not to.

The news came on after the music, and even though Frank could not understand many of the words, the newsreader's voice was comforting. He enjoyed its calm, its efficient tone. He recognized one or two of the place names. *La Unión Soviética. Los Estados Unidos. Inglaterra.* And it felt reassuring to know that all over this madhouse country people were still doing normal things, like listening to the midnight news on the radio. When you are in trouble, he realized, the smallest of consolations are moving.

He poured himself a large glass of rum and settled back into his chair, looking at Eleanor's sleeping face, allowing his mind to drift. He remembered the first time he had ever seen that face, gazing speculatively down at him from the balcony of Saint Michael's church. That was during the first harsh winter after the war. They had both been seven or eight.

That winter the weather had been bitter. The mountains outside Dublin had been silver and white with frost. It was the year the bank had taken the butcher's shop back from his mother. The price of meat had soared and the poor people of the area had simply stopped buying it. Frank's mother could not afford to keep up the payments and the bank had sold the shop to a wealthy man from Kerry. Shortly after that, Frank's father had lost his job at the bakery. Money had gone missing and questions had been asked and no matter what the union tried to do he had been dismissed, a married man with six children, forced to look for another job at the age of forty-eight.

It had been a terrible time in Frank Little's house. There had been ferocious quarrels between his parents because money was suddenly so short. He remembered them having a dreadful argument on the night of his eighth birthday, because they'd had no coal to burn. He remembered sitting with his younger brother on the landing and listening to them fight. He remembered his father running out into the street, shouting. Frank had come down the stairs to find his mother sitting by the fire in tears.

'What's the matter, Mammy?' he'd asked her.

'Nothing, lovie. Go on back up to bed.'

'Are we poor now?'

'Not at all. Go on to sleep, pet.'

When he'd come over to put his arms around her she'd shouted at him to get away and go back to bed. It was the only time his mother had ever shouted at him. The memory still shocked him.

Next day Frank Little had gone up to the Phoenix Park after school. He knew about the coal mountain in the Phoenix Park. Everyone in the city was talking about it. He knew that the government had bought all the coal they could, and that they'd put it all up in the park. Johnny Rea had told him it was to stop the black market blackguards and to keep the factories going.

The coal mountain was guarded day and night by squads of armed soldiers. There were two fire engines there all the time in case the coal caught fire. Frank knew that some of the poor boys in his class went up to the park every day to get coal. It was against the law, and you'd be put in jail if you were caught. But the soldiers would sometimes turn their backs long enough for you to steal a bit of coal.

He had gone up to the park and looked at the huge black mountain. He had talked to one of the soldiers for a while and the soldier had called him 'Captain' and given him a bar of chocolate. But Frank had not been able to take his eyes off that vast mound of coal. There was so much of it, and he needed so little. He thought of the coldness in his house, and he thought of his father shouting at his mother. He thought of the way the coal mountain burnt in his dreams, great fat spouts of red flame spitting into the night sky, and he wanted to cry, because he felt so cold. He looked at the soldier's gun, at his brilliantly polished boots. Then the soldier said he was going over to the trees to smoke a cigarette, and that he would trust Frank to watch his section of the coal stack until he got back. He winked at Frank and strolled away, swinging his rifle behind him. Frank waited for the soldier to disappear, then quickly filled his paper bag with pieces of coal, stuffing two huge lumps into the pockets of his shorts.

When the soldier returned he said, 'Well? Any trouble while I was gone, Captain? Any bowsies?' Frank said no, there had been no trouble at all, and the soldier told him he was a great fellow.

'What's your name?' the soldier asked.

'Francis Little.'

'So, you're a great little fellow then, aren't you? You're the bees knees, aren't you?'

He remembered not being able to think of anything to say. The soldier had laughed and ruffled his hair.

'And what do you want to be when you grow up?'

'I want to have a shop.'

The soldier pulled a face. 'You mean to say you don't want to be in the army and fight for Ireland?'

'No,' Frank said. 'I want to have a shoe shop.'

The soldier had laughed again and told Frank Little he was a gas man altogether.

And on his way home that cold afternoon something odd had happened to Frank. He had been walking along through the park, thinking about the soldier, and about what would happen if that huge mountain were to catch fire, when suddenly he had noticed a movement in a hedgerow across the field.

He'd not been too sure what the bird was at first. But then, as he'd got closer, he'd recognized it. It was a tree creeper. He had only ever seen this bird in books before. But there it was, right in front of him now. He recognized its movements and the colours of its plumage.

Breathless with excitement, he'd begun to walk in a circle around the bird. He'd walked very gently, very softly, because he had not wanted to frighten it away. He had walked in decreasing circles around the bird, and it had taken almost half an hour, and then suddenly he'd been only a few feet away.

He had darted out and grabbed it with his right hand. The bird had gone completely rigid with shock at first. Then it had struggled and flapped its wings and tried to peck his fingers, but he'd held on to it very hard, tears of pain in his eyes, before releasing it into the air. He'd watched it grow smaller and smaller as it flew straight up into the white sky, calling out in a frightened croaking cry. And Frank did not know why, but he had always counted this as one of the important moments in his life.

This was odd. He knew that. But he remembered running home

alongside the Liffey wall, through the dusky streets of Dublin, with a jumper full of coal lumps, his heart thundering, seeing absolutely nothing in the world except possibility and promise. He remembered finding his father in the aviary in the back yard, and he remembered telling his father about this strange bird, and the happy look that came over his father's handsome red face.

Frank and his father had gone into the kitchen and made cups of tea, and doorstep jam sandwiches, and then they'd sat by themselves for several hours while the light had steadily faded outside the window, and they had simply talked about birds. That was all that had happened. He could not remember where his mother had been that day, but he remembered the house being empty, except for his father and himself, and the sleeping baby in the basket by the coal-filled fire, and the golden light of the flames. And he could remember his father talking very excitedly about all kinds of birds. Wrens, jays, pigeons and bluetits, sparrows and eaglets, robin redbreasts and Sandymount snow-whites. He could remember feeling the most exquisite happiness, and he could remember too that, in some odd way, he had begun to count his own real life as beginning on that very cold afternoon in Dublin, in the first harsh winter after the war, the day he had talked to his father about birds.

At midnight the telephone rang. It was the manager. There was an urgent message from Captain Nuñez's office. They were to be at the *Ministerio* at ten in the morning.

Frank smiled into his glass. Things were about to hot up.

12

Avondale

THEY WOULD GO DANCING every Saturday night in Dublin.
They would go to the Olympic Ballroom, the National and the
Metropole, the Arcadia out in Bray, the Stella in Mount Merrion,
the Television Club in Harcourt Street. They would dance to
Dickie Rock, the Indians, Butch Moore and the Capitol, the
Clipper Carltons, the Rhythm Kings, Brendan Bowyer and the
Royal Showband. They would often dance until midnight, and
then they would buy chips on the way home.

They went to concerts of classical music. They went to the
cinema very often, sometimes twice or three times a week. Soon
they were seeing each other every night.

One of Johnny Doyle's drivers was going out with a girl who
worked in the Gaiety Theatre. Sometimes he got free tickets for
the opera and he would give these to Frank because he liked him.
Frank took Eleanor to see *Carmen* and *La Bohème, Turandot* and
The Barber of Seville. He loved the opera. It made him breathless
with excitement and he loved talking to her about it afterwards.
She understood music and she would explain it to him. She knew
all about harmony and counterpoint. She knew about cadences,
about the different key signatures, about sharps and flats and
modulations. She explained all of this and she loaned him records
of her favourite arias. 'Una furtiva lagrima' from Donizetti's
L'Elisir d'Amore, 'Un bel di vedremo' from *Madama Butterfly*,
'Donna non vidi mai' from *Manon Lescaut*. She bought him a book
called *The Lives of the Great Composers* for his seventeenth birthday.

Soon after that, they began to go on cycling trips together, to
Saggart and Portmarnock, Malahide, Rush and Lusk, out to
the lakes at Poulaphouca, to Greystones, and Delgany and

Glendalough. They went to Bray and climbed up to the black cross at the summit of the Head. Once they went all the way down to Arklow and stayed in a little bed and breakfast hotel, in separate rooms, waking up to the smell of bacon frying.

One day in 1956, Johnny Doyle told Frank he was looking for a new driver. It was a great opportunity for a young man, and he wanted to offer it to Frank Little. There was good money in the taxi trade, for a young man who wasn't afraid of graft and hard work. Frank took his driving test and passed it first time.

He started to drive a taxi. He worked hard during the week. He worked all day. He met Eleanor at five o'clock after her work and drove her home to Drimnagh. He would go back out again at ten, picking up fares at the airport or outside the nightclubs and coffee bars. On a Sunday afternoon after Mass he would unscrew the sign from the roof of the taxi and come to collect her. They would drive out for miles into the countryside. He liked being mobile, he told her. Once you were mobile, you were laughing.

They went to see the ancient passage-grave at Newgrange. They went to Clonmacnoise and Mellifont Abbey and they drove around the Boyne Valley. One day at Avondale they walked through the trees for several hours, talking together, listening to the rain splashing on the wet leaves all around them.

In the taxi, on the way back to Dublin, Frank held Eleanor's hand and she laughed as he sang to her:

> Oh have you been to Avondale
> And lingered in her lovely vale
> Where tall trees whisper light the tale
> Of Avondale's proud eagle.

> Where pride and ancient glory fade
> So was the land where he was laid
> Like Christ was thirty pieces paid
> For Avondale's proud eagle.

> Long years that green and lovely vale
> Had nursed Parnell, her grandest Gael
> And curse the land that has betrayed
> Fair Avondale's proud eagle.

13

Families

FOR HALF AN HOUR they sat with Smokes in the dark hall outside Nuñez's office. The simmering heat seemed to dribble from the glossy painted walls. The light bulbs flickered every few seconds and a humming noise was coming from somewhere. When the office door opened, a young sentry with a handsome, frightened face appeared. He gestured for them to come in.

Nuñez was sitting behind his desk, speaking into the telephone. He was wearing glasses now, and they made him look a little older. He had on a black baseball cap that said 'ENJOY YOURSELF' across the front, and under his khaki shirt he was wearing a black vest. He held the receiver between his chin and his shoulder and motioned for them to sit down. When he had finished with the telephone he stood up and nodded at them.

'Your accommodation is satisfactory?' he asked briskly.

'Oh, yes,' Eleanor replied. 'It's lovely.'

He moved to the front of his desk and sat down against it.

'*Señor* Little,' he said, 'I believe you know why you are here.'

'Yes, I do, Captain. I'm here for news about my son. I've been waiting long enough now.'

Nuñez suddenly looked furious. '*Señor*, I have something I would like to share with you.'

He reached over to his desk and snatched up a piece of paper. 'This morning's *Washington Times*,' he said. 'Very interesting.'

He held the paper up to his face and began to read in a loud, chanting voice. 'The boy's parents expressed concern that the Cuban-style Sandinista government is encouraging foreign students to enter the northern militarized zone in order to act as human shields in the event of US military intervention. Mr Frank

Little of Dublin, Ireland, said that the Nicaraguan Interior Ministry had been unhelpful. He hoped that the United States government would take an interest in his son's case.'

'Frank?' Eleanor said. 'What's this about?'

'I never said that,' Frank sighed. Nuñez slapped the paper down on his desk. He took off his glasses, folded them and pointed them at Frank.

'*Señor*, do not think it escapes us that you have been having regular meetings with a certain reporter. This man is a well-known counter-revolutionary, an agent of the CIA, and an enemy of our people. This is not helpful, *Señor*. *Comandante* Borge has asked me to say that he is very disappointed with your actions.'

'Frank?' Eleanor said. 'You didn't tell me about this.'

Frank scoffed. 'Well, I'm sorry now to hear he's so disappointed, Captain. You just tell him to find my son, and I'll stop disappointing him.'

Nuñez stood up and began to shout.

'*Señor*, there are other sons, and other families. Don't you think I have a family?'

'I don't know.'

'I have a family, *Señor*. We all have families and our families are in desperation. Our families are being attacked every day. From the north, from the south, from the sea. We are fighting for our lives. We have better things to do than look for adventurers, *Señor*, while our children are hungry and dying.'

'It's not my fault your children are dying, Nuñez.'

'Do you have polio in Ireland, *Señor*? Do you have typhoid? Do you have cholera, *Señor*, and malaria? Because we have all these things. We have diseases for which you do not even have names, and they destroy our hospitals, and people like your son come to our country to play guitars and talk about peace.'

Nuñez turned to his desk. He snatched up a handful of newspapers and brandished them. 'Nine of our children were murdered by counter-revolutionaries yesterday morning, *Señor*. Nine. The day before there was a bomb in the airport and an elderly *compañero* was crippled. The other day while I was here speaking with you, a counter-revolutionary gang stopped a truck full of women in Bluefields – I say women, *Señor* – and killed them all. Last week a religious sister was attacked and violated for helping the *campesinos* to grow food. Last night, three children were shot dead in the north. One of them was nine years old. Would you like me to continue?'

'I'm sorry to hear that,' Frank said. 'But you'll understand that it's my child I'm talking about here.'

'No,' Nuñez shouted. 'No. It is you who will understand, *Señor*. This is not an adventure playground; we have our people to defend. We did not ask your son to come here. If your son wanted to play the martyr, he may have had to pay the price.'

Frank began to laugh. 'Like what?' he said. 'All these better things you have to do? What are they?'

'Are you so blind, sir?' Nuñez snapped. 'We are building something here. Look around you.'

'Oh, yeah. Socialism. I forgot.'

'You may call it whatever you wish. We wish to feed our people and teach them to read. Do we have your permission to do that, sir?'

'Frank,' Eleanor said, 'what's all this about?'

'I've been Labour all my life, Captain. I've never voted any other way, and, God knows, there've been times I could have.'

Nuñez shouted. 'And you are fortunate, *Señor*, to have had that luxury. Must I tell you again that we are at war here? Can you really not understand this?'

Frank glared at the crucifixes on the office wall. He pointed to them, his finger shaking. 'Blessed are the peacemakers, Captain. Isn't that what the bible says?'

'The hungry sheep look up and are not fed. This too, *Señor*, is what the bible says.'

'Good Christ, you fucking people.'

Nuñez stepped forward. '*Señor*,' he said, 'we *do* like to do things informally here. But I will remind you that you are speaking to a representative of *Comandante* Tomas Borge, the Interior Minister of the sovereign independent republic of Nicaragua. There is also a lady present.'

Frank scoffed. 'If your precious *Comandante* wants to be treated like a leader you just tell him to start behaving like one.'

Nuñez's eyes widened with rage.

'How dare you, *Señor*?' he yelled. 'How dare you? And if you want to be treated like a man, sir, you should start to behave like one also.'

Frank stood up, trembling with anger. 'You little fucking cunt,' he spat. 'Come over here and say that. I've wiped better than you off my boots before now.'

Smokes grabbed Frank's wrists. The soldier ran over and stood in front of him, pulling out a pair of handcuffs. He looked frightened and confused as he pressed Frank down into the chair.

'Take your fucking hands off me, sunshine,' Frank breathed. 'Or you'll be waking up with a fucking crowd around you.'

Nuñez said a few words to the soldier. The soldier stepped back and put away his handcuffs but continued to stare at Frank. Nuñez raised his hands to his face. He took off his baseball cap and threw it on the desk, then folded his arms, breathing heavily.

'Now,' he said, 'we must all take a moment to regain our self-discipline.'

'You just find my son, and spare me your lectures. I'm telling you now, Nuñez.'

Nuñez banged his fist on the desk and began to shout again. 'No, sir, I will tell you. I am in command here. You will understand this. You will stay here for ten minutes and then you will leave. One of my men will drive you to your hotel. You will treat him with respect. You will remain available at your hotel. You will cooperate. There will be no more clandestine meetings, because *we* run this country, *Señor*, and the *Washington Times*, for the moment, does not. Do you understand me?'

'We understand,' Eleanor said. 'We're very sorry, Captain.'

Nuñez cleared his throat and looked at Eleanor as though he had forgotten she was there. He bowed slightly. '*Bueno, Señora*,' he muttered. 'We will not speak of this unfortunate incident again.'

He saluted to her, gathered a sheaf of papers from his desk and walked quickly from the room, taking the soldier with him.

Smokes sighed deeply. 'Jesus, Frank,' he said. 'Big mistake, man.'

Frank scoffed. 'Look, son, sometimes you have to lay things out for these people. Let them know the bloody score.'

Smokes shook his head.

'Frank,' he said. 'The guy's two sons were tortured to death by the *Guardia* in seventy-eight. I think he knows the score.'

Frank stood up, feeling the sweat ooze through his skin. His mouth tasted sour. 'And that's my fault, is it? Everything is my fucking fault. One day I'm sitting in traffic trying not to get a heart attack just long enough to pay his college fees, and next day everything is my fucking fault.'

'I didn't say that, Franklin. Chill out, man.'

'Jesus, you think I spent my twenties studying fucking sociology, Smokes? I was working ten years when I was his age. I had a family and a marriage. There's not one of you kids would know the fucking meaning of responsibility.'

Eleanor came over to him. Her face was very white and she looked frightened. She put her fingers on the back of his wrist. 'Stop it, Frank,' she said. 'Please stop now.'

He pushed her away and glared. 'Don't you dare touch me,' he snapped. 'If he'd ever had something like a mother this would never have happened.'

She smiled, very sadly, as the tears began to come. 'Oh, Frank,' she said, 'Frank.' She picked up her handbag and walked towards the door.

He stared after her. 'Yes, that's it,' he called. 'Walk out, why don't you? You're fucking good at that alright.'

14

Dun Laoghaire Pier

IN THE SPRING OF 1958, Frank Little and Eleanor Hamilton decided to get married. Frank had been working at the taxi office for four years and he was the best driver on the list. There was no job he wouldn't do. People would ring up and ask for him specifically. He had a good reputation and, as Johnny Doyle said, that was worth cash in the bank any day. Frank Little could be trusted and everyone knew it.

They were standing at the end of Dun Laoghaire Pier one warm night in April. They had just been to a dress dance at the Royal Marine Hotel and they were eating fish and chips and watching the beam of the lighthouse gliding across the murky water. He was twenty years old. She was twenty-one.

'Will we get married, Eleanor?' he said to her.

'God,' she said, 'you're terribly serious all of a sudden.'

'Don't be laughing at me.'

She folded her arms around herself then, gazing out at the horizon as though the dark space contained something interesting.

'Is it that you don't want to?'

She was silent for a few moments and then she sighed. 'Well, how could we afford it?'

'We could save. Instead of going out so much. They've new houses up in Sundrive Road. I had a gander at them the other week.'

'Oh God, I see. You've everything planned.'

He put his hand on her sleeve. 'I love you, Eleanor. You know that.'

'Don't be talking like that,' she said.

'Well, I do, Eleanor.'

She looked as if she was thinking now, and after a moment she nodded. 'You know I'm fond of you as well,' she said. 'God help me.'

She turned away from him and stared out at the sea again. When he came and put his arms around her he noticed that she was crying.

'What's wrong?' he asked her.

Suddenly she clenched his hand so hard that he winced.

'Oh Frank,' she sobbed. 'I love you so much it frightens me sometimes. I can't bear to think about it. I hate it when you're not there. It just hurts me so much.'

'But I am here,' he said. She shook her head and laughed through her tears.

'You're such a child,' she sobbed. 'I want to wrap myself around you. Do you understand, Frank? I wish I could just wrap myself around you and never let you go.'

He held her tightly and a warm breeze rushed in from the sea.

'Calm down, Eleanor. I'm here.'

'Don't ever leave me, Frank,' she cried. 'Please don't ever leave me, sure you won't? I can't ever be without you now.'

'Don't be daft,' he said. 'Sure, I've just asked you to marry me.'

They stood clinging to each other in the darkness. Slowly she began to kiss his lips, gently at first, but then harder. She pushed her tongue into his mouth, moaning softly with pleasure. She ran her fingers through his hair and her breath quickened. He kissed her neck. She gasped and took his hands, moving them to her breasts. He kissed her mouth again. He slid the straps of her dress down and kissed her naked shoulders. She pulled the front of her dress down further, baring her breasts completely. She wrapped her arms around his neck and he kissed her nipples. She cried out softly and told him not to stop. He put his hand under her skirt and cupped his fingers gently between her legs. She sobbed and parted her thighs, pushing against him. 'I want you so much, Frank,' she sighed.

When he got home that night, his mother was in bed and the house was quiet. His father had been drinking. He was sitting at the fire with his head in his hands. He nodded, when he heard the news, but he did not look up from the fireplace.

'Well, what do you think anyway, Da?' Frank said. 'Do you think it's a good idea?'

'Don't ask me, son,' his father laughed. 'You're on your way in now, and your old man is on the way out.'

15

Paper Roses

SHE WAS IN THE BEDROOM when he got back, sitting at the mirror and putting on make-up. A pair of her shoes lay on top of the bed. He was relieved to see her, but he found that he was unable to say this. He took out a cigarette.

'So, you're still here?' he said. 'I thought you'd've run off someplace.'

'I'm going to Mass,' she said.

'Oh, sure. Go talk to Jesus. That'll help.'

She took a brush from her bag and began to comb her long grey hair. 'There's no need to be bloody smart, Frank.'

He lit his cigarette and sat down on the bed. The sweet scent of his wife's perfume seemed to fill the stuffy room. When he moved his hand to the back of his neck he found the flesh covered with the hard lumps of mosquito bites.

'Oh, there was a call for you,' she said nonchalantly. 'A woman's voice. She put the phone down when she heard me. Veronica, I suppose.'

He picked up one of her shoes and played with it for a moment.

'I suppose you want me to apologize,' he said, 'for saying those things earlier on.'

She took a lipstick and began to apply it to her mouth.

'I hope you don't think I meant anything,' he said. 'That'd be daft, if you thought that.'

She pouted into the mirror, took a tissue and pressed it to her lips.

'Well,' he said, 'I'm very sorry for any offence, Eleanor. I'd feel very small now, if you were offended.'

She nodded into the mirror but did not look at him. 'What you said was right,' she said. 'I wasn't a good mother, or a good wife. I'll have that on my conscience without you reminding me.'

'No, no. It wasn't right. I got carried away with that fellow.'

'You're like a bloody child,' she said. 'You should be ashamed.'

'I just get a bit frustrated sometimes, Eleanor. I lose my head. I can't seem to help it.'

'Oh, yes,' she said, 'and Frank Little is the only one with the right to be frustrated, isn't that it? God, you haven't changed.'

'I'm very sorry. You know I didn't mean it.'

She turned to him. 'We could all drag up the past if we wanted to, Frank. That's a dangerous game for anyone to play.'

He shrugged. 'Well, I'm sorry for saying that to you, Eleanor, if you're hurt in some way. That wouldn't be intended, God knows.'

He got up from the bed and went to the window. The light seemed to be dying now, melting softly into the green sludge of Lake Managua. He put his fingers to his temples and rubbed hard, trying to massage his headache away.

'I wouldn't mind' – he laughed – 'But this place is only a shagging kip. Just look at it, Eleanor. I mean, what do they see in it, these kids?'

But when he turned back the door was open and Eleanor was gone from the room. He was alone. He called her name, but there was no reply. He walked to the corridor and called out again, louder this time. The dull blue emergency lights glinted in the murk. At the far end of the corridor an old woman in a white dress was on her knees, scrubbing at the floor. She looked up at him and put her finger to her lips, hissing at him to be silent.

He came back into the room, sat down on the bed and picked up her headscarf. He held it to his hot face and sank his fingers into its softness. And just at that moment Frank Little realized something. He realized that he would have killed a man with his bare hands, would have torn a man's heart out and cut out his tongue, if he had to, just to have his son back, and to be far away from this shitty little town and its murderous heat and its silences. If it came to that, he would have done it, with equanimity, with no questions asked, and no doubts.

He knelt down by the bedside, closed his eyes, joined his hands very tightly together and began to pray.

'He's my only son,' he said in a whisper. 'Please. He's my only son. I'm going to die with this heart, and he's the only thing I have. Please. If you're there, if you're listening, help me. I'll do anything you like, but just, please, give me one more chance.'

He bowed his head. Pain chewed at his stomach. Somewhere below him a radio was playing a song by Little Richard.

When she came back from Mass she was in a better mood. Frank had tried the desk for flowers, but they'd had none. So he bought a potted cactus and left it on the bed for her with a note. He said in the note that he was very sorry, and he promised that he would not say such hurtful things to her again.

'Appropriate,' she said when she saw the cactus.

'Yeah, well, they didn't have triffids, you know?'

They went down to lunch at one thirty, in the Augusto Cesar Sandino Banqueting Hall.

The manager smiled and shook hands with them. 'Madame is a perfect vision this afternoon,' he said, and Eleanor blushed and told him to stop. 'No, no,' the manager insisted, 'it is a beautiful day, and Madame is beautiful, and sir is very happy I suppose?'

'Yeah,' Frank said. 'Sir is bleeding delirious.'

The manager seemed to appreciate that. He clapped Frank on the back and grinned like a second-hand car salesman.

When he had shown them to the small circular table on the edge of the dance floor he clasped his hands and explained that thirteen of the fifteen wines on the list were unavailable. It was the political situation, he said, shaking his head very sadly. It just interfered with everything. He took their orders and complimented Frank on his choice of Albanian Beaujolais.

'It is really not too bad,' he said. 'If you drink it very quickly.'

The band played a slow song that seemed slightly out of time. In the middle of the floor a teenage girl in a tight skirt was dancing with a much older man. The man was wearing a black corduroy jacket and trousers which were not quite the same shade of black, and an overblown rose in the rim of his ten-gallon hat. The singer, a tall mestizo girl in a flaring scarlet dress, closed her eyes as she sang, swaying gently from side to side with the flow and ache of the sad music.

> *I realize the way your eyes deceived me*
> *With tender looks that I mistook for love*
> *So take away the flowers that you gave me*
> *And send the kind that you remind me of.*

The trumpeters stepped up to their microphones and began to croon

> *Paper roses. Paper roses.*
> *Oh how real those roses seemed to be.*
> *But they're only imitation*
> *Like your imitation love for me.*

They ate slowly and without speaking. He drank two glasses of wine and she drank water. When they had finished the stringy meat and the stewed grey vegetables, Frank said he wasn't in the mood for dessert. The waiter brought Eleanor a huge hollowed-out orange filled with ice cream. Frank pushed his plate away and lit a cigarette.

'No,' she said, 'I don't mind if you smoke. Thanks for asking.'

'Oh, sorry,' he said, going to crush it out on a saucer.

'I'm joking.' She smiled. 'Smoke. I like the smell of your cigarettes.'

'You do?'

'Yes, I do. It reminds me of Ireland.'

He watched the teenage girl, still dancing with the older man in the ludicrous hat. She was holding him very tightly now and staring lovingly into his eyes. He moved his hands down to the waistband of her skirt.

Frank coughed. 'Eleanor,' he said, 'there's something I want to say to you.'

'Oh, yes? What's that, Frank?'

Just then a group of young soldiers strode quickly into the dining room, spreading out into the corners and standing to attention, their arms straight down by their sides. A murmur ran around the tables and some of the guests stood up.

Three young men in officers' uniforms came in, each of them with two heavily armed guards by his side. One of the men was shy-looking, in thick black-rimmed glasses, like Buddy Holly's. The other two were a little older, both dark and good-looking and so alike that they could have been brothers. Eleanor recognized the young man in the glasses. She had seen his picture everywhere.

There was polite applause from some of the tables, and none at all from others. President Ortega did not acknowledge the applause. He just looked around and began to adjust his epaulettes. The manager rushed over and shook his hand very hard, gesturing towards a table. The President sat down at the table with the two officers. He offered the manager a banknote, but the manager waved his hand away as though he was insulted. He clicked his fingers in the air and three waiters appeared. The other guests went back to their meals.

'Look at the cut of them,' Frank said. 'Would you look at the bloody get-up.'

'What were you saying to me, Frank?'

'Nothing,' he said. 'Forget it.'

'Tell me. You can tell me, Frank. I don't mind.'

He thought for a moment, then leant across the table and spoke with a furtive air.

'It's about Johnny.'

Her expression darkened.

'No,' Frank said. 'No. It's nothing bad.'

'What then?'

He pulled hard on his cigarette.

'Just,' he said, 'just that you know I have my feelings for him. Don't you? Despite all that business.'

Eleanor looked surprised. She put down her spoon and fingered it.

'God, yes, Frank. Of course I know that.'

He was stammering now. 'And, you know, I have my good memories. Of the old days I mean.'

She picked up a napkin and put it to her mouth, staring at the bandstand very intently, as though the music might tell her something.

'Well,' she said, 'you don't have to say these things for a person to know them.'

'Yeah,' Frank stuttered. 'That's my point now, El. These kids now, they're different. They spout all that. It's a love-in with them. It's like the fucking Moonies or something.'

She nodded. 'Some things you don't have to say.'

'Well, I'm with you there, El.' He forced himself to laugh, and the laugh came a little more loudly than he would have liked.

'I mean, God,' he said, 'it doesn't mean a person doesn't have his inner feelings.'

He looked away at the shy little man in the uniform, who was eating a slice of cake and drinking a small cup of coffee. He did not look like a president, Frank thought.

'No, Frank,' she said, 'it doesn't mean that at all.'

He was aware that his wife was looking at him now. He stared into the ashtray and hoped that she would look away. When it was obvious that she was not going to, he allowed himself to catch her eye. It felt like a brave thing to do. He held her gaze, and he tried to tell himself that what he was feeling was not guilt, even though it felt dangerously like it, for some reason which he could not yet fully understand.

She reached across the table and gently touched the back of his wrist.

'We had our days of wine and roses,' she said, 'didn't we, Frank?'

'Yes,' he said. 'We had our happy times.'

She nodded, as though she was thinking about something.

'Nobody need ever think we didn't,' she said.

The music played on and more people stood up to dance.

'Eleanor,' he said, 'you'd better finish up that ice cream before it melts.'

She smiled. She took her hand away from his. He lit another cigarette, even though he did not really want one. And she finished up her ice cream, before it melted.

16

A Wedding

AFTER THEY GOT ENGAGED, Frank and Eleanor began to save
as much money as they could. They stopped going out to concerts
and dances. Instead, they went for long walks and visited each
other's houses. Frank learnt to play the drums from a drunken
idiot called Buckets Boland and he joined a skiffle group that was
run by his cousin. They played at tennis club dances in Ranelagh
and Swords, and sometimes they played at weddings. The money
was very good. He and Eleanor opened a bank account together
and put all their money into it. They saved two hundred pounds
and put down a deposit on a house.

Sometimes they had fights. These were not very serious at first.
They argued about the colour of dresses, about each other's
friends, about politics. Eleanor's family were Fianna Fail. She said
Fianna Fail had got freedom for Ireland, but Frank said Fianna
Fail were no good for the working people, that they only cared
about the farmers and the rich. When he said that, she burst into
tears and shouted, 'Why do you always have to be so clever about
everything?'

After a time Frank realized that his fiancée was more sensitive
than he had thought. He didn't mind. In some secret way he found
it exciting. But sometimes she would flare up and lose her temper
with him over quite small things. She didn't like his workmates.
She said they were coarse and common, and when he tried to
defend them she told him to marry one of them if he loved them
so much. The pattern was always the same. She would snap at
him in an instant, say something cutting and then feel guilty for
several days.

Frank's mother seemed to like Eleanor, but she said she was

definitely the fiery type. 'That whole family were always the same,' his father sighed. 'Seed and breed, they'd cut you in two soon as look at you. I knew the uncle well. He was an evil little tinker.'

'There's nothing wrong with that family,' Frank's mother said. 'They're only ordinary people like ourselves. They had it hard enough.'

'You'll have your hands full with that one, son,' his father said. 'You mark my words.'

'She's grand,' Frank said. 'She has feelings, that's all.'

'Feelings,' his father scoffed. 'God, isn't it great now? Everyone these days has feelings. The whole country is falling to pieces, and everyone is pontificating about feelings.'

The late 1950s were hard in Ireland. Factories closed down and there was scarcely any work. The young people of Francis Street and Drimnagh continued to move away. Three of Frank's brothers went to Australia on the assisted passage scheme. One of Eleanor's brothers went to Boston and her sister went to Coventry. Another of her brothers got married and went off to Chicago the next morning by himself. He was going to send the fare on to his wife when he'd settled down, he said, and everyone thought this was very brave, everyone except Eleanor.

'I don't agree with that,' she said to Frank. 'When you're married, you share things. You share the adventure of things.'

'Don't be hard,' he told her. 'It takes all sorts.'

'You needn't think you'll go off rambling when you're married to me,' she said. 'You're supposed to be together when you're married.'

They had an argument about that too, but they made it up very soon and he told her he'd never go anywhere without her. They danced for hours at her brother's wedding. All the guests said they were made for each other.

17

Maritza Ramirez

THEY WAITED MORE and worried more but somehow a kind of calm became possible for Frank and Eleanor.

On Monday night, Cherry and Smokes came to see them. They sat in the Bar Casablanca together and talked about Johnny. Smokes couldn't seem to remember very much, but Cherry remembered lots of things. The time he'd had all of his hair shaved off for a bet. The time he'd socked an English guy in the mouth for saying the Irish were all drunks. The night Jackson Browne had turned up at one of their gigs and how Johnny and she and Lorenzo had stayed up jamming old rhythm and blues numbers with Jackson, all night long, until the sun had come up over the fishing boats in Rivas Harbour. Five in the morning, she remembered, and there'd been six thousand people in the market square, dancing, singing out 'Baby, Please Don't Go'.

'It was one wild night,' Smokes said. 'It really was a gas.'

'But you weren't there.' Cherry laughed. 'You had diarrhoea, honey. It was me and the others.'

'Course I was there. Don't you remember? Jackson said I was a really hot drummer.'

Cherry shook her head. 'That was earlier,' she said, 'before you got the runs. And he said you were a very unusual drummer, Smokes. That ain't quite the same thing.'

Then there was the time – Smokes laughed at this – when Johnny had walked straight up to the newly crowned Miss Managua at the fiesta in the *parque* and asked her if she wanted to dance. She'd said yes, too, and her boyfriend had got mad, and then drunk, and he'd run after Johnny with a knife, and Johnny'd had to hide up a tree.

Later that night, Guapo came to the Imperial and told them he'd once seen Johnny give away every last dollar he had to a hungry young boy from the slums in the Ciudad Sandino. Then he told them about the time he and Johnny had walked the ten miles out to the airport every day for a week to help unload the planes of their cargo of syringes and drugs, when the boycott had just started and things had been really tough in Managua.

'What?' Frank said. 'Our fellow walk a distance? You're joking me.'

'Sí, Francisco,' Guapo said. '*Verdad.*'

'God, he wouldn't cross the street for a walk at home. You wouldn't get him to walk down the stairs in the morning.'

And then there were the other stories, about all the times when he'd just disappeared, just not turned up for gigs or practices, just taken off for days without saying a word to anyone.

'Yeah, that used to spook me,' Smokes told them. 'Sometimes you could set a watch by the guy. Other times' – he shook his head and whistled – 'like, totally unreliable, man. But he'd never say a word about it. He wouldn't say a damn thing.'

'It wasn't that,' Cherry said. 'He just needed a lot of space.'

'Oh, yeah. Like, I'm not knocking the guy, right? I mean, Johnny was absolutely great.'

'He was real good with people,' Cherry said sadly. 'They trusted him. He used to ask 'em all the right questions and it took me a while to see why.'

'Why, dear?' Eleanor asked.

'So they wouldn't ask questions about him.' She laughed, as though it was absolutely obvious. 'He got real jumpy about stuff like that. He was like a ghost sometimes. He was there, you know, but he wasn't there too.'

'Oh, yeah, Johnny was great,' Smokes said. 'He really was a very interesting person when you knew him as well as I did.'

Suddenly Eleanor stood up and walked quickly from the room. Smokes turned and stared after her, looking surprised.

'Jeez,' he said, 'what's eating her?'

Frank sighed. 'She doesn't like it when you say "was" about Johnny,' he said. 'She has a bee in her bonnet about it.'

Smokes shrugged and tried to laugh. 'Fuck,' he said, 'it's just a way of talking, Franklin. It don't mean nothin'.' He glanced at Cherry but she turned away and shook her head.

'Well it does to Eleanor,' Frank said. 'It does to her.'

Early on Tuesday, Eleanor telephoned Ireland. She spoke to Father Rogan and told him to put things on hold. She called the next-door neighbours, who said they'd been getting terribly worried. Flowers had been arriving from friends and from some of her students. One of Frank's brothers who lived in Melbourne had got in touch to say he'd be coming home to Ireland for the funeral. He was arriving first thing the following morning, with his wife and his children.

But on that Tuesday morning Frank and Eleanor Little were not in the church in Dublin praying over the body of their son. They were sitting by the swimming pool at the Imperial Hotel, when a young woman arrived from the *Ministerio* to say that she wanted to speak to them.

A gang of American reporters sat playing giant chess by the pool, drinking margaritas and laughing, one or two of them drunk, although it was only eleven o'clock.

The young woman's name was Maritza Ramirez. She was dressed very smartly in a black and white trouser suit and a white hat. She was carrying a briefcase.

'I have some news for you both,' she said. 'It may be good or bad. I do not know yet.'

She sat down and they ordered coffee. She opened her briefcase and took out some papers. The dazzling sunlight bounced back off the swimming pool, a painful emerald glare. She unfolded the papers on her lap and began to speak.

'Your son was last heard of in the town of Corinto, in the north. From there he telephoned his *compañeros* shortly before the Contra attack.' She paused and looked at her notes. 'Now, I have to tell you that the body of an unidentified young man was buried there, in Corinto, on the day after the Contras came. He had been very badly burnt in the attack. Identification was impossible. But the dental records you have brought would confirm whether or not this is your son.'

'Good God,' said Eleanor.

'But if he's buried already . . .' Frank said.

Maritza Ramirez peered at him. 'We can arrange an exhumation. That is the word, no?'

'My God,' said Eleanor. 'Frank?'

'But, *Señores*,' Maritza Ramirez said, 'there is also a jail in this town. And it seems that a young European man is being held there. He was arrested in suspicious circumstances shortly after the counter-revolutionary raid. He was in the *zona* without a permit and he was in possession of narcotics. So far, he has refused to say anything to our people. He has a German passport. Now, I must tell you that the German authorities do have a record of a missing citizen. But there are discrepancies. The man in the jail does not fully match the description we have of the missing German comrade. He has also refused to cooperate with our interrogators. This is suspicious.'

'Interrogators?' said Eleanor.

'It is just a word. Since the revolution, we observe the Geneva Convention on all prisoners.'

'It's not a word I like. My son's done nothing wrong.'

'If he was in Corinto without a permission, then he has done something wrong, *Señora*. However, I do not say this is your son. It is a faint possibility only. In any case, we observe the Geneva Convention.'

'Eleanor,' Frank said, touching her knee, 'you heard the girl. It's only a word now.'

Maritza Ramirez continued, 'There are also a number of unidentified bodies, in the hospitals at Granada, Chinandega and Rivas. We are trying to compile a list, but it is difficult. You will have to study this list when it is completed.'

'God almighty,' Frank said.

'And what?' Eleanor said. 'You think one of them might be my son's body?'

The young woman shook her head. 'Perhaps. We just cannot say, *Señora*. Your husband and yourself must make the journey to Corinto first, and then we shall see. It is very hard for you both, I know. *Comandante* Borge has been made aware.'

'How soon can we go?' Eleanor asked.

'The situation is very delicate, *Señora*. The war is all around us. There are active counter-revolutionary units in the hills all around

Corinto. You must wait until the situation is normalized. Then we will find a military escort for you.'

'How long will that take?'

'Eleanor,' Frank said, 'you heard what the girl said.'

'A week, *Señora*. Ten days. Our soldiers are advancing. You will understand, the pressure is on us right now. The American press has been alerted to the presence of foreigners in dangerous areas of our country. They are watching us very closely. We must be careful.'

She pulled a clipping from the file on her lap and showed it to Frank. It was from the *Washington Times*. 'SANDINISTAS PLACE FOREIGN STUDENTS IN WAR ZONE,' the headline said, and Hollis Clarke's name appeared at the end. She offered a handful of cuttings from some other American newspapers. 'LEFTISTS MAKE PROPAGANDA WITH UNARMED KIDS.' 'MANAGUA DENIES HUMAN SHIELD OPERATION.' 'REAGAN SAYS CONTRAS ARE FREEDOM FIGHTERS.'

'This Hollis Clarke,' she said. '*Compañero* Captain Nuñez tells me he is a friend of yours, *Señor*?'

'I wouldn't say that.'

'*Bueno*. We must be very careful. We need the solidarity of the North American people. In these times, we must all be very careful of our friends.'

'I haven't seen Clarke since Sunday,' Frank said, 'when he wrote that.'

Maritza Ramirez nodded. She pinched the fabric of her blouse and pulled it away from her flesh.

'We've come two thousand miles,' Eleanor said. 'Surely you could do something for us?'

'The girl knows that, Eleanor,' Frank said.

'We do understand, *Señora*. We are honestly trying to do our best. You must try to be patient.'

Maritza Ramirez sipped her coffee and winced. '*Ay, Dios mío*,' she gasped. 'When the war is over, we shall drink good coffee again.'

'Yes, it's funny.' Frank laughed. 'It never tastes as good as it smells, does it?'

'My mother' – Maritza Ramirez smiled – 'she says this very often.'

There was a sudden burst of raucous laughter from the swimming pool. The reporters were splashing around in the water and pouring beer over each other.

'This place!' Eleanor said. 'Corinto, you said? Isn't that the place Smokes and the band are going to, Frank? Where Johnny knew that ice cream girl? Remember? Smokes told us last week? They're playing up near there. It can't be that bad, surely, if you're letting *them* go? I mean Smokes is an American. We could go up with them, couldn't we? I think they're going tomorrow morning.'

Maritza Ramirez drank some more coffee. 'Sometimes we do allow foreign *compañeros* to enter the zone,' she said. 'But only if they are residents who are helping the war effort. Even then they need a *permiso*.'

'Oh, for heaven's sake' – Eleanor laughed – 'He's in a rock and roll group.'

'The people need entertainment too.'

'Oh, but couldn't we go up with them? In the van?'

Maritza Ramirez laughed and shook her head very firmly. 'That would not be possible. If your friend is going into the *zona*, he will have had training with weapons. We cannot allow people to go if they are unprepared. Also he will be carrying an American passport. In case of trouble.'

'No,' Frank said. 'They can't allow that, El.'

'Quite seriously,' Maritza Ramirez said, 'you could be killed up there. It is very dangerous. The counter-revolutionaries have penetrated very deeply. They killed a young French comrade just last week. A telephone engineer. A woman.'

Eleanor sighed.

'Of course you're right,' Frank said. 'We know that.'

Maritza Ramirez stood up, smoothed down her clothes and fanned her face with her hand. '*Qué calor*,' she sighed.

'Well, thank you now for coming,' Frank said. 'Thank you for your time, love.'

'*Hasta la vista*,' she said. 'Try to be patient, *Señores*.'

Eleanor watched her walk back towards the hotel. The waiter emerged with a tray of drinks. He seemed to know Maritza Ramirez. He smiled and kissed her on both cheeks. They chatted for a few moments, then they kissed again and she left.

'Lovely-looking girl,' Frank sighed. 'God, some of the people are fabulous, aren't they, El? The ones who aren't too dark, you know, in the face. And they carry themselves very well, now, I must say.'

'Frank,' she interrupted, 'we have to talk.'

'About what?'

'You know right bloody well. You needn't bother coming the innocent with me.'

He sipped his drink. 'Now, look,' he said. 'I know what you're thinking, El, and you're touched in the head. We can't go haring up to the back of beyond under our own steam. We can't go up until they let us. It's dangerous.'

A chorus of electronic bleeps came from the reporters' tables. They all jumped out of the pool and began pulling their trousers on over their swimming trunks.

'Eleanor, be reasonable. We can't. Do you want us to get shot?'

She got up and he grabbed her wrist. She stood limply, listening to him for a moment, tapping her foot on the ground. Then she pulled her hand sharply away.

'Frank Little' – she was bright red in the face now – 'I can't believe you're not ashamed of yourself. And there I was, thinking you were still a man.'

She turned and began to walk towards the hotel. He put his hands to his head. The sun screamed down. He could see it was going to be one of those days.

18

Everything Is Serious

'LAMB CHOP,' CHERRY CALLED from the bedroom. 'Get your cute ass back in here and fuck me again.'

Smokes stared at himself in the mirror. He took a can of deodorant and sprayed his armpits, grinning. Then he stepped out of the bathroom wearing a towel.

'Oh, my God, you're so cute,' she said. 'Get over here.'

'Sweetheart,' he sighed, 'you have such excellent taste.'

She grabbed Smokes by the hair and dragged him down on to the mattress. They kissed hard, wet kisses. They chewed each other's tongues and she sank her teeth into his neck. She put her leg between his thighs and rolled on top of him. He touched her shoulders and her back, smelling her flesh. He could not believe anyone could be so beautiful. He kissed her mouth again and held her breasts in his hands. She gnawed his shoulders. He wrapped his arms hard around her body.

'Cherry, honey,' he gasped, 'I love you so much.'

'Oh, God, Smokes, me too.'

She grabbed his hands and licked them. She put his moist fingers on to her breasts and then between her legs.

'I love you,' she said.

'You make me shake,' he said. 'I'm shaking all over.'

'Shivers down my backbone.' She laughed. 'I want you to make me come, Smokes.'

She held his fingers and moved them over her body. She showed him where she wanted to be touched. He knew, but she showed him anyway, because showing him again was fun and it made them feel close. He caressed her and kissed her and she stroked his soft pink skin. She reached over to the bedside table and grabbed a condom.

'Oh, no,' he groaned.

'*Sí, sí*,' she said.

She held his penis and began to squeeze it gently. She kissed it and licked it, then slipped it into her mouth for a moment, feeling it harden. He put his hands over his eyes and moaned. She laughed. They rolled over and he licked her stomach. The two of them giggled like children, panting and sweating. He slithered his tongue into her navel and she gasped. He gnawed at her thighs. She sat up and began to unroll the condom slowly over his penis.

'I want you inside me.'

He pushed his hair behind his ears, took her face in his hands and held it for a moment. He wanted to shout out loud because she was so beautiful. He kissed her mouth and her nose and her cheeks. When she closed her eyes and sighed, he kissed her eyelids and ran his tongue along her lashes.

'God, now,' she breathed. 'You waiting for Thanksgiving or what?'

She pushed him on to his back again, put her hands on his chest and climbed over him, rubbing gently against his wet thigh. Smokes gurgled with hapless pleasure. He put his hands on her hips. She pushed gently down on to him and they both sighed as they started to move together.

'Oh, God,' he warned, 'I'm gonna come.'

'Not yet,' she said.

'I can't,' he said. 'Fuck.'

He lay flat out and grabbed the bars of the headboard. She leant down and kissed his mouth.

'Think of something boring.' She grinned. 'Think of Trotsky's memoirs.'

'OK,' he panted. 'OK. I think I got it.'

'Now,' she said, moving her nipples against his lips, beginning to grind her hips again. 'I want you to *fuck* me, Smokes.'

'I'll come,' he said.

She leant backwards and pushed down against him, gasping. 'Come on then, it don't matter. Fuck me harder, Smokes. Come in me.'

He put his hands on her breasts and clenched his teeth.

'I'm gonna come, Cherry. I'm gonna . . .'

'Oh, Smokes. Go on, honey. Come in me.'

Five seconds later, the doorbell rang.

'Christ,' Smokes croaked, sitting bolt upright.

'Let's leave it,' she whispered. 'Probably just Guapo.'

He nodded, kissing her mouth again, snuffling with guilty laughter.

There was another long ring on the doorbell, followed by a hard kicking sound. Cherry groaned. The kicking sound came again.

'Jesus,' Smokes sighed. 'I better get it, honey.' Cherry rolled over and started to punch the pillow. 'Hurry up,' she hissed.

Smokes wrapped the sheet around himself and walked through the living room towards the front door.

'Alright,' he yelled. 'Alright, Guapo, you little *cabron*.'

The open door flooded the room with light. His eyes stung. 'Frank,' he gasped. 'Uh, Eleanor. What a pleasant surprise.'

'We won't keep you,' Frank said. 'We can see you're busy.'

'Sorry, Frank?'

Frank nodded at Smokes's sheet. 'You're busy,' he said.

'No, Franklin. I was just, you know, taking a shower.'

'To wash all that lipstick off yourself,' Eleanor said.

'Uh, right.' Smokes found himself wondering whether the whole body could blush.

Eleanor and Frank stepped into the room. Frank took off his hat.

'Great to be young and in love,' he said.

'You're funny, Frank. You're pure vaudeville, OK?'

Frank grinned. 'Eleanor has something to say to you.'

Smokes looked at her. 'OK.' He nodded. 'Shoot, Eleanor.'

'Now, Smokes,' she said, 'we just want a minute, love. You see, we want you to take us to Corinto with you and the *Desperados*. We have it all figured out. They think Johnny might be in the jail up there.'

'Or there's this other fellow,' Frank said, 'this other fellow who was buried there. This woman came, and she told us all about it. She said if he's anywhere, that's where he is. So we'll just tag along with you and the band when you go up tomorrow. That's alright, isn't it?'

Smokes tittered. 'You're kidding me, right?'

Frank shook his head. 'We're not.'

Smokes went over to Frank and punched him playfully on the arm.

'Close, but no cigar, Franklin' — he chuckled, winking – 'You know, Johnny used to try laying shit like this on me all the time too.'

Frank smiled. 'We're not joking, Smokes,' he said.

Smokes looked at him closely. Frank shrugged. Smokes started to get a little nervous.

'OK, cut it out, Franklin. Tell me you're pulling my wire.'

Frank shook his head. 'Eleanor wants you to take us to Corinto. And I do too. We've talked about it.'

'Frank, what are you, crazy? I can't do that, guys.'

'Why not?'

'Eleanor, Corinto is right slap in the middle of the war zone. It's crazy up there. It's filthy. It's just terrible. It's like Hell's Kitchen without the charm. Come on, Franklin. You're jerking me around, right?'

'If you don't take us,' Eleanor said, 'we'll get one of the taxi drivers to do it.'

Smokes collapsed in a frenzy of giggles. 'Eleanor, man, you really kill me. A *taxista* is gonna take you to Corinto, right? And monkeys might fly out of my butt.'

'There's no need for rudeness,' Eleanor said.

Cherry appeared in the bedroom doorway wearing a long white T-shirt with a picture of a pyramid on it. She waved timidly, and Eleanor blew her a kiss.

'Eleanor, honey,' Smokes said, 'I'm sorry, OK, but a taxi driver is no way gonna take you to Corinto. Believe me.'

'Smokes, for two thousand dollars they'd take you to hell and back.'

Smokes's eyes narrowed. 'You don't have that kind of bread. Nobody carries that kind of bread.'

'Oh, Frank's brought plenty of money. Frank always brings plenty of money when he goes away. It makes him feel secure.'

'That's true,' Frank said.

Smokes was beginning to feel very hot now. He sucked his teeth. He felt the sweat beginning to trickle down his back.

'You're kidding me, guys. Am I right?'

He licked his lips and stared at them. Frank shook his head. Suddenly Smokes closed his eyes, chortling with manic laughter. He slapped himself hard on the forehead, turned around to Cherry and pointed at her.

'You slime,' he whinnied, 'you set me up. You told them we'd be here, and you told them to come around and freak the shit out of me. Oh, man, I should've known. What a klutz.'

'No, I didn't, Smokes.'

'We've got it all fixed up anyway,' Eleanor told him brightly. 'We're leaving at dawn on Saturday. We'll be up there in plenty of time for your concert next week. That'll be nice, won't it?'

Smokes went over to the couch and lay down. He put his head in his hands. 'Oh, my good Lord Jesus, they're serious.'

Cherry came in and sat down on a beanbag, hugging her knees. She laughed. 'We'd have to talk to the guys about it,' she said. 'Lorenzo and Guapo. They could get in a lot of trouble.'

'They could get in a lot of jail,' Smokes said. 'We can't do it.'

The sound of thunder cracked the air. Rain began to spill down on to the roof, rattling like applause on the metal slats. Out in the street, the children whooped and screamed.

'There's no way,' Smokes said. 'This is a crazy idea. No way. You heard what Nuñez said about *gringos* being in the war zone.'

'We can't wait any longer, Smokes,' Frank said.

Lightning flickered and the children screamed again.

'No,' said Eleanor, 'we've waited long enough now. Think how you'd feel, love, if he was your son.'

'Tell you what,' Cherry said. 'We'll meet you tonight. Out at Plastic City, you know? Where the McDonald's is? We'll talk to the guys, and we'll see you then.'

Smokes sat up and peered at her. 'Cherry, we can't,' he said in a warning voice. 'Come on. Get real, honey. Are you nuts?'

'Fine. We'll see you later,' Eleanor said. 'We'll leave you love-birds to it now. Come on, Frank. You can show me some of the sights.'

'*Hasta la vista*' – Frank grinned – 'baby.'

Eleanor and Frank stepped back out into the rainy street, closing the door behind them.

Smokes stood up and poured himself a large tequila. He paced up and down the room and lit a cigarette. He drained his glass and poured another drink. He felt wild with worry, breathless and confused.

'I'm fucking dreaming here. This could not possibly be happening to me.'

'Come back to bed, babe,' Cherry sighed. 'Leave the world outside.'

She peeled off her T-shirt. She walked over and stood behind him and kissed his shoulders very gently, digging her fingers into his back.

'Honey,' he said as she wrapped her arms around his abdomen. 'Come on, Cherry, stop, this is serious, man.'

She held him very tightly and closed her eyes, listening to the sound of the rain. She loved him so much. He was helpless without her, but that was alright, because she loved him.

'I know, Smokes,' she said. 'Everything is serious. And this is serious too.'

19

London

FRANK LITTLE AND ELEANOR HAMILTON were married in Mount Argus church on 20 September 1960, by Eleanor's uncle Leo, who was a Franciscan monk. They paid for everything themselves. The reception, the flowers, the dresses, the suits, all the food and drink. Nobody helped them to pay for anything.

Johnny Doyle had a daughter who ran a boarding house in London and Frank and Eleanor went there for their honeymoon. They drank coffee in the Three i's café. They went to see Marty Wilde and his band playing at the Dominion Theatre on Charing Cross Road. They went dancing at the Palais in Hammersmith and they ate out every night.

London was alive with colour and excitement. There were teddy boys and rockers in the streets of Soho, beautiful girls in sloppy Joe sweaters and wide coloured skirts. There were black people and brown people. There were art galleries and lots of theatres. And it was so much bigger than Dublin. It was wonderful, Eleanor said. It was like waking up in a different world.

They did not make love for the first few nights of their marriage. 'Do you mind if we just kiss and touch?' she asked him and he said no, he didn't mind, because he was afraid too.

On the fourth night they were coming home from a play on Shaftesbury Avenue when a thunderstorm suddenly started. Rain lashed down into the streets of the West End. They stepped into a doorway and kissed very passionately, and they both knew then that they would make love for the first time that night.

Eleanor undressed in the bathroom. She put on a nightdress and felt her way to the bed in the dim light. She kissed her husband and felt him lift her nightdress over her arms. She asked him to take off his pyjamas and he did. He held her very close to him for a long time. She touched his penis with her hand. It felt very hard and warm. He put his leg between her thighs. She sighed with pleasure and he rolled on top of her. He put his penis slowly into her and she gasped.

'Are you alright?' he asked her.

She put her arms around his neck. 'Yes,' she whispered. 'Go on.'

'Am I hurting?'

'No, Frank.'

He pushed a little further into her. He tried to hold himself up on his arms so that he would not hurt her. She turned her head and looked away. He felt his climax coming almost immediately and he collapsed on top of her body, crying out with pleasure, and she held him very tightly.

After that, they made love every night for two weeks. They made love until they were sore. And they made love every morning when they woke up, before they went down to breakfast.

They went to see the Tower of London and Madame Tussaud's and Buckingham Palace, and every afternoon they came back and lay down on the bed together and took off their clothes and made love. Then they lay very still in each other's arms, listening to the sound of the traffic outside and the din of the rock and roll music from the little café across the street.

They were so much in love that they wanted to touch all the time. They could not bear even to walk down the street without holding hands. They began to undress in front of each other now. They began to sleep with no clothes on, and to look at each other's naked bodies.

One afternoon they strolled through Hyde Park in the sunshine and turned down a path overhung with ferns and wild roses. Suddenly he put his arm around her waist and began to kiss her throat. She leant back against a tree. He held her face in his hands and covered her mouth with tender kisses. He pushed against her then, and she could feel his body through her thin cotton dress. She laughed and said she thought it was time to go home and lie down.

Afterwards they lay in each other's arms and listened to the classical music on the radio.

'Is it as nice for you, Eleanor?' he asked her gently. 'When we're with each other?'

She blushed deeply and kissed his face. 'It's a nice comfort,' she said. 'You hear such awful stories, Frank. Nobody ever told me what a nice comfort it would be.'

20

Lorenzo Moran

FROM THE OUTSIDE, the Managua branch of McDonald's looked just like any other. Vast glass windows, yellow and green plastic doors, a giant yellow double arch lit up in neon on the roof.

Inside, things were different. There were no hamburgers, no French fries, no apple pies, no chicken nuggets. There was no root beer, no ice cream, no filet-o-fish. There were no straws or serviettes or tinfoil ashtrays. There were tortillas and beers and one kind of milk shake, and that was it. But the queue of gabbling, flirty, denim-clad teenagers stretched all the way out of the door and into the Ciudad Plastica.

When Frank and Eleanor came in, Smokes and Cherry were sitting at a table eating tortillas. Guapo was with them, drinking a beer and whispering in a waitress's ear. He was wearing a trilby hat, a scarlet neckscarf and a black T-shirt with the words THE CLASH stencilled on in red.

There was another man at the table. His skin was black and glossy and he looked a little older than Guapo. He wore a leopard-skin shirt, a white silk jacket and a pair of mirrored sunglasses. He was completely bald. In his right hand he was holding a wooden walking stick with a golden eagle head on the handle. His fingers were covered with gold and silver rings. They were caressing the eagle's beak.

'This is Lorenzo Moran,' Cherry said. 'Lorenzo, this is Frank and Eleanor, Johnny's folks.'

'I'm charmed to make your acquaintance,' Lorenzo said in a beautiful deep voice. Eleanor thought it was the kind of voice that a cello would have if a cello could speak and breathe like a man. He held out his hand and it rested in the air, waiting for someone to take it. Eventually, Eleanor did. Lorenzo raised her hand to his lips and kissed it. Then Frank stepped forward uncertainly and took Lorenzo's hand in his own.

'Yes, man,' Lorenzo said, 'I'm blind as Moses in the desert.'

'I'm sorry to hear that,' Frank said.

'Don't be sorry, brother. The fire of the lord is in my head. There's enough electricity in there to light up Broadway.'

They sat down and Smokes ordered more beers.

'So then, Lorenzo Moran,' Frank said, 'there's Irish in you anyway.'

'My grandfather was from your country.' Lorenzo nodded. 'He was a slaver, in the days of old. But he changed his ways when he met my grandmother. He was swimming in the river one day, in Trinidad, and there she was, with her sisters in the rushes, and he laid his eyes upon her and found grace. They ran away together, and they came to this lovely land.'

'Well now, God, it must be hard for you,' Frank said. 'Being blind, and, you know, black as well.'

'Frank Little,' Eleanor hissed.

'Oh what? I'm only saying.'

Lorenzo opened his mouth and began to laugh, rocking back and forth, banging his stick on the ground. 'It ain't so hard, brother. I got a lot of beautiful angels to care for me.'

'Would they be angels with wings?' Frank asked. 'Or the other kind?'

'Oh, both kinds. Every kind. And you know, man, the blacker the berry, the sweeter the juice.'

'Good man, Lorenzo.' Frank chuckled. 'You've an Irish gift of the gab anyway.'

Smokes cleared his throat loudly.

'Sorry?' he said. 'I mean, are you guys happy? I mean, are we hear to discuss the Emerald fucking Isle or, you know, more important things?'

'Sorry, Smokes,' Frank said.

'Sí,' said Guapo. '*Lo siento*, Marilyn.'

Smokes glared at Guapo and then bent low across the table. He sucked at his milk shake and began to whisper. 'So, look, I've discussed all this craziness with the guys. And I don't know. It's real dangerous, it's stupid, and it's definitely illegal.'

He looked at them both in turn, his childish face attempting seriousness. He shook his head.

'I don't know, they're both fucking nuts, but they're willing to take you with us.'

'You mean it, Smokes?' Frank said.

'Get ready to rock, Frank,' Cherry said. 'It's the no-sleep-till-Corinto tour.'

Hot tears filled Eleanor's eyes. 'Oh, thank you, boys,' she said. Guapo took her hand and squeezed it.

'*De nada*, Eleanor,' he said. 'For nothing, no?'

'OK,' Smokes said. 'Now, here's the deal. From here to Corinto is five hours on the Pan-American Highway. But we can't go that way. It's a pisser, but it's no can do.'

'Why not?' Frank said.

'Two reasons, Franklin. One, it's crawling with military, day in, day out. See, if the Contras ever get to it it's goodnight Vienna, so there's road blocks every five miles. You guys'd be rumbled in, like, an hour.'

'Reason two, we gotta do these gigs. That's the best cover. You come with us in Claudette, just lay low. We go do our stuff, we'll get up there in four, five days, it's all kosher.'

'Where are these gigs?' Frank asked.

Smokes scratched his head. 'I think one in Poneloya. Then, uh, Esteli, is it, honey?'

'Smokes?' Cherry said. 'Why don't you shut up and let me explain it?'

'OK,' Smokes sighed. 'Touchy, touchy, baby.'

Cherry stuck out her tongue at him. 'OK,' she said. 'See, Corinto is due north of here, Frank. We leave tomorrow, that's Wednesday, go by the side roads. We stay off the Pan-Am all the way. We go north up the coast, parallel to the Pan-Am on the Pacific side, up as far as León. We play the festival there tomorrow night. Gig one. Then we turn east. We cross right over the Pan-Am like a river, hope we don't get caught. Then further east, up into the mountains, to Esteli. We got a day off, then gig two, Friday night. After that, north again, way up to the Honduran border, to Ocotal. Gig three, the Saturday night dance. Then west all the way down, west, west, west, down to the Pacific again, and Corinto. We play the seventeenth, that's

Wednesday, hang out, play again the nineteenth, Revolution Day.'

'Yeah,' Smokes said. 'Gig five.'

'Thank you, Sherlock,' Frank said.

'See, we can't go straight up,' Cherry said. 'So we go in a big triangle instead.'

She traced an oblong on the plastic table and drew the line of the journey with her finger. 'Up, east, back around to the sea.' She beamed. 'Like a big question mark.'

A jeep pulled up outside the McDonald's and three young soldiers jumped out. They looked around and then glanced at their watches. They seemed to be waiting for someone.

'Brother Frank,' Lorenzo said, 'your son was a beautiful man. He had a beautiful soul. Great compassion.'

Shouts and wolf whistles came from the counter. One of the soldiers was standing by the queue now, joking with a group of schoolgirls in kilts and blazers.

'You knew him well?' Frank asked.

Lorenzo nodded. 'He was more spirit than flesh. Such a gorgeous heart, but pierced with nails of pain. He was in the world, you know, brother, but the world was not his place.'

Smokes folded his arms and threw his eyes to the ceiling. 'Jesus H Christ,' he sighed.

'What, Smokes?' Cherry said.

'Like, this is Johnny Little we're talking about here, not Mother fucking Teresa.'

'Hey, Marilyn?' Guapo said.

'Don't call me Marilyn, you scumsucker.'

Guapo put his finger to his lips. 'Shhh,' he hissed. 'Marilyn!'

'Lorenzo,' Eleanor said, 'he was a good friend to you?'

Lorenzo hung his head. With his index finger, he pushed his mirror shades tighter on to his face.

'The good Lord has been kind to me, sister. But the day I met Johnny Little, the Lord was being kinder than most. To know that man was a blessed thing.'

Frank reached out and touched Lorenzo's hand.

'Lorenzo,' he said, 'you're a gentleman.'

'Well hey, Franklin,' Smokes said, 'I mean, we all feel the same, man. Me more than anyone. I mean, if the crazy son of a bitch is out there, we can't just leave him to rot in hell, can we?'

Cherry put a finger to her eye and wiped away a tear. Smokes wrapped his arm around her shoulder, and she smiled at him.

'I'm fine,' she told him. 'Just thinking about when we find him.'

'Hey, woman, no cry,' Lorenzo said. 'We are an Easter people, and alleluia is our song.'

'Right on, brother,' said Smokes. 'Now ain't that the truth?'

In the Lobo Jack nightclub, across the little square from the McDonald's, Smokes and Cherry were doing the lambada. The teenagers watched in amusement from the bar, pointing and laughing, and Frank and Eleanor watched too as they swirled across the floor in perfect time with the chugging rhythm. Cherry was wearing a very short red skirt and a sloppy black blouse. She looked magnificent. Smokes looked vaguely ridiculous, the flares of his bellbottoms flapping against his calves. He was a good dancer though. He held her close and pushed her away, and then stepped closer, swirling around her and swivelling his hips. He put his hands on her waist and lifted her into the air. She clamped her thighs around his chest, threw her arms back, and her head too, so that her long hair touched the floor.

'God, now, there's no need for that,' Frank said. 'That isn't about dancing, if you ask me.'

Eleanor sighed. 'Dancing's never been about dancing, Frank.'

Guapo walked over to Frank and Eleanor. He chinked his beer bottle against Frank's, then stood beside them, staring at Smokes, shaking his head from side to side in disbelief.

'Guapo,' Frank said, 'why aren't you dancing?'

Guapo pulled a face. '*No me gusta ese tipo de música*,' he sniffed. '*Preferio el rock and roll.*'

'He says he doesn't like salsa, Frank. He only likes pop music.'

Suddenly the salsa music segued into a U2 song. The young people in jeans invaded the floor, wailing with excitement. They pranced up and down, waving their arms, singing along with the chorus. Guapo ran on to the dance floor and began to rock his head from side to side, stamping his feet and clapping his hands in the air.

Smokes and Cherry came in off the floor, drenched in sweat. They stood beside Frank and Eleanor and watched Guapo dancing.

148

Guapo's eyes were closed now and his hands were clamped on to his swinging hips as he jumped around in a circle.

'Sad, isn't it?' Smokes said.

'Oh, shut the fuck up, Smokes,' Cherry said.

Lorenzo was sitting by the jukebox. A young woman from the Barrio Rubén Darío was stroking his face with the back of her hand and trying to talk to him. She was very drunk and wanted him to dance, but Lorenzo was pretending that he couldn't speak any Spanish.

'*Venga*,' she pleaded. '*¡Baila! ¿Por qué no baila conmigo?*'

'My soul doth magnify the Lord,' Lorenzo whispered. 'And my spirit doth rejoice in God, my saviour.'

'*¿Por qué no baila conmigo?*' she urged. '*¿Por qué no, amor? ¿Por qué?*'

21

Glenageary

JUST AFTER CHRISTMAS 1961, Frank and Eleanor Little moved to their house in Glenageary, one of the new suburbs which had begun to grow up around the edge of Dublin in the late 1950s.

The house had four bedrooms and a garden. The kitchen was very big. There was a living room at the front and another room – 'a lounge', the estate agent called it – at the back. There was more space in the new house than in both of their parents' houses put together.

The neighbours were not particularly friendly. They were all from the country, clannish and curious. But Eleanor and Frank did not care about that because they were so happy together. They bought a good second-hand piano and Eleanor began to give piano lessons to some of the local children. It was an interest for her, Frank thought. Some men did not like their wives to work, but he didn't mind. It was good for a woman to have an interest, he thought, and it was good for a woman to have a little money of her own. He remembered his mother telling him that.

The first time her parents came out to the new house they seemed uncomfortable as they looked around. Eleanor's father hardly said a word during dinner, and her mother would not stop talking about the electric cooker and the size of the bathroom. When Frank got back from driving them home to Drimnagh, Eleanor seemed upset.

'Do you think we've changed, Frank?' she asked him, 'since we came to live out here?'

'Well, I bloody hope we have,' he said. 'There's nothing good about being poor.'

He told her a story about the time his father had been on strike.

His mother had been absolutely desperate for money. There had been children to feed, and there was hardly any money coming into the house. She had given Frank a note and sent him up to his uncle for a loan. He had never seen her look so ashamed, he told Eleanor; he could still see the look of shame on her face.

'That'll never happen to a kid of ours,' he said. 'That's the only way we're going to change, love.'

They went for walks on Killiney Hill and around Dalkey Quarry. Sometimes they walked up the Vico Road looking out at the sea. It was a famously beautiful view; people said it looked like the Bay of Naples. They both worked hard. In the evenings they listened to the radio together, or sometimes they read the newspapers. Most of the time they just talked. They bought a record player and some opera records, then Beethoven's symphonies, Bach's Brandenburg Concertos, Count John McCormack singing Moore's melodies, Handel's Oratorios, and traditional Irish music by Sean O'Riada and Carolan. They made love almost every night.

One day in February 1962, he came in from work to find her sitting in the kitchen, crying to herself. He held her hand and asked what was wrong.

'I went down to the doctor today,' she told him.

'Why, love? You're not sick?'

'No. I'm late.'

'What do you mean, late?'

'Do you not know what I mean, Frank?'

'No,' he said. 'Tell me.'

She turned away from him. 'You know the way a woman can expect something every month, Frank?'

'Oh, that. Yes.'

'Well, it's that. It's my time, Frank. I'm late. The doctor thinks I'm going to have a baby.'

He put his arms around her and began to cry himself because he was so happy. He took her out for dinner at the Killiney Castle Hotel. Afterwards they went dancing in the ballroom.

A baby girl was born in September. She had red hair and green eyes and they called her Catherine Maureen after Frank's mother and Maureen O'Hara. She was baptized at the Church of Our Lady of Victories, Sallynoggin, Dublin.

22

The Cloths of Heaven

THEY GOT UP AT FIVE on Wednesday morning and silently packed a few clothes. Frank shaved in the kitchenette sink while Eleanor showered in the bathroom. When he had dried his face he opened the hotel window and listened to the birds chirping at the light. The sun was spreading across the sky like a bloody egg. He made a pot of tea and toasted a piece of bread. They sat for ten minutes, having breakfast, saying very little, listening to the classical music that preceded the five thirty news on the radio.

Smokes was waiting with Claudette in the car park, a long cigarette dangling from his lips. He was tired and stubble-faced, and didn't say much. He grabbed their bags, opened the back door and muttered something about breakfast. In the back of the van sat his drum kit, an electric keyboard, amplifiers, guitar cases and a thick knot of flexes. There were two double bunk beds. Guapo and Lorenzo were lying on the lower bunks. Guapo was wearing sunglasses. His hands were folded across his chest and he looked like a corpse. A plastic bag of ice was resting on his forehead. Lorenzo smiled as they climbed in, but he said nothing and resumed reading his Braille bible. Guapo muttered in a drunken half-sleep.

A white and dewy haze hung over the city like a fresh sheet. It was early enough to be cool as they moved slowly through the debris of the streets. Here and there, drunks and lovers lay tangled together in doorways. Women poured buckets of water over porches. In the Calle de la Resistencia, they passed a *campesino* leading a mule to the *mercado*. The mule had two churns of milk strapped to its back and a garland of scrawny carrots around its neck. There was hardly any traffic, hardly any noise, just the pleasant quietness of the city in the early morning. News-paper sellers were setting up their stalls. Boys and girls were dragging *gaseosa* carts packed high with jagged lumps of ice through the streets. A line of white-wimpled nuns walked, heads bowed, to the early Mass in Santa María.

They stopped at the Mercado Roberto Huembes to stock up on supplies. The aisles of the market were already busy. Women were sweeping out their stalls and great clouds of sawdust flew up into the air. Men moved in and out of the aisles selling coffee and avocados and oranges to the women. Bulging boxes of blue jeans and T-shirts were being unloaded. Fat wriggling fish in crates gulped dumbly at the dry air. There were black fish and red fish, crabs and scaly slimy creatures with tentacles and no eyes and huge open mouths. There were boxes of apples and fat peaches. There were chunks of scrawny meat and thick strings of sausages.

Many of the stalls had crucifixes hanging over them, beside red and black FSLN flags. Others were decorated with photographs of the Pope and Augusto Sandino and posters bearing revolutionary slogans. Frank and Smokes walked around the aisles and Smokes exchanged jokes and insults with the women. They bought water and bread and a hunk of hard yellow cheese. They bought a cake of soap, a big box of cigarettes, a bunch of bright green bananas, tins of tuna and bars of chocolate. They paid with thick bundles of banknotes. The rate was down again, the traders told them. It was the war. There was nothing anyone could do about it.

Back in the van an argument broke out. Guapo had woken up now and he said he wanted to drive. Smokes was unhappy about this.

'You're hungover, you pathetic shit,' he said, 'or you're still drunk. You're in no condition to handle my baby.'

'*Hijo de la gran puta*,' Guapo said.

'Jesus, Guapo, you're disgusting, man. You're gross.'

Guapo got sulky then. He said that if he couldn't drive he was going back home to bed, where he'd left a Philosophy major from Ohio State University and a large bottle of King of Diamonds rum.

'You're drunk, man,' Smokes said. 'You're gone.'

'Hijo de cien mil putas.'

'Christ, Guapo. You're so fucking gross, man.'

'Listen, brothers,' Lorenzo said, whipping off his dark glasses. 'You don't be cool, I'm the one gonna be driving.'

After ten minutes of arguing Smokes backed down. He let Guapo drive on condition that Cherry sat up front too, to keep an eye on him. He got into the back of the van and sat down with Lorenzo, Frank and Eleanor. 'Guapo can get a little freaked,' he told them. 'He got shot when he was in the army. I think some of it must have gotten to his brain.'

'Brother Guapo is in the groove, man,' Lorenzo said. 'You just gotta tread softly with him.'

'I'd like to tread him softly into a fucking swamp someplace.'

'Tread softly,' Eleanor murmured, 'because you tread upon my dreams.'

'Huh?' said Smokes.

'Yeats,' she explained. '"He Wishes for the Cloths of Heaven".'

Smokes groaned. It was a little early in the a.m. for poetry, he said. He staggered to one of the bunks and took off the sheet, then lifted the mattress out of its frame, uncovering a six-foot length of hardboard. With his fist he knocked on the top of the board and it folded upwards, revealing a gap underneath the bed. This, Smokes explained, was where Frank and Eleanor would have to hide if they got stopped by a patrol along the way.

'How exciting,' Eleanor said, and Frank sighed.

They would have to spend their nights in the camper too, Smokes said. It was too risky for them all to stay in *hospedajes*. Foreigners were supposed to show their passports when they checked in, and the owners might get a little suspicious. It would be hot at night. It would be a difficult journey. Washing would be a problem. Things would be uncomfortable, and there was no mistake about that.

'We may get stopped,' Smokes told them. 'We gotta stay well off the Pan-Am, but sometimes they got barricades on the side roads too. And they might come looking. Just depends how long they don't notice you're gone from the Imper.'

'I didn't think of that,' Frank said.

'I reckon two days,' Smokes said. 'After that, it just depends whether they come looking or not.'

'Well,' said Frank, 'sure, with the war and everything, they won't bother with us.'

Smokes shrugged. '*Que sera sera*. We just gotta roll with the punches, Franklin.'

'You're very good, Smokes,' Eleanor said. 'I know you might get into trouble for this.'

Smokes nodded. He lifted the mattress back into place and folded the sheet, making up the bed. 'Hey, I like trouble,' he said. 'I'm the troublesome kind. Born to be wild, babe, you know what I'm saying?'

Claudette lurched. The engine ground and she began to move slowly forwards, the whole van juddering and vibrating as Guapo tried to engage the gears.

'Let's face it, he's also an American,' Lorenzo said. 'If the worst comes to the worst.'

'What's that supposed to mean?' Smokes said. 'Jesus, you're born in a stable, it don't make you a horse, Lorenzo.'

Lorenzo laughed. 'That's true,' he said. 'The saviour was born in a stable and he surely wasn't no horse.'

'Yeah, well, you remember that, *hombre*.'

Smokes climbed up and lay in the bunk above Lorenzo. He reached into his bag and pulled out a paperback book. *One Hundred Years of Solitude*, by Gabriel García Márquez. He lay on his back and turned the pages, quickly, inattentively, casually.

Eleanor climbed into the top bunk on the other side of the van. She pulled the sheet over herself and then rolled around, shoving her hand underneath the pillow.

'So, Lorenzo?' Frank whispered. 'How's she cutting?'

Lorenzo looked up and smiled, trying to gauge where Frank was sitting. 'Brother Frank,' Lorenzo said, 'and how are you this morning?' He reached out his hand and Frank took it.

'I'm game ball, Lorenzo. And how's yourself? Praying hard, I see.'

He nodded gravely. 'Yes, man. Been reading the good book and praying for Johnny Little. We shall go into the desert and find the child of Israel.'

Claudette reeled sharply to the right, almost pitching Smokes out of his bed. He cursed Guapo.

Lorenzo chuckled deeply. He reached out and groped on the

floor for his guitar case. With gentle fingers he unclipped the clasps and lifted out his guitar. It was beautiful. The body was red and gold, painted with silver stars, and the neck was jet black. Lorenzo placed the strap around his shoulders. Bending forward, listening closely, he began to tune up the machine heads.

'That's a lovely instrument,' Frank said. 'That must have set you back a few bob.'

Lorenzo nodded, but he didn't seem to be listening. His long fingers were running up and down the fretboard, caressing the strings. His foot began to tap rhythmically on the floor. He strummed a few chords and pushed down on the tremolo arm. He nodded his head from side to side as his ringed fingers bent the strings, then he opened his mouth and began to sing, very quietly, in a deep and soulful moan, plucking the treble strings high up on the neck.

> *Get away, Jordan, you get right away.*
> *And get away, Jordan, you river so wide.*
> *I want to cross over, sweet river of Jordan.*
> *And see my Lord Jesus, on the other sweet side.*

'Aw fuck, Lorenzo,' Smokes groaned. 'Can it, OK?'

'Lorenzo,' Frank said quietly, 'I don't suppose Johnny ever said anything to you. About us? About Eleanor and me?'

Lorenzo stopped playing for a moment. His fingers ran across the body of his guitar and he shook his head. 'I'm sorry, brother,' he said. 'Can't help you out with that.'

Frank touched his knee. 'That's alright, Lorenzo. I'm just interested. That's all.'

Lorenzo smiled and began gently to thumb the strings again. Frank went to lie down on the spare bunk. He lay very still, feeling the ground unroll beneath him. It felt very good to be moving. It felt good to be actually doing something at last.

'You alright up there, El?' he called.

She sat up in her bunk, rubbed her eyes and looked around. She stretched her arms out, smiled at Frank, then peered over at Smokes. 'That book, darling?' Eleanor asked. 'Are you enjoying it?'

'What? Oh yeah, man, it's great. I've read all this dude's books, all of them, every word.'

'Only thing you ever read was a cereal box,' Lorenzo muttered.

'I love him, really. These guys down here, you know they really can write, you know? I mean it's a total trip just reading them.'

'Now I've read that one,' Eleanor said. 'I think I prefer *The Autumn of the Patriarch*. What's your favourite one of his?'

'What? Well, this one, I guess.'

'Apart from that one?'

'Well, I love this one. I mean it really is hard to beat this one, for me.'

'I prefer some of his others,' Eleanor said. 'I found that one a bit heavy.'

'Yeah, well,' Smokes said. 'You know, I'm writing a novel myself actually. I don't know if Cherry told you? I'm writing this novel all about my life.'

Lorenzo spluttered with laughter.

'I am,' Smokes said. 'Fuck off, Lorenzo.'

'Brother Smokes been writing this novel since he was in short pants. It's gonna be thicker than the bible when he's done.'

'Shut the fuck up, Lorenzo.'

'And that one you're reading now, Smokes,' Frank said. 'What's the story about?'

Smokes shrugged and wrinkled his nose. 'You'd have to read it, Franklin. I'll lend it to you when I'm through.'

'Well,' Eleanor said, 'isn't it about a family, Smokes?'

'Well, yeah. Obviously. It's about a family. It's like this family and their problems, I guess.'

'Isn't that what all stories are about?' – Eleanor yawned – 'When you think?'

Claudette weaved left and right, straightening up with a wail of brakes.

'Oh, bollocks,' Frank said. 'If we wanted that now, we could have just stayed at home.'

He took out a pen and a piece of paper. He doodled a thin man hanging from a tree, then began, very slowly, to write.

23

A Letter From Frank Little

Nicaragua, Wednesday, 10 July 1985

Veronica, my darling.

I know you will not get this for an age, but I wanted to write to you anyhow. I really wish you were here with me now. I am sitting in this van in the middle of absolute nowhere. The noise of it is unbelievable. It is like an airplane. We are going to find that brat and then I am going to kick some bloody sense into him. After that, I am going to bring him back home to where he belongs. You would want to see this place. It is some set-up, Veronica, I can tell you. The water gets cut off nearly every day. You would hate it. It's not a place for a woman, really.

Herself is asleep now, on the bed effort over there. We have been getting on alright, the occasional ups and downs, but nothing that you would not expect. It is nice to be civilized at this difficult time, but there are painful memories, as you would expect. Cherry is up in the front with that Guapo character. He is a gas man for the ladies, you would want to see him in action. Smokes is asleep. He keeps reaching his hand down into his shorts and scratching his private parts. I wish he wouldn't do that. If he does it again, I will have to wake him up and say something.

We are going to the town where Bianca Jagger came from, Smokes tells me. It is called Léon. She had a bit of bloody sense, Bianca Jagger, if you ask me, in high-tailing it out of here as soon as possible. She is the only famous person that ever came from this place.

158

I miss you, Veronica. I am sorry we had our falling out the other night. It is difficult on the phone, but I really hate when we do not get on. You are very valuable to me. I don't tell you that enough, I know – 'Men' I can hear you saying – but it doesn't mean that the feeling isn't there.

It is very hot here, too hot. Oh God, if I ever see Dublin again, the rain falling on the streets and the black buildings, I don't think I will complain about anything. I was thinking the other night about something that happened to me when I was a child. About one day when I was up in Phoenix Park. There was a strange bird there. A tree creeper. Did I ever tell you about that day? I never thought back then that I would end up here, I must say. Who can tell what is in store for us?

I dreamed about it last night. And I keep thinking about it today, although, God knows, it must have been forty years ago. More. When Adam was a boy, as you would say! I don't know why, but I just wanted to tell you that anyhow.

And I keep dreaming about that son of mine as well. Things were so hard for you when he came to live with us. I know that, love. I never gave you the credit or the thanks you deserved. I never realized it was so hard for you and God knows you were the only mother he ever had. When I think of the nights we drove around looking for him. My God. It was awful what I put you through, and hardly ever a word of complaint. You are such a strong person. I know he never gave you anything except cheek and trouble. It is all past now, I know, but lately I just feel that I never gave you thanks for all you did for us. You are such a pet and I am so very fond of you. I am very sorry for having the row.

How are you keeping? Did you ring Billy Doyle about the car? Tell the lads that they better be working hard or when I get back I'll roast them. Well, I know that they are good lads really. What a terrible time this is. If you were not there, Veronica, I don't know. You are such a strength to me, and I never tell you. You have so many qualities and I am a very lucky fellow to have you in my life. I miss you very much, my dear, and I am longing to see you very soon, when this sad time will be over, and we can be together again.

How are the dogs?

Your fond
Frank

24

An Angel From Sexual Heaven

AT ABOUT A QUARTER TO TWELVE, Claudette shrieked to a sudden halt. Frank woke up covered in sweat to find Smokes dragging open the doors and cursing.

They had stopped on a quiet country road. Silver light sparkled through the dense trees. Cherry was outside, doubled over with laughter. There was a stream flowing by the side of the track, and Guapo was lying face down in it, whimpering and spluttering like a newborn baby.

'He's too hot,' Cherry explained. 'The guy's losing it.'

'Jesus,' Smokes said sulkily. 'Look at him. It's just pathetic really.'

Cherry went down and tried to drag Guapo out of the stream. He rolled over on his back, splashing water over his face and panting hard, then staggered back on to the roadway, dripping with water. He put his hands on his knees, bending over, coughing, retching and shaking his head.

'*Oh Dios mío*,' he gasped. 'I never will drink beer again.'

Eleanor stepped out of the van and offered Guapo the bottle of water. He uncorked it and gulped down a few mouthfuls.

'*Santa María Dolorosa*,' he grunted, sitting down in the roadway, raising the water bottle and pouring water down the back of his neck.

'Jesus, Guapo,' Smokes said. 'Look at you, man. I mean, get a fucking life, you know?'

'*Coño*,' Guapo said.

'What did he call you, Smokes?' Frank asked.

'You don't want to know, Frank,' Cherry sighed.

Lorenzo appeared in Claudette's doorway.

'Well, this is fierce now, Lorenzo,' Frank said. 'This poor fellow is twisted with the hangover.'

Lorenzo looked unimpressed. 'The love of strong wine is an abomination to the Lord,' he said. 'Proverbs.'

'Would you not go and help him up, Smokes?' Eleanor said.

Smokes shook his head and went over slowly to Guapo. 'Sad, sad, sad,' he said. He put one hand on his hip and, without looking, reached the other hand down towards Guapo, sighing very deeply and gazing out over the fields. Guapo slapped his hand away.

'*Tu madre*,' sighed Guapo, 'Marilyn.'

Guapo rose, unsteadily, to his feet and began to walk up and down, holding his head in his hands. Cherry kept trying not to laugh, and then spluttering into helpless giggles. Reluctantly, Lorenzo began to laugh too.

Guapo slapped him on the chest. '*Maricón*,' he said, pushing past Lorenzo and into the back of Claudette. Cherry took the ribbon from her hair and, dipping it in the stream, moistened her arms and face.

'Would you not come into the back, love?' Eleanor said. 'It's a little cooler.'

Cherry nodded. 'You wanna drive, Smokes? I'm just sticking to the damn seat up there.'

He put his arms around her and squeezed her shoulders. They kissed briefly.

'I'm hotter than a hound dog's ass,' she said, wiping her face on Smokes's T-shirt. She took off her shades and went to the back of the van. Eleanor held her hand as she climbed in.

'Now,' said Eleanor. 'I felt guilty anyhow, having all these handsome fellows to myself.'

'Hey, Franklin, babes?' Smokes called. 'Come and ride up front with me?'

'On one fucking condition,' Frank said. 'Just stop calling me that.'

The glare of the sun through the windscreen made the leatherette seats sting with heat. Frank opened a bottle of suntan oil, rubbing some of the liquid into his arms and across his aching forehead. Smokes started up the engine and they began to roll.

'Bit noisy, isn't she?' Frank said.

'Franklin' – Smokes grinned – 'she's the noisiest thing to come out of the Motown since Little Stevie Wonder.'

The dense trees gave way to open fields. A long narrow lake ran along the west side of the road; it was oyster grey in colour. Over on the east side a thick forest of black trees led up towards the mountain. Claudette moaned as they began to strain up the incline.

'Mountains,' Smokes said. 'Nothing but fucking mountains and misfits in this country. Johnny used to say that.'

'Yeah,' Frank said. 'Is that how you ended up here, Smokes?'

Smokes hissed with laughter. He took his hands off the wheel, pulled a pack of Marlboros from his pocket and lit one.

'Came down here in seventy-eight, Franklin. It was just after I graduated school. My cousin and his friend Lenny Wolf were coming down here, surfing. And I was doing nothing, man. Time was going, I don't know.' He paused.

'And there was this chick too; she was absolutely breaking my balls, you know? She was crazy. She really was two chevvies short of a funeral. She wanted me to tie her up all the time. We had a fight one night in Central Park. She pulled a fucking gun on me, and I had to just kick for the end zone.'

'That happens,' Frank said.

Smokes laughed through a mouthful of smoke. 'Yeah, really. Running away from our problems, I think it's called. Like Johnny, I guess. I had a hard time with my old man too.'

Frank took a cigarette from Smokes's pack. 'What do you mean, too?' he said.

Smokes stared straight out of the window.

'I mean, all of us did, you know, Franklin? It was, like, compulsory that your old man was Adolf Hitler.' He paused again. 'Well, I guess Johnny just said you guys didn't always see eye to eye, Franklin. It was nothing terrible. He said you had some fight about a girlfriend of his? After Eleanor left? She was older than him, and you thought she was gonna get pregnant on purpose or something? He just said it was pretty heavy between you sometimes. He said you called this chick a slut?'

'I did not,' Frank said. 'That's not true.'

Smokes shrugged. 'I thought that's what he said. But, hey, I could be wrong, Franklin. I'm sure I'm wrong, man.'

'He told you plenty of bad things I see.'

'No,' Smokes said. 'It was just stupid kids' stuff, Franklin. He wasn't talking about anything big.'

'Yeah, yeah. So what happened then anyway? With you I mean.'

'With me? Well, things got pretty heavy down here in the winter of seventy-eight. The *Guardia* were going crazy, you know? Death squads? The fucking works. You couldn't walk the streets, man; these guys were serious. They'd cut your fucking throat and not think twice. Then the revolution happened July seventy-nine. The General split to Miami and the shit hit the fan. It was fucking chaos, just crazy. Somewhere in the middle, Lenny and his cousin split too, I dunno where. They were freaked, you know?' Smokes shrugged again. 'And I was too, I guess. Being American wasn't exactly fashionable.'

'So why didn't you vamoose as well?'

'Well, Franklin, there's a lotta stuff you don't know about me. I ain't no altarboy, you know?'

'Surprise me.'

Smokes nodded. He thought for a moment, then began to speak again, gripping the steering wheel very tightly and glaring out at the road as if he was expecting something strange to happen.

'See, Frank, I was in a bad way, man. I was strung up higher than the Statue of fucking Liberty back then. Coke, pills, horse, you name it, up my nose, up my ass, into my veins, down my fucking throat. I was a fucking pin cushion, Franklin, I really was. I went down to the floor and then under the fucking boards. I did some stuff I'm not too proud of.'

'Like what?'

'Bad things, man. You wouldn't want to know about them.'

'I'm sorry, son,' Frank said.

'Yeah, well, I'm sorry myself, Franklin. I still have a problem, you know, eating solid food? My stomach's in shit. Still.'

The sound of raucous laughter rang out from the back of the van. Guapo's voice could be heard through the wall. He was singing very loudly and someone was banging a rhythm on the floor. Smokes shook his head when he heard the noise.

'I wish they'd shut the fuck up in there,' he said. 'Guapo does that on purpose when I'm driving. He knows it bugs the crap out of me.'

'And your father, Smokes?' Frank said. 'How do you get on now?'

Smokes nodded pensively. 'He died, Franklin. He died two years ago, and I never saw him. He got an aneurism. I was in the hospital down here, weirding out, with more tubes in me than the New York fucking subway. I couldn't even make the funeral. It was tough, you know.'

'Tough on your mother too.'

'Oh, yeah. Yeah, it was tough on her too.'

Claudette was climbing the steep mountain road now, but her engine was chugging with a satisfied purr. Down in the valley the fields spread out in swathes of colour towards the grey lake and the mountains. Smokes pointed out the Momotombo volcano, smouldering broodily on the distant skyline. People used to worship it, he told Frank, in the old days. The Indians had prayed to it, and made human sacrifices there. And the General had sometimes thrown prisoners into it, from helicopters, to teach the rebel supporters a lesson they wouldn't forget.

'And Cherry?' Frank asked. 'How did you hook up with her?'

Smokes chuckled. 'Jesus, Franklin. What is this? Twenty fucking questions?'

'I'm just curious,' Frank said. 'It's a family trait.'

'Well, Cherry, what happened? I met her in the Imper one time. She was down here on a college trip. There's a lot of that stuff down here. I met her by the pool. She was smoking a joint the size of Kansas, and she asked me if I wanted a hit. Half an hour after we were fucking in one of the corridors. The twenty-fifth floor, actually. The Vaya Con Dios suite.'

'Delightful.'

'Yeah. I guess I shouldn't be talking to you about this stuff, Franklin. You're old enough to be my father.'

Frank shrugged. 'You get broad-minded. Believe me, Smokes, when you drive a taxi, you get broad-minded.'

Smokes glanced in his mirror. He slowed Claudette down a little and pulled in towards the side of the narrow road.

'Well, after that,' he said, 'she went home, and I never called her. There were always a lot of *chicas* around, you know, it was easy come, easy go. But then she started to call. I guess she just got the old love bug, Frank, you know. It was funny. And then one night I got home from a gig and there she was, standing outside my house. Bags, everything. Jesus, she looked beautiful. She was wearing this dress, real colourful. She said she wanted to stay, play in the band, all that. Well I freaked a little, but I guess I did like her. The way she talked, that stuff. I was trying to kick everything and she made me feel like a mensch, you know? She was just OK about stuff like that.'

An open-back truck roared past them full of young soldiers in new sea-green uniforms. It honked its horn and Smokes honked back. The soldiers waved their guns in the air and made thumbs-up signs. One of them was strumming a guitar. Smokes rolled down his window, stuck his arm out and clenched his fist. The soldiers cheered.

'But it ain't that serious,' Smokes said. 'I don't think we got a lot in common, you know, politically? Cherry's pretty middle-class underneath it all.'

'Well, she's a great girl,' Frank said. 'Isn't that the important thing?'

Smokes shook his head. 'Oh, yeah,' he sniggered. 'You don't know the half of it, Franklin. She's an angel from sexual heaven actually. I won the fucking *lotería* the night she arrived on my stoop.'

'I don't want to hear about that,' Frank said.

Loud laughter rang out again through Claudette's wall. Dimly, they heard Cherry's voice shouting 'Stop, Lorenzo. You're crazy, man.' There was a rough banging sound, and more hysterical laughter. Guapo started yelling out the words of another song.

'No, she's a sweet thing,' Smokes said. 'She's great. I just don't know how long it's gonna last.'

'She seems very fond of you,' Frank said.

Smokes nodded. 'Yeah, I know. But you're always looking, ain't you, Franklin? That's guys, I guess. Always looking over the next hill.'

'Well now, you grow out of that. When you get to my age you want to put down a few roots.'

'Maybe.' Smokes laughed. 'But I still got a few years left,

Franklin. My roots ain't going down just yet, man, that's for fucking sure.'

They drove on, straight up the mountain as though heading for the heart of the sun. Frank was beginning to feel hungry now. His stomach rumbled, and he swallowed hard, his eyes suddenly hot with moisture.

'Where are we now?' he asked.

'We're an hour from Morata, Franklin. That's, like, halfway to Léon. You ready for lunch?'

'God, yes. I'd eat a nun's arse through a convent gate.'

'Jeez, Frank,' Smokes laughed. 'You got a real pretty turn of phrase.'

Frank shifted in his seat, feeling the heat burn the back of his thighs. He looked up at the sky, then back down towards the hazy valley, its pale yellow and brown fields marked out by the thin lines of stone walls. A silver river ran along the valley floor, parallel to the broad tan ribbon of the highway. The sun was high now, the landscape devoid of shadow.

'Hey, Franklin,' Smokes said, 'that stuff about my old man. I didn't mean nothin', you know, about you and Johnny or stuff.'

'Yeah, yeah,' Frank said. 'Who said you did?'

'Just to be clear, Franklin.' Smokes nodded, staring straight out at the road. 'Just to be clear, babes, that's all.'

25

A Death

CATHERINE MAUREEN LITTLE DIED of a streptococcal throat infection when she was fourteen months old. It was November 1963, the month that John Kennedy was assassinated in Texas. The whole world seemed to be in mourning, but Frank and Eleanor did not care about that. They were distraught.

On the morning of the funeral the graveyard was blanketed with thick snow. Bells rang in the chapel and the black trees seemed to grasp at the sky. Sleet had poured all night and under the snow the ground had frozen to the consistency of marble. Men in thick frieze donkey jackets had to break the ice with picks before they could dig the grave and lower the coffin into the ground.

Eleanor had nightmares about the tiny white coffin for months afterwards. In the middle of the night, Frank would come down and find her sitting in the kitchen crying. Nothing he said seemed to help her. He tried to be tender; he tried to hold her and kiss her, but his wife was inconsolable. She grew quiet and withdrawn. He would come home from work to find her looking through the child's clothes, weeping softly. She said she did not want to make love any more. She could not bear to be touched. For a time she could not even bear for Frank to sleep with his arm around her waist. Frank talked about this to the priest in confession. He said he was worried. He said his wife seemed to be changing and he didn't know what to do.

The priest said it would be best for Eleanor to get pregnant again as soon as possible. Frank would have to be patient with his wife, but he must also understand that it was best for her to have another baby soon.

'How will I be patient?' Frank asked.

'We men are like light bulbs' – the priest sighed – 'But women are like irons. They take longer than us to heat up.'

'Yes, right. Thank you, Father.'

'Think of your wife's pleasure too,' the priest said. 'That would not be sinful.'

Two months later, Eleanor was pregnant again. This time it was a boy. They called him John Francis after the murdered president and the saint who loved animals.

26

The Well Below The Valley Oh

AT ONE O'CLOCK they saw a little town in the distance, nestling on a cliff that looked down eastward on the purple Pacific. Plumes of white smoke rose straight up into the air over a bowl of white roofs. This was Morata, Smokes said. It was a safe place to stop and get something to eat. He banged on the wall behind him, and shouted, '*Vamos a comer algo*. Come on, homeboys, it's chowtime.'

Closer in, the town looked like something out of a Wild West movie. It had a whitewashed church, a jail with wanted posters papering the outside walls, a barber's shop and a little saloon with a Coca-Cola sign swaying over wooden swing doors. The streets were almost empty, and the wind rushing in from the sea made the doors and windows clatter.

They sat in the saloon, eating cheese sandwiches, grapefruit and fat tomatoes, and drinking the water they'd brought with them. Two young boys were slouching around a pool table, trying to impress a gang of schoolgirls in black and grey uniforms. One of the boys was very good-looking. He had a moody face and a thick quiff of black hair that hung low over his forehead. The other was gangly and flat-footed, but he was the better pool player.

'God help them,' Eleanor said. 'I'm so glad I'm not that age today.'

After lunch, they walked along the cliff path, listening to the suck and flow of the water far below them. The sea had eaten deep into the chalky land, leaving sharp inlets and stark, sandy coves. Frank insisted on holding Lorenzo's arm because the path looked brittle and steep. When they got to the top of the cliff they sat down, panting, and Guapo broke open a six-pack of beer.

'Hey, *gringo*,' he called out to Smokes. '¿*Quiere tomar otra copa?*'

'Don't fucking call me that, Guapo,' Smokes said. 'I'm telling you.'

Guapo laughed and threw him a bottle of *cerveza*.

'You know,' Frank said, 'a fellow once told me that word was Irish. *Gringo*, I mean.'

'How's that, Frank?' Cherry asked.

'Well, apparently there were these Irish chaps in the Mexican war, you see, fighting for the Yanks. When they were captured, they'd all be put in together. And they used to sing this song called "Green Grow the Rushes Oh", to keep up their spirits, I suppose. It's just an old Irish song. You'd hear it in pubs. And the way I got the story was that the Mexicans heard it, Green grow, you see, and they said it as *gringo*. They didn't know what they were saying, but they knew these Irish fellows were green-grows. That's what they called all foreigners after that. *Gringos*.'

'That a fact, Franklin?' Smokes laughed. 'You wanna sing us the song?'

'Oh, don't, Frank,' Eleanor said. 'Please don't.'

'Why not?' Cherry asked.

'Oh, I never liked that song,' Eleanor said. 'It's a song the old tinkers have in Ireland. It's supposed to be bad luck. There was a tinker woman used to come to my grandmother in Galway, and I remember her saying some of the old travellers wouldn't allow it to be sung. They just wouldn't have it.'

'Sure, God,' Frank said, 'I'll give them a little of it, Eleanor. But now Lorenzo will have to pray for us all, to keep the evil eye away.'

He thought for a moment and then started to sing in a faltering tenor voice. The air was slow and delicately mournful. He concentrated hard and they watched him as he sang.

> *He said young maid you're swearing wrong,*
> *For six fine children you have born*
> *At the well below the valley oh.*
>
> *There's two of them by an evil man,*
> *Another two by your brother John,*
> *Another two by your father dear*
> *At the well below the valley oh.*

There's two beneath the stable door
Another two under the kitchen floor,
And two more buried beneath the well,
The well below the valley oh.

Green grow the rushes oh,
All among the bushes oh,
She'll be seven long years all burning in hell
At the well below the valley oh.

Frank stopped singing. Cherry and Smokes clapped. Guapo let out a piercing whistle.

'Way to go, Franklin, man,' Smokes said.

'I can't remember any more now. There's a bit about the devil later. But you got the green-grow bit?'

'God' – Eleanor shuddered – 'that's enough anyhow, Frank. I don't know how that kept their spirits up. The fellows in the war, I mean.'

He laughed. 'It's a strange song alright. But anyway the fellow told me that's where *gringo* comes from.'

'Well, I don't know if it's bad luck,' she said, 'but it gives me the willies anyway. I never liked that song at all.'

At half past two Smokes looked at his watch. They would have to go, he said. They would have to be in Léon by five.

They walked back slowly into the little town. The day was now at its hottest, the thick swarming heat inescapable. Even the flies seemed exhausted and lazy, sprawled out in thousands over the white walls. Lorenzo and Guapo climbed straight into the back of Claudette, but Eleanor sat down on a bench and fanned herself with her hand. Her face was red and puffy, and when she took off her shoes, the straps had left red lines indented across her flesh. She held her left foot in her hand, kneading it and rocking back and forth.

'Are you alright, El?' Frank asked her. 'Do you want a mineral or anything?'

She pursed her lips and blew. 'I wouldn't mind an orange, Frank,' she said, rubbing her forehead and eyes. 'If you can get one somewhere.'

He walked quickly back up the main street of the town, but

most of the shops had shut for the siesta now. The saloon had closed too. He jammed a few coins into a fat Coca-Cola machine outside the saloon, but nothing happened. He tried to ask for a drink in the barber shop, but the barber didn't seem to understand what he was saying.

Hot dry dust blew down the empty street, making him cough. On the way back he noticed an old man standing in the shade of the jailhouse roof, slouched up against the adobe wall, whistling, a scraggy little dog by his feet.

The old man was holding a tray of melting ice creams, and as Frank approached he saluted with a shaking hand. His face was deep brown and craggy; his hooded eyes were bloodshot. He was wearing a greasy black suit, a black bow tie and no shoes.

'*Buenas tardes, hermano,*' the old man sniffed. '*¿Helados?*'

'Yes,' Frank said. '*Hola.*' He pointed to the ice creams and held up six fingers. The old man looked into his face.

'*¿Yanqui?*'

'No, no. *Soy de Irlanda.*'

The old man's eyes seemed to light up. He spat on his hand and held it out. 'You Ireland' – he grinned – 'you put the Queen Victoria out.'

'That's right,' Frank said.

'And now' – the old man beamed – 'the Margaret Thatcher, she must go, *boom*, into the sea.'

'Well now,' Frank said, 'that isn't the way most of us think these days.'

The old man nodded and laughed. He put his fist to his mouth, then snarled and bit, as though pulling out the pin of a grenade. He made a throwing motion and lifted up his arms. '*Boom,*' he yelled, and the dog jumped up. 'And the Margaret Thatcher is in the sea. *¿Correcto?*'

'Oh, alright,' Frank sighed. 'If you say so.' He paid the old man and walked back down towards the car park, chuckling to himself, ice cream seeping stickily over his wrists.

Smokes was sitting up front, with Cherry, peering at a map. The engine was already growling. 'Shift your butt, Frank,' Cherry called. 'You're gonna get left behind.'

When he jumped into the back of Claudette, Guapo and Lorenzo were already asleep. Eleanor was lying on a bottom bunk mopping her arms and shoulders with a damp scarf. Her face was smeared with suntan oil and mosquito repellent. She looked hot and distressed. He handed her an ice cream.

'Oh, lovely,' she sighed. 'Thank you, Frank.'

'Are you alright, Eleanor?'

She nodded. 'Really, I'm fine. It's just the heat. And that song upset me a bit. I'll be fine when I have this.'

'I didn't think it'd upset you,' he said. 'It's only a song.'

'I don't like it, Frank. There's things in that song really give me the creeps.'

'Well, you'd be as wise to have forty winks. Don't you upset yourself about anything.'

She looked up at him. 'You're right.' She smiled. 'I'll have a rest, Frank. You're right.'

He lay down on his own bunk and ate his ice cream.

They drove without stopping for the rest of the hot afternoon.

27

Blue Moon

EVERYTHING ABOUT LÉON reminded Frank of death. This was strange. It was a more commodious city than Managua. It gave an appearance of space, light, almost elegance, with its wide streets, gushing fountains, hot paved squares, vivid white and pastel-coloured Spanish buildings with trellises, balconies and gracious colonnades. But each of these ordered piles of white grandeur was splashed all over with red and black graffiti, and when he looked closely, he could see the cracks, the fissures, the pockmarks left by bullets and shrapnel. Perhaps, too, he was disturbed by the way people looked at him in the streets. They had an oddly knowing look, the way country people do in Ireland, the way they do everywhere. Perhaps it was something else, a strange odour of mould and dampness everywhere. But Frank did not take to Léon. It made him feel uneasy straight away.

While Smokes and Guapo unloaded Claudette, he and Eleanor took a ride in a horse-drawn taxi. They went down to the river bank, where families were sitting in the long grass eating picnics of bread and cold meat, drinking rum and *gaseosas*. It was cool under the trees and the smell of the cedars and pines was sweet. They walked along the forest path until the river flowed out suddenly into a wide circular pool spattered with green leaves. On the bank of the pool a tall wooden crucifix stood wedged into a pile of bricks. The inscription said this was to commemorate a group of students who had been stripped and beaten with mallets by the *Guardia Nacional*, then driven, handcuffed, into the river to drown. The wooden crucifix had been daubed with slogans. *Luchamos Para Vencer. Vivan los Mártires de Léon. Viva Nicaragua Libre. Muerte al Somocismo.*

When they got back to the square the preparations for the festival were nearly finished. Workmen were hammering lengths of scaffolding into a stage. Red and black plastic bunting had been strung from the rooftops of the preposterous buildings and draped down the facade of the vast town hall. Street traders were wandering through the crowd selling fireworks and red flags and photographs of the poet Rubén Darío, whose tomb was in the cathedral. Smokes and the Desperados were hanging around by the speaker stack, drinking bottles of beer and arguing.

'But why *can't* we play some salsa, man?' Smokes was saying to Lorenzo. 'I want to play some salsa. Like, that's a fucking major crime now, is it?'

'The people want rock and roll,' Lorenzo sighed. 'Let my people Go-Go, brother. Give 'em what they want.'

Guapo said something under his breath and tittered with guilty laughter. Smokes put his hands on his hips.

'I heard that,' Smokes said. 'I can too play salsa actually. I've been listening to Tito Puente tapes.'

'Tito Puente?' Guapo said with an incredulous look.

'Yeah. Rubén Blades, Celia Cruz, the works, man. Mambo, salsa, bossa nova, tango, whatever you like.'

Guapo scoffed again and pulled a long face. '*Pobrecita* Marilyn,' he said. '*Pobrecita. El yanqui quire tocar la salsa.*'

Lorenzo laughed. 'I ain't no yankee,' Smokes said. 'Fuck off, Guapo. That's really out of line.'

Guapo came up close to Smokes and grinned. '*¿Oh, sí?*' he said, wide-eyed. '*¿No es yanqui, no?*'

'No,' Smokes said.

Guapo nodded. He glanced at Frank and Eleanor and winked. Then he turned back to Smokes and held out his hand. '*¿Pasaporte? ¿Enséñeme el pasaporte?*'

'Fuck off, Guapo.'

'No, no,' Guapo smirked. '*¿Tu pasaporte, compañero?*'

'That ain't fair, Guapo,' Cherry said. 'What's on your passport ain't what you are.'

Guapo reached out his finger and prodded Smokes in the chest. '*Yanqui, yanqui, yanqui,*' he said. Then he turned away and howled with laughter. '*Yanquita.*' He went to Lorenzo and put his arm around him and the two of them guffawed like schoolboys.

176

'Surrender, Marilyn?' Guapo chuckled. '*¿Se rende?*'

'*Que se rende tu madre*,' Smokes said.

'*Oh, tu madre. ¡Ay, qué bién! ¡Eh! Amigo, este yanqui habla español.*'

Smokes's face was pink with embarrassment. 'You know, you really suck the big one, Guapo. You know that?'

Guapo stuck out his tongue. He started to dance from side to side, clicking his fingers in the air and leering at Smokes. He flounced up and down like a crazed flamenco dancer, one hand on his hip, singing out in a ridiculous squawk.

> *Marilyn, la Marilyn*
> *Marilyn, la Marilyn*
> *Yo no soy marinero*
> *Soy capitán, soy capitán*
> *Soy Marilyn, la Marilyn.*

'You're pathetic,' Smokes said. 'You're the ultimate pits, man.'

'Chill out, brother Smokes.' Lorenzo laughed. 'That music has to be in your blood, you dig? You don't learn it off no tape.'

Smokes scoffed. 'Oh, don't start that jungle fever bullshit, Lorenzo, OK, man? It's just music. It's noise. And don't talk to me about blood, OK? I never like it when you talk about blood. It makes me fucking nervous.'

'OK then, brother. I'm just saying peace, child. Don't take no offence.'

'Well, hey, don't fucking offend me then.'

'Unto the pure,' Lorenzo said, 'all things seem pure.'

Smokes glared at Frank and Eleanor, then sat down on the ground and ripped open a can of beer.

'Jesus, you guys,' Cherry said. 'I mean, it's your culture we're talking about here. Rock and roll is American bullshit.'

'Yeah,' Smokes said, 'it's the music of fucking imperialism. It's like the soundtrack of world domination, man. I mean Elvis was in Uncle Sam's army, you know? You think Gene Vincent voted fucking Democrat?'

'Oh, Smokes' – Eleanor laughed – 'for heaven's sake now, don't be so serious.'

'Eleanor, all I'm saying is their culture should be defended, OK? They don't want to do that, hey, fine by me.'

Guapo clicked his tongue. He turned to Lorenzo and sputtered with incredulous laughter.

'See, Franklin?' Smokes said wearily. 'This is what I get, man.'

Frank nodded. 'Maybe they've had enough of other people defending their culture for them, son.'

Smokes glared up at him and folded his arms. 'Et tu, Frank?' he said.

Frank and Eleanor went and had coffee in a little *cantina* on the edge of the square. They watched a scrawny white horse being led up and down in front of the stage by a little man in black. The waiter came out and told them they'd have to hurry to get a place if they wanted to see anything. The fiesta was to begin at eight.

By seven thirty the square had started to fill up. A murmur of expectant conversation ran around the crowd. Cherry took Guapo and Lorenzo back to the camper to change. Smokes, Frank and Eleanor pushed their way up to the front towards the huge silver doors of the cathedral. Ten lanky soldiers stood on the cathedral steps laughing and drinking Cokes, their M-16s slung across their backs. The clock began to strike eight and the people cheered. Then suddenly, on the eighth clang of the bell, they fell silent. Something was about to happen.

Slowly the huge silver doors of the cathedral swung open. Sonorous male voices could be heard singing inside. Down the steps came a crowd of choirboys in white soutanes, followed by three priests dressed in fabulous heavy scarlet robes, each waving a huge thurible full of incense. Some of the people in the crowd knelt down and crossed themselves. The priests were followed in turn by a group of six men in black suits carrying a hefty-looking bishop in a sedan. The men struggled and sweated under the weight, while the choirboys began to throw flower petals under their feet. Then came three more priests in sky-blue vestments. Finally a huge statue of the Virgin Mary appeared, a ten-foot-tall figure agonizing in white and blue plaster, hands outstretched towards the crowd, tragic eyes fixed on the sky, right foot trampling on the neck of a striking serpent. A stern-looking baby Jesus was sucking at her naked right breast. The child looked old enough to have a pensioner's bus pass, Frank said.

There was total silence in the square now, except for an occasional whistle and the sound of people urging others to be quiet. A clopping sound began to echo against the high walls. It got louder and louder.

A man in a black top hat came riding into the square on the white horse that Frank and Eleanor had seen earlier. He rode around the square once, then came to the front of the cathedral and jumped off. He took a long cane from his scabbard and knocked the back of the horse's legs so that it fell to its knees and rolled over on its side. The man knelt down. He pulled a dagger from his belt, kissed it, waved it in the air, then sank it quickly into the horse's neck.

'Oh my God,' Eleanor gasped.

'Wait, Eleanor,' Cherry said.

The horse screamed and shuddered. Blood jetted from its neck and spilled out into the eggshell-coloured sand. Very soon it stopped moving. The silence remained unbroken except for the clink of chains against the incense bowls. The man in the top hat held a silver bowl to the horse's neck, allowing it to fill with blood. Then he took the bowl of blood and held it up in the air. He swaggered towards the cathedral and, walking steadily and carefully along the bottom step, spilled the blood delicately on to the ground so that it formed a long line. When he had finished he went back and stood with one foot on the dead horse's neck. A priest stepped forward.

'*Deus in adjutoreum meum intende,*' the priest intoned, and the choir sang the response. Then the man in the top hat reached down and took the white horse by the reins. It twitched. It staggered to its feet and kicked at the air. The man took off his top hat and bowed to the crowd. Some of the people yelled, and there was a chorus of angry shushes. The man began to lead the horse back out of the square.

The priest made the sign of the cross three times. Then he lifted the hem of his robe and stepped forward slowly over the brown line of the horse's blood.

The crowd roared with applause. They clapped and cheered and cried out. People drew guns and fired them in the air. The brass band began to play.

They paraded the statue of the Virgin around the square three

179

times. Women and children threw flower petals. Some of them tried to kiss the statue's feet. Others rushed forward and stuck *córdoba* bills into the folds of the Virgin's gown. Glum-looking men stood at the edge of the crowd, watching and muttering to each other. The brass band marched up and down, the drone of their trombones sounding comic and sad.

From the street leading into the square, eight men in black body suits appeared. White skeletons had been painted on to the front and back of their suits and they wore masks shaped like leering skulls. They moved into the middle of the square and began to dance in a circle, holding hands. In the middle of the circle, the tallest skeleton waltzed about with a reaping hook, spinning it, tossing it high in the air, catching it, flashing it around him so that the light flickered off the blade. Then he jumped out of the circle and ran around the edge of the crowd, holding the reaping hook between his legs like a giant phallus. The people screamed with laughter.

Women appeared wearing long black cloaks and painted straw masks. The features on the masks were almost oriental; they had elongated eyes, smiling purple mouths, airholes cut into the flared nostrils and red circles for cheeks. The women whirled in and out of the ring of dancing skeletons, trailing their capes like the wings of demented bats. Smokes told Frank that the women's masks were very old and that nobody could explain their origin. He said that during the revolution the *guerrilleros* had often used them to disguise themselves. Frank shuddered. He tried to imagine what it would be like to see those faces bearing down on you, grinning in murderous innocence – to have that as your last sight on earth.

Later there were speeches. Lines of women and men sat on folding chairs in the cool evening, waving tiny flags and listening as the men in suits and uniforms trooped up to the wailing microphone. The fat bishop was up there too, fanning his face with his purple hat, laughing heartily every time one of the speakers made a joke. An old woman was helped up on to the platform and presented with some kind of scroll. Everyone stood up and clapped loudly and the old woman burst into tears. There were more speeches then. Frank recognized some of the words. *Resistencia. Imperialismo. Revolución.* Whenever one of the speakers roared '*Viva*', the crowd would all scream '*Viva*' back, at the top of their voices, and the men in the crowd would take off their hats and throw them high into the air.

When the speeches had finished, men in orange armbands moved the chairs out of the centre of the square, stacking them up in enormous piles at the edges. Night had fallen, almost imperceptibly. Huge flaming torches were lit on the balconies around the plaza. An open truck full of floodlights backed up to the cathedral. Taped salsa music began to play. Fireworks started to spit and wheeze in the air. The stench of sulphur and smoke descended. Couples shimmied across the plaza, hands on each other's swaying hips. They turned and wheeled, pirouetted and weaved, moving to rhythms that Frank could barely hear.

An announcement came over the speakers to say that the Desperados de Amor would be performing in half an hour. A shout of applause went up. Eleanor said she was sorry, but she was getting a bad headache. Frank took her back to the camper and made her a cup of tea. She told him she was going to have a sleep, that she'd be fine, that he could go off for a walk.

He went back to the square and had a beer, finding it oddly pleasant to be alone. He went to another bar and had a rum and Coke. He ordered another, and then one more. He looked around the plaza, enjoying the coolness of his drink. More people were dancing to the taped salsa music. He recognized one of the tunes with a start. A bossa nova. 'It's In His Kiss' wasn't a rock and roll song after all, it was a bossa nova. He remembered dancing to this song with Eleanor, but he could not remember where. He found his fingers tapping in time on the side of his beer bottle. He tried to remember the words. *If you want to know if he loves you so, it's in his kiss.*

Suddenly, out of the corner of his eye, he noticed a tall thin man standing in the shadows at the front of the cathedral. The man was wearing a calliper on his right leg. His arms were very long and he was holding a walking stick over his shoulder like a rifle. Underneath his armpits, dark sweat stains had spread through the fabric of his white suit. The tall thin man seemed to be staring very intently at him.

Frank turned away and ordered another drink. When he turned back to look, the man was still staring. He felt uncomfortable now. He took his drink from the table and walked out into the

181

square. A young girl approached him, smiling. '*¿Gringo?*' She beamed. She was wearing a tight red shirt, a short skirt and red stiletto heels. She could not have been more than fifteen, he thought. Her face was a pantomime of lipstick. He turned away from her and said nothing. She took his hand and kissed it. He laughed. She nibbled at his fingers and pushed her long hair away from her eyes.

'My house,' she said, pointing towards the centre of the town. 'Happy times. Thirty dollars.'

Frank looked at the girl. She was heartbreakingly pretty. Her hair was dark, and sweat had made strands of it cling to her cheekbones. Her skin glowed in the firelight. She raised her eyebrows and, taking his hand, pressed it against her breast. 'Stop,' he said. She put her hands behind her back, pushed her breast against his hand and moved her body. He took his hand away. She leant forward and kissed his neck. Her breath smelt of mint.

'You and me?' she whispered. 'Happy times?'

'No, no, love. I don't think so.'

'Yes, baby.' She grinned, pouting her reddened lips. 'I do everything you like. Thirty dollars.'

'No,' he said more firmly. 'Go home, can't you?'

Her eyes flared with anger. '*Perro,*' she sneered, turning away. She walked through the crowd in the direction of the cathedral, towards the long-armed man. Frank watched her. She seemed to be arguing with the man now. Suddenly the man lunged forward and slapped her across the face. She burst into tears and ran off into the plaza. The man turned and stared at Frank, a look of fury on his face. After a moment, he grinned and tipped his hat, pulled a fat cigar from his pocket, bit the tip off and spat it away. Then he cupped his hands and lit the cigar, the yellow matchlight flaring against his face.

Frank began to walk across the square. It was getting late, but he did not feel like going back to Claudette's stuffy heat. The plaza was packed with people now; there were drunks everywhere. The flower petals, strewn all over the cobbles, had been crushed by hundreds of dancing feet; a gorgeous aroma was rising up into the air.

He turned off the plaza through a black stone arch and into another quieter square that was almost empty. All down one side were stalls selling some kind of spicy-smelling food. The echo of the music sounded odd as it bounced against the high walls of the buildings. A young boy was standing by a huge dark statue of a swordsman on a horse. He was selling newspapers. '*Barricada*,' he called softly, '*La Prensa*', '*Barricada*', '*El Nuevo Diario*'.

Frank walked across the greasy cobbles, enjoying the unexpected coolness and the sound of the gurgling fountain. He dipped his hand in and smeared his wet fingers across his face. He lit a cigarette, flicking the match into the water, then walked on. At the far edge of the square, he stepped through another stone arch and began to wander down a narrow side street.

He saw the young girl in the short skirt again, up ahead of him now, walking slowly, arm in arm with a soldier. They stopped in the orange light of a café window and kissed. The soldier put his hands inside her shirt, cupping her breasts, and she laughed. They walked on and turned a corner. Frank followed. He saw the girl open a door and pull the soldier inside by the hand.

Frank walked towards the door and stood outside for a moment. There was no sound except for the distant thud of drums and bass guitar. He touched the metal plate on the door. It was warm.

He turned and walked back. But he felt drunk now, and heavy, and suddenly he did not know where he was. He was not sure which way he had come. He stumbled in the dark and turned down another shadowy side street. Somewhere a radio was playing. The urgent voice of a sports announcer and the roar of excited applause came down from an upper window. Yellow light spilled out through the slats and shutters. He felt uneasy.

He came to another corner. A young couple were huddled together in a doorway, making love. The girl was silent as the boy thrust against her. She had her hand on the back of his head. The boy was groaning as though in terrible pain.

Frank walked on again, faster, turning corners, desperately wishing to meet someone who could show him the way back to the plaza. He heard applause and distant music. He kept trying to walk towards the sound of the music, but the farther he walked the more intense the sensation of spiralling inward became. He walked on. Turned more corners. He felt his heart thump. The music in the square seemed to be growing more distant.

He stopped and looked in the window of a butcher's shop.

Hefty lumps of meat were laid out on marble slabs. At the back of the shop a line of scrawny pigs hung suspended from metal hooks, eyes bloated and black, red mouths open. A cat was moving languidly across the tiled floor, lapping the pools of seeping blood which had collected under the carcasses. It arched its back in pleasure. Frank watched. The focus of his eyes shifted. Suddenly, in the window's black reflection, he saw a man walking slowly towards him.

He turned quickly and saw the man stop in the shadows. He felt his breath quicken. He recognized the man immediately. He was thin and tall, with long arms and a white suit. Frank called out, but the man stood still and said nothing. He called again. The man began limping towards him, banging his walking stick against the metal calliper on his leg and cackling with laughter.

Frank felt afraid now. He walked on again. He was sweating and his mouth was dry. He quickened his pace. Suddenly he saw a narrow passageway, barely wide enough for an adult body to pass through. He stopped. Out of the corner of his eye, at the end of the passage, he could see light and colour and movement. He paused, pulled his cigarettes from his pocket and lit one. He turned. He could not see the man now, but he could still hear his laugh. He took a deep drag on his cigarette, held his breath, then darted into the alley and began to run.

He ran hard. Lines of damp laundry slapped against his face and he heard himself panting. He heard the click of the man's feet behind him. He ran faster, as fast as he could now. He heard a woman scream. He tripped and fell against a pebble-dashed wall. He grunted, staggered back up and ran towards the light, almost swooning with fear, and then suddenly the square burst into colour before him. He looked over his shoulder, but saw nobody. He ran into the square and towards the dancing crowd.

There was Smokes, on the stage, thumping his drum kit and doowopping sulkily into the microphone. There was Cherry, hammering her electric piano. There was Lorenzo, prowling up and down the stage, wrenching a screeching solo from his guitar. The sound was rough, but couples were dancing and young boys were at the front of the stage punching the air. Frank felt safe again. He crossed into the middle of the plaza.

Lorenzo moved to the front of the stage, urging the audience to dance. He held his hands to his mouth and hollered and the young boys yelled back. Lorenzo put his hand to his ear, pretending not to hear. They yelled again. Lorenzo slung his guitar over his back and raised the collar of his leopard-skin jacket. He strolled up to the microphone and grabbed it. The crowd went berserk. He started to sing 'Great Balls of Fire'.

The boys and girls put their arms around each other and heaved up and down. They danced around the plaza and clapped their hands in the air. Cherry and Guapo pranced across the stage and started to jive together. The audience whistled and screamed with laughter. Smokes started bashing the cymbals. Lorenzo came back to the front of the stage and thrust his legs wide apart, grabbing the microphone again. He fell to his knees and leant his head far back. Cherry bopped up and down, pumping at the piano. Lorenzo raised one hand in the air and began to yowl again.

Frank found himself smiling as he looked around. People were weaving and twisting. Two nuns were waltzing by the cathedral steps and all the white-robed choirboys were standing in a circle, nodding their heads and playing air guitar. By the time Frank left the Plaza de Armas Lorenzo and the Desperados were on their fourth encore and there were five thousand people dancing. He felt light-headed and unsteady and still a little drunk.

In the car park behind the cathedral, Eleanor was sitting in Claudette's doorway, wearing short-sleeve pyjamas and reading by torchlight.

'Jesus,' Frank said, 'Lorenzo is fairly stirring them up out there.'

'Yes. I was listening. They're great, aren't they?'

She glanced up from her book. 'Are you alright, Frank? You look a little pale.'

He scratched his head and shrugged. 'This queer fellow followed me earlier. I don't know who he was. It gave me a bit of a turn.'

'Oh, Frank!' She laughed. 'You've such an imagination.'

They got into the back of the van. Eleanor poured some tea and began to take off her make-up, humming to herself as she cleaned her face with tissues. Frank uncorked a bottle of rum and swallowed a mouthful.

'And they played "Blue Moon" earlier on,' she said. 'It was lovely. Cherry sang it with Guapo.'

She hummed the melody, waving her fingers from side to side as she sang. Then she closed her eyes, smiled and folded her arms.

'God, that was a great one in our day, wasn't it, Frank? "Blue Moon?"'

He sipped his hot tea. 'Yeah,' he said. 'That one was big, but I never liked it too much.'

She leant in close to her mirror and looked at her face. She held her long grey hair in a bun above her head, then let it fall through her fingers.

'Frank Little,' she sighed, 'you haven't an ounce of sentiment in you.'

'I never did.'

She began to comb her hair. 'That's true. You never did. But you made up for it, I suppose.'

He sat down on his bunk and gazed at her long straight back, her bare arms, her delicate hands. He lifted the bottle and took another shot. 'Yes,' he said, 'I made up for it in other ways.'

She drew the comb through her hair a hundred times. And when she turned around again Frank was already asleep.

28

The Santa Maria

HE WAS THE BRIGHTEST of children. He was beautiful looking, with a thick mop of curly brown hair and a wide freckled face. He was lively and happy and he loved school. The old nun, Mother Lawrence, said he was destined for great things. At the age of five, he could read like a seven-year-old. By the time he was seven, and in junior school, he could draw Christopher Columbus standing on the deck of his ship, the *Santa María*.

Frank and Eleanor Little loved their son. They talked to him about school and tried to answer his questions. They helped him with his homework and, wherever they were going, they took him with them. They made sure he wanted for nothing. They bought him Ladybird books and helped him with the words. Frank thought his wife mothered him too much, but he didn't mind. When he saw her sitting with her arms around him, stroking his hair and reading him stories, it filled him with a joy that he couldn't even begin to describe. One night they took him to a play at the Abbey Theatre and he sat between them, wide-eyed with excitement, holding their hands and giggling all the way through. There was no sound in the world that made Frank feel as happy as his son's laughter. On the way home in the car that night, he realized that he had everything he had ever wanted in his life.

The arguments began when Johnny had just started attending junior school in Willow Park. They started about very small things. If Johnny came home from school with a torn jumper she would shout at him and then Frank would get annoyed with her. He would tell her to leave him alone, that boys went through a roughneck phase and you just had to let them be. She would say that Johnny was too delicate for horseplay, that she didn't want him breaking something and having to go to hospital. They argued about how hard Frank was working. She wanted him to come home earlier at night, but he said he had to work evenings to make real money. And sometimes Frank would be late home from work and Eleanor would be so upset with him that he could not understand it. There were times when she was so angry it would take him half an hour to calm her down.

One day in the summer of 1969 Frank was asked to drive a man up to Belfast. It was an emergency, the man said; his father had died of a heart attack and there was no train until the next afternoon. The man pleaded with Johnny Doyle. None of the other drivers wanted the job, so Johnny Doyle asked Frank to do it, and Frank said yes because he felt sorry for the poor man.

But it was July 1969. Catholics in Northern Ireland were being burnt out of their houses. There was talk of sending in the British army to keep the Catholics and Protestants apart. When they got across the border Newry was in flames. They drove on to Belfast and the streets of the city were burning. There were police everywhere. There were gangs of armed men in black Balaclavas, smashing windows and setting cars on fire. Frank had never seen anything like it. He had never felt fear like he felt that night. He dropped off his passenger and drove straight back to Dublin, exhausted and shaking with nerves. He thought about the poor people in Northern Ireland. He could not understand why the Irish government would not send in the army to protect the Catholics. He drove without stopping. He kept thinking about how lucky he was, to be going home to a warm house, to his son and his wife. Everything in his life was worthwhile because he had a home to go to. It was only an accident of fate that he was so lucky and other people were not.

When he got back to the house she was sitting at the kitchen table in tears of rage. She seemed to have been drinking. There was a sour smell of alcohol on her breath; there were shards of broken glass on the kitchen floor. She said he didn't love her. She said he had never loved her at all. She accused him of seeing another woman. At first he was so shocked that he couldn't speak. Then he began to shout back at her. She picked up a cup and threw it against the wall. Their son came down into the kitchen, crying. It was July 1969.

In September that year Eleanor's father died in a car crash. On the night the coffin was brought to the church they went up to her mother's house and she got drunk on sherry. Frank was very surprised. He had never seen his wife drink before. He couldn't understand what she was doing, but he said nothing because he knew she was upset. Next day she refused to go to her father's funeral. She sat at home by herself and got drunk again.

She continued to drink then. Whenever they went out she would drink a lot, and he noticed that she would drink anything. Beer, spirits, wine, she didn't seem to care. She would drink anything, and sometimes she would get sick. On Christmas Eve, 1970, she got drunk and told him to shut up in front of three of the other drivers.

Things began to get steadily worse for Frank and Eleanor. They seemed not to agree about anything any more. They began to argue about wallpaper. They began to argue about money. They argued all the time about their son.

He was not doing well in school now. He always seemed to be in trouble. There were complaints about his behaviour. He was cheeky to his teachers and aggressive towards the other boys. The priests said his language was atrocious for a child. They said they didn't know where he was picking it up, but it was the language of the inner city, not the kind of language you would want in a school where decent people sent their children. Frank scolded his son and Eleanor said he was too strict with him. She would say that Frank had no love in him, that the way he treated the boy was unnatural. She began to accuse him of never having wanted a child. She used to shout this at him. 'I don't know why you got married if you didn't want children.'

They were both working now. He was driving his taxi and she was giving piano lessons. But the government put taxes on everything and money was hard to come by. There were wars in faraway places and that pushed up the price of oil. Petrol was expensive now, and sometimes you had to queue for hours to get it. Insurance was expensive too. There were strikes and more price rises. Their mortgage went up, slowly at first. Then it doubled.

Frank joined the taxi drivers' union. He worked hard during the day and at night he went to meetings. He stood for election for the local union, as secretary first, then chairman. Johnny Doyle made up a slogan for him. *Think Big: Vote Little*. He went on the radio. He organized demonstrations. When a taximan was knifed to death one night in Parnell Square, it was Frank Little who went on the television to talk about it.

Johnny Doyle died the year after that, and his wife put the taxi company up for sale. She said she'd sell it to Frank at a good price because she knew how much her husband had liked him and she knew he was reliable. Frank tried to discuss the idea with Eleanor. At first she was angry; she said he spent far too little time at home as it was. She wanted to know why he had to go out working such long hours when other men could be at home with their families. They fought about it for a month. Then she seemed not to care any more. He tried to talk to her again, but she told him to do whatever he damn well liked. He got a loan from the bank and bought the company.

He knew that his wife was drinking every day now, but he said nothing about it because he was afraid, and because he did not know what to say. She began to hide bottles around the house. He would find them in drawers, under beds, in the cupboards. Before long, he began to dread opening a drawer or a closet because he knew he would find an empty bottle wherever he looked. She started to buy cheaper cuts of meat, margarine instead of butter, so that she could spend more money on drink. She began to buy mints to cover the smell of her breath. One night he plucked up the courage to ask her about it and she flew into a terrible rage. Shortly after this, he found out from a neighbour that Eleanor had stopped giving piano lessons. There had been a problem with the man's child; the girl had gone home and told her mother that her piano teacher had been drunk. Frank said nothing. He did not want to humiliate his wife.

One day in 1972 he came home in the middle of the day to find her drunk and naked in the bath, crying bitterly. He held her in his arms. He lifted her out of the bath and put her into a dressing gown. He stayed at home with her until she was sober and then he begged her to see a doctor. But she told him she couldn't bring herself to see anyone. She felt ashamed, she said; she felt wicked.

That night she locked herself in their bedroom and got completely drunk again.

Frank began to panic. He stopped inviting people to the house. He deliberately caused an argument with his brother so that he and Eleanor would not be invited to his home any more. He went around the house searching for bottles and pouring their contents down the sink. He had nightmares about bottles tumbling endlessly out of cupboards.

Eleanor didn't understand what was happening to her. The man she loved began to look at her with distaste. The only man she had ever made love to seemed suddenly to hate her. The night of her niece's wedding he got drunk himself and told her she could make a little more of her appearance. They stopped sleeping together.

Slowly, the arguments grew worse. A terrible violence crept into them. Frank and Eleanor Little began to say things that only people who have once been in love can say. They shouted. They screamed obscenities and curses. They poured scalding words over each other. They accused each other of dreadful things. She told him she had never wanted to marry him. She accused him of adulteries. He accused her of neglecting the child who had died. And then they simply stopped speaking.

For three months in 1974 they did not speak at all. Their eleven-year-old son passed messages from one to the other, until Frank could not bear the frightened look on his face any more. It was a look that felt as if it would tear him to pieces.

He told his wife that they were making life very hard for their son. He told her that he loved her, that he wanted to sort everything out. He said he wanted to start again. They tried then. They took a holiday together in Mallorca; they went to Valdemosa, to the monastery where Chopin died. It was a very beautiful place, hot and bright, with the sweet smell of the orange groves drifting down from the hills.

She got drunk every night. They argued almost every day.

29

Faith

THE MORNING AFTER the festival of Léon, Frank slept late, and after they'd eaten breakfast, Smokes and Eleanor went for a walk through the streets. The squares and avenues around the cathedral were ankle deep in tattered bunting, crushed flowers, blackened fireworks and empty plastic bottles. Men were hosing down the cathedral steps. Bedraggled young girls were wandering home in black satin trousers and flouncing skirts made of chiffon and silk in fluorescent yellow, candy-floss pink, raging red and iridescent blue. Gangs of schoolchildren ran around the Plaza de Armas, separating cans from glass bottles and loading them into black plastic bags. American reporters stood in the sunlight jabbering into television cameras.

'Well, Smokes,' Eleanor said, 'that was only great last night. Lorenzo's a fabulous singer, isn't he?'

'Oh, he's OK, I suppose. You guys shoulda heard Johnny.'

She laughed. 'What I heard was great anyway.'

'Yeah, yeah,' Smokes said. 'We were OK. But when we had Johnny we really were something.'

They walked across the hot square and turned into a tiny cobbled side street. It was narrow and dark and smelt of stewed cabbage and stale beer. Halfway down, two old Indian men were sitting on the ground, playing dice and smoking long pipes. They smiled up at Smokes and Eleanor and one of them took off his sombrero. 'Buenos días,' he said.

Further down in the darkest part of the street they stopped by a pair of oak doors. The panels were black and intricately carved. Devils and dragons danced across them, chasing terrified men and women. A witch laughed as she pushed a man with an erect penis into a vast cauldron. Over the doorframe, a grinning skull and crossbones motif was carved into the same black wood. From behind the doors they heard the sound of sawing. It was a satisfying sound, pleasant to listen to.

Suddenly the big doors opened. A happy-looking man came out, smiling, bowing and nodding to Smokes and Eleanor. Inside the light was soft and yellow. Three young boys were working in the dim glow, each of them whistling as they hammered nails and measured lengths of wood. The little room was full of coffins.

'Here's a guy making good bread.' Smokes chuckled. 'Plenty of folks dying around here.'

'You know, Smokes,' she said, 'he might have another customer soon enough.'

She went to walk on, but Smokes did not follow. When she turned around, he was staring at her, grinning uneasily. 'Actually, Eleanor, I hate to lay this on you.'

'What?'

'Well, you know, that mightn't be such a bad idea.'

Smokes looked embarrassed. He began to speak quickly, in an agitated voice. He told her that Corinto was a really terrible place. Every kind of supply was scarce, he said. Corinto was too close to the border. Whenever they built something the Contras blew it up straight away. Bricks and mortar were like gold on the black market. Wood was like diamonds. He'd been really worried about this, but he hadn't wanted to say anything. He'd been thinking about it since they'd left Managua. People up in Corinto didn't have coffins when they died. They just got wrapped in a sheet and put in the ground or burnt. People up there would think coffins were a waste of wood when you could build a cot for a child or put a floor in one of your rooms. He wasn't saying it was right or wrong, just that this was how things were in Corinto. It was a very tough town. It was dirty and the air was black from the oil wells, and people didn't have money to spend on coffins. But he'd been thinking, about what they would do with Johnny, if the worst turned out to be true. He hadn't been able to get it out of his mind. There'd been a terrible scandal back in March, when a Swiss paediatrician who'd been killed in a skirmish had been brought down to Managua in a plastic bag, his body rotting on the back of a truck. His wife had turned up at the airport to collect him with a man from the Swiss embassy. When she'd seen what the heat and the crows had done to her husband's body she'd fainted right there on the runway.

'Good Jesus,' Eleanor said.

Smokes clenched his fingers. 'I know, Eleanor. It's heavy, I know. But, Jeez, we wouldn't want to bring Johnny back to Managua in a plastic bag. In this heat, too.'

He nodded at the door of the carpenter's shop, mumbling. 'I just think . . .' He fell silent and looked away.

'Oh, God, Smokes, I couldn't. I don't think I could do that.'

He sighed. 'This is the last place we'll find an undertaker, Eleanor. I just think you and Franklin should know it. We leave here today, we're in bandit country. They won't have a coffin for him, Eleanor. Not in Corinto. It just ain't that kind of place.'

They walked back to the van and found Frank. He was stripped to the waist, shaving in a basin of soapy water. Lorenzo was kneeling on the ground, praying silently, nodding his head and knocking his chest with his hand. Cherry was lying in the shade of the camper in a bra and underpants, drinking from a water can. Guapo was frying up beans and rice on the gas stove. They asked Frank to come for a stroll with them, and on the way they told him why.

'We want to buy a coffin for him,' Eleanor said.

He stopped walking and laughed out loud. 'What? You're mad, the pair of you.'

'Franklin, look. We just want to be ready for the worst.'

'You're joking me now, aren't you?'

They said no, they weren't joking.

'But he's alive, for Christ's sake. I'll have no part in this. Are you both sick or what?'

Smokes put his arm around his shoulder, but Frank pulled away.

'No,' he cried out. 'No, Smokes. I won't. He's alive.'

Smokes shook his head. 'We can't bet on that, Franklin.'

'Jesus, kid. Whose side are you on? I can't figure you out sometimes.'

'I'm on your side, man. You know that.'

Frank scoffed. 'God, maybe,' he said.

Smokes looked him in the eye. 'Frank,' he said quietly, 'I'm gonna pretend you didn't say that.'

'Give us a minute now, love,' Eleanor said. 'Just give us a minute to chat about things.'

Smokes glared at Frank again, then strolled slowly down the street, hands in his pockets, kicking at the ground. He leant against a lamppost and bent his head low.

'Well,' Frank said, trying to laugh, 'everyone's against me now. Sure, I don't know what to say now.'

Eleanor breathed in deeply. She looked at him and said nothing.

'I want no performance, Eleanor. No carry-on about coffins or death. This is getting sick.'

'Frank, pet, just listen to me.'

He closed his eyes and shook his head. 'He's alive,' he snapped. 'He's alive. He has to be. I don't want to know about anything else. He's alive and any damn individual who thinks otherwise needn't say anything to me.'

She interrupted him, speaking loudly.

'Frank, I hope to God that he is. I'd do anything if he was, you know that. I'd die myself, if I could, and that's God's truth.'

'Oh, don't start with your bloody nonsense. There's no need to go making a bloody Greek tragedy out of it. That little messer is as alive as you or I.'

'But if he's not, Frank?' she insisted. 'What if he's not?'

When he opened his eyes his wife was crying softly. Her lips were quivering, her face was twisted and her shoulders shook as she tried to hold back the tears. Her moist eyes looked up at him, pleading like a frightened child's.

'No son of ours is going to be thrown around like a tinker. Please, Frank. He's our flesh and blood. We didn't do everything we did for that to happen. For decency's sake. We have to think of what's right. Please,' she sobbed. 'Oh, please now, Frank.'

And something in her imploring face suddenly filled him with dread. It took him back. He saw her on the night of their first argument, standing in Francis Street in rainy lamplight. He saw her on a terrible night when the police arrived at their house. He saw her on the night before she finally went away. He tried to steady himself and make these pictures fade. He clenched his fists and looked at her. He could take it. He was strong. He was a man. He searched for words and began to say them. She looked up at him again, and suddenly, in her weeping and fearful eyes, Frank Little saw an unspeakable thing. He saw a face that he recognized. He saw the face of his only son.

'Christ,' he sighed. 'Alright, alright, Eleanor.'

He went to touch her shaking shoulder and his hand felt awkward as a spanner. He wanted to hold her now, so much that it scared him. He looked at her, trembling, and he wanted to take her in his arms and hold her close and feel her sobbing until her tears had cried themselves out. He wanted to put his arms tight around her, but for some reason he could not. He felt shocked and frightened. He felt absolutely alone.

'Thank you, Frank,' she said. She took a tissue from her handbag and dried her face.

'I'm sorry, Eleanor. I didn't mean any offence.'

'God, look at me,' she sniffed. 'Making a holy show again.'

Smokes was staring at them from the end of the street. Frank looked at him, feeling wild with shame and confusion. His head reeled with the pain of memories.

'Sweet Jesus, El,' he croaked, 'how did we ever come to this?'

She took his hand in hers, squeezing it tightly and gnawing her lip. She sobbed again, shaking her head from side to side. 'Courage, Frank. The past is the past now, after all.'

In the courtyard, the carpenter was sitting with his feet on a table, reading *La Prensa* and drinking coffee from a jam jar. He jumped up when he saw them coming in. He took his measuring tape from around his neck and held it in his hands, hopefully eyeing them up and down.

Smokes chuckled. 'He thinks it's one of us,' he said. 'People up here do that. Poor folks especially. They start paying for their coffins while they're still alive.'

'They don't just do it here,' Frank said. 'My poor mother saved up for years.'

'Tell him who it's for,' Eleanor mumbled.

'*Usted no entiende, Señor. Es para su hijo.*'

The carpenter pursed his lips and nodded, then stepped forward and clasped Frank's hand. He shook it very vigorously, nodding at the ground. Then he bowed to Eleanor and pointed inside his workshop. He beckoned for them to follow.

In the back of the sweet-smelling shop a young boy was working on a rocking chair with an adze. Another boy was planing down an oblong piece of teak. There were wooden statues of Virgins and martyrs and long black wooden crosses. A beautiful young woman in white overalls was kneeling in front of a wooden Child of Prague, lovingly colouring its ferocious eyes with white and blue paint. They stepped through a door at the side and into a darkened storeroom. It smelt heavily of sweat and wood shavings. The carpenter flicked the light switch. This room, too, was full of coffins.

Some of the coffins were laid around the floor, lids on top or standing vertically inside them. Others had been placed on end. There were coffins stacked up high in the corners, covered in thick dust. There were coffins in all kinds of wood, some dark and varnished, some painted white or red. There were coffins made of chipboard, mahogany and rough planks of cedar.

Eleanor pointed to a smooth casket in pale yellow pine.

'*¿Cuanto es?*' she asked calmly.

The carpenter scratched his head. 'Seven hundred, *Señora.*'

'*¿Córdobas?*'

The carpenter raised his eyebrows.

'*Dólares, Señora.*'

'*Es muy caro,*' she said. 'Very expensive.'

From the other side of the storeroom, Frank called to her. 'El, What about this one?'

The coffin was covered with carved angels and cherubs playing flutes and lyres. The lid had three carved panels, the Bethlehem manger, the Crucifixion, and Christ rising up through a cloud, holding a book in one hand and pointing to heaven with the other. The interior was lined with thick red velvet and black silk. The nail-heads were brass and cross-shaped.

'I like this one,' Frank said.

Eleanor pulled a face. 'It's a bit much. Do you not think it's a bit much, Frank?'

'What's wrong with it?'

She looked away. 'I'd just prefer something a bit simpler. That's all.'

'*¿Cuanto?*' he asked, ignoring her.

'*Mil dólares, Don,*' the carpenter said.

'Frank, for heaven's sake, a thousand dollars.'

'We'll take it,' he said. 'It's the best one.'

'Frank, please. A thousand dollars. He saw us coming now.'

'We'll take it,' Frank said. 'We want the best one.'

He opened his wallet and began to count out crumpled hundreds on to the coffin lid. He licked his finger and counted again, checking the amount. 'Now,' he said, 'let's just get out of this place.'

The carpenter grabbed Smokes by the elbow and whispered in his ear.

'Franklin, he's saying that if we bring the body here, he'll embalm it.'

The carpenter nodded. He pinched his nose between his finger and thumb and pulled a horrible face. Then he spoke to Smokes again.

Smokes coughed. 'He's saying there'll be no smell. If, you know, he embalms it.'

The carpenter pocketed the banknotes and began to write out a receipt.

'You're a shagging robber,' Frank muttered. 'You should be wearing tights over your face.'

The carpenter grabbed Frank's hand and shook it.

'I suppose we're to carry the thing ourselves,' Frank said. 'Tell him we're not bloody skivvies, will you, Smokes?'

The carpenter went to the workshop door. He clapped his hands and shouted and the two young boys rushed in. The carpenter pointed at the coffin and barked out an order.

The boys carried the coffin through the litter-strewn streets of Léon, all the way across the Plaza de Armas and down the Avenue Santiago Arguello. Frank and Eleanor walked in front and Smokes walked behind. Nobody said anything. Groups of men and women stared in silence from the *cantinas*. One of the women made the sign of the Cross. The cathedral bell clanged for noon.

When they came to the car park Lorenzo was sitting in Claudette's doorway, strumming his guitar and humming. Guapo was leaning down to comb his hair in the wing mirror. When he saw the coffin he stood up straight and shaded his eyes with his hand.

Cherry appeared in the doorway, her long wet hair wrapped in a white towel. She put her hands on Lorenzo's shoulders and squeezed them. He laughed. Then she looked up at Guapo and followed his gaze. 'Oh shit,' she said.

'What is it, sister?' Lorenzo said. '¿Qué pasa?'

'*Francisco y Eleanor, hermano,*' Guapo said. '*Tienen un ataúd.*'

Lorenzo stood up quickly. He was shaking. He took off his guitar and laid it on the ground, picked up his stick, closed the buttons on his silver jacket and began to walk away. He went straight past Frank and Eleanor without stopping, then around the corner of the cathedral.

'Lorenzo,' Eleanor called.

'Let him go, Eleanor,' Frank sighed. 'Leave him.'

'See,' Smokes said. 'Now that's Lorenzo for you. That's the *Nicas* all over, you know. They're great people, but I gotta say they really can't handle a fucking crisis.'

They carried the coffin to the camper van and put it down. 'You got it then?' Cherry said. Smokes nodded.

'*Madre de Dios,*' Guapo sighed, staring at it.

'A grand,' Frank said. 'Bloody robbers, that's all they are here.'

Guapo started to get excited. He said the coffin wasn't coming into the back of Claudette. He wouldn't have it, he said, not where they were sleeping. It would bring down bad luck and Lorenzo would start raving about the devil and, anyway, it was a horrible thing to look at. Cherry argued, but Guapo would not be persuaded. '*Nunca, nunca, nunca,*' he kept saying. 'No, Cherry.' The carpenter's boys stood around, looking confused and smiling.

'Well,' Smokes sighed, 'there's only one place else.'

The boys climbed up on to Claudette's roof. Smokes and Guapo lifted the coffin and pushed it up to them. The boys hauled it up and tied it to the rack with thick twine, in between the two surfboards, one of which was electric blue, the other white, with a beautiful cartoon woman painted on it. The sun roared down over the cathedral.

After the boys had left, Frank and Eleanor sat in the back of the van with the others, trying to talk about the day's journey. Smokes said they'd be crossing over the Pan-Am and heading up north-east into the mountains towards Esteli. They talked about the miles they would have to travel, each of them aware of the terrible object that lay above them, and aware of the terrible thing they had done. They talked about maps. They talked about roads. They talked about heat and food and crisp white bed linen. They talked about everything, except the one thing they wanted to talk about.

At half past two, Lorenzo appeared by the gable wall of the cathedral, walking very slowly, tapping the iron railings with his stick. Guapo stood up and started to walk towards him. 'No, Guapo,' Frank said. 'Let me.'

Frank walked over to where Lorenzo was standing. They stood in the cathedral's shadow for five minutes, speaking very intensely. From time to time, Lorenzo lifted up his walking stick and pointed it towards the sapphire-coloured sky, shaking his head. Then Frank punched him softly on the shoulder and Lorenzo nodded. He put his hand on Frank's arm and they began to walk slowly over to Claudette, linking arms like old lovers.

'Lorenzo, *hombre*,' Guapo called. '*¿Qué tienes?*'

Lorenzo stopped. He lifted his stick in the air and brandished it. 'Lift high the banners of love,' he said. 'And beat me, big Daddy, eight to the bar.'

Cherry rushed over to Lorenzo and took him by the hand. She kissed his bald head and his face. Guapo took his other hand and the three of them climbed into the back of the camper. Smokes peered at his watch, cursing to himself. He opened the cab door and climbed up into the driver's seat.

'Frank,' Eleanor whispered, 'what did you say to him?'

He shrugged. 'I told him to have faith.'

'That's all?'

He picked up the water bottle and began to drink.

'Have faith, but expect the worst,' he said, wiping his mouth with his sleeve. 'That way, if the worst happens, you're not in for any surprises.'

Claudette's engine began to roar. In the back, Guapo was already singing. His terrible wailing voice filled the car park as he clapped his hands and crowed. *Well, Lordy, Lordy, Lordy, Miss Claudy. You know you look so good to me.*

'And is that what you still believe, Frank?'

'No,' he said quietly. 'The little messer is alive, Eleanor. Apart from that, what I believe doesn't matter.'

30

Mothers

MY SWEET JOHNNY LITTLE, I know you are dead. I am your mother and I can feel it now, like death, like my own death. When I close my eyes, I see the smile of death on your gorgeous mouth. I breathed life into you and now your life has drained away. Like all mothers, I know about death.

My beautiful child, you are dead now, and I am here in a strange place, with a man who is strange as blood. I do not know or care about this place, full of masks and guns. We are here to find you and to take you home. To put you in the earth in a silent place. That is all I can think about now.

What can I tell you about my grief? Only that there is no word for it. It has no language. It has no shape. Only that I would die nine times to have you back. You were the inside of my life and now you are gone and my life has no inside. I will never see your gentle face again.

Because, Johnny Little, your fingers are sinking into the clay. They are clutching the earth as once they clutched at my breasts, and your sucking frantic mouth is full of earth now, and your lips are dust, and your lungs are weeds.

Johnny Little, my own darling. My treasure and my only love. You will never know the harshness of this journey. Your poor father, the impenetrability of his moods. His sudden and terrible enthusiasms. His obscene hope. He is a moth flying into a window. A man trying to move through a mirror. And all for nothing.

Because you are dead now, Johnny Little, my sweet boy. Bloody flowers are growing out of you. You pierced me and tore me on the night that you came. You are tearing me through again now.

My child, my beloved, my only pleasure. My hands will never touch your face again. I see death when I think of your mouth. I hear its sigh. I hear its promise. And I want to lie down with death then, fall asleep in its arms for ever.

31

The Stars And The Planets

OUTSIDE LÉON THE ROADS quickly became steep and narrow
as they began to climb again, the sea behind them, past fields of
bubbling mud, up towards the ring of grey volcanoes that
stretched out towards the eastern horizon. Momotombo loomed
closer now. Its slopes were green shale and yellow granite and
clouds of thin purple smoke came belching out of the crater. It
dominated the surrounding country, leering down like an angry
schoolteacher. It looked alive and vicious and the landscape
seemed to bow down and die as they approached it. There were
no more lush trees. There was little vegetation of any kind. They
moved closer to the steaming mountain and up on to a plateau of
black and grey scalded soil. The land looked like the surface of
the moon now, the earth pockmarked, dotted with tiny lakes
and outcropping white rock. Smokes explained that the volcano's
poisonous gases had long since rendered the fields useless. They
passed tiny shacks made of packing cases and scrap metal. Women
and men were working around the huts, unloading trucks of seaweed and shovelling it into the ground. Aka-47 rifles were jammed
into the dead earth like fence posts. Here and there, a scrawny
pine or blasted olive tree nodded down as though pleading for
mercy before the vast and treacherous peak.

Lightning flickered low in the sky. Claudette roared across the
dead land and rain lashed down into the fast-flowing river that
ran alongside the gravel road. The sky seemed to change from
blue to seagull grey. Rain spattered on the van's roof and washed
over the windscreen. Thunder exploded high above them. And
then the rain became so heavy that Smokes had to pull over. He
was afraid the storm would cause a mudslide, or an avalanche. It

was getting serious now, he told them. They could get washed off the road, and in this neck of the woods they couldn't count on being found too soon.

They sat in the back of the van, playing poker and listening to the rain battering the roof. They talked about music and about Ireland, and then the rain got so loud that they couldn't hear one another any more, so they just stopped talking and continued dealing out the cards. When the rain finally stopped, a misty yellow light hung over the lowlands, bathing everything in softness, blurring the edges of the mountain and the plain. Creamy clouds drifted slowly across the sky. They rolled back like curtains, revealing the blue behind, and when the clouds finally broke up, the drenched landscape looked absurdly beautiful.

Guapo climbed up on to Claudette's slippery roof and covered the coffin with a dirty tarpaulin, wrapping it very delicately, as though making up a bed. Then he slithered back down again and drank some hot tea, and changed out of his damp T-shirt, flexing his biceps and chuckling in the chilly breeze.

'OK,' Cherry said, looking up from the map. 'This here's the tricky bit. The Pan-Am's coming up real soon.'

They drove two or three miles along the road leading eastwards until they saw the wide perpendicular sweep of the highway two hundred yards in front of them. Smokes stopped the van again. He and Guapo jumped out and went to stand under a dripping tree, talking and smoking. Finally Guapo nodded and began to walk ahead towards the highway. Smokes jumped back into the cab and Frank went up front to join him.

'OK, Franklin,' Smokes breathed. 'Get ready now. Hold on to your fucking toupee, man.'

Up ahead, on the edge of the Pan-Am, the ground was already almost dry and it shimmered in the heat. Guapo walked out on to the hard shoulder. He looked right and left, then whipped around, whistled and beckoned. Smokes jammed his foot down and the van sped forward. 'Here goes,' he yelled.

They drove out quickly, crossing straight over the highway and on to the side road leading up to the east. Guapo ran after them. They opened the back doors and let him in. Behind them and to their left, the highway stretched into the distance, a thin white ribbon winding up into the mountains towards Honduras.

'*Vámonos*, Smokes,' Cherry yelled.

'OK, Franklin?' Smokes said.

Frank nodded, his heart beating hard. Smokes slapped his thigh.

'Drives you fucking crazy, I know, man. Corinto's only an hour up there, but we gotta take the long way round.'

'It doesn't drive me crazy,' Frank said.

'Yeah?' Smokes laughed. 'Franklin, something tells me you're not the kind of guy likes taking the long way round.'

'Tortoise and hare.' Frank shrugged. 'You get philosophical after a while.'

The road was a churning mess of mud. They drove very slowly for the rest of the afternoon, taking it in turns to sit up front with Smokes, who was beginning to look very tired now, black rings etched around his weary eyes. Far in the distance they saw a line of army observation towers stretching out at regular intervals towards the south. The land seemed fertile again, laid out in vast square fields planted with corn and olive trees.

Fifty miles south-west of Esteli they picked up some news on the crackling radio. There was Contra activity in the hills all around the town; the townspeople were preparing for an attack. Smokes groaned and brought Claudette to a halt.

He said they'd do better to camp out in the country and not go into the town until the next morning. That would be safer, and it would still give them plenty of time to set everything up for the gig the next night. Everyone agreed, so Smokes and Cherry climbed back up front and drove on for another hour. They pulled up finally by the side of a short, narrow lake ten miles or so to the south of Esteli. In the late afternoon sun, the lake was the colour of creamy coffee.

Guapo and Cherry went into the woods with machetes to collect some kindling. Frank went down to the lake with a towel and a change of clothes. He peeled off his damp shirt and his trousers and walked slowly into the water. The floor of the lake was crusted with tiny stones. Frank allowed himself to fall quickly forward. The cold water took his breath away and he pulled himself through it with steady strokes. He swam out to the middle, then trod water and floated on his back, staring straight up into the sky. He thought about the nights when his son used to come and watch him learning to swim in the pool at Willow Park. When he closed his eyes, he could almost hear the splash of the pool and the echoing laughter, the cheerful sound of young boys shouting encouragement to their fathers.

When he crawled back to the shore and climbed out of the lake, the sun was beginning to set behind the mountain. He peeled off his wet underpants, dried himself and put on his fresh clothes. He felt better now, and he sat on a warm damp rock and smoked a cigarette, looking up at the bright stars beginning to prick through the clouds.

When he got back to the van, Eleanor was lighting a fire. In the middle of the field, Guapo was staring up at the darkening sky through a telescope. Lorenzo was kneeling beside him, swigging from a bottle of beer. The air seemed very still and Guapo was speaking in a voice breathless with excitement.

'*Puedo ver los astros y los planetas lejanos. Veo a la Osa Mayor y la figura del cazador, Orion. A Venus la veo encima de la montaña, y Martes resplandeciente en el agua del lago. Júpiter, Saturno . . .*'

Frank listened to Guapo's voice, enjoying the sound of the beautiful words he was saying. It made him feel happy to hear them.

'*¡Oh!*' Guapo said. '*Hermano, hay tantas estrellas esta noche. ¿Las ve?*'

'*Sí, hombre,*' Lorenzo sighed. '*Sí.*'

'What are they doing?' Frank whispered to Smokes.

Smokes shook his head and chuckled. 'They're stargazing, Franklin. They do this shit when we're on the road. Every night Guapo looks up at the stars, and I guess, I dunno, I guess he sorta describes them to Lorenzo. It's just a thing they do together. He's talking about the planets and shit. Weirdsville, Arizona, huh, Frank?'

'It's not weird,' Cherry said. 'Why is it weird?'

'Oh, come on, babe!' Smokes giggled. 'It's not like he can fucking see them or anything.'

'Jesus, Smokes,' Cherry said. 'You really can be a heartless shit sometimes, you know that?'

They filled a copper pot with the last of their drinking water. Cherry peeled some onions and bananas and threw them into the pot. They put the bread on the glowing grill and opened two cans of tuna fish. Guapo had a bar of chocolate which he broke into pieces and shared around.

When they had finished eating, Lorenzo sat in the firelight strumming his guitar. After a while he began to play a delicate classical piece which Eleanor recognized as a Bach prelude. He leant into the guitar and stroked the strings, whistling an elegant harmony as he plucked the fugue and counterpoint.

'Beautiful,' Eleanor said. 'That was really lovely.'

'Lorenzo Moran,' Frank said, 'who taught you to play like that?'

Lorenzo grinned and put his guitar down. He said that wasn't really his kind of music and, anyway, it was a very long story. Frank clapped him on the knee. He said it was going to be a long night and they had all the time in the world for stories. Lorenzo opened a bottle of *cerveza Victoria* and swallowed a mouthful. He cocked his ear and listened for a moment to the sputtering fire.

'They walked in the midst of the flames' – he smiled – 'But they praised the Lord of Israel.'

He sat back hard against the rock, put his hands on his knees and began to speak.

He was from a small town on the Costa Atlantica. The town was called Bluefields, he said, and everyone there spoke English. It was a beautiful little place, on a sea the colour of iodine. The sea was jumping with lobsters and crabs and giant fat barracudas and the trees were heavy with fruit. There were coconuts and mangoes and oranges the size of melons. There was white cheese and thick cream. There were great big ships from Mobile and Cuba and Spain. The sailors brought money into the town. They brought wine from Europe, radios and refrigerators from the United States. There was a big school in Bluefields. There was a hospital, the only one for miles around. There were people of all colours in the town. There were blacks, whites, mulattos, *gringos*. There were all kinds of Indians, mestizos and Ramas, Miskitos and Garifunas and Sumus. There was a Chinese tailor and a Frenchman who ran a *glaceria*. There were Italian nuns and Argentinian bullfighters. There was a Cuban dance teacher and a drunken guitar maker from Mississippi. And there was a crazy black Irishman, Michael Moran, Lorenzo's father, who worked in the gold mine when things were good, and who bare-knuckle boxed in the travelling rodeo when they weren't.

Bluefields was full of all kinds of music, Lorenzo said. There was ska and reggae, bluebeat and bebop jazz. There were church choirs and barber shop quartets. There was swing and jive in the dance halls, mambo in the bars, boogie-woogie piano playing in the dockside cathouses. When the island people came in on a Saturday night, there was calypso and merengue in the Red Pepper and Spanish Danny's Juke Joint. And there was rock and roll music on the radio from Miami. It was a paradise, he said. It was a wonderful place to grow up in.

'Well, one day,' Lorenzo told them, 'I was sitting in my mother's kitchen. It was just after my eyes started to go. I was nine years old and she was baking, I think, and the kitchen was full of the smell of bread – wonderful smell – and we were just listening to the radio. I believe I was doing homework. It was something normal. And all of a sudden, man, I hear the most magical sound. I jump up out of my chair and I looked at that radio. I couldn't believe the noise coming out of that box. My hair stands *up*, man. That was back when I had hair to stand up.

'John Lee Hooker' – Lorenzo grinned – 'And, Jesus, that brother was making the guitar talk. He wasn't fast now, and he wasn't fancy, but I never heard a noise like that in all my days. It was pure spirit. It was like nothing else. And I was gone, man. I was nailed to the wall, blown away. I stopped doing my homework pretty damn quick.'

Eleanor and Frank laughed as they opened their bottles of beer and lemonade. Lorenzo smiled too.

'Well, in school, those old nuns didn't like that. They beat my fingers with rulers. They whipped me and they chastised me, but nothing would do me any good. Lorenzo was going to be like John Lee Hooker and that was all he knew. So, after six months, my mother sent twenty dollars to her cousin in New York, and I got a guitar for Christmas. It was a little Hofner, with one pick-up. It was red. I remember that. I guess that's the last colour I remember, my eyes being so bad by then. And my father bought me a chord book somewhere, but I couldn't read it. So, at night when he came home, he'd get the book and we'd sit out on the porch and he'd put my fingers on the strings and show me the chords and the scales. And man, I played those chords till my fingertips bled. Then he showed me how to plug it into the radio.

I blew the tubes and I nearly drove my poor mother crazy.'

Everyone laughed again. Lorenzo scowled and shook his head.

'But nothing would come of it. I was small as a child. My hands were weak and I couldn't make the shapes. And I had no feeling for the music. I was too young, I guess. When I was a child, I saw like a child, like Saint Paul says. Well, my mother used to clean house for this guy called Little Arturo, who ran a honky-tonk down in the boondocks. Little Arturo was a big blues fan, you know, although my father used to say he dressed like an FBI man. I'm saying he dressed square, you know? He's passed away now. He gave my mother a box of records one time, and she gave 'em to me. Big heavy shellac things. Like china plates. Ray Charles and Sonny Terry. Lightning Hopkins and the Howling Wolf. Muddy Waters doing "I'm a Rolling Stone". And I was just in heaven, man. I spun those things till the grooves was smooth as glass. I loved all that stuff, but there was still nobody could touch John Lee.

'So I tried and tried, every night, but my eyes got worse, and my playing stayed the same. My folks did all they could for me. But there were nights when poor Lorenzo cried himself to sleep.'

Lorenzo paused. He took off his sunglasses and looked up at the sky. Picking up his beer bottle, he took a swig from it. His voice deepened and he spoke in a more serious tone.

'And then, one night, I had a strange dream.'

'Oh, Jesus wept, Lorenzo,' Smokes sighed. 'Not this one again.'

Lorenzo ignored him. 'I'm sitting in a beautiful church, full of silver light. Angels singing, you know? But I'm feeling low, man, low as Job. I'm crying out to Jesus, but my prayers were as dust in the ears of the Lord.'

Lorenzo stopped again. It was getting darker now. The fire spat and crackled and orange light was reflected on his face. He stared into the fire as though he could see it. He lowered his voice and held out the palm of his hand. Breathless he whispered, 'And suddenly, man, I hear this sound. Like a great big puma growling outside the church. Like no sound I ever heard before, brother, but I'm not afraid. I step up and I go out and the night is full of smoke. And there's this long black Cadillac, man. Long and black and sleek, like an animal, and the engine is going, and the window rolls down. Smooth. This hand comes out and it's wearing a white glove, and the window is black as the night. And the hand beckons to me, and I go over. And I look in. This dude is sitting there, in a tuxedo and a top hat. And the cat's smiling. He takes off his hat. He points at me. And, saints alive, man, do I jump back in the alley.'

'Why?' said Frank. Lorenzo turned to face him.

'Because this cat's got two horns, man. On top of his head, like an ivory crown.'

'Yeah, yeah, yeah,' Smokes muttered. 'And Elvis is pumping gas in Albuquerque.'

'I'm saying Satan himself is sitting there, brother, right down there on the back seat, proud as the Jack of Hearts.'

'Oh, Lorenzo' – Eleanor laughed – 'Stop that.'

But Lorenzo was not listening. He licked his lips as he continued and his voice began to tremble. He stood up and stepped towards the fire. His voice croaked. He began to speak more quickly, sounding nervous now, and frightened.

'I go, Jesus, help me, and the cat just laughs. He laughs in my face. And his voice is like nails on a slate, man. And he's hissing and spitting like a crawling king snake. He goes, child of mine, your precious Jesus has taken your eyes. Nothing I can do, but I can give you vengeance. I can give you the gift of the devil's music. But I want your soul, he goes. I want your soul and that's my only price.

'Oh, I feel the power of Jesus stir within me, telling me not to listen. But what the wise man shuns the fool will see as righteousness. I step forward, Christ have mercy, and I take the devil by my own right hand. He laughs, and I see hellfire in his eyes, but it's too late.

'He says, now you're mine, child. You remember the face of the Prince of Darkness, because when your time of dying comes, you will see my face again. You will see this Cadillac waiting to take you, and I will give you a key. You will come to the devil's Cadillac, and you will step right in. And then you and me's gonna be taking a long, long ride.'

Lorenzo stopped speaking. He was breathing hard.

'The very next day,' he whispered, 'I could play the guitar the way I do now. That was twenty years ago. No word of a lie.'

Lorenzo sat back down, looking shocked and exhausted. He sat very still, with his mouth a little open, and then he took a long drink of beer. He pulled a huge white handkerchief from his breast pocket and wiped his face. Frank began to laugh. 'You're an awful chancer now, Lorenzo.'

'Oh, yeah? Well, when I woke up next morning, brother, you look what I had in my hand.'

'Here we go,' Smokes sighed.

'*Cállese*, Marilyn,' Guapo snapped. 'Shhh.'

With shaking fingers, Lorenzo opened the top buttons of his shirt. He reached inside and grasped the chain from around his neck. He unhooked it and held it out in his hand. Dangling on the end of the chain was a silver-coloured car key.

'This is the key to Satan's Cadillac,' Lorenzo snapped. 'And if I'm lying, Jesus strike us all down dead this moment.'

'My God,' Eleanor said.

'Oh, come on, Eleanor!' Smokes laughed uneasily. 'If you believe that, I got some swampland in Florida for sale.'

'Yes,' Frank said. 'Sure, you could have got that anywhere.'

Lorenzo hung his head and buried his face in his handkerchief. 'Oh, ye of little faith,' he said. 'My saviour paid my reparation, but I sold it away for a three-chord trick.'

He stood up slowly and began to make his way back to the van. The fire crackled and hissed. After a moment Guapo stood up too. He packed his guitar into its case and glared down at Smokes.

'*Gracias*, Marilyn,' he said quietly, then he spat into the fire, turned and went to follow Lorenzo.

'Well, the guy's fucking crazy.' Smokes laughed. 'He lives in this fantasy world, you know? He makes all this shit up. It's sad.'

'And what about you, Smokes?' Cherry said suddenly. 'You make stuff up all the time.'

'I do not.'

'You do too,' she snapped. 'Everyone knows it. Only difference is the stuff you make up is so fucking cheap, if you ask me.'

'Well, babe, I'm not the one talking about the black dude who sold his soul to the fucking devil. You think he even made that up himself? It's the oldest story in the damn book.'

Cherry stood up, looking angry. 'Jesus, Smokes, where're your fucking feelings? Don't you have any?'

'Sure I do.' He giggled. 'What? You got the world monopoly on feelings now?'

'You know,' she said, 'it's no fucking wonder about you and Johnny. He got your number right, man.'

'Don't start about that now. Just butt out.'

'What about him and Johnny?' Frank said.

Cherry began to gather up the cups and plates.

'It's nothing, Franklin,' Smokes muttered. 'Cherry just gets upset sometimes.'

She turned to him and pointed.

'Cherry's not fucking upset,' she shouted. 'This sick mother got jealous, Frank. We took a trip together one time, me and Johnny, when Smokes was away. We went down to Rivas to see the fucking volcanoes. He got back and accused us of sleeping together, you know, me and his best fucking friend? That's how sick he is. That's the kind of stuff Smokes makes up.'

'Shut up, Cherry, OK?'

'You gonna put that in your fucking novel, Smokes?'

Smokes laughed and shook his head. 'It was a guys' thing. Johnny understood.'

'He did not understand. And I didn't understand. There you go again, Smokes. Fucking fantasy land. You're so full of shit it's coming out your ears, man.'

He looked at her. 'Jesus, Cherry,' he sighed, 'you're sad, honey, you really are.'

'No Smokes. What's sad is everyone knows I'm right. Everyone except you.'

She gathered up the rest of the plates, turned and walked towards Claudette.

Eleanor smiled nervously at Smokes, then stood up and yawned. 'Well,' she said, 'I'll never sleep now. These stories about the devil would give you the willies.'

Guapo emerged from the van, bare to the waist. He said he and Smokes would sleep out in the field, that Frank and Lorenzo could share Claudette with the two women.

'Grand,' Frank said. 'That's OK with you, Smokes, is it?'

Smokes looked at him, shrugging. 'Lorenzo,' he said, 'I love the guy, Franklin, but he's wired to the moon.'

Suddenly a dull, flat *thud* echoed over the fields. This was followed by a louder sound, like the smash of falling crockery. Smokes and Guapo ran to the edge of the clearing. The sound was coming from the direction of the town.

'*Los Contras*,' Guapo said.

Rapid popping noises filled the air, like corks being pulled out of bottles. Flashing white light illuminated the silhouettes of the mountains and red and yellow tracer fire soared into the sky. Shrill whistling sounds sang across the dead fields. Sometimes there were long intervals between the sounds. At other times they followed one another in rapid succession.

'It's happened,' Smokes said quietly. 'It's them.'

They climbed on to Claudette's roof and stood silently watching the bombs fall on Esteli. The attack lasted for about half an hour. Then came the distant wail of sirens, rolling in and echoing across the lake. Small fires had started on the hillside just behind the town. One by one they went out and then everything was quiet again, except for the shrieking of startled birds.

'What should we do, Smokes?' said Frank.

'Get some sleep, Franklin. Nothing else we can do.'

Guapo and Smokes took their groundsheets from their rucksacks and rolled underneath Claudette. Frank climbed into the back. It was stuffy and hot now, and the tiny space smelt of feet and sweat.

He lay in the darkness listening to Guapo and Smokes mumbling and snapping at each other beneath him. After a while they went quiet. Eleanor started to snore softly.

He fell into a light sleep. Pictures of his childhood flickered through his mind. He saw his father's handsome laughing face, his brother on his first motorbike, his mother dancing through a long room with a strange man who was not his father.

He was woken by the sound of a twig cracking outside in the field. He told himself it was nothing. Another sharp *crack* made him sit up. His heart was pumping fast. He looked at the door. He kicked on the floor to waken Smokes and Guapo. He waited. For maybe a minute nothing happened. Then, very slowly, the handle on the door began to turn.

Frank's heart fluttered. A teenage boy stood in the doorway with a pistol in his hand. He was breathing heavily and looked panic-stricken. He coughed.

'*¡Manos arriba!*' he said.

'*No entiendo,*' Frank said.

'*¡Ponga las manos arriba!*' the boy said, more sharply, jerking the gun up and down. Eleanor and Lorenzo sat up in their bunks. Cherry stirred but kept on sleeping. Frank stepped out of bed and put his hands above his head.

'Frank?' Eleanor said uncertainly. 'What's going on?'

'Put your hands up,' Frank said. 'Both of you. Quick.'

The boy stepped into the van. His face was bloody and tired. A septic-looking gash ran down his right cheek. He had a black bandanna tied around his forehead and he was wearing a tattered blue uniform. He walked towards the bed on which Cherry was lying. With the barrel of his gun he raised the sheet. He looked down at her, then whirled around and pointed the gun again, wiping his mouth with the back of his hand.

'*Algo de comer,*' he hissed. '*Déme algo de comer.*'

He wanted food, Lorenzo said. Frank moved slowly to the table, picked up a loaf of bread and handed it, at arm's length, to the boy. The boy began to gnaw at it, swallowing hard and rubbing his lips with his right sleeve. His eyes were wild. They darted around the camper as though he was looking for something.

'Where are the others?' Eleanor asked.

'Don't worry about the others,' Frank said in a loud voice. 'I'm sure the others are fine.'

The boy took a step towards him. '*Silencio,*' he snapped.

Frank looked out into the field. In the murky firelight he saw Guapo creeping towards the door, tiptoeing along as though walking on broken glass. Guapo caught his eye and raised his index finger to his lips.

'Cigarette?' Frank said brightly, reaching for his pocket. 'American cigarette?'

'*¡Manos arriba!*' the boy screamed. Cherry sat up. 'Smokes?' she called.

In one sudden movement, Guapo was inside the van. He chopped the boy in the back of the neck, grabbing his gun at the same time. The boy fell forwards. Cherry screamed. Smokes jumped into the van, waving his rifle. Guapo grabbed the boy by the heels and started to drag him out of the door. Lorenzo stood up and staggered.

When Frank got out into the field Smokes was sitting astride the boy's chest, pressing down on his neck with the barrel of the gun. Guapo was kneeling too, pulling hard on the boy's hair.

The boy was struggling like a trapped animal. He spat and kicked, and when Guapo put his hand over his mouth he sank his teeth into it. Guapo howled and punched him in the stomach. The boy groaned with pain. Guapo clenched his right fist and began to pummel him in the face, still dragging hard on his hair.

Frank shone his torch on the boy's face. His eyes were wide with fear and he was crying now. 'No me maten,' he kept pleading. 'No me maten, por favor.'

'Get something to tie the little motherfucker,' Smokes yelled. 'Franklin. Get a fucking rope. I hope the policia kick seven shades of shit out of you, pal.'

'Smokes,' Eleanor said, 'would you not just take his gun and let him go? Sure, he's only a boy.'

'Only a boy, fuck. This boy wants to slit your throat, Eleanor.' Frank glanced at her.

'Well, won't it be awkward?' he stammered. 'I mean, there'll be questions. Me and Eleanor aren't supposed to be here, after all.'

'No way, Franklin,' Smokes said. 'We got him now.'

Smokes took the gun off the boy's throat. The boy jumped up, still crying. He held his hands in the air, weeping and shaking. '¿Me va a matar?' he wept. He joined his hands and went down on his knees, hugging at Smokes's legs. 'No, hombre. ¿Por favor?' he begged. '¿Por favor?' He lay down flat and kissed Smokes's feet. Guapo growled a curse and stepped forward. He grabbed the boy by the hair and pulled him up on to his feet. He took out his knife and held it to the boy's throat.

'Come on, Guapo,' Cherry said in a trembling voice. 'Don't do anything crazy.'

'No,' the boy whimpered. 'No quería hacer daño, hombre.'

'Let him go,' Lorenzo said. 'Justice is mine, says the Lord.'

He came forward and put his hand on Guapo's arm. 'Hombre,' he said. Guapo released the boy, pocketed his knife and walked away. The boy lunged forward and grabbed Smokes's hand, kissing it. Smokes stepped back and wiped his hand on his shirt. He pointed his gun in the direction of the woods. *'Fuera,'* he said quietly. *'Vayase a la mierda.'*

The boy began to walk away slowly, afraid to turn his back. Then, suddenly, he wheeled around, stumbling, and began to run. Smokes opened his mouth and screamed. He unclasped the safety catch on his rifle. He pointed it high in the air and began to shoot, and he laughed as the gun danced in his hands. Eleanor put her palms over her ears. Halfway across the field, the boy began to duck and weave from side to side, running hard, until he came to the edge of the woods and disappeared. Smokes kept shooting.

'Stop it,' Lorenzo shouted.

Smokes turned and glared. Guapo ran at him, snatched the gun from his hands, ripped the magazine from its socket and threw it on the ground. *'¡Basta!'* he snapped. Then he turned and stalked past Cherry, got into the back of Claudette and lay down on the floor with his hands over his eyes.

Cherry was shaking now and sobbing quietly into Eleanor's shoulder. Smokes knelt down and picked up the magazine.

'You shouldna done that, Smokes,' Cherry wept.

He stood up. 'Oh yeah? Well, I didn't notice you helping out, honey.'

'Real brave, ain't you, Smokes? Real brave with a fucking gun in your hand.'

'Jesus Christ Almighty,' Frank said. 'What kind of place is this?'

Smokes turned and stabbed at Frank with his finger. 'Nobody asked you to be here, Frank. That's the kind of place it is, the kind of place you shouldn't fucking be in, OK?'

'OK, kid. Jesus, relax.'

Smokes snapped his hair out of his eyes. 'Fuck. Relax, Frank. That's beautiful. Relax, from you. You know, you get in a snot, the world's supposed to stop fucking turning, man. Everyone's supposed to be so fucking scared. You're gonna teach me to relax, Frank? Like you taught Johnny?'

'What's that supposed to mean?'

Smokes looked away, shaking his head. 'Jesus Christ, man, if I had a father like you.'

'Smokes, don't,' Cherry said. 'Shut up.'

Frank laughed. 'What, son? You'd run off to some dump and get yourself killed too? Just to teach him a lesson?'

When Smokes turned there were tears in his eyes. 'Fuck you, Frank,' he sobbed, and he stepped back and walked across the field into the darkness.

'I think,' Eleanor sighed, 'we should all go inside now, and try and get some sleep.'

'But what if he comes back?' Cherry said.

She cradled Cherry in her arms and stroked the back of her head. 'He won't come back, love,' she said. 'We've given him a chance, so he'll give us a chance now. That's the way people are, you know.'

She glanced up at her husband. He was standing by the campfire with his hands on the back of his head, staring into the flames, breathing very heavily.

The sky was tinged with yellow light. The birds croaked and screamed in the trees. They sounded vicious now, the beautiful birds. They sounded as though they were laughing.

32

A Cold Day In Hell

THEY SLEPT UNEASILY and woke up early. Just after dawn, Frank went down to the lake for a swim, but the water was so cold that he couldn't bear it for long. When he got back to the van, Smokes was studiously ignoring him.

Claudette started up with a breathless chug and they began to head for Esteli. The land became increasingly cultivated as they approached the town. They passed fields of blooming orchids, pink and white chrysanthemums, and dark red poppies, all swaying gently in the breeze. The telephone pylons reared above the flowerfields like giant metal crucifixes.

They drove down the Avenido Bolívar and into the centre of the town. Esteli was alive with talk of the Contra attack. Two hundred *guerrilleros* had moved in on the coffee *cooperativas* in the hills to the north, but the *campesinos* had been well armed, and an army infantry unit had arrived just after the attack had started. All the *campesinos* had survived. Two soldiers and thirty-six Contras were dead. About fifty had been taken prisoner.

The star of the evening's show, Carlos Mejia Godoy, had arrived with his band from Massaya. He was standing in the middle of the main square, smiling, kissing babies and signing autographs. Carlos was a hero of the revolution, Cherry said. He'd been outlawed and jailed in the time of the General and now he was like a god to the ordinary people. There was no one to touch Carlos for popularity, she said. The guy was just king of the pile.

After breakfast, Cherry took Eleanor to see the prehistoric stone carvings down in the park. They could only just make out the grinning androgynous figures. Afterwards they walked around and looked at the flowerbeds. The morning was fine now and hordes of schoolchildren ran around in the sunshine, splashing each other with water and tearing up the gorgeous flowers. There was a puppet show in the arbour by the pond and a fat clown was handing out sweets and fruit to the children. He blew kisses to Cherry and Eleanor and they waved back at him.

They sat down in the shade and began to talk. Eleanor said she was worried about Frank and Smokes's argument the night before, that she hoped they'd make up and not make everything more difficult than it already was. Cherry said she was sure things would be OK. She'd been around Smokes long enough to know that he never argued for longer than twenty-four hours. He just didn't have the patience for it. Or the brains, either. Eleanor laughed.

'You have him well trained, love.'

'He depends on me.' Cherry shrugged. 'See, he used to take drugs and I got him to quit. Smokes is that kind of guy, you know. He needs someone around. He just can't survive on his own.'

'And tell me now,' Eleanor said, 'do you think you're going to stay with him long-term?'

Cherry thought for a moment. 'I dunno. I got a lot of faith in Smokes, I guess. He's just gotta learn to cut the crap. But I figure he's got a good heart, deep down.'

'He has a bit of a temper as well, Cherry.'

'Yeah, well. Old Frankie's pretty hot-headed too, ain't he?'

Eleanor laughed. 'You don't have to tell me, pet. I've been on the receiving end a few more times than suits me.'

She looked at the children screaming around the fountain.

'Eleanor,' Cherry said, 'what happened with you guys? Do you want to say?'

Eleanor smiled. 'Oh, well, that's the million-dollar question.'

'Don't you wanna tell me, Eleanor?'

'Well,' she said, 'things just didn't work out for us, dear. We got married too young, I think. We were very impetuous. I mean, we loved each other so much, but when you're that age, you think that's all you need.'

'So, how'd you guys meet?'

She flicked back her hair. 'Well, I always knew him, I suppose.

We grew up together. He was a very good dancer actually, that's what attracted me to him first. He was a nice-looking fellow alright, but he could dance like an absolute angel.'

The clown was walking on his hands now. He flipped himself back up on to his feet. 'Hoopla,' he cried out.

'And when you got married?'

'Oh, he was a very good husband. Very responsible, very serious about things. His mother used to call him the Pope, you know, when he was a boy, because he was so serious about everything. I used to laugh at that. But he was gentle to me, very soft. Oh, we made such plans, the way you do when you're young. God, the things we talked about, when I think of it now. And he didn't run around, you know. He was home every night. He was very kind to me. We knew nothing, of course, about the physical side. But even that didn't seem to matter, at first.'

'Really, Eleanor? That didn't matter?'

Eleanor shook her head. 'When there's love there, you can overcome anything.'

'And then you had Johnny?'

'Yes, we did. And he was a marvellous father. The nights he stayed up with him, rocking him to sleep, and he'd have to go out and drive a taxi the next day. I found him one night, down in the kitchen, asleep at the stove, and the baby asleep in his arms. I always remember that.'

She smiled sadly and sat back hard against the bench.

'Oh, they were lovely days then. We used to make love just all the time.' She paused, laughing. 'God, we were terrible. Sometimes he came home in his taxi, and we'd just jump into bed, in the middle of the afternoon, with the baby right there in the next room. And we went out together, you know, to plays and concerts, things at the union. And it'd be lovely looking at him, with everyone talking to him and thinking he was wonderful, and knowing that we would be together when we went home. And waking up beside him, and feeling him next to me, all drowsy in the mornings, you know, the way men are in the mornings? He made me feel like no woman on earth. Do you know, he cried sometimes when we made love. He used to cry like a little baby because, he said, he was so happy. He was always a terrible charmer, of course. Flowers, perfume, you name it. He brought home a bunch of red roses every Friday night. It was a terrible waste, really.'

'It sounds nice,' Cherry smiled.

Eleanor nodded. 'Yes, it *was* nice, I must say. We were blessed to have those days.'

She sighed deeply and hugged herself, as though she was cold. And when she spoke again, her voice was hesitant and nervous.

'But we had a little girl who died, you see. I don't know if Johnny ever told you?'

'No. God, he didn't.'

'No, well, it was before he was born. She would have been a big sister to him. Catherine, her name was, a lovely little thing, the reddest hair, really red-gold hair like you read about. The poor little mite died. She got a throat virus and died.'

'Oh, no, Eleanor.'

'And when she died, love, something strange happened to me. In my mind, do you know?'

Over by the pond, the clown was tearing off his baggy blue suit. He ripped off the jacket and stepped out of his trousers, tripping up on his huge yellow shoes. Underneath he was wearing a ludicrous blue military uniform. Eleanor looked at him and tried to smile again.

'Go on, honey,' Cherry said.

'Well, love, I started to drink then, you see. A lot of it was my own fault, to be honest. I just started to hit the bottle. I don't really know why. I suppose it was curiosity too, at first. And I'd be bored. It was just after my father died. I'd be bored and I had too much time to think about the past. My father and I fell out, you see. He was very hard on us as children. Anyway, Frank would go out to work and I'd have nobody at all to talk to until he came home.

'Well, at first I went into bars, or up to the golf club. But women didn't in those days. There was a name for a woman like that. And people started to talk. They knew me in the shops and there'd be smart remarks. So I'd walk all the way down to Dun Laoighre then, to get a drink. I'd sit in this bar that looked out on the sea, with Johnny beside me in the pram, and I'd be drunk at half past two in the afternoon. People would be making comments. And it went from bad to worse. I fell over in the street

221

one time. It was Christmas Eve, and a man had to drive me home in his car. I was so ashamed of myself, I locked myself in the bathroom and I just cried. Frank wouldn't notice, of course. He'd come in tired and he'd just want a dinner put up. I really think he didn't even notice at first.'

She paused and started to twist her bracelet.

'You didn't hear the word alcoholic in those days. You didn't hear the word addiction. Not in Ireland anyway. There were all sorts of words you wouldn't even hear. That was the worst thing. I felt like the only woman in the world who was like that.

'And I often tried to stop. I went to a priest about it. But then, before too long, I was taking drink into the house. I was like two different people, love. I'd know the drink would send me mad. I'd *know* that, you see, but I'd just find myself taking it anyway. It got to the stage where a bottle wouldn't be safe. Sometimes Frank would get beer and all kinds of wine, from the regulars in work, at Christmas, you know. He didn't drink much then, so it was always there, in the house, and I'd be there in the day by myself. I felt very lonely. I don't know why. I had an awful lot, when you think of some girls. But the drink made me feel strong, I suppose, or numb, maybe. I don't really know. Life was very thin for me, I don't really know why. The old drink softened it a little.'

The clown pulled a giant pair of spectacles from his bag and put them on his head with an elastic band. He began to stumble forwards, reaching for the screaming children with outstretched hands, staggering from side to side, wobbling and falling.

'But of course,' Eleanor said, 'things got worse then. I've heard a lot of alcoholics now, one way and another, telling their stories. I go to AA, you see. Well, they'll all tell you the same story, every last one. They'll all say it started with the odd little drink to make life easier. But it always gets worse. It gets a grip on you.

'I had to stop giving the piano lessons. There were complaints from some of the parents. I never told Frank that. I just told him I was fed up doing the lessons, I was so ashamed. But this one little girl had gone home to her mother and told her about me. The husband came up to the house and gave me an awful dressing down. I didn't know where to look. Well, Frank would give me a little money then, you know, for myself. For stockings or personal things. He hated me having to ask him for money, so he would give me a little, just for me. Well, I spent it all on booze, Cherry. There was one time I didn't have a hairdo for six months. I didn't look after myself. My appearance went off, and a man doesn't like that, when a woman lets herself go. Then the fights really started. About little things first. It was around the time Johnny started going to school. I was a bit over-protective at first, I suppose.'

She stopped speaking for a moment. She took one of Cherry's cigarettes and lit it. She stared into the distance, trying to concentrate.

'The physical side stopped shortly after that. He wouldn't want to touch me any more. He started sleeping downstairs on the couch. And I'm afraid we said awful things to each other, in front of poor Johnny too. When I think of his poor little face. He'd throw himself in between us and he'd beg us to stop. He'd beg. He saw things no youngster should ever see. Things being thrown around the kitchen. Plates, everything. Heard terrible language from the two of us. I would just lose any self-respect, you know. He had a terrible start in life.'

Her voice began to tremble.

'And then I reached the lowest days of shame. There were times I took it all out on the poor little fellow. I swore I'd never strike a child of mine, but somehow the rage would come down on me. I lost all dignity really. I'd be screaming like a madwoman and I'd be hitting him. And I don't mean a slap now, I mean violence.'

'Eleanor,' Cherry said gently, 'he never told me.'

'Oh, yes. God forgive me, but I'd knock lumps off the poor child. The neighbours all knew about it. There was trouble in the school too. He'd be going in with bruises. Frank would go mad, of course. He never lifted a hand to me, but I must say now, I think he was often close to it. He'd *shake* with the rage, you know. He'd stand there and just shake and roar at me. It's a terrible thing to see. A man shaking like that. He'd scream like a woman. The police were involved, more than once.'

'And when did he leave?' Cherry asked.

'Oh he didn't leave, pet. That wouldn't be Frank at all. No, I did. We parted alright, a few times. He went to live with his brother for a while, but he came back then and we tried to start again. For Johnny, really.'

'I thought Frank left,' Cherry said. 'I was sure Johnny said that.'

'No, love. I left. It got too much. I was afraid I'd do the poor child a damage, I really was. I went over to my sister in Coventry. Her husband was in the army, so he'd be away a good bit. She helped me an awful lot. She was a nurse, you see, so I suppose she had come across it a bit. She took me to see a doctor in the hospital. A coloured fellow, he was; from Bangladesh, I think. He was a lovely man anyway. Very understanding. They put me on anti-booze tablets. I got into a twelve-step programme then and I joined AA, and I started to see this counsellor fellow. I just hibernated for two years. I disappeared really. Nobody knew where I was.'

'God, Eleanor, how terrible for you.'

'Ah, no, it was lovely in a way. We had some lovely times, myself and Molly. We'd go out to the pictures at night and Mass every morning. And I'd give her a hand, you know, with her little Niall and Vincent. Her husband Matty is a lovely man. He's from Wales. He didn't ask a question about me being there. I never even rang Frank for ages. He must have been climbing the walls. I would just send him a card from time to time. I came home to Dublin in 1979, but I never went back to Frank in the end.'

'Why not?'

Eleanor's eyes flooded with tears.

'Why not, Eleanor?'

She raised her fingers and wiped the tears away. 'Oh, well, my sister found out there was another person in his life by that stage. I was hurt, I suppose. But I had to let him go. Sometimes that's love, you see. Letting go. I thought he was entitled to a bit of happiness in his life. So I just got my own little place then and I was better off really. I'd got a bit of money from Daddy's life insurance and Frank gave me a hand with the rest. He insisted, you know. He's funny that way. He'd never ring you or anything, but he can't give up what he thinks are his responsibilities.'

'Did you ever think about anyone else?'

Eleanor waved her hands, as though brushing away a mosquito. 'Oh, there was a fellow once, a few years ago. I met him at

AA. He went to the same meeting as me, in Blackrock. I was fond of him, I suppose, but he was a bit too keen. Roman hands and Russian fingers, do you know? Too keen in that department. And he wouldn't tell you the truth to save his life. I mean, he wouldn't be up there with Frank.'

She laughed. 'A fellow would want to be decked out in diamonds before I'd look at him now.'

'Men,' Cherry said.

'Oh, no, I like men. Men are lovely, I think. I can see the beauty in men. Their strength, you know, and the way they go on. But they'd tell you that night was day if they were let.'

She paused for a moment, looking into the middle distance, and her eyes filled with tears again.

'No, I never loved anyone like I loved Frank Little. I really did fall for him. He was everything in life to me and we thought we were it. But we lost our love somehow. It's the worst thing that can happen to a person.'

She pulled a tissue from her handbag and wiped her eyes.

'I'll say a little prayer, love, so that it'll never happen to you. It was the most awful thing to happen. We could have made a lovely life together, I must say.'

Cherry reached out and took Eleanor's hand.

'And you don't drink now?'

Eleanor smiled. 'Oh, no,' she said. 'No, thank God. I gained sobriety on Johnny's birthday. It was the seventeenth of September, 1982. I haven't touched a drop since then. I don't even have the wine at Mass.'

'But that's great, Eleanor. You should be real proud.'

'Oh, yes, it is. But, you see, I'll never be cured, love. Frank never liked me to say I was an alcoholic, you know, but I am really. It's more than a disease. It's a curse. And when the drink comes into a marriage, the love goes out the door.'

The children were screaming with laughter now as the clown chased them up and down the bandstand stairs.

'They say you never get over the desire,' Eleanor said. 'I still have my moments, even now, though I know all the harm it's done.'

'Well,' Cherry sighed, 'I guess everyone's an addict for something.'

'No, dear.' Eleanor smiled. 'Oh, I don't think so. I really don't think that at all.'

Fifteen minutes before the concert started, the Desperados de Amor were still in their dressing room arguing about what to play.

'Understand this,' Smokes said, 'this is my fucking band, and I want to play some fucking salsa.'

'Brother,' Lorenzo sighed, 'the people don't want that.'

'I don't give a fuck what the people want, Lorenzo. If they don't want it, they should. Sometimes you lead from the front, man, know what I'm sayin'? That's what Marx said.'

'Which one, man?' said Lorenzo. 'Harpo or Chico?'

Guapo took off his bass. He sat down, lit a cigarette and opened a can of beer. He wasn't going to go on, he said. He was not going to be told what to do by a fucking *gringo* with long blond hair.

'Guapo, *hermano*,' Lorenzo pleaded.

Guapo closed his eyes. '*No*,' he said. '*No, no, no.*'

'Well, fine,' Smokes said. 'That's just fine. Cherry, you can play the bass parts, can't you?'

'Come on, babe,' Cherry said, but Guapo just shook his head.

'Lorenzo?' Smokes said. 'You in or out?'

Lorenzo sighed again and strapped on his guitar. 'OK, Smokes.' He shrugged. 'Let's get it over with.'

Guapo glared up at him. '*¡Traidor!*'

'Come with me, brother,' Lorenzo urged. Guapo turned away and puffed hard on his cigarette.

At half past seven the Desperados de Amor came on and the concert started. When they launched into '*Abre Tus Ojos*' the crowd seemed completely bewildered. Nobody danced. Cherry tried to keep up with Smokes, but the right hand part was too intricate and her left hand kept missing out on the bass beat. And Smokes's voice sounded absolutely dreadful as he sang

> *Oye, abre tus ojos*
> *Piensas arriba*
> *Que todas las cosas buenas*
> *Que tiene la vida*

226

Lorenzo kept playing seventh blues chords that sounded completely wrong. Halfway through the second number a slow hand-clap began. After the first two-minute drum solo, the crowd started to boo. A beer bottle came flying through the air and shattered on Smokes's drum kit. The crowd laughed and clapped.

Smokes stopped playing. He stood up and yelled into his microphone, 'Hey, Esteli? *¿No quieres bailar?* Let's dance, no?'

'No,' roared the crowd.

'*¡Bailemos! ¡Venga!*' Smokes yelled. '*¡Nos vamos!*'

Somebody roared '*¡Váyase a casa, gringo!*' and the audience hooted with laughter.

The chant began very quietly at the very back of the hall. *Yanqui Go Home*. Soon it was taken up by other sections of the crowd. *Yanqui Go Home*. It began to echo against the walls and the roof. It got louder. *YAN-QUI GO-HOME*. Louder still. *YAN-QUI GO-HOME*. A minute later, every single person in the little hall was stamping, clapping hands in the air and yelling '*YAN-QUI GO-HOME. YAN-QUI GO-HOME. YAN-QUI GO-HOME*.'

'Shut up,' Smokes howled. '*Eso es la musica de la lucha de clases, y la cultura que luchamos para defendir.*'

'*YAN-QUI GO-HOME. YAN-QUI GO-HOME. YAN-QUI GO-HOME*.'

'*¿Por favor, compañeros?*' Smokes said in a bewildered voice.

They started to sing it to the tune of 'Amazing Grace'. *Yanqui Go Home, Go Home, Go-oh Home*. A young woman at the front of the crowd got up on to her boyfriend's shoulders and began to conduct. *Yanqui Go Home*. They started to sing in harmony. Lorenzo took off his guitar and sat down on top of his amplifier.

Guapo strode on to the stage, chuckling, his bass guitar around his neck. The crowd stopped singing and they cheered and whistled as he bowed to them. Smokes stepped out from behind his drum kit. He pointed at Guapo.

'If he plays,' he said to Cherry, 'I'm fucking leaving.'

'Fine. You do that, babe. I'll get Frank up here to play the drums.'

'You wouldn't fucking dare.'

'*YAN-QUI GO-HOME*.'

'I would too. Johnny said he was a really hot drummer, Smokes. You remember, don't you?'

Suddenly the house lights sprang on. The crowd groaned and jeered.

'You wouldn't dare do that,' Smokes said. 'This is my band.'

'What, honey? You afraid Frank's gonna be better than you?'

The people began the slow handclap again. More bottles were thrown at Smokes. He dodged from side to side, staggering, trying to avoid them, but this only seemed to encourage the crowd. Bottles started to rain down. Someone picked up a folding wooden chair and flung it with a clatter on to the stage. Cherry looked out at the audience and touched Smokes's hand.

'Come on, Smokes,' she said. 'Just get up there and fucking play, willya?'

'*YAN-QUI GO HOME. YAN-QUI GO HOME.*'

Guapo came over and grinned. He nodded his head at Smokes's drum kit. 'Marilyn,' he said. '*¿Nos vamos?*'

Smokes sighed. He stepped back behind his drum kit and started to batter the cymbals. The crowd yelled. Guapo went over to Lorenzo and shouted in his ear. Lorenzo beamed and turned up his amplifier. He stepped up to the microphone and pounded into the intro to 'Tutti Frutti'. The crowd screamed with applause. The lights went out again and people started to dance.

The Desperados played 'Twenty Flight Rock' and 'Something Else' and 'Rock and Roll Music'. When they dedicated 'I Fought the Law' to Ronald Reagan the crowd hissed and howled with laughter. They did 'Lucille' and 'Peggy Sue' and 'Jumpin' Jack Flash' and 'Heartbreak Hotel'. After the first encore two young men came on to the stage and sang 'All I Have To Do Is Dream'. They were absolutely terrible, but when they finished there was a huge round of applause. Then Carlos Godoy came on and jammed with the Desperados, doing a punchy reggae version of 'Twist and Shout'. He looked odd, this fat little man in his poncho and cowboy boots, skanking around the stage and waving his sombrero. When the song was over the crowd went wild again. Smokes threw his arms around Carlos Godoy, kissing him on both cheeks. He lifted Carlos's hand in the air and waved it.

'*¡Seguimos al frente!*' Smokes bawled into the microphone.

'*¡No pasarán!*' yelled the crowd, and Carlos Godoy laughed out loud, embracing Smokes, as his own band trooped on behind him. He sang gentle songs by Victor Jara, and songs by his brother, Luis

Enrique Godoy, and he sang 'Blowing in the Wind', strumming delicately on his Spanish guitar. When he sang '*Nicaragua, Nicaraguita, La Flor Más Linda*' the crowd lit candles and waved cigarette lighters above their heads. Carlos bowed low and applauded them. His band struck up again and the crowd roared as they recognized the introduction.

> *Ella es bonita*
> *Pero mentirosa*
> *Ella es bonita*
> *Pero tú me quieres, tú me quieres, corazón.*

Eleanor stood backstage watching with Smokes and Cherry, sipping an orange juice, swaying gently from side to side with the music.

'*Mentirosa*,' she said. 'What's that now, Cherry?'

'It's a liar, Eleanor. It's Carlos's big hit. It means you're cute, but you're full of shit.'

Cherry winked and turned towards Smokes.

'Hey, dreamboat, Carlos is playing our tune.'

'Oh, funny,' he said. 'Funny. You oughta be in the movies, Cherry. Anyone ever tell you that?'

When the concert was over Smokes was in a vile mood, even though he kept pretending to be cheerful. Lorenzo and Guapo said they wanted to go for a drink with two big Finnish women they'd met earlier on at the sound check, and Smokes said he thought he'd better go with them and make sure they didn't get into any trouble. Cherry laughed and said yeah, that was really likely. He sighed. She ruffled his hair and kissed him, then took out her purse and gave him twenty dollars.

'Go on,' she said. 'But don't get too smashed, OK? We gotta start out early tomorrow.'

Frank and Eleanor walked around the square with Cherry, looking at the stalls selling iguana-skin bags, lacework and earthenware pots. They bought a bag of oranges and a couple of fat pears.

The golden roof of the church was lit up with gorgeous red light. They crossed the plaza and sat on the steps. Cherry took out a penknife, peeled the fruit and handed around juicy segments.

Frank pulled out his camera and began to take pictures of the sky.

'They'll be nice for Veronica,' Eleanor said. 'To give her an idea.'

'Yes,' he said. 'I didn't think of it that way.'

A young woman at the front of the plaza seemed to be gazing at Frank now. She was so thin that the bones in her arms protruded through her light brown flesh. She was wearing a shabby black pinafore dress and a yellow ribbon in her hair. Her feet were bare, wrapped in bloodstained bandages. She moved cautiously forward and touched him on the wrist, then began to speak to him, urgently, in Spanish, pointing at his camera. She had five young children with her and a baby in her arms. All the children looked pale and hungry and the young woman's face was tired. She pointed at her children, then at Frank's camera. She pulled a *córdoba* note from her pocket and scribbled an address on it, pressing it into his fingers.

'Frank,' Cherry said, 'she wants you to take her kids' photo and send it to her when you get home.'

'Yes, alright. Why not?'

'You'd make her night, Frank. It's a big deal to have a photo of your kids around here.'

Frank looked at the young woman and nodded. The woman beamed. She took a comb from the pocket of her dress and pulled it through her hair. She licked her hand and rubbed at the face of the grubbiest little boy. Then she stood on the church steps and arranged the children around her, lifting up the baby in one arm and one of the toddlers in the other. They stared curiously at the camera and the baby started to cry. The woman undid one of the buttons on her pinafore and, pulling down the material, began to feed the baby, stroking the back of its tiny head. Frank clicked off ten pictures and walked towards her. She smiled at him. Her teeth were black and twisted.

He ruffled the baby's downy hair. 'Aren't you a great fellow now,' he said, and the baby closed its eyes and sucked at its mother's breast, stretching out its tiny hands in pleasure. 'You're a great man,' Frank said. 'You're the broth of a boy, aren't you?'

Eleanor and Cherry came over to talk to the young woman. She told them that her husband had been killed by the Contras the previous year. He and his brother had been in the army and their unit had been sent up into the mountains. They'd both been killed by a land mine the week before they'd been due to come home. Tears filled her eyes and she wiped them away.

Eleanor and Cherry continued to talk to her while Frank pretended to rummage in his bag for another film. He zipped open the pocket, crumpled up two fifty dollar bills and shook hands with the woman, covering her hand with his, pressing the notes into her palm. When she saw what he had given her, she looked away and started to sob. He closed her fingers with his own and cooed at the baby. He lifted him from her arms and swung him up in the air, gurgling at him. The other children laughed out loud and the baby whimpered with fear. He gave the baby back to its mother and it chuckled. The young woman's tearful face lit up with happiness. 'Gracias, hombre,' she said. 'Stop that,' Frank whispered. 'God bless now, love.' She took his hand and kissed it.

He watched her walk away across the plaza with her children, then turned to look at Eleanor.

'God, it's desperate, isn't it? It'd break your heart the way some people have to live. Do you remember when you'd see women like that in Dublin?'

'Ah, no,' Eleanor said. 'They wouldn't be as bad as that, Frank.'

'God, they would so, Eleanor. My Christ, there was a poor woman who used to come up to us in Francis Street. Mary Molloy was her name. My mother used to try and give her a cup of something, although she had little enough herself by then. She was put away in the end, the same poor Mary.'

'That's because she was touched in the head, Frank.'

'She was not, Eleanor. She was only a poor woman trying to look after her children.'

'Well, I'm not saying she wasn't, Frank. But she was simple, the dear creature.'

'She was sane as you or me, Eleanor. And how the fuck would you know anyway?'

She laughed nervously. 'I never saw anyone in Ireland as bad as that girl there, Frank.'

'Jesus, I'm telling you I did, Eleanor. I wouldn't bloody well lie to you about it, would I? Holy bloody Ireland is no place to be poor, I can tell you.'

'God, Frank, nobody's saying you're lying.'

'Well, you never bloody listen, Eleanor. It was our house she was in anyway, not yours. God knows she wouldn't have been let in the door there, your old man was such a streak of misery.'

'Frank, don't say that.'

'What? Is it Sir Paddy Hamilton of Drimnagh? That fellow had more airs than a bloody orchestra.'

Eleanor took a step towards him. 'What has my father got to do with anything?'

'A job in Guinness's and he thought he was something right enough. Don't think I don't know what he thought of my parents. More airs than you like.'

'Hey, *compas*,' Cherry said. 'Chill out, will you?'

'Her ladyship here doesn't like to see poor people. Thinks it's below her. Thinks she's Princess fucking Diana.'

'Oh, Frank,' Eleanor snapped, 'don't talk such bloody rubbish.'

He turned and glared at her. 'You know, Eleanor, if there was an Olympic games for talking rubbish I know who'd win every fucking medal.'

He felt his temper rise, the muscles tightening in his throat. Anger surged through him.

'I mean, do you ever listen to yourself? Do you ever listen to your stupid voice, Eleanor? Because now, if you listened for five minutes, you'd know why nobody can stand you.'

She turned away from him, looking shocked. He folded his arms. 'Yes, that's it. Stand there like a fool. Don't say anything.'

Music started up on the square again. Someone was shouting over a microphone. She whipped around to face him.

'Frank Little,' she cried, 'there'll be a cold day in hell before I ever feel another tenderness for you.'

'Oh, well, I'm shaking.'

She turned and walked off into the crowd. Cherry called out after her, but she didn't stop. The church bell began to clang.

'Frank,' Cherry sighed, 'Jesus, Frank.'

'Leave me alone, Cherry, will you?'

'Frank, honey, you shouldn't do stuff like that. Don't you know that?'

He turned on her. 'What? I'm a fucking male bastard, right? Go on, kid, if it makes you feel better, say it. That's what it's all about with you kids, isn't it? Feeling better?'

Her eyes were flashing now as she pushed her hair out of her face. 'Jesus, Frank, I feel sorry for you. You haven't a damn clue about people.'

He laughed out loud. 'Oh and you do, right? You're Sigmund fucking Freud, I suppose.'

By the time he had finished the sentence Cherry was already walking away. He zipped the camera into his bag, went into a bar and ordered a bottle of rum. He drank it all and smoked eleven cigarettes. He thought about his mother, about the night he had found her crying in the kitchen because the house was so cold. He drank remorselessly. He closed his eyes and saw his mother's face. He heard his father running out into the street and slamming the door. He felt the alcohol coursing through his veins and he went out into the plaza again.

The night was hot and humid and he was still raging inside. He went into a little cinema and sat down in the back row by himself, his mind reeling with drink.

The cinema was empty except for a few courting couples. He sat in the dull red light, listening to the laughter, feeling very hot now, his jaw heavy. He was suddenly tired. When the film started he found it was dubbed in Spanish and he couldn't follow it. His mind began to wander again. He thought about the day he had taken Johnny to see 'My Fair Lady' in the Plaza Cinerama Theatre on Parnell Square. He clenched his fists hard, trying to think about something else, but the memory persisted.

It was the day of Johnny's seventh birthday and he had promised him a trip to the cinema. That morning he and Eleanor had an argument and she locked herself in her bedroom. Frank told his son that she just wasn't feeling well, that she wanted them to go to the pictures without her. Halfway through the film, Johnny started to cry and Frank took him outside. His son sat down on the path and wept for about half an hour, refusing to tell his father what was wrong. Frank didn't know what to do. He was frightened and confused. He sat down beside his son and put his arms around his shoulders and waited for him to stop crying. Passers-by stared at them. He remembered the vague and curious

233

looks on their faces, but he had not cared at all about what they thought. He had only cared about his son.

They had bought ice creams then and gone for a walk in the Garden of Remembrance. It was a cold day in September, and they walked up and down by the pond and he pointed out to his son where the names were carved, all the names of the brave men who had died for Ireland. Then they went up to look at the big black statue of the children of Lir. He told his son the story of how the children of Lir had been turned into swans by their wicked stepmother. For nine hundred years they had lived on a lake in the middle of Ireland until Saint Patrick had come to the country. When they heard Saint Patrick ringing his bell they resumed their human form. But it was not a happy story. For the children of Lir were now nine hundred years old. They had aged in a second and collapsed on the side of the lake and died. But it was alright, Frank said, because Saint Patrick had made them Christians in their dying moments.

Suddenly the film rolled to a stop and the lights came on, stinging Frank's eyes. The courting couples stood up and began to leave. He wondered what was happening. A man in an usher's uniform ran into the cinema, waving a torch. '¡Salga, hombre!' he shouted, beckoning towards the door. 'Rápido, rápido.'

Frank hurried out into the street. He recognized the dull thudding sounds. Blue and orange light was flashing in the sky behind the hills. As the sirens began to wail he ran down the Avenida de Revolución Eterna towards the field where Claudette was parked.

Guapo was standing in the field in his shorts, smoking a cigarette and clutching his rifle, staring up into the mountains as though he could see right through the darkness. Smokes was standing behind him with a bottle of beer in his hand. He looked terrified. Cherry emerged from the back of Claudette and went over to stand by Smokes, putting her arm around his waist. She did not look at Frank.

Frank climbed into the back of the van. Lorenzo was asleep and snoring. Eleanor was sitting up in bed. She was holding the sheet to her neck and looked afraid.

'Eleanor?' he said, slurring her name. 'Are you alright?'
She avoided his eyes and looked around the van.
'Eleanor, I'm sorry. You know I didn't mean anything.'

When she turned to face him she had tears in her eyes. 'You just leave me alone, Frank,' she whispered. 'You're the cruellest person I ever met in my life.'

'I'm sorry,' he said. 'I'm sorry, Eleanor.'

'Let me *be*,' she shouted. Lorenzo muttered in his sleep.

He tried to apologize again, but she lay down and ignored him, rolling around to face the wall. After a moment she pulled the sheet up over her head, her body shaking with silent tears.

He watched the sheets of silver light flickering in the clouds and the spears of red tracer spurting up over the hills. He sat very still, smoking cigarettes, waiting for the sirens to stop.

33

Collaborators

THE MORNING AFTER the battle the sun came up hot and early over Esteli. They walked into town and had breakfast on the balcony of a little *comedor* on the Calle de Reforma Agraria. Eleanor tried to make conversation with Cherry and Lorenzo, but Lorenzo seemed in an odd mood, and Cherry was very tired. A black and white television was on in the corner, showing a Tom and Jerry cartoon with the sound turned down. A sudden commotion in the street startled them. A shout went up. The shopkeepers came running to their doorways.

There was silence then and dust rose into the air. A thin man came riding down the street on a scrawny black horse. There was a rope attached to the horse's saddle and it was dragging the bleeding corpse of a young man dressed in a blue Contra uniform. The man dragged the body as far as the church steps, then dropped the rope. The horse reared up on its hind legs.

The body had left streaks of dark blood in the sand. It lay face down, twisted and ridiculous, on the stone steps of the church, the left arm wrapped around the neck, an oozing wound in the back crawling with flies. The man's boots were ripped, revealing blackened toes. Eleanor looked up at the sky and saw six tiny black dots in the clouds. The vultures were beginning to circle.

An old priest with white hair descended the steps of the church. He went down on his knees and took the hand of the dead young man. Some of the people began to hiss and boo and an old man spat on the street. '*Me cago en la hostia,*' he shouted. The priest snapped around, glaring into the crowd, and the old man cursed again as he walked away.

The priest turned the body over and it leaked dark blood over

236

the white steps. He shook his head and took the crucifix from around his neck, kissed it and touched the dead boy's lips with it. He folded the arms across the body and closed the eyes. Then he took a little black book from his pocket and knelt in the sunshine, touching the boy's head, praying in whispers.

After a few moments the crowd began to disperse, leaving the priest still praying over the dead boy. Two nuns came out of the church carrying white sheets. They stood still, heads bowed, fingering rosary beads, until the priest had finished. Then they knelt down on the steps and began to wrap the body in the sheets.

'Smokes,' Eleanor said quietly, 'why did they do that? Why did they bring that poor boy in here like that?'

'They do it to discourage collaborators.'

'I thought all these people were supposed to be on the same bloody side,' Frank muttered.

Smokes sat down and said nothing.

'There's supposed to be rules,' Frank said. 'Even in war, there's things you don't do. Sure, everyone knows that.'

'Frank,' Smokes sighed, 'that guy probably killed more people than Teddy fucking Kennedy.'

Cherry sniggered, a little too loudly.

'It's not right,' Eleanor said. 'That's a human being. He has a mother too. He has a family.'

'I ain't saying it's right, Eleanor. It's just the way things are.'

'Well, I agree with Eleanor,' Frank said. 'Even a louse deserved something.'

He glanced over at her. Still she refused to look at him.

'Can we go now?' she said. 'I'm really not feeling the best.'

Down in the street the church doors opened. The two nuns and the old priest began to manoeuvre the body up the steps while patches of blood seeped through the linen.

Half an hour later, Smokes and Cherry were down at the back doors of the concert hall helping Guapo to pack away the gear when a very attractive blonde woman stepped out of the crowd, shielding her eyes with her hand.

'Hey, Smokie,' the woman said. 'Is that you?'

He pretended not to hear.

'Hey, Smo-kie,' she called. 'You still listening to Abba?'

He stood up and turned. 'Oh, my God, hi!' He grinned. 'How are you? God, what a surprise.'

She laughed. 'Yes, yes. So did you ever get my lipstick off your window? You were great last night by the way. You were a lot better last night, I think, than the other night I met you.'

Smokes tittered frantically. 'Ulla,' he said, 'this is my girlfriend, Cherry Balducci. Umm, Ulla, I don't know your second name?'

'Planker.' Ulla smiled. 'I didn't know you had a girlfriend, Smokie.'

'Oh, yeah, yeah. This is my main squeeze, you know? So, how's the old teethpulling? Ulla's a dentist, Cherry. She's, you know, pulling out molars for the revolution.'

'How nice,' Cherry said.

'Yes,' said Ulla a little nervously. 'Yes, right, well, nice to see you again anyway, Smokie. *Ciao, bambino.*'

Ulla turned and walked away. Smokes lit a cigarette, knelt down and started unravelling the cables.

'God, look at this mess,' he said. 'This is really a terrible mess.'

'Smokes, who was that?'

'Who? Oh, just this dentist. I met her with Eleanor. She was on the same flight.'

'While I was away?'

He felt the sun on the back of his neck. 'Yeah,' he said. 'While you were away. I think so.'

He stood up, turned around and beamed at her. He noticed Guapo silently chuckling at him by the doors of the hall. He started untwisting the flexes again.

'Look at this fucking mess here. Jeez, we really oughta get a roadie. You think Keith Richards has to do all this shit himself? No way, man. No way.'

'So, what happened, Smokes? Did you fuck her?'

'*What?*' he whinnied. 'Jeez, Cherry, what are you, nuts?'

'My God,' she said, 'you're lying. I can't believe you're lying to me.'

Smokes whimpered with nervous laughter. He looked her in the eye.

'I'm not lying. Honest to God, baby. I wouldn't lie to you. You know that.'

He tried to kiss her, but she pulled away, eying him with

contempt. He touched her chin and looked at her very tenderly.

'Come on, sweets. I wouldn't lie to you, honey.'

'Honey,' she said, 'you are a scumsucking, pathetic, dick-brained little shithead and you would lie until piss turns to Pepsi.'

Guapo grinned at him, closed his eyes, stuck out his tongue and drew one finger slowly across his throat.

'Cherry,' Smokes said, sounding offended, 'Jeez, why do you get off on hurting me so much?'

A flock of white larks descended, squabbling, into the square. She unpeeled his fingers from her face.

'Smokie,' she said, 'I think you'd better start telling me the truth, man. Or, so help me, I'll get out that Aka and I'll blow your fucking balls all the way back to Bleeker Street.'

34

Holyhead

ONE WARM NIGHT in the summer of 1976, when she had been married for sixteen years, Eleanor Little told her husband that she wanted to leave him. They sat in the living room of their beautiful house, weeping in each other's arms, trying to talk about what to do. He begged her not to go. He pleaded with her until she said she would stay.

They tried again. But drink had taken her over now. She would wake up sweating and hot and thirsty. Her sweat would smell of whisky and gin, and her first thought every day would be about how to get something to drink.

One morning Frank found Johnny in the bath with his arms and legs blackened with bruises. He made his son tell him who had done this to him. He woke his wife up and screamed at her. He told her if she touched him again he would kill her.

He began to take his son to his own mother's house regularly, eventually for days at a stretch. Eleanor accused him of trying to take him away from her. They spent night after night fighting.

One day Frank's father came into the office and asked him what the hell was going on. Johnny had been so scared the day before that he had cut the flex of his grandparents' telephone with scissors, so that his mother would not be able to ring him. He had been sick with fear, Frank's father said. He was getting up at night and vomiting because he was so afraid. He had been telling his grandmother about some of the things that were going on in the house.

'It isn't right, Frank,' his father said. 'This isn't the way it's supposed to be, you know.'

Eleanor kept drinking. She was staying in bed all day now.

Frank and Johnny hardly ever saw her any more. One night there was a ferocious argument. She fell down the stairs and bruised her face so badly that when the police came they took Frank away for beating his wife and he spent the night in a cell in Dalkey police station.

Next morning was 20 September 1977, Frank and Eleanor's seventeenth wedding anniversary. Eleanor woke up early. Johnny was still in bed. She got the first bus down to Dun Laoghaire and waited for the bank to open. She took three hundred pounds from their joint account, walked down to the pier in tears and bought a ticket for the boat train to London.

She posted a card from Holyhead station. 'I'm sorry, Frank,' it said. 'I'm going away now. I will always love you both, but I just can't go on like this.'

35

A Dream of Ice Cream

WHEN CHERRY ARRIVED BACK at Claudette by herself Eleanor thought she looked in a very bad mood. She didn't say anything, but she was red in the face and she was chewing her nails and chain-smoking. When Eleanor approached her she smiled and said nothing was wrong. But when Smokes returned, looking white and exhausted, it was obvious that they'd had an argument.

'Better hit the road,' he said, attempting enthusiasm. 'It's only twenty miles to Ocotal, but the sooner there the better.'

'Fucking putz,' Cherry breathed.

Guapo appeared ten minutes later. He seemed to understand what was happening and he said he would sit up front with Smokes. '*Marilyn y yo*,' he said. '*Ella es mi amor*.' Eleanor sat in the back with the others. Cherry pulled a Walkman out of her rucksack, turned her back to the others, clamped the headphones over her ears and closed her eyes.

They drove down to the doors of the hall and Smokes and Guapo loaded up the van. Then they headed out of the town, travelling north now, up towards the border. They passed through the tiny towns of Achuapa and Condega, San Juan de Limay and Pueblo Nuevo. Tall, dense evergreens blocked out the light and the air was heavy with the scent of eucalyptus and pine resin.

They passed through Yalaguina and into Somoto, then turned on to the sandy road to Ocotal. All along the roadside, battered tanks lay rusting in the ditches. They drove for about ten miles, passing timber huts with panting dogs slumped in the porches and over a creek full of weed, where flat boats bobbed at creosote-stained mooring posts. A line of red pines stood stark against the sapphire glow of the sky.

They drove into the town and parked Claudette down by the river. Jagged plum-coloured rocks broke through the surface of the foaming water. When they stepped out of the van the heat sucked the breath out of their lungs, and the air smelt of honeysuckle. Ocotal was a clean, whitewashed town, with red-roofed adobe houses, a line of shops and a white wooden church surrounded by trees with whitewashed trunks. Some of the shops had delicate gold jewellery in the windows. There were posters advertising tours out to the gold mines on the Río Coco. There was a school and a small health clinic. Everything felt orderly and calm. For a town in the middle of a war zone it seemed incredibly peaceful.

They had *refrescos* in the Café La Cabana, sitting in total silence. Frank refused to take his sunglasses off, even though the light was dim in the back of the café. When he asked for the salt, Smokes passed it to him without looking up from his food. 'Well,' Eleanor sighed, 'we're all a little tired today.' Still nobody said anything.

When Cherry went to the bathroom, Eleanor followed.

'Cherry, love,' she said, 'is there anything ailing you?'

Cherry said no, there wasn't, she just wasn't feeling too good. A touch of Somoza's Revenge, she said, clutching her stomach. And her period was coming on too.

'Oh.' Eleanor nodded. 'Being a woman is the hardest of all, and what sympathy do we ever get?'

'Yeah, really.'

Eleanor filled the sink with hot water, took a bar of soap from her bag and washed her face and her throbbing hands. 'You're not having a row with himself, love? You can tell me to stop being a busybody now, if you like.'

Cherry looked away. 'It's nothing much worth talking about.'

When they'd finished eating, Cherry and Lorenzo went back into the town to buy water while Guapo and Smokes started to unload the guitars and amplifiers. When that was done they strolled off to get a beer. Frank stayed behind counting out his money and pretending to look for something. Eleanor sat on a shaded park bench reading a copy of *Newsweek* which she'd found on the side of the street. After a while he came over to her.

'What's up with Cherry?' he asked.

'They had a tiff.'

He nodded, sitting down on the bench beside her. She crossed her legs and turned away. 'God, all these rows,' he murmured. 'And there's really no need for any of them.'

She flicked the pages of her magazine.

'Eleanor,' he said, 'I suppose it wouldn't matter if I apologized again?'

She shook her head. 'That's too easy, Frank. You say what you damn well please, and then you think sorry takes it all away. You were always the same.'

Across the river, a young woman was leaning out of the top window of a tall pink stucco building, banging a rug against the wall.

'Please,' he said. 'I'm very sorry, Eleanor. You don't deserve to be spoken to like that. I don't know what comes over me.'

She turned to look at him.

'You wouldn't bloody speak to Veronica like that. She wouldn't put up with your hurtfulness, I hope.'

'I'm not talking about Veronica.' He paused, wiping the sweat from his eyebrows. 'I'm talking about you, Eleanor.'

'God. That makes a change anyway.'

'That's not very fair.'

She scoffed. 'Don't you talk to me about fairness, Frank. I sometimes wonder if you'll ever know what those times were like for me.'

'What do you mean by that?'

She peered down at the river and took off her glasses.

'What do you mean, Eleanor?'

She pursed her lips. 'Well, then, do you think it was nice for me, Frank, when you went off with Veronica? And before that, when I needed help, and you weren't there?'

'Where was I?'

'You were very closed. You knew I had a problem and you never did anything to help me. You let me lose my self-respect.'

'That's not true, love.'

'You know damn well it is.'

'It isn't Eleanor, love. I often asked you to see a doctor. If you needed any kind of help it could have been arranged.'

She raised her voice. 'See? That's the whole point. You asked

244

me, but you never said you'd come with me, no. You thought paying for everything was enough.'

'That's not what I meant.'

'You should have helped me, Frank. You don't ask a drowning man if he'd like to be saved. You do it.'

'I tried to help you, Eleanor. I wasn't very happy either.'

She pulled a tube of suntan oil from her pocket and began to smear the contents on her arms.

'I really don't blame you,' she said. 'You just couldn't bear it that I wasn't what you thought. That's what made you unhappy. You couldn't bear it that I wasn't perfect because Frank Little would have to have the perfect wife, because Frank Little and his poor bloody family are so perfect too. You let everything go and you said nothing. That was your way of accepting it. You turned out to be very cold, Frank. I never thought you would, but you did.'

'God, now, Eleanor,' he said, 'that's not how I remember things.'

She nodded angrily. 'And you thought love was finding some-one exactly like you. And it's not, Frank. It's not.'

'I was very fond of you, Eleanor. I mean, if you think back a sec, I was mad about you.'

'After we had Johnny,' she said, 'did you ever once ask me how I felt about anything? Did you ever ask me for an opinion? Did you ever tell me I looked nice?'

He looked down at the ground. The chestnut-coloured asphalt was soft under his feet.

'I'm sure I did. Of course I did.'

'Well,' she said, 'I don't remember that.'

'Eleanor, I always thought about you, love. I never . . .'

'And when Catherine died?' she interrupted. 'Did you think of me then, Frank?'

He felt the sweat trickle down his spine. 'Of course I did. God, what do you mean, Eleanor?'

She closed her magazine and stood up. 'We'll say no more about it. I'm the fool to even care any more.'

He gazed up at her and tried to laugh. 'But there's two different stories going on here, Eleanor. I mean, we can't both be right after all.'

She looked down at him, shaking her head.

'That's the really sad thing about you, Frank. You don't even realize that we can.'

She put on a scarf and went off to Mass.

He sat by himself, feeling shocked. He ran her words over again in his mind. They were not true, he told himself. How could they be true? She was the one who had not understood. He had tried, time and again. When other men would have walked out, he had stayed. He thought about the nights he had held their child in his arms and listened to him crying. The mornings he had begged her to stop hurting their child. He thought about the loneliness he used to feel in those days, the loneliness of knowing that the biggest risk in his life had been a terrible mistake. The sickening dread that used to gnaw at his gut when he would realize this. He had married the only woman he had ever loved and it had been a mistake. But yet it wasn't a mistake. He had Johnny at least. He thought about the days he had worked fifteen hours only to come home and sleep alone on a couch in the front room. He thought about the lies he had told and the spite he had fought against, the fear and the guilt and the shrieking rage, and through it all Johnny had been the only consolation. Whatever else had happened, there had always been Johnny. That, and the knowledge that he had tried to do his best. And now she wanted to take even that away. He sat by himself and wondered why.

When Smokes and Guapo came back from the bar they looked gloomy and tired.

'Frank,' Smokes said sulkily, 'we found a *hospedaje* where they won't ask no questions. It'd do us all good to sleep in a bed tonight.'

'Oh, great, son. That'd be a treat alright. We'll just wait for the girls and Lorenzo to come back.'

Smokes nodded. 'Guapo'll take you later. I have to go see a guy.'

'Come on and sit down, Smokes. Just for a minute.'

'I said I have to see a guy, man. Someone has to keep this fucking show on the road, you know? OK?'

He grabbed a notebook from the van and stalked off towards the town. Guapo sat down on the bench and lit a cigarette. He winked at Frank and giggled.

'Marilyn fight with the Cherry,' he explained. 'He is crazy now.'

Frank tried to smile. 'Oh, well, that happens.'

Guapo nodded. 'Oh, *sí*. It happens. *Es verdad*.'

The day was getting hotter and they went to sit in the back of Claudette. Guapo opened bottles of beer and gave one to Frank. Then they took out a deck of cards and began to play poker for matchsticks. But Frank couldn't concentrate. His wife's words kept coming back into his mind. What had she meant? Why was she saying all these things to him now? What difference did it even make now?

'Guapo, son?' Frank said. 'Did Johnny ever say anything to you about us? About Eleanor and me?'

Guapo looked up blearily. '*Sí*, Frank,' he said. '*Claro que sí*.'

'Can you tell me what he said?'

'Oh, Frank. *Pero es muy difícil. No sé las palabras en inglés*.'

'Could you try, Guapo?'

Guapo pulled a face. He looked around and grinned.

'*Bueno*,' he said. '*Me contó un cuento una vez*.'

'*No entiendo*, Guapo,' Frank said.

Guapo looked around again. He stood up and went over to Smokes's bag, rummaging in it for a moment. He picked out Smokes's paperback copy of *One Hundred Years of Solitude* and pointed at the cover.

'*Un cuento*,' he said.

'A book?'

'*No, no, hermano*,' Guapo said, flicking through the pages.

'A story then?'

'*Sí, sí*. A story. Johnny. The story is what you tell to him? When he is sleeping?'

'Sorry?'

Guapo folded his hands together and placed them against the side of his face. He paused, then closed his eyes and made a loud snoring noise. 'When he is sleeping.' He beamed. 'He is a little boy.'

'A bedtime story?' Frank said. Guapo pointed his finger and nodded.

'*Sí*,' he said. '*Eso es*.'

He scratched his head and searched for words.

'*El cuento trabata de un rey*, Frank. *¿Sabe?*'

'No.'

'*Un rey, hombre*. He live in *un castillo. Un palacio enorme*.'

'I don't understand, Guapo. A castle, is it?'

Guapo clicked his tongue. He looked down at the table and put his head in his hands, drumming his fingers against his cheeks. And then suddenly he smiled. He reached out and began to shuffle through the playing cards. '*Momentito*,' he said. He found a card and held it up. It was the king of hearts.

'This man, Frank,' Guapo said. '*¿Cómo se llama?*'

'The king? Is it some story about a king?'

'*Sí*. The king. *Tiene mucho dinero, OK?*'

'He's rich?'

Guapo nodded.

'He is rich. But not the happy man, Francisco. His woman, she is beautiful.'

Guapo picked up the queen of clubs and raised his eyebrows.

'The queen,' Frank said.

'*Sí*. The queen is very beautiful. And the boy.'

He tapped his finger against the jack of hearts.

'That's the jack,' Frank said. 'You mean the prince.'

'*Sí, sí. Su hijo*. Prince. *Bueno*, the queen is beautiful. The little boy also is beautiful. *Pero al fondo está triste*.'

Guapo pointed towards his heart. '*Aquí*,' he said. '*En su corazón*. He is sad, man. *¿Verdad?*'

Frank nodded. 'I understand.'

'*Ay, es difícil*,' Guapo sighed. '*Bueno*, the king. He talk to *el Señor. ¿Me entiendes?*'

'The king talks to a man?'

'*No, no*,' Guapo said, exasperated. '*¡Dios!*'

Guapo pointed upwards. He made the sign of the Cross, joined his hands and raised his eyebrows again.

'Oh, yes, Guapo. God. I understand.'

'The king talks to the God. And everything he touch with his hand will be *helado*.'

'Ice cream?' Frank said.

'*Sí, hombre*.'

'He wants everything he touches to be ice cream?'

Guapo clicked his fingers. '*Exacto*.'

'When he touch with his hand, he want ice cream. The God

says, no. The king says, *sí, sí*. The God says, OK, bad news for you, King, but it will be ice cream.'

'Alright, Guapo. I have you.'

'OK, he is a happy man now. He touch the table. Ice cream. The chair is ice cream. Everything is ice cream. But, then, the bad news. He touch his woman and his prince and they are ice cream. And *mañana, mucho calor*. The sun is hot. And they are water now. His woman and his prince.'

'They melt?'

'*Correcto*, Francisco. They melt. And so the king is *loco*.'

Guapo shrugged. '*Eso es*. Is the story.'

Frank laughed, unsure what to say.

'*¿Me entiendes, Francisco? Mi inglés es fatal.*'

'No, no, I understand you, son. I just don't remember telling him that story.'

'*Yo no sé*, Frank. *Eso es lo que me dijo.* He say to me, is the story he remembers. He sees this story in his dreams.'

'Really? I don't remember that now.'

'*Sí.* And in the north Johnny has a woman. She is in the house of ice cream and he is in love.'

Frank looked up at him.

'What?' he said.

Guapo wrapped his arms around himself and began to make kissing sounds.

'He is in love, Francisco. *Una mujer en el norte.* In Corinto. Where we go soon.'

'But Smokes told me that wasn't serious.'

Guapo rolled his eyes. '*Pero, sí.*' He nodded. 'The Johnny say it to me, not to the Marilyn. He is in love, like the songs.'

'What songs?'

'Each night,' Guapo crooned, 'I ask the stars up above. Oh, why must I be a teenager in love?'

'And what's her name? This woman.'

'Pilar,' he said brightly. '*Se llama Pilar.* She is in the ice cream house. *La Glaceria Elvis Presley, se llama. Me gusto mucho el nombre.* She is beautiful like the queen.'

'And Johnny told you he was in love with her?'

'Oh, *sí*.' Guapo chuckled. '*Pero a veces no decía la verdad. A veces fue un embustero. ¿Entiendes?*'

'No, Guapo. I'm sorry.'

'*Mentiroso*. Many stories, Francisco.'

'Oh, well. I know that alright.'

Guapo sniggered and hung his head. Then, after a moment, he reached out and began to shuffle through the playing cards again.

'Here is your prince, *hombre*,' he said. 'How is he called?'

Frank looked down at the card.

'That's the joker, son.'

'*Sí*.' Guapo grinned. 'Johnny the joker. *Exacto*.'

36

Let It Be Me

ELEANOR LEFT THE CHURCH and walked around the little town of Ocotal. It was hot, but this was the part of the day she liked best, the two hot hours before the rain. Soldiers were walking up the main street, nailing notices to the lampposts. The notices bore the words *Servicio Militar Popular* at the top in red letters. They said that all notified men had to be in the church square at seven thirty in the morning, and that buses would be waiting there to take them to the training camp at Rivas. *¡PATRIA LIBRE O MORIR!* the notices announced in conclusion.

Eleanor went into a little café and ordered a *cortado*. She sat outside in the shade of the canopy and slipped off her sandals, feeling the warmth of the pink tiles against the soles of her feet. A gentle breeze blew down the street, raising clouds of fine white dust. The light was deepening to the colour of copper. In the distance she saw Frank and Guapo walking quickly southwards out of the town in the direction of the violet hills. They were striding along purposefully, swinging their arms. Frank was carrying his camera and wearing a hat. She was going to stand up and call out to them, but she changed her mind and just watched them go.

A fat green iguana loped across the street. It was exactly the colour of avocados, she thought. She watched as it eyed the world, scuttled forward, then stopped again, its black tongue flicking at flies. A young boy wandered past selling roses and oranges and carrying a parrot in a white cage. The parrot was hopping from leg to leg, squawking gloomily. It was for sale too, the boy said, but nobody wanted to buy it. She gave him five dollars and he ran into the café and came out again, clutching

a guitar. He sat down on the steps and sang her a song about
Nicaragua.

> *A través de las páginas fatales de la historia,*
> *Nuestra tierra está hecha de vigor y de gloria*
> *Nuestra tierra está hecha para la Humanidad.*
> *Pueblo vibrante, fuerte, apasionada, altivo;*
> *Pueblo que tiene la conciencia de ser vivo,*
> *Y que, reuniendo sus energías en haz*
> *Portentoso, a la Patria vigoroso demuestra*
> *Que puede bravamente presentar en su diestra*
> *El acero de guerra o el olivo de paz.*

The song was by Rubén Darío, he told her. He had learnt it in
school. He was the only one of his family who could read properly. Rubén Darío was a very famous Nicaraguan poet and he had
travelled all over the world. He was going to travel himself, the
boy said. He was going to be a sailor when he grew up. He was
going to sail around the world like Rubén Darío. He would go
to Africa and see the pyramids. He would sail to Zanzibar. He
would sail to the North Pole and see igloos.

Eleanor bought him a Coca-Cola. He said he was trying to
teach the parrot to speak, but it wouldn't. Some parrots could
recite poems, he said, and others could tell the time. There was
a parrot in a zoo in Ecuador that could read your mind and do
multiplication. But this parrot would not even say hello in the
mornings. It was a dunce. He laughed and tapped the side of his
head.

She asked the boy why he didn't just let it go. He shrugged
and poked a twig through the bars of the cage. Because he liked
the colour of its feathers, he told her, and because it had taken so
long to catch.

That night, Frank sat at the bar in the Centro Cultural Carlos
Fonseca knocking back glasses of iced rum and Coke and looking
down over the balcony at the dance floor.

The hall was filling up now for the Saturday dance. Taped
guitar music stuttered out of the speakers, but nobody seemed to
be listening. The young people stood around in groups, talking,

laughing and whispering to each other. The hall was alive with the murmur of expectant conversation. The smell of toothpaste and beer and cheap perfume drifted through the room. After a while a few policemen arrived, but that didn't seem to cause a problem. They wandered around in the crowd, kissing girls, shaking hands with the boys, sucking on bottles of rum.

At half past nine on the dot, the main lights went out and the white spots sprang on. The crowd cheered as Smokes took the stage alone. He bowed low and sat down behind his drum kit, pulling the microphone to his mouth.

'*Buenas noches,*' he shouted. He waved his beer bottle and took a swig. He held his sticks in the air and clicked them together. '*Uno, dos, tres, cuatro,*' he yelled. '*Vamos a bailar.*' He bashed the cymbals. He whooped into the echoing mike. He stamped down hard on the bass pedal, pounding out a steady chugging rhythm. The crowd roared and began to dance, clapping along in time.

Smokes thumped hard for a minute or two and then Guapo ran on and plugged into his amp. He bopped from side to side, slapping out a throbbing bass figure. The crowd yelled again as Lorenzo strode lazily on to the stage, a cigarette stuck to his lower lip, his guitar already round his neck. He nodded briefly towards the crowd and lashed out a couple of bar chords. He strolled up towards the speakers and the screaming feedback wailed. Cherry came on then, waving. Somebody threw a bunch of red roses. She blew a kiss, rolled up her sleeves, hunched over the electric piano and began to hammer the keys.

The young people screamed and stamped. They put their arms around each other's shoulders and jumped up and down. The floorboards shook. Smokes thundered on the snare drums. Lorenzo bounded up to the microphone and began to sing 'Jailhouse Rock'.

The thump of the drums echoed around the tottering town hall. Lorenzo's guitar wailed. Guapo's bass throbbed up through the floorboards. Almost everyone in the room was dancing now. The girls were wearing mid-length flouncing skirts, tight bodices and ribbons in their hair. Silver crucifixes glittered on their necks as they caught the light. The boys had on blue jeans and lurid shirts. They swayed and pranced and snapped their fingers, opened the buttons on their cuffs and rolled up their sleeves. Some of them danced in rings. Others danced with the girls, jiving and twisting, lifting them high in the air, swinging them around in their arms.

Alone at the back of the hall, Frank ordered another glass of rum. He drank it in one slug and called for a half-pint bottle. He looked around again at the heaving, colourful mass of bodies, but he couldn't see Eleanor anywhere. He watched the Desperados de Amor and drank until the bottle was almost empty.

Slowly the night seemed to melt into a blur of colour. The young people were holding each other now, slow-dancing under the revolving mirror ball. There were others in the dark corners too, kissing passionately, pushing their bodies together. He remembered what Guapo had told him. Tomorrow these young men would be going to the war. Tonight they were misbehaving. Tonight they were saying goodbye. He looked down at them and realized then that for many of them this would be the last time they would ever dance, or hold another person in their arms. It would be the last time they would get drunk and scream and hug their friends and jump around. The last time they would listen to loud rock and roll music and kiss someone they cared for or someone they shouldn't have been kissing at all. The last night in Ocotal.

He looked up at the stage. Smokes was standing at the microphone, singing 'Let it be Me'. He was completely soaked with sweat, bedraggled hair stuck to his scalp. His shirt was open to the navel and his eyes were closed as he sang. Cherry and Guapo were singing in harmony, their mouths so close that they were almost kissing.

I bless the day I found you
And promise to stay around you
Now and for always
Just let it be me.
Don't ever leave me lonely
Promise you'll love me only
Now and for always
Please let it be me.

Frank was very drunk now. His head felt heavy, his neck weak. He closed his eyes and a swishing sound filled his ears, like waves breaking over wet sand. He tried to remember something. He saw a man walking down a beach on a cold sunny day in Bray, holding a young baby in his arms. He saw the pastel blues of bathing huts and the pinks of raspberry ripple ice creams. He heard the harsh cry of seagulls, the crunch of shoes on broken shells and dried seaweed. And he remembered a story about a king who had once wished for heaven, only to have it melt away in his hands.

The whine of an electric guitar burst into his consciousness, screeching out a Chuck Berry solo. When he opened his eyes, Lorenzo was up close by the microphone, legs spread wide, shaking his head and spitting out the words to 'Roll Over Beethoven'.

'*Nos vamos, compañeros*,' Smokes was yelling. 'Get up and fucking dance.' Cherry was clapping a tambourine in the air and Guapo was whooping into the microphone.

But the young people of Ocotal were not jiving any more. The music was wild and loud, but they were dancing very slowly now, and some of them were not dancing at all. Some of them were drunk. One or two were fighting. And some were standing in the middle of the dance floor, underneath the revolving globe of mirrors, their arms around each other, their heads on one another's shoulders, crying.

37

A Human Heart

AFTER HIS WIFE HAD LEFT HIM, Frank's life began to change very quickly. He could not sleep any more. He grew afraid of the dark. He could not sleep with the light off in the bedroom that he had once shared with her. He would wake up shaking from nightmares.

His son was thirteen then. Very quickly, he seemed to change too. He grew sullen and stopped talking to his father, sometimes saying nothing at all for a whole night. He began to wear black clothes; he would wear nothing unless it was black. It would infuriate his father more than almost anything else. 'Black bloody clothes,' he'd say. 'Here comes Father Johnny Little again.' He would tell his son that he looked like a bloody corpse or a Christian Brother, but his son wouldn't even laugh. He would sit with his eyes fixed on the television, flicking from channel to channel with the remote control, refusing to say a word.

He tried to encourage his son to bring his friends home from school, but Johnny never would. He couldn't bring his friends home here, he told his father. He would laugh, bitterly, when Frank asked him why. He would laugh as though the answer was obvious, and soon he could not say the word *here*, meaning home, without a sneer appearing on his lips.

One day Frank got a telephone call at work from the head priest at Johnny's school. The priest wanted to know where Johnny was. He had not been attending classes. Was he ill? Was there something wrong at home?

That night Frank asked Johnny what he had been doing with himself for the last month. He just wanted the truth, he said. There would be no punishment: he simply wanted to know. Johnny told him he had been walking the streets, getting the bus into town to play the gaming machines in the amusement arcades on the quays, hanging around in the Dandelion Market, the Botanical Gardens in Glasnevin, or the bowling alley in Stillorgan. He'd had a row with one of the teachers.

His father laughed. There was nothing wrong with the occasional mitch from school, but there were exams coming up and Johnny would have to think about them. He made his son go back to school. He made him promise to say if he was ever in any trouble. There was no problem that couldn't be sorted out, he said, if they were friends, and if they were honest with each other.

'I could never talk to my old man,' Frank would say. 'I don't want that for you and me, son. Do you understand?'

Johnny would nod but never say anything.

For a while, he did go back to school and he seemed to do quite well. The art teacher said he was very good with his hands. He liked History and English too. He got a good report at Easter and won second place in an essay competition. He was picked for the debating team. And then one May morning Johnny came down to breakfast and told his father he just didn't want to go to school any more. Frank laughed.

'Son, you're fourteen. Why do you think I'm out on the streets day and night? It's so you don't have to do the fucking same.'

'I'm fifteen,' Johnny said. 'I want a job. I want to go to London and get a job in a recording studio. You're always going on about how you left school when you were bloody three or something.'

'I was thirteen, and anyway that's different, son. It was a different time in those days.'

'Funny how it was alright for you, and it isn't for me.'

'Don't say that to me, Johnny. Now your mother's gone, we have to be buddies.'

His son rolled his eyes. 'Funny how everything was so great in bloody Francis Street.'

'God, what's up with you these days, Johnny? Do you miss your mother, son? Is that it?'

Johnny shook his head. 'No,' he said. 'I don't. And nothing's fucking well up with me.'

'Now, don't you speak to me like that, Johnny. Don't use that language with me.'

'Oh, right. Funny how it's alright for you to use it. I heard you use it often enough.'

'Yes, well,' Frank said. 'You do as I say, son, not as I do.'

Johnny and Frank began to have terrible arguments. Johnny would curse at his father just to annoy him. He would steal money from the pockets of his father's jacket and then lie about it. He would go the whole weekend without saying a single word. The head priest rang up again. Johnny would have to be expelled, he said, if he didn't start coming to school every day.

Frank stopped working nights so that he could be at home with his son. They began to learn to cook together. They made simple things, lasagna, casseroles, spaghetti carbonara. He began to drive him to school again, the way he had done when Johnny was a child. He would wait outside the school gates to make sure he had gone in. He would wait for a quarter of an hour and then drive to work.

For his sixteenth birthday, Johnny asked for an electric guitar. Frank took him into McCullough Piggot's in Suffolk Street and they got the most expensive guitar in the shop, a Gibson Les Paul. His son's friends began to come around to the house every night then. They had guitars too. Some of them were older than Johnny, and they seemed a little rough. They also wore black clothes and one of them wore a dog collar. But they were only middle-class kids going through a phase, Frank thought, and, anyway, there was never any harm in music. They would sit in the front room playing loud raucous guitar for hours, the same three chords over and over again, but Johnny seemed to be happy. Frank bought him a Marshall amplifier for Christmas. 'Fuck,' Johnny said when he saw it. 'Happy Christmas, Da.' He hugged his father for the first time in two years.

But Frank was not happy. He was not sleeping well and he was tired all the time now. He felt depressed and anxious, permanently in the grip of some kind of vague terror that he could not understand. At work, he began to lose business. Worse, he began not to care. He would get up in the middle of the night and worry about dying. He tried to hide all this from his son, but sometimes he couldn't. And even though Johnny was more communicative, he found himself snapping at him, for the smallest things. He went to see the doctor and started to take anti-depressants.

And then he began to work nights again. He would start at seven or eight, when people were going out for the evening. The other drivers couldn't figure it out. There wasn't another boss in the whole city who worked nights. But Frank Little would work until two or three in the morning, when the nightclubs closed down on the Leeson Street strip. Then he would go for coffee in the Manhattan in Rathmines, or the Gigs Place, or some all-night joint on the Northside full of drunks and prostitutes and off-duty special branch men. When the sun began to come up Frank would drive home. It was the only time he felt content, driving alone through the empty streets of the city. He would go home and make himself tea, sometimes watch a video. He would go to bed at five or six, exhausted. He could sleep then, because there was no darkness to be afraid of any more. At eight thirty or nine the sound of traffic outside would wake him, and he would stagger out of bed, wash, get his son up and ready for the day. Then he would drive him to school and go to work again.

One morning he drove a human heart all the way from Dublin airport to Saint Vincent's hospital in Elm Park, where a dying young man was waiting for a transplant. He sped through the streets of Dublin, a police motorbike up ahead of him on the road, and he thought about the heart on the back seat of his taxi. He wondered what would happen if he just stopped his car and cut that heart open with a knife. He wondered if it would tell him something he didn't know about people and what they were really like.

At ten in the morning he would go home and back to bed. He would sleep until two or three in the afternoon, wake up then, numb and stupid with tiredness, lungs rattling with nicotine. He would shave and take a long shower, and at four o'clock he would drive down to the school, collect his son, bring him home, then make his dinner, watch a few hours of television, check that Johnny was studying, and go back out to work.

One day in 1979, one of the drivers knocked on the door of Frank's office. He said he didn't want to interfere, but some of the men had been talking, and he thought there was something that Frank should know. A week before, one of the other men had been called to McGonagles nightclub in Anne Street at three o'clock in the morning. There had been a punk rock concert at the club. Johnny had been there and he'd been very drunk. The driver had seen him, he was sure. There had been a fight and the police had been involved. He didn't want to interfere, the driver said, but he just thought that Frank should be told. He had sons himself, he said. It was very late at night for a sixteen-year-old to be out on the street.

Frank confronted his son and they fought. Johnny admitted that he had been going into town late at night, sneaking back home before Frank got in. Frank warned him that he would forbid him to go out at all if he had to. He took away Johnny's guitar and locked it in Eleanor's old room.

They began to fight almost every day then. And there were times when Frank lost his temper completely with his son. One morning they argued viciously about the best way to boil an egg and Frank slapped him hard in the face. Johnny left the house that morning and didn't come back for three nights. Frank was wild with worry. When Johnny came back, he held him in his arms and they agreed to make a new start.

One afternoon shortly after that, Frank got a phone call from the police. His son had been arrested in Switzer's for stealing a Christmas candle. He drove down to Pearse Street station to find Johnny locked up in a cell. He said he had wanted the candle as a present for his mother.

When Frank got his son home from the station he dragged him into the kitchen and hit him. Johnny exploded with rage. He stood up and punched his father in the chest and threatened to break his jaw. They held on to each other as they pushed around the kitchen. They argued and shouted late into the night.

The next morning they went to the juvenile court together. The magistrate said Frank would have to give an undertaking to be a responsible parent; otherwise his son could be taken away from him and put into care. There was a very dangerous road ahead for Johnny Little, the magistrate said. In another year he would not be a minor any more. In another year he could be sent to prison.

Once again, they tried to make up. They promised that they

would try to be friends. Frank gave the guitar back. He said he'd allow Johnny to play in a band, even if it meant staying out late during the week, if only Johnny would just tell him the truth. Johnny agreed. Frank bought him a new stereo.

Frank tried to meet another woman. He thought it would be good for Johnny to have a woman's influence in his life. On a Saturday night he would shave early and put on aftershave and go to one of the hotel bars where he knew middle-aged people went to meet each other. He was a taxi driver. A taxi driver got to know secret things about a city – where you could drink after hours, where you could pay men to get someone shot, where middle-aged people went to try and meet each other.

But he had no way with women. They made him nervous. He didn't like disco music. He felt stupid, a man of his age, dancing around to disco music. Once or twice, he met women he liked, but after about ten minutes he could not think of anything to say to them. One night he danced with a woman called Rita and she invited him back to her flat in Raheny. He left her waiting while he went to the toilets to pour cold water over his face. He stood in one of the stalls for almost ten minutes, staring at a graffiti scrawl that said FUCKING UP THE IRA, before deciding that he couldn't do it. He slipped out into the car park without even saying goodbye and drove home.

Johnny got into trouble at school again and was suspended for a month. One night, shortly after he went back, Frank caught him smoking a joint and threw him out of the house. When he returned next morning, Frank didn't ask where he had been. His son started going out with an older girl whom Frank didn't like at all. He began to slope around the house with the same old sullen expression on his face. He went out every night with his guitar under his arm, refusing to say where he was going.

Frank would try to sleep, with his light on and his radio playing quietly, waiting for Johnny to come home. All night long he would listen to the sports channel or the BBC World Service, to news of wars and disasters and earthquakes in strange faraway places with exotic names that he knew he would never see. He wondered if he would be lonely for the rest of his life.

Then he began to go out at night again, because he could not bear to be alone any more. He knew it was wrong. He knew he should have been at home every night, waiting for his son, but he couldn't stand the loneliness. He would do anything not to be alone in this house full of memories. He telephoned friends he had not seen in years. He contacted people he did not even like and went out with them for long nights in smoky pubs. They would always want to know what had happened between him and Eleanor. He would come home drunk, close his front door and straight away feel crushingly lonely again, as though he had not spoken to anyone in days.

He stopped swimming. He began to put on weight. He began to let his appearance go and to drink too much whisky. He began to take valium and mandrax. He was prescribed stronger anti-depressants. One night he was so lonely that he drove to the lanes behind Mount Street where he knew the prostitutes lived. He sat there for two hours, trembling with nerves, trying to summon up the courage to ring one of their doorbells.

He stopped washing every day. He wore his dirty clothes until they stank. The drivers at work would joke about it; they would pinch their noses when he left the room. There were nights when Frank drove his taxi down on to Sandymount Strand and looked out at the sea, wishing to Christ that he had the courage to drive his car in and drown himself. Things Frank Little would never have thought about he began to contemplate now, as a matter of course.

One afternoon in 1980 his son came home drunk from town with a Mohican haircut and a tattoo of a broken heart on his wrist. When Frank saw the haircut he nearly lost his mind. He and his son fought terribly. He hit his son in the mouth and Johnny threatened to kill him. He said it was all Frank's fault that his mother had gone away. He screamed and raged. He picked up a glass and smashed it against the wall. Frank found himself crying.

'You little fucking bastard,' he wept. 'How can you hurt me like that?'

His son tried to apologize, but Frank slapped him away.

'Go to your mother, you little fuck, if you fucking love her so much. You're like her anyway. Why don't you just fucking go with her and let me be?'

Later that night Johnny knocked on the door of his bedroom. He came in and hugged his father and told him he was sorry.

Frank put his arms around his son and the two of them sobbed with desperation.

Johnny began to stay at home then. He began to cook for his father. And whenever his band was playing he would insist that his father came along. Frank went to see them – the Bitter Pills – playing in the Project Arts Centre, the Baggot Inn, the Magnet Bar in Pearse Street. They always played support, to the Bogey Boys, the New Versions, the Brush Shiels Band and the Radiators from Space. Once they even supported U2. Frank loved to watch his son dancing around on the stage, although he couldn't understand this music at all and the volume made his ears throb. He liked being around his son's friends. He liked talking to them, liked the way they were enthusiastic about everything and never asked any questions. He began to feel a little better and to take care of himself once more. He began to go swimming again, every day, in the heated pool in Fitzpatrick's Castle Hotel in Killiney.

One night that summer he was driving down Dawson Street in a freak hailstorm when a middle-aged woman flagged him down outside the Mansion House. They got talking. She was a widow with a grown-up daughter who was married to a vet and living in Australia. She worked in Kenny's Shoe Shop on Grafton Street. Frank liked this laughing Dublin woman. He liked her voice, its kindness and its warmth. He drove her out to Churchtown and just before she got out of the taxi he asked if she wanted to have a drink with him sometime. She said yes, why not, that would be nice.

That night he told his son about Veronica Grady. He said he hoped Johnny didn't mind, and Johnny laughed and said of course he didn't. The next Saturday they went into town together and Johnny helped his father pick out a new suit and a couple of ties in a trendy shop called Alias Tom. The ties were a little more colourful than Frank would have liked, but his son insisted. 'Go crazy, Da,' he said, laughing. He would want to be looking his best, Johnny said. He would want to be looking well for his date.

They went to dinner in the Grey Door in Pembroke Street and talked for so long they were the last to leave. The week after that they went to the opera. They got tickets for 'Evita' and went to that. They went to see the Bitter Pills playing at an outdoor concert in Blackrock Park. On Stephen's Day that year they went to the races in Leopardstown. Frank loved being with this woman. She made him feel human again. She made him feel like a man.

After three months, Frank and Veronica decided that they wanted to live together. It happened very simply. She said she was looking for a commitment. She was having a lovely time, she said, but she had come to care very deeply for Frank, and she wasn't a girl any more. Frank said that was fine. He was looking for commitment too. They talked about him selling up and moving in with her and they wondered what was the right thing to do. Sometimes when he thought about Eleanor he would have an attack of guilt. He would discuss it with Veronica and she always seemed to understand. She was never unpleasant about it. Once they were truthful with each other, she could put up with a lot, she told him. In time he came to feel that he could tell this woman anything. It was something to do with age, he knew. Young people talked about honesty, but older people could actually *be* honest. He told her this and she laughed. He thought about Eleanor again, but she had never even telephoned after all. She was probably with somebody else herself, for all he knew. Frank began to think about the future. It was exciting. The prospect of not having to live life from one week to the next filled him with joy. It was not as exciting as being young again, but it was certainly the next best thing. And in the end they agreed that it was more simple for her to move in with him.

Johnny never got on with Veronica. She was relaxed with him. She said she didn't mind where he went or what he did. She said he was old enough to make his own decisions, and as time passed he seemed to resent this. It was odd, but Frank noticed that Johnny seemed actually to want her to be angry if he came home late or cursed. His son began to pick arguments with Veronica. He would leave the room if she argued back. Soon, if she criticized him at all, he would go upstairs and pack a bag and leave the house. There were many nights when Frank and Veronica drove around the streets of Dublin trying to find him. Veronica tried to be patient, but sometimes she would tell Frank that she thought it would be better for her to move out again. She was not Johnny's mother, she said. She could never be his mother, that was too much to ask of her. There were nights when he had to plead with her not to leave him. She told him she didn't want to go, but that something would have to be done about Johnny.

Frank quarrelled bitterly with his son. He said he loved Veronica and wouldn't have her life made difficult. He asked Johnny if he wanted to live with them, or go and find his mother in England. Johnny was seventeen then. He didn't want to live with anyone, he said. He hated his father and his mother.

'You fucked me up,' he yelled. 'The two of you fucked me up. You never gave a damn about me.'

Frank threw him out of the house that night and told him never to come back.

A few nights after Johnny left, the telephone rang. It was Eleanor. She had come back to Ireland and was staying with her sister in Chapelizod. She knew about Veronica, she said, and she didn't want to come back to Frank anyway. He asked if she wanted to meet and she said no. He said he wanted to explain about Veronica. She told him she wished him the best, but that she wasn't interested in explanations. They talked on the telephone for nearly an hour, the two of them numb with loss. They wondered where they had gone wrong. They said all the things that people say when they lose their love. They had worked hard. They had done all the things that people are supposed to do. But Frank and Eleanor had simply lost their love, in the way that happens sometimes, almost imperceptibly, when luck runs out and the dream of love melts away into nothing more than a set of arrangements.

Johnny came back to his father's house for a week. He and Veronica fought again and he said he wanted to go and live with his mother. He said he was sorry for hurting Frank's feelings, but he thought that if he could get to know his mother things would calm down in his life. Frank said he understood. He and his son agreed that they would meet each other every Saturday morning.

Some Saturday mornings Johnny would turn up at the car park of the Victor Hotel. Other mornings he wouldn't. Frank would sit by himself, waiting for hours, before going back home to Veronica. And some Saturdays he was so hurt that he would not go home. He would go to a film for the afternoon. He would sit in the cinema and watch the same film twice over to fill in the time. Sometimes he would drive out into the countryside by himself. He would drive to Glendalough and walk around the lakes. He would drive out to Poulaphouca, Greystones, Delgany, Avondale, the places he had gone to with Eleanor before they were married. When he got home he would lie to Veronica about all the things he and Johnny had done. He would tell her how well they had got on with each other. He would lie because he was so hurt and because he could not bear her sympathy any more.

And then things seemed somehow to improve again. His son began to see him a little more often. They went for drives and walks together. Sometimes they went to the matinée of a play. Johnny was in his final year at school now. He seemed to be getting on well with his teachers and to have some good friends. He was enjoying living with his mother, he said. It was nice to have a chance to catch up. He began to talk about university. He thought he would like to study law.

His son was having difficulty with his studies, so Frank paid for him to have extra tuition in a private school in Leeson Street. He made him promise to try for the place in university. He told him that he would pay for him to take a trip to America, if only he got a place in university.

Johnny sat the Leaving Certificate and scraped a place doing arts at UCD. The night he got his results, Frank suggested dinner with Veronica in the Guinea Pig, an upmarket restaurant in Dalkey. Johnny turned up late and very drunk, with a sullen girl who was wearing black lipstick and a low-cut dress. He refused to speak to Veronica. He refused even to acknowledge that she was there. When his father asked him not to smoke in between courses, he stood up cursing and walked straight out of the restaurant with the girl. They didn't see each other again for three months.

And then, one night at the end of the summer of 1982, Johnny rang his father's house to say that he had run away from his mother. They had not been getting along, he said. They had been fighting every day for months, and his mother didn't understand him at all. Nobody understood him, he said.

They met that night, in Bowes pub off D'Olier Street. Johnny had been crying and was very upset. He went back to Frank's house after closing time and stayed for a week. Frank arranged to get him a flat in a modern block near the university and told him he would pay for it.

In October that year Johnny started attending UCD. He liked it, he told his father, but he couldn't decide what he wanted to do. He started with English and history and then moved to philosophy and politics. After Christmas, he moved again, to sociology. He got involved with the students' union. He was arrested one day for occupying the office of the Minister for Education. He failed his first-year exams and repeated them in the autumn. He failed again.

The night he told his father about this they had a furious argument. Frank asked his son where his life was going. He told him he was a spoilt little brat. That he was selfish. That he was a coward and wanted to cling to all the pain of his past, because it was easy to do that.

None of this mattered any more, Johnny said. He was going away to Nicaragua to pick coffee. Everyone else was talking about it, but he was going to do it. He would be back in three months and he would get his life together then. But he would do it without his father, he said. He would live his life without his parents now. It was September 1983. He never wanted to see his parents again.

38

Desperadoes

FRANK WOKE UP with the mother of all hangovers, fully dressed, except for his right shoe, which was dangling by its knotted lace from the back of the chair. The string-pull fan on the ceiling was turning, *click, click, click*, but one of the blades was missing. An empty bottle of rum stood on the dresser, obscuring his view of a grotesque and bleeding Sacred Heart. He licked his lips and coughed. When he tried to sit up, pain shot across his eyes and he collapsed back on the pillow, groaning out loud. He could not remember coming back to the *hospedaje* and getting into bed. Through the white shutters he heard the sonorous clanging of the church bell. Already he could hear people singing hymns. It was Sunday morning.

Clutching his head, he sat up. The room lurched. He stood up, walked precariously to the window and pushed open the stiff shutters. Silver light blazed in his eyes and a hot breeze blew in from across the herb garden. A rush of nausea threatened. He bent his head low as his eyes flooded with hot moisture. His mouth felt sour. After a moment, the feeling passed. The hymn was getting louder now, floating up from the little white church at the bottom of the hill. Vaguely, he recognized the tune, but not the words.

Downstairs in the breakfast room, Smokes was in a bad mood. Cherry was still not speaking to him. She hadn't said a single word to him since Esteli. When he'd rolled over against her in the middle of the night, she'd unpeeled his hands from her breasts and wedged two long pillows between their bodies. This morning, when they'd got up, she'd gone straight out for a long walk. He'd tried to talk to her. He'd tried to apologize, but she just wouldn't listen. She was going for a walk and that was that. You could always tell when women were pissed at you, Smokes reflected. All of a sudden, they wanted to walk everywhere. It was a very pedestrian situation.

He glanced up and saw Frank come into the room looking like death warmed up. His face was white and his hands were shaking. He didn't say anything to Smokes. He sat down at the table and poured himself a cup of coffee. He lit a cigarette and gazed out of the window, tapping the ash on the floor.

'Jesus, Franklin,' Smokes said, 'you look like barfsville, Arizona. You shoulda laid off the jungle juice, man.'

Frank put his head in his hands. 'You were right there,' he muttered. 'I feel like shite.'

Smokes caught his eye. 'You'll be OK, Franklin.' He chuckled. 'Hang in.'

The waitress came in with bread rolls and grapefruit juice and coffee. Frank ordered an avocado. He splayed his fingers against the side of his head. His chest was aching now.

'Oh, yeah.' Frank nodded. 'I'll be OK. I'll be fine in a little while.'

The food came. They bent their heads and ate, hungrily and in silence, listening to the soft sound of the singing still drifting up the hill from the church.

In the back row of the church of San Felipe del Norte, Eleanor wasn't feeling too well. She had bad stomach cramps and a sharp headache. She knelt down and bowed her head. The cramps pulsed through her. She joined her hands and listened to the wailing of a baby. The priest stepped forward to the altar. '*El cuerpo de Cristo*,' he said, and the altarboy rang a tiny handbell. The baby's cry echoed round the church. The priest lifted the host above his head.

He ate the host and wiped the rim of the chalice with a white cloth, then held it up. '*La sangre de Cristo*.' He swallowed the wine. The little bell rang again and the congregation stood up. The wheezy old organ began to puff and play. The priest conducted the singing, joining in with a strong tenor voice. He had turned up for Mass on a motorbike, wearing tight leather trousers, and stood in the porch with his helmet in one hand, greeting people as they arrived, one eyebrow ever so slightly raised. He was very handsome, Eleanor thought. He had dark brown hair and beautiful fingernails. His eyes were like black olives and he had a very sensual mouth. She wouldn't have minded leaping on to the back of that motorbike and speeding off into the mountains with him. She would have given him a run for his money, she thought, bending her head and shivering in hot embarrassment, wishing the pain in her gut would melt away.

Behind the little church, Cherry Balducci was walking through the marketplace. It was still early. It was quiet and cool, and the air smelt of damp foliage. Two young men in silk *camisas* were standing behind a stall selling jewellery, tiny heart-shaped boxes, wooden ornaments, crystallized orchids and pink shells. They were talking quietly together. When they saw Cherry they smiled and nodded and one of the men jumped up. 'Hey, beautiful' – he grinned – 'You look so pretty today. You wanna buy something?'

'No,' she said. 'Just looking.'

He clicked his fingers, suddenly looking excited. '*Mira.* You play the rock and roll? Last night? *Muy linda.*'

'Yeah.' She nodded.

'"Roll Over Beethoven?" *¿Verdad?*'

'Yup,' she said, 'and give Tchaikovsky the news.'

He clutched at his chest. '*Linda amorcita*, such a beautiful music. Such a beautiful lady. You break my heart if you leave. Stay with me. Stay with me for ever. I have colours for your pretty hair. I have rings for your fingers.'

He grabbed a handful of scarlet and blue ribbons and caressed them.

'Very beautiful,' he sighed. 'Like your eyes, *amor.*'

'Yeah, right.' She smiled. 'Look, I gotta go.'

'*No. No. ¿Por qué, amor?* Where you going? You wanna ride? I drive you, *chiquita.* I got a big long car, long and black. Ridin' along in my automobile? *¿Verdad?*'

She laughed. '*Me voy a Corinto.*'

The young man pulled a face. 'Very bad there. Very bad for the pretty ladies. You stay with me here. We ride up to the *lago* in my car. It's a beautiful thing. Why you going to Corinto?'

She looked down at the stall and touched the cool, flesh-coloured shells. 'To look for a friend of mine. A guy who disappeared.'

The young man was still smiling, but the expression in his eyes had darkened. He nodded at Cherry, then looked over his shoulder, gnawing his lip. He peered up and down the aisles between the stalls and then, with a brisk nod, he beckoned her to approach.

'*Amor*,' he hissed, 'you wanna talk with the priest. Not much happen in Corinto he don't getta hear.'

'The priest?' she said, and he nodded gravely.

'OK.' She shrugged. He stepped back and sat down, sliding his arm around his friend's shoulder and beginning to whimper. '*Oh, Jaime, mi hermano*, such a pretty thing she is. *Ay, chiquita, te quiero con toda mi alma*. Don't go. You break my heart into tiny pieces.'

He winked and jerked his head for her to leave. 'Oh, pretty woman, walkin' down the street. I kiss you. I make love to you. You leave me all alone and I cry.'

She smiled, turned around and walked off up the hill towards the *hospedaje*.

In the tiny blue bathroom of the Hospedaje Fidelma, Lorenzo was standing in the shower. He turned the creaking tap and water began to dribble out. He clutched for the soap, then swivelled around, arching his back. He rubbed the soap over his chest, under his arms and around his neck, and began to sing.

> *Amazing grace, how sweet the sound*
> *That saved a wretch like me.*
> *I once was lost, but now am found,*
> *Was blind, but now I see.*

He let the water pour down over his bald head, yelping at the heat. He rubbed the soap between his legs and up and down his back. He sang again, louder now, listening to the echo of his voice.

> *Twas grace that brought my heart to fear*
> *And grace my fear relieved.*
> *Oh, how precious did that grace appear,*
> *The hour I first believed.*

Down the corridor, in his hot bedroom, Guapo rolled over and touched the girl on the arm. She opened her eyes and smiled. He kissed her neck. She put her hands on his face, laughing, and slid her tongue between his lips. She rested her head on his chest and he combed through her hair with his fingers. She sighed, climbed out of the bed and stretched. He told her she was the most gorgeous woman he had ever seen. She rolled her eyes, grabbed the warm sheet, wrapped it around her body and went to the window.

She pushed open the shutters and looked out. The smell of pine and orchids drifted into the room. Guapo came over and stood behind her, wrapping his strong arms around her waist. She turned and kissed him hard on the mouth. The sheet slipped to the floor. Their flesh touched. He caressed her shoulders and told her she was beautiful.

'*Mentiroso*,' she scoffed.

'*Oh, sí, sí*,' he said. '*Muy, muy bonita.*'

He knelt down on the floor and kissed her thighs. She leant back against the hot windowsill, closing her eyes, grasping his thick brown hair with her fingers.

When Eleanor came back from Mass she thought Frank looked dreadful. He was sitting at the table in the shabby dining room reading a paperback. The curtains were drawn and the light in the room was dim. There was an odour of fried oil. The ashtray on the plastic tablecloth was already full of butts. He glanced hopefully up at her.

'Eleanor,' he said, 'I have to talk to you.'

'I'm not in the mood for conversation, Frank.'

'Please, El. It's important. Would you not sit down?'

She stayed standing. 'What's so important all of a sudden?'

The sun slipped through the curtains, casting a lozenge of tangerine light across the threadbare carpet.

'Well,' Frank sighed, 'Guapo's after filling me in on this young one up in Corinto. He says Smokes is wrong. He says Johnny was doing a heavy line with her. Pilar, her name is.'

She said nothing. He narrowed his eyes and squinted in the gingery glow.

'Well, I just think maybe we should try to find her, El. Guapo says she works in this place that's named after Elvis, if you don't mind. What do you think?'

'Frank,' she said, 'I think you should do whatever you like.'

She turned away from him and walked out of the room, almost bumping into Smokes, who was coming in carrying a high-hat cymbal and snare stand. He peered after her, sighed and sat down at the table.

'Yo, Franklin,' he said. '*¿Qué pasa?*'

Frank put his fingers to his face.

'Guapo told me a bit about this bird, Pilar. He seems to think it was moonlight and bloody roses with her and Johnny. You said Pilar too, didn't you? Last week in Managua?'

'I said it *might* be Pilar, Franklin. I dunno.'

'Well, Guapo thinks it was a big thing anyhow.'

Smokes shook his head and laughed. He picked up a fork and drummed it lightly against the cymbal. 'I'm telling you, man. Every single damn thing that guy says is a crock of shit.'

'Stop making that fucking noise,' Frank told him, 'or you'll be having that fucking fork surgically removed.'

They rolled slowly out of Ocotal, down the mountain road and across the white sandy plain. The road was a swirl of red dust under a silvery blue sky. They passed a line of Indians walking towards the town with bundles of traditional blankets and tall stacks of straw hats tied to their backs.

They drove back down to Somoto and out on to the western road until they came to the tiny ghost town of El Espino. A flock of shaggy sheep observed them as they drove slowly through the litter-strewn streets. The listing wooden ruins of the Hotel Almeria leered down at them, windows shattered, doors hanging from their hinges. Further down the street was an abandoned filling station with a yellow Shell sign swinging from a rusty chain. Foxes and lizards scurried for shelter, scared by the noise of Claudette. There was a burnt-out church, its blackened rafters and joists crumbling. On the edge of the main street, next to the church, was a marble grotto with a headless statue of the Virgin Mary sprayed with graffiti breasts and genitals. An elegant swan wandered around the grotto flapping its wings at the mosquitos.

At the end of the main street the paving stopped. Smokes pulled over and walked round to the back of the van. There was no more road, he said, not even a dirt track. There was just mud and cinders for maybe fifty miles. It was going to be a very rough ride. 'Batten down the hatches, guys,' he said. 'We're gonna be rockin' and reelin'.'

He climbed back up front and revved up the engine. Claudette sprang forward, heaving and tumbling like a ship in a storm. They bounced around in the back, laughing at first, then lying down on the bunks and clutching hard on to the bed frames. 'Shake it, baby, shake it,' Lorenzo said, chuckling, 'and Jesus slow us down.'

After they had been driving for about an hour, Eleanor started to wince and shudder. The pain flared up and shifted suddenly into the pit of her stomach. Slowly it started to spread. It moved into her thighs, down the backs of her kneecaps and across her calves. Pain gripped her spine. She stood up in the back of the van, clutching her stomach, sweating heavily. She had a vinegary taste in her mouth. Her skin felt raw.

'Eleanor?' Frank said. 'Are you alright?'

She nodded. The pain burst like an egg in her gut. She struggled to the back of the van and knelt on the floor. Her mouth opened. She bent her forehead. Her breakfast came up in a sticky green mess.

'Oh, my God,' she gasped. 'I'm sorry.'

Cherry jumped up and thumped on the wall. Smokes honked the horn. She hammered on the wall again, calling out for him to stop. The van swerved and skidded to a halt.

'I'm alright,' Eleanor said. 'I'm fine now. Let me get something to clean this.' She went to stand, cried out with pain and staggered to her knees again. Frank took her hand. She hung her head and vomited, more violently this time.

'What did you eat last night?' Frank asked.

'Just some shrimp.' She flinched. 'And a salad.'

'Eleanor,' Cherry said, 'we're miles inland here. You can't trust the fish, honey. I told you that.'

Eleanor began to cry with humiliation. She put her hands to her face and sobbed. 'It just looked so nice. I'm sorry. I was so hungry.' She clenched at the air and threw up again.

They helped her outside and she sat down in the shade of the van, retching and groaning. 'Oh, God,' she muttered. 'Oh, my God. I'm sorry.' Frank knelt down in the dirt beside her and held her hand in his own. 'You're alright,' he said. 'Cough it up.' He stroked the back of her head as she gagged again, spitting thick saliva into the dust. 'Guapo,' he called, 'bring some water out here.'

The sun blazed down on Claudette. Cherry made Eleanor stick her fingers down her throat so that she would throw everything up. Eleanor retched and vomited until her chest and throat were burning. Afterwards she lay flat on her back in the middle of the road. A dull rhythmic pain hammered inside her head. She looked up at the scorched blue sky. She could see the black dots circling around again. She was a middle-aged woman from Ireland. She was lying on her back in the middle of the day in the far north of a strange country. There were vultures flying overhead.

A bolt of pain seared through her stomach. Her eyes filled with tears. She grabbed at Frank's arm and cried out loud. Her face flared with heat and she shuddered.

'You're fine,' he told her. 'You're going to be grand, pet.'

'Oh, Jesus Christ,' she moaned, 'help me. Father in heaven, take this away.'

Black clouds formed in the corners of her eyes. She felt light streaming through her body. Light came pouring through her and a roaring sound filled her head. She thought she saw her son's face leaning over her, blocking out the opaline glare of the sun. He looked older than she remembered. He looked like her husband. Her son's face was bleeding now. Blood was trickling from his dark lips. His face shifted like a reflection in water. He had a beak. He had a sharp, bloodstained beak. Like one of those birds in the sky.

Her son, she laughed, was one of those birds in the sky.

They lifted her back into the van and let her sleep for a couple of hours. She kept shaking and muttering, throwing the sheet off her body. Cherry sat beside her and tried to pour a little water between her lips. Guapo cleaned up the back of the van where she had been sick. He scrubbed down the floor with cold water and Lorenzo dried it with a newspaper.

'*Pobrecita*,' Guapo sighed, putting his hand on her hot forehead.

Smokes began to get worried. He kept pacing up and down, glancing at his watch. Time was getting on, he said. They would have to make a move soon. They didn't want to get stuck out here in the wilds, where anything might happen, and nothing could be counted on.

'Yes,' Frank agreed. 'We'd better head on. I'll stay in the back with herself for a while.'

Smokes helped Lorenzo up into the cab, then jumped in himself. Lorenzo slapped him on the thigh and told him everything would be alright, not to worry. Smokes nodded. 'The night is long,' Lorenzo said, 'but the day of mercy will surely come.' Smokes chuckled reluctantly. 'Right on, man. Let's take it to the fucking bridge.' He pulled a tape from the dashboard, rammed it into the stereo and clapped his hands on the wheel. 'OK,' he whooped, 'let's rock and fucking roll.' He stuck the key into the ignition and turned it.

Nothing happened. He turned the key again. Silence. 'Claudette?' Smokes tittered. 'Let the good times roll, honey.' He twisted the key. Nothing. 'Come on, babes,' he urged. 'Don't you get evil on me now.' He turned the key a few more times. 'Come on,' he yelped, 'come *on*, you fucking witch. *Now*. Hit it.' But Claudette refused to move an inch.

'Fuck,' he sighed, jumping out of the cab. Frank was already standing in the road.

'Hey, you know anything about engines, Franklin?'

'No, Smokes,' Frank said. 'I've been a fucking taxi driver for thirty years, so I wouldn't know anything about engines.'

Smokes told him this was no time for sarcasm. Frank opened the bonnet. A cloud of steam jetted out. Something was hissing loudly. 'Sweet Mother of the Divine Jesus,' Frank sighed. 'What a fucking sight.'

'Can you fix it, Franklin?' Smokes asked anxiously. 'Can you fix it, Franklin? Can you?'

'Your radiator's leaking, son. But that isn't your problem.'

Frank stretched his hand into the engine and winced. He looked at the steaming pile, pulled the dipstick out of the block and peered at it, shaking his head. 'You're low on oil too.'

'Is that it, Franklin?'

Frank pushed past him and jumped up into the cab. He twisted the key, gently, then hard. Nothing happened. He sighed.

'It's your electrics, Smokes. Could be your battery. There's no charge getting to your spark plugs. Do you have a spare?'

'A spare?'

'A spare battery, son?'

Smokes clapped his hands to his face and began to walk up and down. He stopped suddenly and clenched his fists. He kicked hard at Claudette's front right tyre, then howled with pain. Guapo jumped out and laughed.

Frank climbed down from the cab and looked at the engine again.

'Oh, and your fan belt's loose as well, Smokes. The rubber's rotting away to shit.'

Smokes limped back over. 'Is that serious, Franklin?'

'Well' – Frank shrugged — 'only if you mind her seizing up and falling to pieces. Only if you intend, you know, driving her at all. I mean, if you just want to leave her here . . .'

Smokes interrupted. 'That means yeah, right?'

Frank nodded, slamming the hood closed. 'That means yeah, Smokes. But your electrics now, that *is* fucking serious, until we get to a garage anyway. There's not enough juice in her to power a dildo. She's banjaxed.'

Smokes scratched his head and stared out over the fields. Suddenly he beamed. 'We could go back to Ocotal, Franklin. It's only thirty miles.'

'Only thirty miles? Are you fucking serious, Smokes?'

'Well, we could try it, couldn't we? Come on, Franklin.'

Guapo chuckled again. He strolled past Smokes, making a kissing sound, and jumped up front to talk to Lorenzo.

'Thirty miles is some stretch in this heat, son.'

Smokes put his hands on his hips. 'Well, what do you suggest, Frank?' He pouted. 'I mean, like, lay it on me, babes.'

Frank shook his head. 'I don't really know,' he muttered. 'Maybe Lorenzo could say a fucking prayer.'

A loud moan came from inside the back of the van. When Frank went to investigate, Cherry was leaning over Eleanor's shaking body and a sour stench was rising up from the bed. His stomach turned. Cherry looked up. 'Frank, she's got diarrhoea.'

'Oh, sweet bloody Jesus. That's all we need now.'

'It's just the shits, Frank. Ain't nothing to get upset about.'

Cherry laid Eleanor back down and gently rolled her on to her side. She picked up a towel and began to unzip her skirt.

'What are you doing?' Frank gasped. 'You can't take off her clothes like that.'

She turned and snapped. 'What the fuck you want me to do, Frank? You want to leave her like this?'

'No, of course not. But Eleanor's funny about things like that.'

She pushed her hair behind her ears and held out the towel, her eyes flaming. 'You want to do it, Frank? Well? Do ya?'

He turned and walked out of the camper. Smokes was squatting in the road talking to Lorenzo and Guapo.

'What's shaking, Franklin?'

'Oh, nothing. Eleanor's got a dose of the runs.'

'Probably good, man. Get it all out, you know? Nothing like a good crap when the old microbes are attacking the end zone.'

'Sorry, do you mind, Smokes? That's a lady you're talking about.'

Guapo and Lorenzo had a suggestion. They thought there was a sugar cane *cooperativa* about five miles to the south. They could walk down there and see if the *campesinos* had a tractor or maybe an earth mover. Sometimes the government hired them out, Guapo said. And sometimes the *campesinos* managed to club together and buy one. Smokes looked unconvinced. But it was possible, Guapo insisted; it was worth a shot.

'Lift up thy chariot, O Lord,' Lorenzo muttered, 'and deliver thy servants to the promised land.'

'Jesus, Lorenzo,' Smokes sighed. 'Enough already, OK?'

Smokes took his Aka from Claudette's cab. He led Frank into the field and showed him how to unhook the safety catch and how to push the magazine into the barrel and fire the gun. 'Just in case of emergencies, Franklin,' he said. 'But don't waste any bullets, man, because I'm going to kill myself when we get back.'

Smokes and Guapo took a water bottle and set out for the *cooperativa*. Frank lay down on the grass. Lorenzo came over and laughed. 'Fear not, brother Frank,' he said. 'The Lord moves in mysterious ways.' Frank scoffed. 'I wish he'd fucking move us to Corinto.' Lorenzo clicked his tongue, put on his straw hat and stepped gingerly into one of the swaying fields.

Cherry emerged from the back of Claudette, wiping her hands on a flannel. She poured some water over her hands, rubbed them with soap and dried them on the thighs of her jeans. 'I fixed her, Frank,' she said. 'She'll be more comfortable now.'

Frank felt his face flush. 'Thank you, Cherry. Come over and sit here beside me.'

They sat down on the side of the road and drank some warm water from a bottle. There was no sound around them except for the fidgeting of the cornfields.

'Hey,' she said, 'sorry for yelling you out, Frank.'

'Oh no, love, I'm sorry. Thank you for helping us out there.'

Lorenzo was wandering through the field now, leaning down low, smelling the wild yellow flowers. He looked completely engrossed in what he was doing. He moved slowly, swinging his stick in front of him. He bent over suddenly, plucked a flower and stuck it into the pocket of his leopard-skin jacket.

'That guy,' Cherry sighed. 'Sometimes I think the elevator just ain't travellin' to the top floor.'

Frank laughed. 'Yes, he's a bit touched alright.'

'Well,' she said, 'he's an angel really.' She paused. 'You know, Frank, he really did love Johnny a lot. It was real nice to see them together.'

He felt himself tense up. 'Well himself seems to be very popular alright. All these love stories. You all seem very soft on him.'

'Well, see, I was in a lot of trouble once and Johnny really helped me out. He's a sweet thing.'

He turned and peered into her glittering eyes. 'What happened to you?' She looked at him, searching his face.

'You can trust me,' he said. 'You needn't worry.'

She nodded and looked away. She picked up a flat stone and dropped it from one hand to the other.

'Well, see, I slept with this guy,' she said suddenly. 'Not Smokes. It was this guy from France. He was here for a while. He said he was some big deal in the government over there. We got smashed in the Imper one night, and stuff just happened. I didn't want to tell Smokes about it. I thought he'd be real pissed, so I didn't want to tell him. It was just a dumb thing that happened.'

'Wow,' Frank said.

She nodded. 'Yeah, Frank. Wow is right.

'So we did the wild thing, me and this guy. Wasn't even that great, you know? And then a few weeks went by and I missed my period. I still didn't worry. But then I missed the next one too. I started to weird out. I went to the *mercado* and got a kit. I remember I took a cab home and I poured a real big tequila. It was early in the morning. I had the drink. Then I went to the bathroom, and I did the test. And Jeez, Frank, I practically died.'

She sighed deeply and took a cigarette from his pack. She lit it, inhaled a few pulls, and then went on.

'Smokes was away just then. Up here, I think. Johnny found me one night down in the *barrio*. I was real freaked, Frank, you know. Talking about doing all kinds of stuff.'

'And it definitely wasn't Smokes? The father?'

She wrinkled her nose. 'No way. Pumping junk into your veins ain't too good for your sperm count. Smokes can't have kids, you see. It's a thing between us sometimes.'

'I didn't know. I'm sorry.'

She nodded. 'I didn't have the money to get back to the States. Matter of fact, things were pretty tough back then for money. My trust fund hadn't been fixed, you know, so we didn't have too much dough.'

'Your trust fund?'

'Yeah. That's what me and Smokes live on, Frank.'

'But I thought he wrote for the papers.'

Cherry tapped the side of her head. 'In here, Frank. That's where Smokes writes for the papers.'

'Good God.'

'So anyway, see, I had no money, and so I had to have the operation here. Johnny knew about this quack down in Massaya who'd do it for a bottle of Wild Turkey and fifty bucks. He went down there with me while Smokes was still up here. I don't know, Frank, I felt real bad. My folks are Italian, you know. I was raised Catholic. But I just had to do it. It just wouldna been right for me.'

She shook her head and dragged on her cigarette, trying hard not to cry. Her lip was trembling now and a tiny knot had formed in her chin.

'So, see, we go find the quack's place. It was over a bar. I walk into the guy's room. It's maybe the size of Claudette and I can smell the booze off the guy from across the room, Frank. He's just sitting there, smiling at me, dressed in this black suit, you know, like a preacher, and he's putting on these rubber gloves. I can hear music coming up from the *cantina*. The Rolling Stones. And there's a table there, covered with a white sheet. There's a couple of glass bottles full of coloured stuff.'

She pulled hard on her cigarette.

'And there's a pair of secateurs, Frank. There's a pair of secateurs on the guy's fucking table.'

Frank shuddered. 'Jesus.'

'I just ran out that door, Frank. I ran out and Johnny came, and I changed my mind then. I decided I was gonna have it, gonna just tell him, you know? I was screaming and crying, man. Johnny and me talked it all out. We stayed up all night, just talking, and I was so scared, but he said he'd stick around, no matter what. Next day we came back up to Managua. Smokes got home late from the mountains and we just went to sleep. He was tired, you know? He had a touch of something too. And anyway, in the night, I woke up.'

Her voice lowered to a whisper. The long leaves rustled in the trees. Her face looked tense.

'I woke up, and the moon was shining in the bedroom window. It looked real pretty. It was quiet. I remember that, the quietness of everything. The stillness and the colour of the moon. I felt kinda small, I guess. There were all these stars in the sky and Smokes was fast asleep, with his arm around me.'

She crushed her cigarette out in the dirt, folded her arms and looked straight ahead of her.

'And I was bleeding, Frank. See, I just started to bleed, you know, in the night? I just started to bleed. And by the time the morning came, I lost it.'

A flock of blue parrots flapped noisily over Claudette's roof. They turned and wheeled in the blue sky, flying out in a wide arc over the whispering fields.

'Jesus, Cherry. You poor thing.'

She began to chew her fingernails.

'See, I really wanted that baby, Frank. It's the weirdest thing. I was gonna get rid of it, but then I really wanted it. I think I must've wanted someone to love. Except for Smokes. Someone else to love, you know? Someone to need me.'

'Sure, that's only natural, pet. That's what we all want.'

She nodded. 'Johnny never told anyone. He's loyal as an old puppy, you know? If he says it, you can count on it. He's a real doll.'

Her breath shuddered as she cupped her hands to her face.

'And Smokes still doesn't know?'

She shook her head and picked up a handful of earth, letting it trickle through her fingers. He sighed deeply and she glanced up at him. 'I suppose you're real shocked now, Frank? Are you?'

He laughed. 'I suppose I am. A little. But I think you're a very brave girl, Cherry.'

He reached out awkwardly and took her hand. She squeezed his fingers and looked quickly away over the fields, nodding her head.

'Well, not really. It's circumstances, is all. People do stuff. Sometimes you don't get the chance to debate about it.'

In the middle of the field, Lorenzo stood up and yelled. He turned towards Claudette and waved his stick in the air. They called out to him and he laughed and went back to the flowers. They lit the last cigarette from Frank's packet, passing it in turns from one to the other.

'Well, God,' he sighed, 'everyone has a love story about that fellow. I'll have to put them all in a book some day.'

'Some book, Frank.' She smiled. 'It's gonna be thicker than a telephone directory.'

'I'll make a million out of it,' Frank said.

'Yeah. Maybe you will, Frank. Maybe you'll win the Pulitzer Prize, huh?'

She slipped her feet out of her sandals and began to knead her toes. Her movements were graceful and her hands very gentle. It made him feel happy just to look at them.

For two long hours there was no sign of Smokes and Guapo. The storm clouds began to roll in from the mountains, blackening the sky and blocking out the sun, reducing its light to dull yellow rays oozing down reluctantly through the gloom like thick soup forced through a sieve. The birds began to chirp and scream in the fields.

'The rain is coming now,' Lorenzo sighed. 'The ark's gonna sail pretty soon.'

In the back of the van, Eleanor began to moan again. She lifted her wrists to her face and coughed. Cherry went and rolled her over on her side again. She dabbed her forehead with a damp cloth and Eleanor quietened down. Lorenzo looked worried. He said she was going to get dehydrated if they didn't get some liquid in her soon. They stood over her, slowly trickling the rest of the drinking water between her lips. She lapped it up like a suckling baby. Then they opened a bottle of warm *cerveza* and passed it around between them.

Frank stepped out of the van and looked back down the dusty road. Way in the distance, at the vanishing point of the track, he thought he saw something moving. He squinted, then stepped back into Claudette and grabbed Guapo's telescope. 'Say nothing' – he laughed – 'We might be in business.'

Thunder cracked in the sky. He rushed back out and put the telescope to his eye. 'I can see Smokes,' he called excitedly, and then, almost immediately, the tone of his voice changed. 'Oh, no. Oh, *no*. Oh, sweet mother of God. I don't believe it.'

He handed the telescope to Cherry and she peered through it. Smokes and Guapo were walking slowly along the road, looking very red in the face, both stripped to the waist and puffing hard. Behind them, two *campesinos* were chivvying a team of fat white oxen along the road.

'Jesus H Christ,' Cherry sighed, 'it looks like an episode of "Bonanza".'

They watched the group approach. The *campesino* man was huge and broad with a pointed head and arms like hams. The woman walking beside him was small and wiry. There were six oxen harnessed together with leather straps and reins. Two of them had wooden yokes over their vast muscular shoulders. There was a scrawny mule too, tied to the harness with a rope. Smokes and Guapo waved. The *campesinos* were dressed in grey peasant tunics and the woman had on a straw hat. The man had a thick rope wrapped around his chest. He was carrying a metal hook. They were both barefoot.

'*Hola, compañeros*,' panted Smokes as he came up to them.

'Yippie aye fucking yay,' said Frank.

'Now, Franklin, I told you about sarcasm, dude. I know what you're thinking, but these babies are gonna see us through.'

'I thought you were getting a fucking tractor, son. It's up a fucking mountain nearly all the way to Corinto.'

Smokes shrugged. 'Nearest tractor is back in Ocotal. You feel like a stretch of those pretty legs, Franklin?'

'It'll be OK, Frank,' Cherry said. 'It's a pretty gentle mountain. We're already pretty high up.'

The *campesino* man shook Frank's hand, nodded his head and said '*Mucho gusto, hombre.*' The woman said nothing at all. She had a hard country face, piercing eyes and skin like old leather. A large wooden cross hung around her neck.

The man took an earthenware jug of water from around the neck of the mule. He uncorked it, raised it to his lips, drank deeply and gasped. Then he wiped his mouth with the back of his hand and offered the water around. Frank stepped forward.

'Wouldn't do that, Franklin,' Smokes said. 'Not till it's boiled, babes. No way is that water sweet.'

Frank nodded at the huge *campesino*. 'Your man looks healthy enough to me.'

Smokes shook his head. 'These are country people, babes. They get used to it. You're gonna make yourself puke like a one-armed bandit.'

'Smokes,' Frank said, 'I have to have a drink. I'm sorry.'

He took the canister from the *campesino*'s hands, wiped the neck with his sleeve and swigged from it. The *campesino* slapped him on the back.

The oxen were all a foot taller than Frank, fat, cream-coloured beasts with mean expressions on their faces and dented iron bells around their necks. The mule had a moth-eaten, wiry look. Lightning flickered. Thunder boomed in the sky, making the ground shake. Suddenly the clouds parted and warm rain began to hiss down into the fields.

The big *campesino* looked up at the sky and made the sign of the Cross. He laughed and held out his hands, with his palms facing upwards, and he shouted above the roaring rain, '*¡Hay bastante lluvia! Gracias a Dios.*'

'Much rain, Franklin. He's thanking God for the rain.'

'Right,' Frank said, feeling the damp soak through his cotton shirt. 'Tell him if he likes the fucking rain he should come and live in Ireland.'

The *campesino* woman stared at Claudette as if she had never seen anything like it before. She touched the painted pictures with her fingers and she laughed. She looked up at the surfboard with the image of the half-naked woman on it, then scowled and looked away, shaking her head.

The man unwound the rope from his torso, then took another length from his canvas bag. He clamped the metal hook to Claudette's front fender and looped the ropes around it, tying them with thick knots. He and his wife began to push the oxen into place. He attached the ropes to the two wooden yokes.

The sky was a mess of deep greys now, so that it looked as if dusk had fallen even though it was only mid-afternoon. Hunger gnawed at Frank's stomach and his temples drummed with pain. 'OK, Franklin?' Smokes yelled. He nodded and made a thumbs-up sign. The woman appeared with two heavy switches cut from a wild olive tree. 'People get ready,' Smokes shouted. Guapo, Frank and Lorenzo took up their positions behind Claudette.

'*Uno, dos, tres,*' breathed the *campesino*. '*Y vámonos.*'

The oxen bellowed at the sky. The *campesinos* thrashed at their backs with the switches. Guapo, Lorenzo and Frank leant hard against Claudette, groaning, digging their heels into the mud. Up front, Cherry and Smokes bent low, grabbing on to the fender, hauling, gasping, soaked through with sweat and rain.

'*Vámonos, pues,*' the *campesino* roared. He grabbed the front ox by the halter and yanked hard at it. Nothing happened. He took a length of rope and slapped hard at the ox's flanks. The ox danced in the reins, bellowing with pain and fright. '*¡Adelante!*' the *campesino* shouted. '*¡Vámonos, hijos de puta!*' Very slowly, Claudette's thick wheels began to turn. Her springs creaked. She felt heavy. She resisted, as though biting down deep into the muck. And then, suddenly, she lurched forward. Frank staggered. His hands slithered across the glossy wet surface of the back door and he fell face down in the mud, gurgling and choking. He could hear Smokes laughing at him. When he got to his feet he was covered in oozing muck. He wiped his eyes. Claudette was still moving. He just didn't care about anything else.

Claudette moved forward slowly, ponderously. They groaned and panted, but they could do nothing to speed up her progress. The *campesino* kept coming back and harassing them. '*Hombres*,' he'd say, '*empujen más fuerte. ¡Más fuerte!*' He'd clench his fist and grimace. Once, he ran hard at Claudette's back and she jumped forward as if she'd received an electric shock. He was one seriously large motherfucker, Smokes said. You wouldn't want to fuck with that guy, not in any sense of the word.

After a few minutes, the slope gradually decreased, eventually becoming almost imperceptible. There was less mud now and Claudette gathered a little momentum, which made her easier to manoeuvre. The *campesino* stopped thrashing the animals and he danced along the track in front of them instead, waving bundles of straw and urging them on. Dusk fell quickly. They were moving up the spine of the mountain now, with the Pacific miles ahead to the west. A vivid sunset streaked the sky. A long meandering valley lay in a huge curving sandstone fault on the southern side of the road. A mile or so up to their right, the fields swooped upwards and the wall of the jungle rose stark as a green cliff.

Cherry suggested they should take it in turns to watch over Eleanor and rest for a short while. Frank went in first. He held her hand and mopped her sweating face. He got out the map and looked at it by torchlight. There was Corinto, straight ahead and over the mountain. Managua lay to the south, on the banks of the lake. Honduras was on the other side of that patch of thick jungle. If they walked off the road and turned right they'd end up in another country in less than an hour.

After ten minutes he leapt back out into the rain. It was Cherry's turn for a rest now. She clambered into the van, shuddering with cold, and peeled off her wet clothes. She dried herself with a dirty towel and put on dry underwear, new jeans and a sweatshirt. She poured some of the *campesinos*' water into the kettle, lit the gas stove and put the kettle on to boil, then sat down on Eleanor's bed and stroked the side of her face. She could hear Guapo singing 'Raining in my Heart' and the others yelling at him to shut up.

She smiled. Eleanor rolled over towards the wall and started to snore and Cherry pulled the clean sheet up over her. Claudette lurched foward, rocking gently from side to side. Cherry made tea for everyone and took it out. Then she went back inside and lay down on a bunk.

Some time later, Lorenzo pulled the door open and climbed into the back. Cherry sat up. Lorenzo was clutching something in his hands. He went to the stove and poured out a jug of bubbling water. He dropped whatever he was carrying into the water, then groped for a spoon and stirred the liquid.

'What's that, Lorenzo?' Cherry yawned.

He grinned. 'Juju medicine, sister. The male parts of the deadeye flower, a couple of roots, mixed with some crumbs from bread made on Good Friday. It never goes stale. Cures anything. I carry it with me all the time.'

'Jeez, Lorenzo.' She laughed nervously. 'I don't know.'

He ignored her and knelt down on the floor. Joining his hands and bowing his head, he whispered, 'Anoint the hands of thy servant, oh Lord. And send down tongues of healing fire.'

He took off his leopard-skin jacket, rolled it into a ball and placed it under Eleanor's head. He touched her eyelids. Very gently he pinched her nose, so that her mouth gaped open. Slowly, delicately, he poured the yellow liquid between her lips.

She began to moan. Her hands clutched hard at the sheets and her teeth chattered. Lorenzo put his hands on either side of her face.

'Lorenzo,' Cherry said, 'you sure about this, baby?'

'Faith, child of grace,' he hissed. 'After the storm comes the sweetest calm.'

Eleanor's body juddered. She tossed her head from side to side, lifting her hands up in the air, and then, very suddenly, she went still and limp and she sighed. Her mouth opened. She began to breathe deeply, regularly. Lorenzo lifted her head and took back his folded jacket. He moved the hair out of her eyes, kissed his thumb and traced the sign of the Cross on her forehead. Then he put his jacket on and stood up.

'Get her some lemonade in the morning, sister. Break a fresh egg in it. She'll be whole again.'

Cherry looked at Eleanor's sleeping face. 'Wow, Lorenzo. That's pretty good, man.'

'Nothing to do with man. Man is as nothing to the lion of Christ.'

He moved over to the door and opened it to the rain and wind.

'Hey, babe,' Cherry called, 'you don't do anything for broken hearts, do ya?'

Lightning flashed in the sky. The oxen groaned. Lorenzo turned in the doorway.

'Physician,' he said to her, 'heal thyself.'

He stepped out into the night and closed the door behind him.

The rain was getting worse. Thunder crackled and fork lightning ripped the purple and charcoal sky in two. The *campesinos* had two oil lamps and a couple of torches. They were trying to light up the road ahead of them, but in the gloom the flashlights were almost useless. The night was full of screeches and cries. They could hear monkeys whooping up in the jungle.

Smokes was getting bored. To pass the time, he started to tease Guapo about the girl he'd met the night before. He baited and heckled until Guapo finally revealed her name. Cordelia Portillo, Guapo sighed, and Smokes clapped him hard on the back. Guapo pushed him away and his eyes took on a moody and serious look. He said he had fallen in love with Cordelia Portillo. Smokes guffawed and said Guapo fell in love with a different girl every night of the week. Guapo shook his head. She wasn't like any of the others; she was the kind of person you wanted to stay with for ever. Smokes scoffed, but Guapo insisted he was serious. He wanted to go back to Cordelia Portillo when all this was over. He wanted to marry her and that was just the way it was.

Smokes laughed out loud. He leant his back against Claudette and pushed hard, wincing with effort. He said the day Guapo got married he'd eat his stonewashed bellbottoms. But Guapo refused to joke about it. He said he was fed up with being independent. Being single was too much hard work. He thought sleeping around was wrong. People got hurt, he said, and he was tired of being involved with that. 'Oh, come on, man,' Smokes panted. 'What are you now, a fucking priest?' He started to chant then, '*Padre Guapo, Padre Guapo*', and Guapo said '*Tu madre, yanqui*,' and the two of them suddenly slipped and fell in the muck.

Frank pushed all his weight against Claudette's back doors. He said he agreed with Guapo. In his experience, it was bad for people to be on their own. It made them selfish and it meant they had nobody to share things with. 'You need that,' he panted. 'Through good times and bad. You need the adventure of all that.' Smokes said this was all sentimental hogwash. The rain was gushing down in sheets now. 'Looks like it's you and me then, Lorenzo,' Smokes called. 'Bachelor boys to the end, huh?' Lorenzo shook his head gravely. 'I too would like a companion, if the Lord so chooses to bless me. Saint Paul says it is better to marry than to burn with desire.'

'And are you burning with desire, man?'

Lorenzo nodded and grunted. 'Often, brother. The spirit is willing but the flesh is weak. Praise God.'

Suddenly Frank felt nauseous. His stomach began to pulse and throb. He ran forward, vaulted the hedge like a man half his age and fell to his knees, fumbling desperately with the buttons of his trousers. He pulled them down and yanked at his underpants. He squatted on the long wet grass. Shit began to pour out of him. He moaned and rolled over on his side. He grabbed a handful of grass and tried to wipe himself clean. Suddenly his bowels opened again, all over his hands. Groaning with disgust, he knelt forward in the rain, dipped his fingers into a thick puddle of cold mud and wiped them on the flattened grass. He stood up, eyes moist, arms trembling and aching. He looked around the dark wet field, feeling utterly miserable. He would have happily shot somebody to be in a warm bed in Dublin with a glass of hot whisky beside him. He wiped his mouth with the back of his sleeve, ran out to the road and caught up with Claudette.

'OK, man?' Smokes called. Frank nodded, putting his shoulder against the rear door. 'Just taking a leak.'

Cherry came out of the van wrapped from head to foot in black plastic rubbish bags. She swapped places with Guapo, who shook his head like a dog and went off dripping to sit in the van. Cherry said nothing at all to Smokes. They pushed. They heaved. Suddenly the road levelled again. They took their hands off the van and walked along panting, trying to regain breath and sense. They stood in the muck and Claudette continued to move slowly forwards. Cherry leant over, hands on her knees, coughing. Then she stood up straight and raised her face towards the falling rain. Smokes stepped towards her and tried to put his arm around her shoulders. She turned away but did not shrug him off. He held her hand. 'Please,' he said, 'please, Cherry. I need you.' Slowly and still without looking at him, she twined her fingers through his. He put his arms around her and leant his forehead against her chest. 'I'm sorry, Cherry. I swear to God I'm sorry.' She sighed, lifted her arms and put them around his neck, pulling him close.

'Yeah, well, do it again, jerk, you'll be more full of holes than a pound of fucking Gorgonzola.'

From down the road, Frank called out, 'This isn't the back row of the fucking movies, Smokes. Quit the sweet nothings and push the fucking thing.'

They stopped at three in the morning and sat in the back of the van drinking hot tea and shivering. The *campesino* said he had never been to Corinto and never intended to go. It was an evil place, he said, full of lust and wickedness. Everyone there was diseased and depraved. There were no churches in Corinto; all the churches had been burnt down and destroyed. Smokes laughed and said this wasn't true. He told them he'd been to Corinto plenty of times. The *campesino* shook his head fervently. He knew men who had been to Corinto. His own brother had been there once. If you looked at a map of Corinto, his wife said, you wouldn't find a church anywhere because the people there had burnt all the old maps and made new ones, without any of the churches marked on them. There were witches and devil-worshippers everywhere in that town. There were people in Corinto who would murder you for no reason. It was like Babylon of old. It was Sodom and Gomorrah. It was bad luck for a person to go into Corinto. '*Un infierno sobre la tierra,*' the *campesino* said with a scowl. It was a hell on this earth. It was a place that God had forgotten.

The woman warned them not to stay in any hotel in Corinto. She had heard stories about the things that went on in the hotels there. And it would be a very brave person who slept in a bed in that town, she told them, when you thought about what went on in those beds. She looked up at them and asked if they knew what they would find in those beds, those terrible beds in Corinto. She held out her hands and squirmed with disgust, wriggling her fingers.

'*Animalitos,*' she winced, and her husband nodded in agreement.

'*Un purgatorio,*' he said.

'It sounds a bit like Portlaoise,' Frank said.

'Chill out, Franklin.' Smokes laughed. 'We got a good place to crash in Corinto. Ma Baker's. We always stay there. I figure she's got the hots for Guapo.'

'*Tu padre,*' Guapo sighed.

'Only *animalitos* in Ma Baker's beds gonna be us.' Smokes giggled.

'Speak for yourself,' Cherry said.

Eleanor was sleeping soundly now. Smokes took his turn to watch her and the others stepped back out into the gale.

They pushed all night, and the rain poured down relentlessly. Once, the tarpaulin came loose from Johnny Little's coffin, and it slapped in the whistling wind like the wings of a terrible angel. Guapo started singing again and Lorenzo joined in on the harmonies. They sang 'Wake Up, Little Suzie' and 'Hey, Bird Dog' and 'Ebony Eyes' and Frank said the Everly Brothers would be whirring around in their graves, if they were dead, and consulting their lawyers, if they were alive, and either way, if Guapo and Lorenzo didn't stop soon, he was going to shoot the pair of them and leave them in a ditch to fucking die.

The road steepened and then levelled out suddenly and once again Claudette seemed to get a little lighter. She was rolling forward almost gracefully now. The last rolls of thunder echoed over the distant hills. Cherry sang 'Blue Moon' and everybody clapped when the song was over, even the *campesino* and his wife, both of whom looked wide awake still, bright-eyed and nimble-footed.

And then, just before dawn, the rain suddenly stopped. Silence descended over the countryside, a silence so intense that it seemed as though the rain had been stopped by some violent act. They pushed on, aching with tiredness now. The bells clanked around the oxen's necks as the animals trudged through the mud. And then, slowly, the pink light of dawn began to spread out over Nicaragua like watercolour paint spilled over a white page. The sky turned yellow and green. It began to fill with turquoise and bronze light, a long arc of peach-coloured cloud, a spiralling swathe of soft pinks and variegated reds. The volcanoes loomed up dark in the distance, a gentle breeze coaxing their smoke towards the south. Creamy clouds emerged from the gloom. The birds began to chatter and warble. Flies buzzed at the animals' swishing tails. Away to the north, up by the expanse of jungle, they saw a slick tawny puma padding along the crest of the hill with one of its cubs in its mouth. The light turned golden over the valley and then all at once the scarlet sun exploded over the blackening mountains, filling the sky with whiteness and space. The larks rocketed up into the air.

A few minutes later, they came to the peak of Ponte Negro. Below them in the valley lay the orange haze of a town; beyond that, the violet expanse of the Pacific. Fishing boats were carving white lines across the water. A long grey military ship sat anchored on the farthest edge of the bay. A helicopter hovered in the air above it, then lifted at a diagonal, taking off in the direction of the mountains. They lit cigarettes and looked down over Corinto and the new morning was cold and tangy with salt.

'Hell on earth,' Smokes sighed. 'Never thought I'd be so damn happy to see it.'

39

Corinto

THE *CAMPESINOS* ASKED for twenty dollars, but Frank said it wasn't enough and gave them a hundred. When they tried to refuse he insisted, and eventually, after ten minutes of arguing, they took the money, still seeming very reluctant.

'*Bueno.*' The man shrugged. '*Buena suerte, compañeros. Esperamos que lo encuentren.*'

He and his wife shook Frank's hand. Then they turned around and began to walk slowly back eastwards, flicking at the oxen with their sticks.

Claudette freewheeled precariously down the winding mountain road, creaking and whining as she went. Down below them they saw the grey strip of the Pan-American Highway running into the town from the south. 'Praise the Lord,' Lorenzo said. 'For mine enemies shall be cut down like the grass.'

They rolled down the hill towards Corinto and turned into the forecourt of a tiny garage. It had one petrol pump, a squat fat Coca-Cola machine and a tumbledown shack with posters of Betty Grable and Lauren Bacall taped to the windows. Smokes and Frank got out and knocked on the shack door, but nobody came.

The birds were whistling in the early morning quiet, but nothing else in the town seemed to be moving. Smokes strolled over to the edge of the forecourt, kicking at stones. He lay down under an olive tree and tried to nap. Guapo paced around, staring up at the mountains through his telescope. Lorenzo came over to him and squatted down, putting his hand on Guapo's shoulder.

'*¿Qué ve, Guapo, hermano?*'

'*Bueno, veo la montaña hermosa. Es muy verde, y por encima el cielo es azúl. Veo todos los olivos, llenos de pájaros, y el río.*'

'*¿De verdad?*'

Frank watched for a while as Guapo described what he could see. Then he went to the other side of the forecourt and found a rubber hose pipe connected up to a rusty tap. He turned the tap and water dribbled from the end of the hose. He dragged it back over towards Claudette and began to spray her clean, splashing her filthy sides, her windows, her mud-caked tyres. Cherry sat up and peered blearily out through the side window.

'Well, madam,' he said, 'are you alright there?'

'I could sleep for a week, Frank. I'm bushed.'

When he had finished cleaning the van Frank sat on a barrel and watched Lorenzo and Guapo again. Guapo seemed to be getting more excited now as he described the different colours of the sky and the fields. He stood up and pointed his telescope towards the centre of the town. He spoke very quickly, but Frank could pick out the names of some of the colours. *Roja* was red. *Negro* black. *Rosa* pink. He thought how strange it was that you could understand the shape of a language, even when you knew hardly any of the words. He felt he knew what Guapo was saying, although he could not have written it down.

He had always liked the sound of different languages but had never found time to learn them. He could speak a little Irish, but that was all. He sat in the forecourt and remembered driving his son to school when Johnny was only seven or eight, going over his Irish with him in the car. They had a routine together. It was after things had got so bad that Eleanor would never be up in the mornings. He remembered it very clearly.

In the mornings, when he got up, he would go into his son's bedroom and open the blinds to wake him. 'Oh, Lothar,' Johnny would groan. It was a pet name he had for his father. There was a cartoon strip called 'Mandrake the Magician' in *The Evening Herald*. Mandrake the Magician had a friend called Lothar and Johnny had said he looked like his father and had started calling his father Lothar then, for a joke.

'You're a monkey,' Frank would say. 'Do you know what my old fellow would have done to me if I called him that?'

'Yes,' Johnny would say with a yawn, rubbing his eyes.

'He'd've boxed you from here to the other side of the world.'

'And what would he have given me for Christmas?'

'A doll, a drum, a kick in the bum, and a chase around the table.'

'That's right, son. That's right. You remember that now.'

Frank would take him into the bathroom and make him clean his teeth and wash his hands. He would tell him the Irish words for teeth, hair, comb, and the words for water, and sink and soap. He would make him repeat the words. Then he would let Johnny watch him shaving. Johnny would sit on the edge of the bath and look up at his father shaving and he would hum to himself while he watched. After that Frank would make him hold out his hands, so that he could see if his fingernails were clean. '*Bun ós cionn*,' he would say then. He always said it in a cross voice because it made Johnny laugh. '*Bun ós cionn*.' 'The other way around' that meant in Irish, and Johnny would giggle and turn his hands palms down. Then he would take his son by the right hand and shake it and they would say their rhyme. They did it every morning. It was just a small thing they did together.

> *Shake hands, shake hands, shake hands, brother*
> *You're a rogue, but I'm another.*

After this they would go downstairs and make breakfast. Frank would ask his son the Irish words for milk and sugar and spoon, and Johnny would tell him. He would sit there in the kitchen with his son, eating corn flakes, and they would exchange words in Irish, speaking in very quiet voices so that they wouldn't wake up Eleanor. Then Frank would make Johnny a sandwich for his lunch. He would ask him if he knew the Irish words for bread, butter, cheese and apple. He would put the sandwich into a Tupperware box. He laughed at the memory of his son's lunchbox. It had a drawing of a spaceship on one side, a black knife and fork on the other.

When he'd made his son's lunch, they would slip out together and get into Frank's taxi, and on the drive down to the school he would ask his son the irregular verbs in Irish, and Johnny would recite them. *Abair, beir, clois, ith, tabhair.* He knew them all. *Tar, teigh, feic, dean, bí, faigh.* Then sometimes he would make Johnny get out his Irish book and read to him. The book was called *Daithí Lacha*. It was about animals that could speak Irish.

He would tell his son how important it was to learn Irish. He would tell him how people were almost ashamed to be Irish when he was growing up, how they had no interest at all in learning their own language, because they knew that they would all have to go away to get work in the end. In the old days everyone had to go away, to England or America, even to Australia sometimes. They would have to go to the other side of the world sometimes, because everything was so hard in the country. But things were different now, Frank would tell his son. Better times were coming for Ireland now. Good times were coming for everybody.

Johnny would laugh then. He would say he didn't like Irish, that he thought it was boring. 'Maybe,' Frank would say, 'but when you're older you'll need it. You'll need it if you ever want to go to university.'

'I don't want to go to university.'

'Well, *I* want you to, son. You're to get a good job, so you can look after me when I'm old and poor.'

And Johnny would laugh. 'Oh, Lothar.'

He would make him say goodbye in Irish too. He thought it was important; he wanted to get him into the habit. When they arrived at the school gates, Frank would say '*Slan leat anois*', and his son would kiss his father, and murmur '*Slan leat, a Lothar*', jump out of the car and run up the path to school.

There had been many mornings, after things had got bad at home, when Frank had worried himself half to death about his son. He would watch him running up the path to school and wonder what would become of him, and wonder too if there wasn't some way of returning things to the way they had once been. It was a time in his life when Frank had felt desperately alone.

He sat in the forecourt of the little garage and remembered one particular morning when he had dropped his son off at school. It was just after Christmas one year, and bitterly cold. There was frost on the window of the car. It was so cold that morning that they'd had to pour water over the windscreen.

'*Slan leat a mhic*,' Frank said. His son looked up at him and suddenly burst into tears.

'What's the matter?' Frank said.

'Are you going to go away, Lothar?'

'What? What do you mean? Of course I'm not.'

His son's face twisted up as he cried.

'I don't want you to go away. You told Mammy you were going to go away.'

'I did not. When did I say that?'

'You said it last week when you were fighting. I heard you saying it.'

'I was only play-acting, son. I'm not going away. Where would I be going?'

His son began to sob even more bitterly then. He wiped his eyes with the back of his hand. 'You don't like Mammy any more. I think you're going to go away.'

He leant across and put his arms around his son, holding him as tightly as he could.

'Oh, son, I'm not,' he said. 'I'm not, Johnny.'

His son's body was shaking from crying. The wind whipped up the dead leaves and blew them against the windscreen. He hugged his son harder.

'I'm not going anywhere, Johnny, son. I'm not.'

'Is Mammy going to go away?'

'Don't be dense. Of course she's not. She's going to stay here with us. Where do you think your mammy would be going?'

'I don't know.'

'Well, exactly. Your mammy would miss us if she went any-where. She wouldn't want to go anywhere.'

He took his son's hands and squeezed them.

'Don't you love your daddy?'

'Yes.'

'And you love your mammy too, don't you?'

He nodded and started to cry again.

'Well, they love you. They're your best friends, aren't they? Sure, they'd never go away. Why would they go away?'

'You're always fighting each other, Lothar. You're always shouting at each other. It's always about me.'

'Johnny,' Frank said, 'Mammy and me are friends too. But you know the way you have fights with your friends sometimes? I mean, even you and me have little fights sometimes, don't we? And we're the best of old buddies.'

Johnny flung himself at his father and clung to him. 'Oh, please, Lothar,' he wept, 'if you go away, won't you take me with you? You wouldn't forget me, sure you wouldn't, Lothar? Please?'

He held his son's quivering body and looked out at the winter street. He felt tears sting his own eyes, but he blinked them away. He kissed the top of his son's head and listened to the sound of the storm blowing up outside. And he asked himself how any of this had ever happened. There must have been one day when things had started to go wrong. There must have been one moment. Why had he never been able to see it? There must have been a reason, but he had not been able to locate it. He had married the only woman he had ever loved. It was the bravest thing he had ever done. They had had dreams. They had made plans. Now he was thirty years old, sitting in a car with his arms around his weeping, terrified child, and the one thing he knew for certain was that he understood nothing at all about his life. 'I won't go away, son,' he said. 'And if I ever did, I'd take you with me.'

He remembered it all very clearly. But there had been no reason, he told himself now. He knew that. He was in a town he knew nothing about, in a strange country, with people he did not know, still trying to find the son who had wept in his arms on that cold morning so many years ago, and there was no reason for any of this, except bad luck. It was a terrible truth that sometimes things had no reason to them. It was why people had invented God. He knew this now, but it still shocked him that the beauty of love was so bound up with its cruelty, that sometimes those two things came together. Nobody had ever told him about the loneliness of being a father. Nobody had told him about any of this. If somebody had only told him it would have been so much easier to understand.

Guapo finished telling Lorenzo what he could see. He stood up and began to wander around the forecourt, looking bored, then he gaped at Smokes asleep under the tree and giggled. 'Hey, Francisco,' he called, winking. He went over to Smokes and nudged him with his foot. 'Mar-ilyn,' he cooed. 'Oh, Marilyn?' Smokes woke up, swearing and mumbling. He picked up a handful of earth and threw it at Guapo. 'Fucking peckerhead,' he said.

'*Coño*,' Guapo replied. They came over and sat on the ground beside Frank.

On a hill at the far end of the town, nearest the sea, stood a tall white opulent-looking building. Guapo pointed it out to Frank. He said it was the new prison. He said that's where Johnny was and he smiled. 'I hope so, son,' Frank sighed. 'You know,' Lorenzo murmured, 'maybe he's looking down at us now. Could be he's standing at his window and thinking, who's those folks down there in that crazy old automobile?' Frank tried to laugh. He said Johnny would never be up this early.

It occurred to him that they were nearing the goal of their journey now and a sudden wave of fear swept over him. What if Johnny wasn't there? What if the man in the prison was not his son? What if his son was lying dead in the basement of some hospital far away? Or in some patch of scorched jungle crawling with vultures? He had a sudden image of his son's body, the body he had held in his arms so many times, twisted now like the corpse of the Contra boy in Esteli, battered, stinking, an object you would use to frighten the innocent, leaking blood, oozing entrails into the hot earth. He shuddered and tried to put the image out of his mind. They sat in the sunshine and waited for something to happen.

At about half past seven a very thin man in overalls came walking slowly down the road. Behind him came two scrawny children holding hands with each other. The girl was about thirteen. Her face was very pale and her dirty blue dress was torn. She was barefoot and there were streaks of grey mud on her legs. The little boy was about five. He was wearing shorts and a pair of big floppy sandals. He had a mop of untidy black hair and was carrying a plastic spade in his hand. The man stopped in the road and beckoned to the children. He turned into the forecourt of the tiny garage, carrying a toolbox and a bundle of keys.

'*Buenos días, hombres,*' he said in a sleepy voice, '*¿Cómo le va?*'

'*Tenemos un problema, compa,*' Guapo said. '*Creemos que la batería está descargada.*'

The man looked at Claudette and laughed. His thin face and the backs of his hands were covered with boils and white-tipped carbuncles. His skin had the texture of a shrivelled apple. He had pale lips and a drooping moustache, and long straggly hair under a black baseball cap. His eyes looked bloodshot and sore. Some of the pustules around his mouth were flecked with blood.

'*La batería*,' Smokes explained.

The man shrugged. '*Oh, no hay problema.*'

The children went over to the olive tree and sat down. The little boy began to dig into the sandy earth with his spade. The mechanic unlocked the door of the shack and went in, moving very slowly as though he was in pain. He came out with two plastic beakers of water and gave them to the children.

Guapo and Lorenzo said they would walk down to Ma Baker's and try to find some rooms. Cherry jumped out of Claudette and said she'd go along with them.

'*Hasta luego, Marilynita,*' Guapo said.

'*¡Y tu madre!*'

The mechanic laughed at them. He opened up Claudette's bonnet, wincing, and lifted out the battery. He put it down on a concrete block and connected it up to the charger. He nodded. The battery was completely flat. It would take about an hour to charge up, he said.

'We'll wait,' Frank said.

The mechanic shrugged. He looked under the hood again, reached in and pulled out the dipstick. He wiped it on his overalls, then peered at it and shook his head. He got a can of oil from the shack and filled up the engine. He took out the spark plugs and checked them, then threw them away, went back into his shack and found two more plugs, brought them out, sanded them down vigorously with a nailfile and screwed them into Claudette's engine. He unscrewed the carburettor and took it out. He held it up to his mouth and blew hard into it. He took a rag from his pocket, wiped the carburettor clean and put it back in.

Over in the shade of the trees the girl suddenly shouted. The little boy stood up and bawled 'Papa.' He ran over to the mechanic and wrapped his arms around his legs.

'Isabel,' the man called out. The girl came over to her father and looked sulky as he began to scold her. She grabbed the boy by the hem of his shorts and led him back over to the tree.

The man smiled at Frank and Smokes. '*Los niños,*' he said, shaking his head. He went down on his knees and began to fill the tyres with air.

'God,' Frank said, 'tell him he's a brave man to bring his kids to work with him.'

The man laughed gently. He shook his head again. His wife had died of malaria the previous year, he told them, and he made the sign of the cross. He had three more children at home and the oldest was looking after them. But the oldest was only fourteen, he said. It was too much for her to take care of them all.

Smokes yawned and the mechanic grinned warmly up at him.

'*¿Cansados, hombre?*'

'*Sí,*' said Smokes, '*muy cansados.*'

The mechanic stood and beckoned towards the door of his shack. '*¿Le apetece un café?*' he said.

'*Bueno, no gracias.*'

'*Oh, sí,*' the mechanic urged, '*un cafelito, nada más. ¿Por favor?*'

'What's he saying, Smokes?'

'He wants us to have coffee, Franklin. I told him no. He probably can't spare it.'

'Son,' Frank sighed, 'do you not know a thing about people?'

'What you mean, Franklin? He probably ain't got too much coffee, is all.'

'Well, Christ almighty, you can tell you were never poor anyway.'

Smokes giggled nervously. 'I don't get it, Franklin.'

Frank turned to him. 'Jesus, you don't rub it in, Smokes. You don't refuse a person's hospitality.'

They went into the shack and sat down together. The mechanic turned on the radio and they listened to the news. Fidel Castro was going to make a state visit to Managua and Ronald Reagan had asked Congress for more money for the Contras. The mechanic filled a kettle with water and lit the little paraffin stove. He opened a drawer, took out a small loaf of bread, broke it into three pieces and offered some to Frank and Smokes.

Frank took a packet of cigarettes from his pocket and lit one up. He noticed the mechanic looking at them and he held out the packet.

'Will you have one?'

'*Oh, no, no gracias.*'

'Go on,' Frank said. '*¿Por favor?*'

'*Bueno, gracias,*' the mechanic said. He took the cigarette from

Frank and sniffed it. 'American cigarette.' He nodded, putting it behind his ear. '*Muy rica.*'

'Take the packet,' Frank said. 'Go on. I've plenty more.'

The mechanic's eyes widened. '*Gracias,*' he said, and he took the packet from Frank. He stared at it for a moment, like a child with a new toy. He took out a cigarette, lit it on the stove and took a deep drag. He spluttered and started to cough.

'*Ay, Dios mío,*' he said, wiping his eyes. '*¿Es muy fuerte, no?*'

'*Sí,*' said Frank. 'Very strong. Very bad for your lungs.'

The mechanic smiled and pointed at himself. '*Me llamo José Ortega,*' he said.

Smokes chuckled. '*¿Igual que el Presidente?*'

The mechanic threw his eyes upwards. '*Oh, sí. El Presidente.*' He laughed and gestured around the shack. '*El presidente de petroleum.*'

Frank introduced himself and Smokes. The mechanic wiped his fingers on his overall, stood up and shook hands with both of them. '*Mucho gusto, hombres.*' He smiled, then peered at Frank.

'*Pero* Little?' he said to Smokes. '*Eso significa pequeño in español. ¿Verdad?*'

'*Sí.*'

'*Pero es grande,*' José Ortega said, clenching his fist and laughing. '*Está hecho un roble.*'

'He says you're a big strong guy, Franklin. He doesn't think you should be called Little.'

'*Sí,*' the mechanic said. '*¿Francisco el grande, no?*'

'*Sí,*' Frank laughed.

'I'll tell him you're going on a diet, Franklin.'

'I wouldn't, son,' Frank said. 'I don't think you talk about diets when a fellow's kids are hungry.'

José Ortega poured out three cups of coffee. '*¡Salud!*' he said, and they clinked their mugs against his. He sat down again and began to talk. He told them his wife had died in April the year before. He shook his head. She had always been very strong, he said; she had never been sick in her life. But two years ago there had been an outbreak of malaria in the town. It was carried by a terrible breed of mosquito, he told them. They had come from Africa, these mosquitos, and nobody could figure out how they had managed to get all the way over to Nicaragua, but they had come to Corinto, millions of them. It had been awful. You could see them everywhere. You could see clouds of them in the sky. You could put your hand out and they would come down and cover it, so that you would not be able to see your flesh any more. At night it was impossible to sleep because of the noise. In the end, things had got so bad that they had to empty the fonts in the cathedral because the mosquitos were breeding in the holy water.

He thought it was something to do with the oil himself. The air in the town was full of oil from the refinery, and somebody had once told him that bad air attracted these mosquitos. He thought it was the oil, but some of the old people said the mosquitos were a curse on the town. He wasn't so sure about that, but you certainly couldn't make a living in Corinto any more. This town was no good now. He hoped that his children would go away somewhere when they were older; he hoped they would go to America. The war was terrible, he said. To see the people fighting with each other was terrible. A few years ago everyone was on the same side, in the fight against the General. Now the very same men who had fought side by side were killing each other. It was wrong. It was like a family turning on itself. It was a very sad thing for Nicaragua. José Ortega poured out more coffee and he asked them why they had come to Corinto.

He listened to Frank's story, shaking his head with disbelief. 'Cristo y María,' he kept saying. He asked for the name of Frank's son, but then shook his head and said he had never heard of him. There was a girl too, Frank said, and they thought her name was Pilar. The mechanic shook his head again. It was a very popular name. There were lots of Pilars in Corinto. His wife's sister was called Pilar and so was his youngest daughter. But he could ask around, he said, if it would help. He knew a lot of people in the town and the people he knew could all be trusted.

He told them to be very careful about asking questions. Things were dangerous in Corinto now. The town was full of Contra spies and government agents and you just couldn't ever be sure if people were telling you the truth about themselves.

José Ortega looked at them for a few moments, then stood up and went to the door of the shack. He peered out into the road, waved to the children, closed the door, then came back and sat down. He leant forward, beginning to speak again, very quietly now, almost in a whisper. His eyes were nervous.

'Franklin,' Smokes said, 'he says there's a guy in the town we should see. He says if anyone knows about Johnny, this guy will.'

'Really? What's his name?'

José Ortega gnawed his lip. He took off his cap and ran his fingers through his dirty hair.

'Can he not give us the name, Smokes?'

The mechanic held his coffee mug in both hands as though he was cold. He stared into it, then looked up through the window and out into the road, shaking his head.

'*Bueno*,' he sighed suddenly. '*Es cura*.'

Smokes chuckled with surprise. 'He says he's a priest, Franklin. That's all he can tell us.'

'Smokes?' Frank said. 'Did Cherry say something to you about a priest before?'

'I dunno. Did she?'

'I thought she did,' Frank said. 'Some fellow in Ocotal told her there was a priest in Corinto worth chasing up.'

'Maybe, Franklin. I dunno.'

The mechanic swallowed hard. He pulled a dirty white handkerchief from his pocket and held it against his mouth, mopping it up and down his face. He glanced at the handkerchief, flecked now with yellow and red stains, crumpled it and put it back in his pocket.

'Where would we find him, Smokes? This priest? I mean do we go to the church or what?'

José Ortega laughed bitterly and shook his head.

Smokes shrugged. 'He says we should go down to the pier and ask around in the *cantinas*. Just ask anybody for the priest.'

'I don't understand. Could he help us find him maybe?'

The mechanic stood up very suddenly.

'*No, no, no*,' he snapped. '*No puedo hacer eso. No puedo. Tengo que pensar en mis hijos.*'

'Jeez. He says he's got kids, Franklin. He says he's gotta think of his kids.'

The mechanic began to cough, shaking and wincing with pain. He pulled the handkerchief from his overalls again and wiped his face and the back of his neck, breathless now. Thin watery blood was seeping from the cracked skin at the corners of his mouth. He folded the handkerchief in half and ran it quickly across his lips, shaking his head from side to side. He put his hands to his forehead.

'Jesus, Smokes. Tell him to relax, will you? Tell him it's OK.'

'*Lo siento*,' the mechanic said.

'We'd better head on, Smokes. Tell him thanks for the coffee anyway.'

José Ortega looked away. '*De nada*,' he said.

When they went back out on to the forecourt the morning was already quite hot. Light seemed to catch the mountain, picking out seams of mulberry blue and gold in the granite, reflecting back down over the bowl of the town. The concrete steps around the petrol pump were stained dark brown and an army of insects buzzed around in a spiralling cloud above the stains.

José Ortega took the battery out of the charger and put it back under Claudette's bonnet, connecting up the terminals. Then he climbed into the cab and started the engine. Claudette hummed and chugged. He jumped out, slapped the bonnet and wiped his blistered face.

'*Ahora no hay problema*,' he said.

Frank reached into his pocket and took out a bundle of *córdobas*.

'Ask how much we owe him, Smokes.'

The mechanic looked away, apparently embarrassed, then came up close to Smokes and spoke quietly to him. Smokes nodded.

'Frank, he wants to know if we got any food. He says his kids ain't eaten anything except bread for two days.'

'Jesus,' Frank said. 'I don't think we've any food left.'

The mechanic nodded. He held up the palms of his hands and stepped back, as though surrendering to something. '*OK, sí*,' he said. '*No hay problema*.' He took off his cap and scratched his head, looking up towards the hills, before turning to Smokes again.

'He wants to know if two dollars is alright, Franklin.'

Frank opened his wallet and took out a twenty, folding it.

'Here, Smokes. Give him this.'

'*No, no*,' the mechanic said. '*No tengo cambio*.'

'*Sí*,' Frank said. 'Go on. It's OK.'

'*Pero . . .*'

'It's alright, pal. Tell him it's OK, Smokes, will you. Tell him to keep the change.'

The mechanic stared at the twenty dollar bill. He pursed his lips and blew softly. '*Gracias, pues,*' he said. '*Gracias, hombre. Muy amable. Muchas gracias.*'

'*Por nada,*' Frank said.

He began to speak again, pointing over to his children.

'He says there's hardly any food in the town, Franklin. He gets paid in *córdobas,* but you gotta get dollars for the black market.'

'We understand,' Frank said. 'He's grand. Tell him he doesn't have to explain.'

They turned around and went towards Claudette.

'Franklin,' Smokes said, 'he don't want us to say he told us about the priest. If anyone asks.'

'Alright. Tell him it's alright.'

'He wants us to promise, man. We gotta keep his name out of it.'

'We will,' Frank said. 'Don't worry.'

José Ortega looked relieved as he stepped forward and shook Frank's hand.

'OK,' he said. '*Mucho gusto, hermano.*'

The children came out from behind the olive trees and ran over to stand beside their father. He put his blistered hands on their shoulders.

Smokes put Claudette into gear and they eased slowly out of the garage. They drove down towards the south pier, found the little *hospedaje* and pulled up. The others were waiting inside. There were only four rooms to spare, the *Señora* said, all with twin beds. They booked the rooms and paid thirty dollars. Guapo and Lorenzo took one room, Smokes and Cherry the second. Frank took one and booked Eleanor the last.

In the back of Claudette, Eleanor was still sleeping. Frank wrapped her in the sheet, and he and Guapo lifted her out, panting and staggering as they carried her up the two flights of stairs. They laid her down on the bed and opened the window. Cherry came in and said she'd put her into a fresh pair of pyjamas.

'OK, love,' Frank said. 'If you would. Thanks.'

The little dining room had a spectacular view of the west of

Corinto and the ocean. The town was a huddled spiral of black-ened buildings, grey slanted rooftops and aluminium chimneys with wide metal urns at the top. It looked conspiratorial some-how, and irredeemably ugly, but the sea beyond had the texture of silk and was a deep sapphire blue. Gulls whirled and played above the water. Guapo had a map of the town spread out on his knees. When he saw Frank he grinned and pointed to where the prison was marked.

Guapo said he had an idea. He knew an army corporal who was stationed somewhere up around here. They had been in the mountains together before the revolution and this guy owed him a favour or two. Guapo said he'd go into the town and find a bar where the soldiers drank. He'd be able to pass himself off as a local, he said, because he'd once had a girlfriend who lived down the coast in Poneloya and he knew how to talk in a northern accent. 'Meera.' He grinned. 'Booenas deeas, hermaaano.' Like a sheep, he said, and he chuckled. The people who lived in the north talked like sheep. Maybe he could find this corporal. Maybe he'd be able to get them a pass into the prison.

Smokes said he didn't think this was a great idea. They didn't want to get the military or the police involved. The police and the military were all party members and you couldn't expect them to do any favours. They could all get arrested for bringing Frank and Eleanor up here without a permit, and they really didn't want that. Guapo began to argue with him. Smokes laughed back scorn-fully. He said something that Frank didn't understand and then suddenly Guapo lost his temper and thumped the table with his fist as he spoke.

'No fucking way, Guapo,' Smokes said. 'You don't tell me what to fucking do, man. You don't run things here.'

Guapo threw the map down on the table, stood up and began to shout, prodding at Smokes's chest. Smokes slapped his hand away. They began to push each other and curse. Lorenzo stood up and touched Smokes on the arm.

'Brother,' he said, 'you take the beam out of your own eye, and not the speck out of your neighbour's.'

Smokes turned, his voice shaking with anger.

'Butt out, Lorenzo. I'm warning you. You just save that bible shit for the marines.'

Frank began to panic. He knew that Guapo and Smokes were about to have a fight. He had seen people fight before and he knew when it was too late to stop them. Lorenzo stepped towards Smokes and tried to take him by the arm. Smokes elbowed him away. Lorenzo stumbled and fell, crashing against the wall and knocking a framed picture to the ground.

Guapo sprang across the room at Smokes, grabbed his shirt and snarled at him, pushing him up against the wall. Frank moved towards him. Guapo put his hands around Smokes's throat and screamed. The *Señora* came rushing into the room. Lorenzo got to his feet and lunged out to grab Guapo's arms. '*No, hombre,*' he panted.

Guapo pulled away from him. Frank stepped between Guapo and Smokes and held out his hands. Guapo jerked his thumb at Smokes and yelled again, spittle flying out of his mouth.

'*Stop it,*' Frank shouted.

Guapo turned towards Smokes and spat on the floor. He sat down at the table and lit a cigarette with shaking hands.

'Jesus,' Frank said. 'What's going on here, Smokes?'

Smokes's face was florid with anger. He ran his finger around the collar of his shirt. 'Nothing, Frank. Guapo's just being a stupid dumb fuck as usual.'

'*Cobarde,*' Guapo said quietly. '*Váyase a tomar por culo.*'

The *Señora* gasped with horror.

Smokes turned to Guapo again. 'Here's the thing. I'm fucking telling you, man, you knock it off or you'll be fucking sorry.'

'*Tu madre,*' Guapo said, '*yanqui.*' He pulled hard on his cigarette.

'Come on, Smokes,' Frank said. 'We're all tired. Come on and we'll get some air.'

'I don't want fucking air, Frank. He's calling me a fucking coward, man. Like, I don't think we should get the fucking military involved and the guy calls me a fucking coward. Like, fuck it, we could get our asses shot off here.'

'I know that, son,' Frank said. 'Come on. Come on with me.'

'*Cobarde,*' Guapo shouted as they left the room.

They walked down the steps and into the front garden. Smokes was still breathing hard and quivering with rage, his eyes narrowed. He stopped on the path and lit a cigarette. 'That little creep,' he spat. 'He thinks he's fucking Che Guevara.'

'Yeah, son, I know. Come on, now. We're all just tired.' Frank put his hand on Smokes's shoulder. 'Let's just relax.'

Smokes sighed and allowed Frank to lead him down to the street. As they went out through the gate and made to turn towards the town, they heard a man's voice calling out behind them. When they turned, the street seemed to be empty. The heat haze shimmered. They could see nobody. '*Hombres*,' the voice hissed again.

José Ortega stepped out of the bushes at the front of the house. He took off his cap and ran his scarred fingers through his hair. He looked as if he wanted to be asked something. Suddenly he stepped towards them and began to speak in an urgent whisper, his eyes darting up and down the road.

'Oh, no, man,' Smokes said. 'This is fucking nuts.'

'What is?'

Smokes put his hands on his hips and stared down towards the sea. He shook his head wearily.

'He says he's been thinking, Franklin. If we can give him some dough, he'll help us find this fucking priest. He says he's embarrassed to ask for money, but his kids need food.'

'Well, that's fair,' Frank said. 'Is that not fair?'

Smokes shrugged. 'He wants us to pay him now.'

'How much does he need?'

José Ortega whispered to Smokes, looking mortified.

'Fifty bucks, Franklin.'

Frank took out five tens and handed them over. The mechanic crumpled the notes without looking at them and stuffed them into the back pocket of his overalls.

'*Gracias, hombre. Lo siento.*'

'He's gonna set it up tonight, Frank.'

'Where?'

'Some bar down on the pier. He says he knows people there.'

'What's it called?'

'*Las Diez Copas*,' José Ortega whispered. '*Se llama Las Diez Copas.*'

'Tell him I'll be there.'

'Franklin, listen,' Smokes insisted. 'I really dunno about this, man. This is getting *crazy* now. We don't know what we're into here.'

'Tell him I'll be there, son. I'll go by myself.'

'Jesus H, I'm not *saying* that, Frank. What is it with you guys? You all have to act the fucking hero.'

Frank looked at him and tried to make his voice sound conciliatory.

'I'm just trying to find my son, Smokes. If he was your son, you'd do the same.'

A motorbike sped past, raising a cloud of white dust. José Ortega turned his face towards the house. Smokes spoke to him again and the mechanic pointed at Frank, then at himself.

'He says he wants to help you, Franklin. He says you helped him and now he wants to help you. Like, I'm practically in tears here.'

Frank stepped forward and took the mechanic's hand. '*Gracias, José,*' he said. '*Gracias.*'

'*OK, Francisco, sí,*' the mechanic whispered. '*Hasta luego.*' He turned and began to walk quickly back up in the direction of the garage.

On the way into town they passed a tall white church on wooden stilts, splashed all over with red and black graffiti. A rectangular sign hung down over the canopy with the words *¡CRISTO VIENE!* painted on it in gold. Frank laughed. If Christ was coming to this town, he said, he was sure as hell going to be kept busy. Smokes said nothing.

Men and women were scurrying through the streets on their way to work. The foghorn blasted down on the dockside. The air was heavy with the stench of crude oil and the streets were thick with black mud. There were wooden footpaths and rows of small concrete shops with metal gates in the windows. Many of the shops had queues outside even though they were still closed. Lined along the waterfront were five vast black oil containers. They had skulls and crossbones painted on them in yellow and the word *PELIGROSO* in red. A couple of soldiers in grimy uniforms were slouched outside a grey two-storey building that had bars in the windows. They were stopping people and checking their papers. Another soldier was searching a man who was standing up against the wall, hands outstretched, legs spread. A dark green armoured personnel carrier was parked by a jeep in front of the building. A young woman in tight pink shorts and a T-shirt was leaning against the back of the jeep talking to a policeman. Frank and Smokes doubled back and crossed the street, then walked back down again without looking over at the soldiers.

The refinery belched huge stinking flames into the sky, so that Corinto looked gloomy, even though the day was sunny and bright. They walked straight through the town, past the school and the graveyard, until they came to the low hill where the *prisión* stood. A winding lane led up towards the main gates. They stood in the middle of a copse of wild olives, looking up at the building through the leaves.

It was an enormous white *hacienda* with grey fluted pillars, a broad staircase leading up to the door, long shuttered windows, an elaborate cornice with carved figures and a white balcony full of plants. It looked ridiculously tasteless, the kind of house that a country and western singer would put up and that coachloads of hick tourists would come to photograph. There was a vast flagpole on the roof, but no flag. When Frank peered through the leaves, he could see young men in leather jackets and jeans lounging around on the steps with soldiers. It didn't look like any jail he had ever seen, but Smokes explained that the old prison had been burnt down one night in a riot. This house had belonged to a first cousin of the General and now it had been requisitioned by the government. It was only used for special prisoners, sex offenders, traitors and foreigners.

They walked a small distance up the gravel lane, taking it in turns to watch the road and peer up at the house. Smokes scanned the upper windows, but all the shutters seemed to be closed. Sprinklers played over a pale green lawn that rolled down to the gates. Plovers and seagulls were pecking at the grass.

Suddenly, behind them, they heard the roar of a motorbike coming up the lane. 'Fuck,' Smokes said. He looked wildly around for somewhere to hide but there were thorny thickets on both sides of the road.

The motorbike sped around the corner and came to a stop, its tyres biting hard at the gravel. A woman soldier in black leather boots stepped off. Her face was very dark.

'*¿Qué pasa, hombres?*' she said cautiously.

Smokes shrugged. '*Nada,*' he said.

She walked towards them.

'Tell her, Smokes,' Frank said. 'Go on.'

'*Bueno, compañera, queremos hablar con el preso irlandés.*'

The soldier shook her head. '*No hay ningún irlandés aquí. Hay muchos extranjeros, pero no hay nadie de Irlanda.*'

'*¿Está seguro?*'

She folded her arms and stared. '*Sí. Seguro.*' She was watching them very carefully now. A ticking sound came from the motorbike.

'She says there's no Irish prisoner here, Franklin.'

'Ask her if we can see the German.'

'Frank,' Smokes said through grinning teeth, 'we gotta split.'

'Ask her, Smokes.'

The soldier stepped forward. '*¿Tienen ustedes permiso?*' she said. '*No.*'

She held up a finger and pointed towards the town. '*Fuera, pues.*'

'*Por favor,*' Frank said. '*¿Por favor?*' He took a step towards her.

The soldier stepped sharply back. '*¡Fuera!*' she snapped, putting her hand on her holster.

'OK, OK,' Smokes said. '*Nos vamos.* Come on, Franklin.'

They turned around and began to walk down the lane. The soldier stood by her motorbike, watching them, until they had rounded the corner. Then they heard the bike start up again and roar up the lane towards the *prisión*.

'Fucking lesbian,' Smokes muttered.

'Come on, Smokes,' Frank said. 'She could probably get the high jump for even talking to us.'

They trudged down the lane and back into the stinking town, passing a boarded-up cinema with long sheets of corrugated iron nailed into the doors and windows, and posters for American films still hanging in the dusty glass frames. The sun was a hard white disc in the sky. They went into a tiny café on Calle Pancotal and drank bitter coffee. Bloated cockroaches scuttled through the sawdust on the floor. A huge red plastic lobster hung from the roof. The walls were completely covered with picture postcards of faraway landmarks, the pyramids, the Eiffel Tower, the Taj Mahal.

Smokes said he was feeling very tired. The long night on the road was catching up on him. He said he wanted to go back to the *hospedaje* and crash for a while. Frank's head was beginning to throb with exhaustion, but he said he wouldn't be able to sleep and there was just no point in even trying. He felt gripped by some vague panic. His instincts told him this had all been a mistake, that his son was not here. He thought about Nuñez. The people in the hotel would have discovered that he and Eleanor were missing by now. He wondered if Nuñez had sent anybody after them. For the first time it occurred to him as a reality that they could be arrested at any minute. There were soldiers and police everywhere in the town. Any one of them could take him away and put him in jail. There wasn't much time. Something would have to be done.

'Son,' he said, 'listen, maybe we should find that Diez Copas place. The gaff your man was telling us about.'

Smokes sighed. 'Why, Franklin?'

'Well, if we could hook up with this priest fellow . . . You never know. He might be there now.'

Smokes looked into his eyes and Frank could sense his nervousness. It was so palpable now that he felt he could reach out and take it in handfuls. He had seen fear too often not to recognize it. It loomed up in Smokes's expression like an old adversary. It was a look he had seen many times, on his son's face, on his wife's, more than once in the mirrors of cars. There was a way you held yourself when you were scared. There was a darkness behind the eyes, a look that was infatuated with its own vulnerability. It was a thing actors never got right. When people were afraid they looked half alive; they didn't look excited. Smokes peered up at the red lobster as though suddenly captivated by it. His lips worked against his teeth.

'You know, Frank,' he said, shaking his head, 'I never liked this town. I always figured something bad could happen here.'

Frank attempted a laugh. 'Nothing bad's going to happen to you, kid. I'm lucky.'

'OK, man.' He nodded. 'I hope so. Because I feel my luck running low now. Like the oil in the engine, you know?'

'Engines are different, son. They're controllable.'

'Yeah, well. This better start feeling controllable too, Frank. I sure as hell could live with controllable.'

313

He said he wanted another coffee and then they'd go down to the pier.

At half past nine Eleanor sat up suddenly in bed, a startled expression on her face. She stared around the little room, but when she saw Cherry sitting by the dressing table, thumbing through a magazine, she smiled.

'Are we here, love?' she said in a hoarse, sleepy voice.

Cherry came over to the bed. 'We're here, Eleanor. How are you feeling now?'

Eleanor lay back on the white pillows. 'What dreams I had,' she said, touching her eyelids with her fingers. 'Good heavens, the terrible things that you keep in your head.'

'Now that's true,' Cherry said.

She sat up again. 'Love,' she said, 'I want to find that girl. That Pilar.'

'Now, honey,' Cherry said. 'I dunno about that.'

'No. You don't understand, pet. Guapo told Frank all about it. He said they were close, Johnny and this Pilar. He said she worked in an ice cream place. It's named after Elvis.'

Cherry poured some fresh lemonade into a glass. She turned her back to Eleanor, broke an egg into the drink, came over and held the glass to Eleanor's lips. 'Now, you just take it easy, honey,' she said. 'And maybe we'll do that tomorrow.'

Eleanor sipped at the thick liquid, grimacing. Then she rubbed her eyes and yawned. 'I'm going to find her now,' she said. 'It would be nice if you came with me, but I'll go by myself if I have to.'

Before Cherry could answer, Eleanor had stepped out of the bed. She went to the window and pulled open the curtains, gasping at the view of the sea. She went into the bathroom, washed herself and put on some clothes.

'I feel so funny in my head.' She laughed. 'So light.'

Cherry held her arm as Eleanor eased her way slowly down the stairs, gripping hard on the banister. 'What a lovely little place now,' she said when she saw the breakfast room all laid out with white tablecloths and clean sparkling glasses. The *Señora* brought coffee and a big jug of orange juice. The men were not here, she said. They had all gone out and were running around. That was all men were good for, running around thinking they were important. Eleanor nodded. 'Well, we're better off on our own.' She smiled. 'You'd get fed up of men too.'

They drank more coffee and then the *Señora* brought a bowl of salty soup and a bread roll. Eleanor ate a few mouthfuls and said it was delicious. The *Señora* looked pleased.

'We'll go now,' Eleanor said, 'and we'll find this Pilar.'

'But, honey,' Cherry said, 'we don't know a thing about her.'

'We do, love. She works in this ice cream place. Guapo told Frank all about it.' Cherry sighed.

'And anyway,' Eleanor said, 'I feel like an ice cream now after my lovely food. I think an ice cream would be the ticket.'

Eleanor went out to the hall and asked the *Señora*'s daughter to telephone for a taxi. When it came, the *Señora* and Cherry helped her down the steps and into the back seat. Cherry jumped into the front and the driver peered across at her bare legs. She pulled down the hem of her miniskirt and told him they wanted to go to the *glaceria* that was named after Elvis Presley. He laughed. There was no such place in Corinto, he said.

'*Sí*,' Eleanor said.

'*Creo que no, amor.*'

'*Sí. La Glaceria Elvis Presley.*'

The driver got out and went up the steps to speak to the *Señora*. They stood on the porch talking together for several minutes, but the *Señora* kept shaking her head and shrugging. She called her daughter out to the porch, and the driver spoke to her, then nodded, saluted and came back to the taxi.

'*No hay*,' he said. 'The *Señora*, she does not know.'

'Oh, dear,' Eleanor said. 'Are you sure?'

He pursed his lips. '*Bueno, momentito*,' he said, picking up his radio.

'*¿Compañeros?*' He chuckled. '*¿Dónde está la Glaceria Elvis Presley?*'

There was silence for a moment and then the radio crackled.

The driver turned around to look at Eleanor. He grinned. One of the men thought there was a Glaceria Elvis Presley on the road to Chinandega. It was about fifteen miles away, up in the hills.

'*¿Nos vamos, amor?*'

'*Sí.*' Eleanor nodded. '*¿Cómo no?*'

He looked at Cherry and winked. '*Nos vamos,*' he said. Eleanor called out of the window and told the *Señora* where they were going.

By the time Frank and Smokes got to the north pier the tide had gone out. An abandoned fishing smack lay sunk into the dark green mud, mast broken, keel encrusted with bright yellow barnacles. They walked down the pier, past rows of small *cantinas* and bars. None was called the Diez Copas. They stopped an old man who was shuffling back up the pier towards them and asked him for directions, but he said he had never heard of a bar with that name. They walked on, staring over the pier wall at the sludgy floor of the harbour. There were rusted bicycle frames and battered prams lying in the mud. Crabs scuttled through the rocks attacking the long black eels that lay stranded and jerking in the shallows. Frank and Smokes walked down towards the end of the pier, where the rock floor seemed to sink down steeply into a trench, giving way to greasy-looking water. Then down at the very end, in the shadow of the lighthouse, they came to a squat rectangular block of cement bricks, painted light and dark blue in a rigorous chessboard pattern. There was no sign over the door, but there was a huge tarot card painted on the gable wall, facing out towards the sea. The card was the Ten of Cups.

'I guess we're here,' Smokes said. 'The joint ain't exactly jumpin', huh, Franklin?'

The thick steel front door was locked with three heavy bolts. The shutters in the windows were closed and the side door was boarded up with wooden planks. They knocked hard on the door, but nobody came. They went around the back. The rear seat of a car was standing on a row of adobe blocks, facing out to sea. Used condoms were scattered on the ground in front of the seat. A pair of black scorpions scuttled around, nuzzling at the condoms, tails high in the air.

They went back around to the front door and Smokes kicked it. From inside they heard the crash of breaking bottles and the frantic growl of a dog. They could hear it running hard at the door, thumping repeatedly against the metal. It sounded big and heavy.

'*Está cerrado,*' a voice called out.

When they turned around, they saw a young man sitting on an upturned dustbin by the water's edge with his back to them. He had one arm. He was holding a fishing rod and staring down into the shallow water. A transistor radio sat on the stone beside him, playing country and western music.

He did not look up at them when they approached. He said he was a barman at the Diez Copas and the place wasn't open just now. It was closed all day, he said. He wasn't sure when it would be open again. When they asked if he knew a priest who went there the one-armed man shrugged. He didn't know any priests. He didn't think there were any priests who came to the Diez Copas. He'd lived in the town all his life and he'd never once seen a priest in the Diez Copas. It wasn't the kind of place you'd expect to find a priest.

'OK,' Smokes said. '*Gracias.*'

The young man sniggered without lifting his gaze from the water. He peered hard at it, as though he could see right down through the floor of the sea to whatever lay beneath.

'*No hay curas aquí.*' He laughed. 'No priest here, *yanqui.*'

The Glaceria Elvis Presley was a long thin clapboard building, painted candyfloss pink and lurid yellow. There was a big neon ice cream cone on the roof and a Sandinista flag sellotaped to the door. In the front room, a couple of teenagers were sucking at milk shakes, laughing and joking together. There were pictures of rock and roll singers on the walls – Jerry Lee Lewis, Buddy Holly, Little Richard with a giant pompadour hairstyle. Behind the counter hung a long framed mirror with a picture of Elvis Presley painted on it. He was wearing a red jacket and sneering, his black hair hanging in his eyes, a beautiful white guitar slung low around his hips. There was nobody behind the counter. One of the teenagers smiled across at them. 'Pilar?' said Eleanor. '*¿Dónde está Pilar?*' The boy pointed towards a door that led out to the garden.

The garden was alive with vivid wild flowers. Nightingales were warbling in the trees and a smug peacock strutted up and down, flashing its tail and pecking at the ground. There were little wooden tables painted white. Some of the tables had people sitting at them.

A young woman was making her way through the tables, collecting up empty glasses. She was tall and lithe and very beautiful, with prominent cheekbones, a large mouth and glittering dark brown eyes. Her hair fell in black ringlets across her shoulders. She was wearing a loose white blouse, jeans and a red apron. When she saw Eleanor and Cherry sitting down she came straight over to them.

'*Buenas tardes.*' She nodded shyly. She had a notebook hanging on a piece of twine from her belt. She picked it up and pulled a pen from behind her ear.

'*¿Entiende inglès?*' Eleanor asked.

'*Poquito.*' The girl smiled. '*¿Qué quiere?*'

Eleanor leant forward. Very lightly, she took the young woman by the wrist. The woman looked down at her.

'Pilar?' Eleanor said.

The woman nodded. She looked curious. 'Pilar Hernandez. *¿Por qué?*'

'My name is Little,' Eleanor said. 'Eleanor Little. I'm looking for Johnny, my son.'

Pilar Hernandez pushed her hair out of her eyes. She sat slowly down at the table. She asked if anyone had a cigarette.

When Frank and Smokes got back from town, Guapo and Lorenzo were sitting on the balcony strumming their guitars and working out the harmonies for 'Ruby Tuesday'. They sat down, ordered beers from the *Señora*'s daughter and began to tell Guapo and Lorenzo about the Diez Copas. Guapo was still in a bad mood with Smokes and he refused to look him in the face.

Outside a low rumbling sound began, like the roll of distant thunder. Smokes stood up quickly and leant over the balcony. Four army motorbikes came droning up the street, sirens wailing and lights on. The riders jumped off and ran to the corners of the junction, holding up their hands to stop the traffic. Coffee-coloured dust clouds rose into the air. Children ran out of the houses. A long line of open-back army trucks came rumbling up the street in a fume of diesel. The trucks were full of soldiers singing loudly, punching the air and waving rifles. There followed three dark green fire engines, a phalanx of beetle-shaped armoured cars and a rocket launcher mounted on the back of a low-loader.

'Jesus fucking wept,' Smokes said. 'Something's up here. This place is gonna be just crawling with military by morning.'

The *Señora*'s daughter brought out the beers. Smokes sat very still, staring at the table.

'Be still, brother,' Lorenzo said. 'Be still and know that I am God.'

'Ain't God I'm worried about, man. Ain't God at all.'

Frank took a sip of beer and stood up, yawning. He told them he was going to try to get some sleep.

'OK, son?' he said, and Smokes nodded absent-mindedly.

'Yeah, Franklin. Go for it.'

'So, I'll see you in a little while?'

'Yeah, Franklin, yeah. Catch you later, babes.'

He walked from the balcony, leaving Smokes and the others sitting in silence. Guapo picked up his guitar and started to strum it again.

'Brother,' Lorenzo said, 'you know, if God is for you, the nations are a drop in the ocean.'

Smokes nodded. 'Yeah, yeah. I know, Lorenzo. I know all that, man.'

Sixty seconds later Frank appeared in the doorway with a frantic look in his eyes.

'Where the fuck is Eleanor?' he said.

'Is he alive, love?' Eleanor asked. 'Do you know if my son's alive?'

Pilar looked away, her face liquefying to tears. Eleanor reached across the table and rested her hand on her wrist.

'*Yo no sé*,' she sobbed. '*Creo que no.*'

'Eleanor,' Cherry said, 'she doesn't think he's alive.'

'But tell her about the prison, Cherry,' Eleanor said. 'Tell her what they said to us in Managua. I mean that he might be up in the prison.'

An expression of disbelief came over Pilar's face as she listened. She shook her head. '*No*,' she said. '*No creo.*'

'Eleanor, she can't believe he's alive and didn't try to contact her.'

'It's possible though,' Eleanor said. 'Surely to God, it's possible, isn't it?'

'*No*,' Pilar said again. '*No es posible.*'

Eleanor sighed. 'Ask her did she know him well, Cherry.'

Pilar began to speak with great intensity, and so quickly that Eleanor couldn't follow, and Cherry had to translate almost everything she was saying. She seemed to be very frightened. She kept glancing over her shoulder, her long fingers twisting the edge of the tablecloth.

'He was real sweet,' Cherry said, 'but he could be cold sometimes. Like ice cream, she's saying. Sweet and cold. She met him after a concert, about a year ago. It was in Puerto Sandino, down the coast. She was there with her sister and her brother-in-law. She met Johnny coming out of a bar and they went dancing together.

'She's saying it wasn't serious at first. He was real gentle, and he was fun, but it wasn't serious. They were both happy with that. She had just split from her husband. He ran off to Miami with some girl from the next town. Johnny used to come and see her sometimes. He'd ride up from Managua on his motorbike and they'd go for trips into the mountains. And dancing. He really liked to dance, she's saying. And then after a while, she's saying, they started to fall in love.

'And at first that was OK too. But he never wanted to introduce her to his friends. Sometimes he seemed to want to run away from them. Sometimes they fought about it. He was real secretive. Sometimes she thought he was some kind of spy. Other times, she thought he had another girlfriend somewhere, and it felt like she was having an affair with a married man.'

'Yes.' Eleanor nodded.

Cherry continued. 'She didn't like it. He met all her family, and they really liked him. But he wouldn't allow her to meet anyone. She says he was a guy who lived *en dos mundos*. In two worlds. She couldn't figure it out. He seemed to want to live in this bubble. But after a while she got used to it. Her friends all said it was wrong, but she didn't really care. She was in love with him. She liked being with him. They made plans to get married, she's saying. They were going to get married next year, Eleanor. In February.

'So they tried to save some money. He was gonna take her away somewhere. Maybe back to Ireland. He said Ireland was a beautiful country. But saving money was real hard, and they sometimes fought about that too. He was real moody, she's saying. Sometimes real gentle. Other times full of this awful

320

anger. She says he could go without speaking for days on end.'

'Like Frank,' Eleanor said. 'Like his father.'

'On the night of the attack he was in a real bad mood. There was something on his mind and she couldn't find out what it was. He kept jumping up and looking out the window, she's saying. He kept staring up at the sky, as though he was expecting something bad to happen. When the bombs started to fall, he went down into the town with a gun. He wasn't going to do anything crazy, he said; he just had to see a guy. He told her he would be back before too long.'

'But he didn't come back?'

'It was the fourth of June,' Cherry said. 'It was the last time she ever saw him.'

'Does she know what happened?'

Pilar began to bite her fingernails. She stared into the middle distance, looking absolutely terrified.

'She's real scared, Eleanor. She says he knew this dangerous guy. She don't wanna talk about it. She says she can't say nothing else. This guy is real powerful in the town.'

Pilar looked over her shoulder. A man in a red suit was wandering around wiping the tables. She waited for him to go back into the *glaceria* before leaning forward again.

'*Es un hombre peligroso,*' she whispered. '*Está loco. Todo el mundo le teme.*'

'A dangerous man. A man the whole world fears.'

'*¿Cómo se llama este hombre?*' Eleanor asked.

Pilar shook her head. '*Por favor,*' she muttered. '*No puedo. Es contrabandista por la Contra.*'

'He's a smuggler, Eleanor. He smuggles stuff to the Contras in Honduras. She and Johnny had a bad argument about it.'

Eleanor nodded, shocked. 'Did she try to find out what happened when he went missing?'

'She went to the hospital, but they didn't have him there. She thought about going to the police then, but she couldn't. Because of the Contra stuff.'

'And he was definitely involved in smuggling? Is she sure?'

Pilar nodded her head. '*Creo que sí,*' she said bitterly. '*Y por la Contra. Por los mercenarios.*'

'It doesn't sound like Johnny,' Eleanor said.

Pilar's eyes widened with anger.

'*Por los hijos de putas que ataquen los pobres.*'

'For the bastards who attack the poor.'

Pilar bowed her head and said something quietly, shaking her head as she spoke. Cherry listened, tears suddenly welling up in her eyes.

'*Creo que está muerto.*'

'She thinks Johnny's dead, Eleanor.'

The wind made the *malinche* tremble and dance. Eleanor nodded again. She felt very calm now, and that surprised her. She felt a little weak, but her heart was beating steadily.

Suddenly Pilar put her hands to her mouth. Her lips trembled, and her fearful brown eyes flooded with tears. She mumbled something through sobs and gasps for breath. She put her hands to the side of her head as though she had heard some loud and terrible sound. She whimpered and choked out the words.

'Oh, fuck,' Cherry said.

She stood up and went over to Pilar, wrapping her arms around her neck, and Pilar gripped her arm.

'Oh, the poor mite,' Eleanor said. 'God help her.'

'Eleanor,' Cherry said quietly, 'Pilar's pregnant. She's four months pregnant with Johnny's kid.'

The *Señora* came back from the market to find Frank red-faced and frantic with worry. She laughed and told him to calm down. She said the two ladies had just gone off for a drive. They'd got themselves a taxi and gone to eat some ice cream. It was only twenty miles away, she said. It was a nice little village up in the hills. There was really nothing to worry about. It was a lot safer than going into the town.

'Fucking ice cream at a time like this.' Frank laughed. 'God. You have to love women all the same.'

Smokes walked up and down the porch kicking at stones, his hands deep in his pockets.

'Son,' Frank said, 'I'm feeling bad for landing you in all this.'

'Listen, Franklin. The joint is gonna be crawling with military by the weekend, man. That's all I'm saying. There ain't too much time.'

'You can go back home if you like,' Frank said.

'No,' Lorenzo said. 'We cannot go home.'

'Well, no,' Smokes said. 'I mean, obviously, no. Like, am I talking about going home here?'

'It's alright,' Frank said. 'You've done enough, Smokes.'

'Frank, who's fucking talking about going home? Jesus.'

Smokes sat down at the table and lit a cigarette. 'I mean we gotta do this gig Saturday night. We gotta stay until Saturday.'

Lorenzo slapped his hand on the table. 'We will stay until the time comes to go. There is a time for all things, but the children of Israel shall be free and the faithful shall see Paradise, sayeth the Lord.'

'Yeah?' Smokes snapped. 'Well, maybe I don't want to see fucking Paradise as soon as you, Lorenzo.'

'Maybe you don't, brother. Maybe that's your damn problem.'

'Now, come on lads,' Frank sighed. 'Come on. We've been up all night and we're all jacked. Let's just all get a bit of kip and not be fighting.'

Smokes stood up and stubbed out his cigarette. He said he was going to bed.

When Frank woke it was nearly six o'clock in the evening. He had slept so deeply that he had a bad headache. He got out of bed, splashed his face with water, brushed his teeth and tried to find some clothes that were not too filthy to wear. When he was dressed he zipped open his holdall and filled his wallet with banknotes. His money was running low. He had less than a thousand dollars left.

When he came out of the room, Smokes was waiting for him in the corridor, leaning on the wall and smoking a cigarette.

'Now, listen,' Frank said. 'You don't have to come with me, Smokes. I understand.'

Smokes sighed and put on his sunglasses. 'Shut up, Franklin, OK? Just shut the fuck up and let's go.'

Downstairs the *Señora* told them that Eleanor and Cherry were still not back. But they were not to worry. The women had telephoned a while ago to say that they were fine, but they hadn't wanted to wake anybody up after the late night. They would be home in a little while. They would be home in time for supper.

Frank and Smokes walked back up past the white church and

into the town. The sky had darkened to purple, with red and black slashes across it. A silver half-moon hung low over the horizon and fat flames spurted high from the oil stacks down on the docks. The air was thick with the noxious stink of iron and petrol. Music blared out from every *cantina* door. The main *avenida* was full of prostitutes wearing red miniskirts, low-cut blouses and high-heeled shoes that looked ridiculous in the muck. The streets were crowded with people; there were sailors and soldiers everywhere, roaring, fighting, singing songs. And there were herds of black cows in pens by the dockside wall, lowing in terror at the gushing yellow oil flames.

The Diez Copas was full now. It smelt of beer, smoke and sweat, and as they walked in, some of the men turned and stared. The room was suffused with dull red light and the jukebox in the corner was playing a slow raucous blues with the bass turned up too loud. On a tiny stage at the end of the room, a thin middle-aged woman was dancing in a sequinned miniskirt, a red bra, black stockings and a face mask of a tiger's head. A young man in a cowboy hat was gaping at her. Nobody else seemed to be taking any notice.

The one-armed man they had seen earlier on the dock was standing behind the bar wearing a scarlet silky waistcoat and a necktie with blue parrots on it. He didn't look happy to see Frank and Smokes; he shook his head and cursed when they asked for a drink. Frank took a twenty dollar bill from his wallet and slapped it down on the counter. 'Tell him we want a fucking beer, Smokes.' The one-armed man stared at the banknote, then reached down and took it. He groped under the bar, pulled out two bottles of beer, opened them and banged them down on the counter. He leant close.

'*Ustedes,*' he said. '*¿De dónde?*'

Smokes nodded at Frank. '*Irlanda,*' he said. '*Y yo soy norte-americano.*'

The barman's face relaxed. He winked. 'You wait,' he whispered.

'*Muchas gracias,*' Frank said, raising the bottle. 'Tell us, is the padre not here yet?'

'*No padres aquí,*' the barman snapped. '*Si quiere un cura vaya a la iglesia.*'

'If we want a priest we should go to a church. I think you're bugging him, Franklin.'

They sat at the bar drinking their beers, while up on the stage the stripper gyrated, swivelling her hips in time to the music.

'I feel bad, Franklin,' Smokes said. 'I'm feeling really spooked out, man.'

'Relax, kid,' Frank said, chuckling. 'Enjoy the view. We'll all be laughing about this soon. You and me and Johnny together.'

'I dunno, Franklin. Say if, like, this guy in the slammer ain't him? That broad said there were no Irish prisoners.'

Frank glanced at him. 'Smokes, look, mistakes get made. Most of these people have never seen a European in their lives, except in the fucking pictures.'

Smokes scoffed. 'You've been here what, a month, Franklin? You're a fucking expert now?'

Frank allowed himself a smile. 'All I'm saying is don't lose heart, son. You lose heart, there's nowhere else to go.'

Up on the stage, the woman in the mask was peeling off her bra. She held her thin breasts in her hands and turned to the wall. She had a tattoo of a rose in the middle of her back. She stepped out of her miniskirt and peeled her pants down over her thighs. Then she sloped off the stage and the music stopped.

They waited for half an hour. The bar gradually filled up until it was over-crowded. They drank some more beer. Night was falling now. Sweat poured down Smokes's face and he looked transfixed with fear.

'Will you relax, Smokes,' Frank said. 'For Jesus' sake. You're giving me the fucking heebies.'

'Frank,' he breathed, 'I never thought this would happen. I never thought I'd be stuck up here in a goddam dump like this.'

'Me neither kid. But I never thought I'd drive a taxi and get a heart condition either, and I did anyway.'

'Maybe, Franklin. But I'll tell you one thing, man. I don't ever want to see this town again when we're through.'

'Join the club,' Frank said. He swigged hard and belched.

'Jesus H,' Smokes said. 'They all drink like that in Ireland?'

'Aren't you very smart? We're the land of saints and scholars, you know.'

'Yeah, right.'

'Well, we are. Who d'you think civilized the whole of Europe?'

Smokes rolled his eyes. 'Who, Franklin? Tell me.'

'The Irish. The Irish monks, of course. Sure, when they were only lousy pagans over in England, we were building cathedrals. And wasn't it Saint Brendan discovered America, never mind that other blow-in, Columbus?'

'Bullshit,' Smokes said.

'You don't know your history, son. Did you never read the history of the church, no?'

'Franklin,' Smokes said, 'I'm Protestant.'

'So what? Wasn't Jesus Jewish?'

'What the fuck has that got to do with it, man?'

The one-armed man brought more beers, then strolled back down the bar. Smokes lit a cigarette and stared at the match burning in his fingers as though the flame was some sudden miracle he was trying to understand.

Suddenly the barman came back down the counter. He glanced at Frank, and nodded towards the door.

'Outside now, *hombre*,' he whispered.

'Shit,' Smokes said.

He stared at the ceiling as though some strange sound was emanating from it. He scratched his nose and sucked hard on his cigarette. 'Shit,' he said, closing his eyes.

Frank and Smokes both stood up. The barman lunged forward and clamped his hand over Frank's.

'*No*,' he hissed. '*Uno sólo.*'

'You'd better go, Smokes,' Frank said.

'*What*?'

'Well, I won't understand the lingo, son. I'd be useless.'

'Frank, I . . .'

'Smokes, look, I'll be right here. Just shout if there's any hassle.'

Smokes turned and took a swig of his beer. His face was pink and wet with perspiration. He turned again and looked at the door.

'Oh, well,' he sighed, 'damn the torpedoes.'

'OK,' the barman whispered. '*Uno sólo. No debe seguir, hombre.*'

'He says you're not to follow, Franklin.'

'OK, son, right. Good luck.'

'Don't wish me luck, Frank, OK? It makes me fucking nervous.'

Frank watched as Smokes walked out of the bar. He waited for a moment, then turned and craned his neck, trying to look through the window. Over in the shadows by the edge of the pier he thought he could see Smokes's long thin back. He seemed to be talking to a man in a black coat, but the condensation was fogging up the glass, so it was hard to make anything out.

The barman grinned at him, running his fingers through his straggly hair. Then he leant in close and spoke slowly.

'Hey, *Irlanda*,' he said.

'What?'

He held one finger in the air. 'It is a long way to Tipperary. *¿Verdad?*'

'Yeah,' Frank said. 'It is.'

The barman nodded. 'To the sweet girl I know. *¿Verdad, Irlanda?*' He laughed and wiped his lips with his tie.

'Very good,' Frank said. 'You're bleeding hilarious.'

'*Sí.*' The barman grinned. '*Cristo y María.* For you, *Irlanda*, it is long way to Tipperary.'

Frank waited for five minutes. A thick cloud of cigarette smoke hung under the ceiling of the Diez Copas. The barman kept staring at him and smiling. Frank's heart pounded. The stripper came back on to the stage and the blues music started up again.

The door opened and Smokes came back in. He walked straight up to the bar, picked up his beer bottle, took a swig from it and wiped his mouth with his sleeve. He gasped as he clutched Frank's hand.

'We're in business, Franklin,' he choked. 'This dude in the prison, with the Kraut passport? *He ain't German.*'

Frank sat down, breathing hard. He felt a thundering sensation in his chest. His son was alive. Tears burned in his eyes. His son was alive. He drank some more beer. He wanted to find Eleanor and tell her. His son was alive. He hung his head and tried not to cry, but the tears came anyway.

'Was it the priest?' he said.

'One of his homeboys,' Smokes panted. 'Mean-looking mother with an Aka.' He put his hand on Frank's thigh.

'Franklin, listen to me. This guy in the prison, this guy with the German passport. The priest's *hombre* won't say if it's Johnny or not, but he can get us in there to see him.'

'When? When, Smokes?'

'Tomorrow, Franklin. But it's gonna cost.'

'How much?'

'Five hundred for the in, Frank. For the priest. After that, if it's Johnny, we talk again. It's gonna cost more to get him out.'

'That doesn't matter, son. Here, do you have to go back out to him with the dough?'

Smokes nodded towards the barman. 'No, no. We just give it to Lord fucking Nelson here.'

Frank reached into his pocket and pulled out his wallet, extracting four hundred notes and two fifties. He folded them, looking at the barman's face.

'Franklin,' Smokes said, 'I think we should talk about this.'

Frank put the banknotes on the bar. 'You'd better count it,' he said.

The barman sniffed and shook his head. With delicate fingers, he peeled the banknotes off the damp counter. 'No, no. You are my good buddy, *Irlanda*. Is OK.'

He stuffed the soggy banknotes into his breast pocket.

'Goodbye, Piccadilly.' He grinned. 'And farewell, Leicester Square.'

'OK,' Smokes said. 'OK, Franklin. So, we gotta wait here for five minutes and then split.'

He leant his elbows against the bar and began to watch the stripper. She was wearing nothing but stockings now and thrusting her thighs against the corner of the jukebox. The blues music pounded out. Frank stood up and began to button his jacket. He glanced at his watch and noticed that his fingers were trembling.

'We'll have to go and tell Eleanor,' he said.

'He said to wait for five minutes, Frank.'

A crowd of men began to gather around the stage. The woman put her hands on her hips. She danced over to the jukebox, picked up a beer bottle and waved it in the air. The men clapped. She licked the cap on the bottle top and rubbed it across her breasts. She put the neck of the bottle into her mouth and began to push it slowly in and out between her lips.

Frank craned his neck to see out the window again, but the

glass was so steamed up now that it had become opaque. His son was alive. He knew it. He ran the words over in his head. His only son was alive.

'Let's go, Smokes.'

'Wait another minute, Franklin, OK? I wanna go home with my kneecaps intact, you know?'

Frank looked at his watch. 'Look, we have to go, Smokes. I can't stand this gaff any more.'

They stood up and began to move towards the door. The naked woman knelt down and parted her legs, putting her hands behind her back. The men crowded around the stage, pushing each other and jostling, yelling and stamping, clapping in time with the music. And then, suddenly, the bar exploded with drunken cheers.

'*Hombres*,' the barman shouted. Frank turned in the doorway, breathing hard. In the dull red light, the one-armed man grinned and raised his glass.

'*Venceremos*,' he called.

They closed the door on the roar of loud applause. A stinking breeze swept up from the sea.

They looked around, but there was no sign of anyone. The pier was completely empty. They walked quickly back up towards the town, then stopped for a moment to catch their breath. Smokes lit a cigarette. They stood at the edge of the pier and stared down into the black water full of cardboard boxes, matted seaweed, old tyres.

'Well,' Frank said, 'your friend must have slipped off.'

'I guess. Jesus, Franklin, he was one tough-looking honcho.'

Frank beamed and clapped his hands together. 'But Johnny's alive, Smokes. I told you, didn't I? He's alive.'

Smokes shook his head. 'I'll believe it when I see it, Franklin. I dunno about this. I'd trust this priest guy 'bout as far as I'd spit a rat.'

'We've no choice, Smokes. We've nobody else to trust.'

Smokes sat down on a bollard. 'I'm not so sure, Franklin. I'm sorry, man.'

They stared out at the dark blue sea. The foghorn bawled and ropes rattled against metal masts.

'Well, don't be sorry, son. I mean, even if you're right, there's nothing to lose now.'

Somewhere in the distance, a police siren was wailing. The silver beam of the lighthouse swept out across the water.

'Except five hundred dollars, Franklin. It's a lot of bread. For five hundred dollars I'd wanna be meeting Jesus Christ. I'd wanna be putting my fingers in the fucking wounds, you know?'

Frank laughed. 'I wouldn't say that too loud, son. In this town, it could probably be arranged.'

When they got back to the *hospedaje*, Eleanor and Cherry were waiting in the dining room. There was a young and very beautiful woman with them. She had the most marvellous black hair, all hanging down in ringlets around her neck.

'Eleanor?' Frank said. 'You're feeling better?'

'Frank Little, where in the name of God were you? This is a friend of Johnny's. A special friend.'

'Oh,' he said. 'Is it Pilar?'

Pilar gazed up into Frank's face as though she recognized him. He went over and took her hand.

'*¿Es usted su padre?*' she said.

'Yes. I'm his father, love. I'm delighted now to meet you.'

'Frank,' Eleanor said, 'I think you should sit down.'

'You're feeling better anyway? You're looking a lot better after your ice cream. Doesn't Eleanor look well, Smokes?'

'Yeah. Eleanor looks great, Frank.'

Frank sat down and poured himself a cup of coffee. Pilar smiled at him. He caught her expression and laughed.

'Well, God, he has an eye for a pretty face anyway, fair play to him. How the blazes did she find out we were here?'

'Frank, Pilar has some bad news for us. She thinks the news about Johnny is bad.'

Frank scoffed. 'God, would you get away out of that. Sure, haven't I just paid out good money to see him?'

'What do you mean? Who did you pay?'

He chuckled. 'Oh, now, that doesn't matter. You leave all that to the men. You girls are better off thinking about your ice cream.'

'What do you mean, Frank? What have you done?'

'We're going to see him tomorrow in the jail, Eleanor. It's really as simple as that.'

Eleanor looked up at Smokes. He shrugged and turned away.

'It's a lovely name, isn't it?' Frank said. 'Pilar. That has a lovely ring. You could write a lovely song about it.'

'I don't think you understand, Frank.'

'Don't start, Eleanor. I'm not in the humour now.'

'Frank, please.'

'Don't.' He laughed. 'Don't tell me I don't understand. I'm warning you now, Eleanor.'

There was a silence. He put his cup carefully back on the saucer and looked at her.

'I don't mean to be short with you,' he said. 'But we're seeing him tomorrow. It's all arranged now.'

40

Prisoners

MORNING CAME, bright with rain, over the sweep of Corinto Bay. Frank got out of bed, still numb and reeling with tiredness. He switched on the radio and turned the dial until he found some music. It was a Cole Porter song, sung by Ella Fitzgerald. He listened to the music while he washed and shaved, and it made him feel a little lighter. He swayed gently from side to side as he sang along, thrilled by the cleverness of the words.

> *In shallow shoals, English soles do it,*
> *Goldfish in the privacy of bowls do it*
> *Let's do it, let's fall in love.*

He smiled. If people could think up words like that there was still some hope for the world.

His skin felt clean and raw. He opened the bathroom cabinet and took out a glass bottle of yellow liquid, removed the stopper and sniffed it. It smelt of lemons. He dabbed a little of the liquid on his face. His skin stung.

He sat on his bed and began to smoke a cigarette. He found himself thinking about Ireland. He thought about the dirty streets of Dublin filling up with early morning traffic. He thought about the drive into work, about queues of schoolchildren at bus stops, the sound of Gay Byrne's voice on his radio show, the taxi drivers laughing at each other, calling each other names in the back room of the office, getting ready to go out for the day. He thought about the chink of milk floats, and he closed his eyes. He would have liked to hear that sound now, the simple sound of milk bottles chinking in crates, and the realization amused him. But

332

then suddenly it occurred to him that it wasn't morning in Dublin. It was evening, and people would be going home now. He loved going home at five o'clock after work. He loved getting into his car and turning on 'Today At Five' and listening to the politicians being interviewed. It made him feel very content, though he didn't know why. Every day he tried to do the same thing. He would buy a can of Coca-Cola, get into his car, light up a cigarette and turn on 'Today At Five', knowing that the day's work was over and he was going home. He liked to know what was going on. He liked being able to talk to Veronica about what had been on the news. He took another long drag on his cigarette. He wanted to go home.

When he went down to breakfast the empty room looked sparklingly clean. There was a brown foolscap envelope sitting on his plate and his name was written on it, printed very carefully in large letters, along with the word *URGENTE*. The *Señora* came in, bringing bread rolls and a jug of water. She managed to make him understand that she hadn't seen who had brought the envelope. It had been lying on the porch when she'd come back from the market. She stood looking at him while he opened it.

The envelope contained an official-looking form filled in with Frank and Eleanor's names in untidy handwriting. The form had been rubber-stamped twice, and scrawled on the back were the words *Prisión, 7 pm, dos personas.* He groped in the envelope, but there was nothing else. The *Señora* peered at him. She raised her eyes questioningly and said something. He wished he could speak even a little Spanish. He showed her the form and she shrugged and smiled and brought him a pot of coffee.

He ate alone, looking down into the town. The sea was greener this morning and spread out in lightening shades towards a chain of rock formations and distant islands. A dark green tank peeped out into the street like a curious animal awakening from hibernation. It edged forward and rumbled into the Avenida Lenin. A soldier wearing black headphones was standing in the turret, peering down at the sea through a pair of binoculars.

Two young boys were walking along the street, arm in arm, delivering newspapers. Frank watched them. One of the boys had a bag slung over his shoulder. From time to time he would take a newspaper out of this bag and give it to his friend, who was a little younger. The younger boy would fold the paper and run up into one of the porches with it. Then he would come out and walk on with his friend, and they would start again. He watched them gradually make their way up the street. They looked very content, these two boys. The sky was flecked with streaks of dark blue and orange. The town was very still. In the clean, crisp light, it was as close as it was ever going to get to being beautiful.

Smokes came down after a time, looking gaunt and dishevelled. His face was dark with stubble and his eyes were circled with light grey rings. He said he hadn't slept at all. He had been awake all night, thinking about Johnny. He had been trying to figure out why Johnny had never told him about Pilar Hernandez and how serious things were between them. He couldn't figure out how to feel about it, no matter how hard he tried to understand. 'Jesus, Franklin,' he murmured, 'I thought we were friends, you know? It just bugs the shit out of me.'

Frank sighed as he poured Smokes a cup of coffee. 'I've known the guy twenty-one years, kid. There's nothing would surprise me about him any more.'

Smokes leant his elbows on the table and stared into his coffee cup. 'I just thought we were friends, Frank. I don't understand it. Like, I think I know the dude, then it turns out he has a girlfriend and a kid coming and he's working for the fucking Contras. Jesus.'

'Who knows what goes on?' Frank said. 'Everyone has a surprise, son.'

Smokes shook his head. 'But the Contras, Franklin. That's bad, man. That's major league low-rent.'

When Eleanor came down she was in an odd mood. Frank showed her the pass and she nodded and looked away and said she would make sure to be ready when the time came. He had expected her to be excited, but she didn't seem to be. He was going to say something about it, but he decided it would be better not to. She was just in an odd mood. It was the strain of everything. It was not a crime to be in an odd mood, after all.

'Well, now,' he said, 'I'm after hearing a great old song on the radio there. One of the old standards. It made me think of that time we were at the dinner dance with Billy Boland. You know? That time he stole the ice bucket out of the hotel?'

She nodded.

'This fellow, Smokes,' Frank said, 'he was a gas. He used to nick things just for the laugh. Myself and Eleanor went out with him and his fiancée this one night, you see, and Billy was wearing this huge overcoat. Out he comes anyway into O'Connell Street, and underneath the coat he has this big bloody ice bucket, and a sign off the wall. This Way Out, it said. God, Billy was mad as a hatter. He was astray.'

He looked across the table at Eleanor.

'There was another time. He worked in the same office as me, and he was making the tea. It was one time when Johnny Doyle, our boss, was away. I met Billy on the stairs and he had this big tray full of cups of tea, and he says to me, Frank, what do you think would happen if I threw all these cups of tea over the banisters? Well, of course I told him I didn't know. Next thing he takes the tray, full of tea, and he just fucks it over the banisters. Jesus, tea all over the place, up and down the walls, broken cups everywhere. And then Johnny Doyle's office door opens and he comes out. He wasn't gone away after all, do you see? He just stands there looking up at Billy with a face like thunder. And Billy is shitting bricks. And he suddenly grabs his chest, you know, and he starts groaning, and he throws himself down the stairs as though he's after having a heart attack.'

Smokes grinned. Frank laughed and stirred his coffee.

'Did you ever hear what happened to Billy afterwards, El?'

'No, Frank. I never did.'

'Well,' he said, 'didn't he get married and go away? Canada, wasn't it, that he went to?'

'I said I don't know, Frank.'

'I think he got married,' Frank said, 'and went to Canada. I heard something about Toronto. He was a gas man anyway, the same Billy, wasn't he, Eleanor?'

'Yes,' she said. 'He was.'

Smokes and Frank finished their breakfast while Eleanor ate a little bread and half an avocado. Frank stared at her, wishing she would say something, then glanced at Smokes. Smokes pulled a nervous face. Eleanor kept eating, looking down at her plate. Frank clapped his hands together and asked her what she was going to do today.

She was going to spend the day with Pilar, she told him. They were planning to go for a long walk in the hills, maybe take a drive up to see the Cosiguina volcano and the thermal springs. 'I thought you might like to come up with us,' she said.

'Well, I thought I'd just leave the two of you alone for the day.'

She stopped eating and asked him to pass the coffee pot.

'I mean, I'll go if you like,' he said. 'But you know me for sightseeing.'

'No, it's alright. Cherry's coming with us anyway.'

She dabbed her mouth with a napkin and laid her cutlery carefully across her plate. Smokes began to whistle. Eleanor asked Frank for some money. She wanted to get a few things for Pilar in the market.

'Oh, right,' he said. 'Of course.'

He took out his wallet, gave her a hundred dollar bill and told her just to ask if she needed more.

'I shouldn't have to ask, Frank,' she snapped. 'She's practically family now, after all.'

Smokes stood up, yawning ostentatiously. He said he'd catch them later and strode out of the room.

'What's the matter with you today?' Frank asked. 'Did you not sleep?'

'Nothing's the matter, Frank. If I'm not bloody tap-dancing you always think something is the matter.'

She folded up the banknote, put it into the pocket of her shirt, then began to eat the other half of her avocado.

'Well,' he said, 'do you want me to drive you to the market?'

'No, Frank. I'm after ordering a taxi.'

He picked up a fork and played with the leftovers of Smokes's breakfast. She took an emery board out of her handbag and started to file her nails. He fingered the tines of the fork, looking at her. 'Are you thick with me or something?' he said.

'Oh, for God's sake, stop it,' she said. 'A person wouldn't have a minute's peace around here without being bloody quizzed.'

After lunch, Lorenzo went back to bed, saying he was tired and still hadn't recovered from the long night crossing the mountain. Frank and Smokes walked into the town with Guapo. They strolled across the Ponto Icaco and down to the beach, talking about Johnny. Smokes was still upset that Johnny hadn't confided in him. He just couldn't figure out why he'd told Guapo and not *him* all about Pilar. 'I know the guy was quiet,' he said, 'but, Jesus, you tell your friends everything, don't you? You tell your friends the truth?' When he said that, Guapo raised his eyebrows and laughed out loud. Sometimes you did, he said, and sometimes you didn't. It all depended on what sort of friends you were talking about.

They strolled back up to the plaza and went into a *cantina*. It was small, with wooden benches arranged at long wooden tables. Two young foreign women came in with rucksacks on their backs. They were both blonde and they had on shorts and hiking boots, and one had on a T-shirt decorated with the Southern Cross of the Australian flag. They ordered beers and put some money into the jukebox. The sound of sweeping violins began. Guapo whistled to himself as he gawped at the women. He stood up and shimmied across the room, crooning the words of the sentimental song. When he got to their table he knelt down on the floor and started singing even louder. They stared down at him with a mixture of curiosity and embarrassment.

'Look at the antics.' Frank chuckled. 'That fellow will get himself shot one day.'

'They'll get shot too,' Smokes said, 'if they're up here without a permit.'

Frank turned, grinning. 'Who'd shoot them though?'

'For sure, yeah,' Smokes said, 'who would, man? Not me.'

Frank watched as Guapo continued to sing. The two young women smiled and then Guapo suddenly leapt to his feet, grabbed two plates from the table and started to juggle them, still singing. The barman called out for him to stop. Guapo sat down between the two women and pulled a face at the barman. The women laughed and called out for more beer.

'I've a few brothers in Australia myself,' Frank said. 'In Melbourne. I always meant to go over, but I never got around to it.'

'You should go, Franklin,' Smokes said. 'Maybe all the babes over there look like those two.'

'I was going to go once, but I was never sure what they'd think,

337

you know, about Veronica and me. They're a bit old-fashioned.'

'I got a brother in West Point,' Smokes said. 'He's an imperialist son of a bitch, but, hell, he has his moments.'

'Everyone has their moments,' Frank said.

'I guess, Franklin. Max used to be a great card player, actually. People thought he'd take after my dad.'

'Your old man played cards?'

'Oh, yeah. He played cards for a *job*, Franklin. That's what my old man did. Didn't I ever tell you that? Oh, yeah, he was pretty shit hot. He went all over the world playing poker.'

'Go away,' Frank said.

'No, straight up, Franklin. Card players go on these cruises, you know? It's like a circuit. He'd go play for six months, make enough bread to sit on his ass for the rest of the year. He took me on one of them one time. It was a big ship, you know, real smooth. I'll always remember it. We're sitting on the deck one day, we're down in Florida or somewhere, and there's a big game going on. My dad is betting. He has the jack, the queen, the king of hearts, right? He shows me his hand and goes what do I think. Like, I'm ten, man, I haven't a clue, you know, but he shows me and I'm happy as a clam. He asks me what'll he do, bet or fold, and I say bet. So he goes OK, flashes the cash, buys two cards. The dude pulls out the ace of hearts and the fucking ten, Franklin. Won three and a half grand in cash. Lost it all the next night.'

'Jesus,' Frank said, 'what a way to earn a crust. I'm sure your mother wasn't too mad about that carry-on.'

Smokes shrugged. 'They fought a bit, you know? He couldn't keep it in his pants, I guess. But they dug each other too. I mean don't you fight with Veronica, Franklin?'

Frank sipped at his beer. 'We've had our ups and downs alright. Johnny and her had terrible run-ins. Asking a woman to bring up someone else's kid is dicey.'

'But there's never been nobody else?'

Frank laughed. 'I did meet a woman a few years ago. She was a lovely bird. She would have done me very well. She was my own age and she liked singing. Knew a lot about music. She was like Eleanor that way.'

'So, hey, did you do the wild thing, Franklin?'

'We went to the opera once, on the QT. It was a Saturday night, when Veronica was away, and we went to see *Carmen* together. Veronica doesn't like opera, you see. She finds it a bit much. But that was the height of it. She was a very attractive person, but it just didn't feel right to me.'

'Franklin, I'm surprised at you, man. Variety is the spice of life, ain't it?'

'No,' he said. 'Monogamy is the spice of life, son.'

Smokes cackled with laughter.

'And, anyway, I think betraying someone is a terrible thing to do. When you get a bit older it's worse. You've got to know a person very well, you see. It's not like when you're young. When you're young you just tumble into bed and everything is grand. When you're older you're a part of the person's life. You have your obligations to that.'

Smokes shook his head. 'Jesus, Franklin, you really are one righteous mother.'

'I'm just a stayer, son. But I don't know if I'd change it, even if I could.'

'I don't think I'm a stayer, Franklin.'

'Yeah, Smokes, well, it takes all sorts.'

Smokes went up to the bar and ordered another round of beers. From across the room Guapo pointed at him and whispered something. The Australian women laughed. 'Hey?' they shouted. 'Marilyn?'

Smokes brought the beers back to the table and said he wanted to go and join Guapo. 'Come on over with me, Franklin,' he said. 'Nobody ever got pregnant talking, huh?' Frank said he was happier by himself, but he told Smokes to go ahead. Smokes picked up his beer and sloped across the *cantina* to Guapo and the two women.

Frank tried to read a newspaper, but he could not concentrate. He kept looking at his watch and every minute felt like an hour. He stared down at the sea and found himself thinking about the time he had gone swimming with Johnny at Sandycove Beach. He thought about how cold the water had been that day, even though it was June and the weather had been hot and sunny. There had been an Irish tricolour flag flying from the roof of James Joyce's tower. He had thought that odd, for some reason, but he couldn't remember why. Was it something to do with his father? Hadn't his father once said that James Joyce had done nothing but run Ireland down for money? But there was the Irish flag anyway, flying on top of the tower.

And there had been some nuns on the beach, that was right. Johnny had laughed at the nuns, all sitting on the beach in their long black robes and sensible thick shoes. Frank had told him to stop, even though he had found the nuns funny himself. On the way home they had stopped to buy fish and chips in Glasthule, he remembered that, and then he and Eleanor and Johnny had sat out in the back garden eating them, and Eleanor had been wearing a red bathing suit. Johnny had gone off to play with his friends. Then Frank and Eleanor had gone into the house, in the middle of the afternoon, and they had gone up to their bedroom, and they had made love, and he had covered her breasts with kisses while the sun beamed in through the window, warming their bodies. He remembered it very well. It was the day he had noticed the Irish flag on the Martello tower in Sandycove and thought it an odd thing to see. It was the last day they had ever made love.

When they finally left the *cantina* Frank felt quite drunk. Gangs of soldiers were digging pits and filling sandbags. Radio speakers had been put up on all the main street corners and they were blasting out military music and speeches. There was a sense of urgency in the air. People were standing in groups around the radio speakers, talking and listening. The radio announced that strict rationing would be introduced at the weekend. Coupons would be distributed for milk, meat, coal, wood, soap, salt and bread. There was a speech by the local party leader. Hard times lay ahead for Corinto, he was saying, but the people would triumph in the end. In the Calle Grande soldiers were handing out weapons and rounds of ammunition to gangs of clamouring men and women. In the central plaza, coaches and trucks stood throbbing and spilling out diesel fumes. Children and old people were queuing up to get into the coaches. Smokes stopped and stared at the queues. He looked nervous and distracted.

'What's going on now?' Frank said.

Smokes turned to look at him, swallowing hard in order to get the words out. 'They're evacuating people, Franklin. They think the Contras are coming again.'

They went back to the *hospedaje* and lay down for a few hours.

The *Señora* called them at six o'clock and they ate a meal of greasy cold meat and shrivelled lettuce. Lorenzo said he still wasn't feeling well. His stomach was aching and they'd run out of Lomotils. They ate in silence, listening to the solid ticking of the grandfather clock.

When Frank went back up to Eleanor's room, she was sitting on the bed, wearing white slacks and a creased cream shirt. The wind had whipped up and outside a light rain was falling.

'How was Pilar today?' he asked her.

'Oh, she was alright, I suppose. We saw the volcano. She invited me over to meet her mother tomorrow.'

'That'll be nice.'

She nodded and looked up at him. Her face looked tired and her eyes were rheumy.

'Eleanor?' he said. 'Do you think you'll be alright?' His jaw still felt heavy from the afternoon's drinking.

'Yes, Frank,' she said, 'I'll be alright.'

He glanced at his watch. 'Will we head so?'

'Yes.' She nodded. 'I'm ready to go now.'

Smokes drove Frank and Eleanor through the narrow streets of the town. There were people everywhere, strolling out for the evening, some of them with rifles over their shoulders. When Smokes turned into the Calle de la Luna he stopped and cursed. A barricade had been set up across the street and it was too late now to turn around. They edged slowly forward, but the soldier just took one look at Claudette before waving them through. Smokes heaved a deep sigh.

'There, you see.' Frank laughed. 'I told you I was lucky.'

Smokes drove to the end of the gravel lane and stopped the van, his hands quivering. He offered to wait for them, but they told him they would walk back. They would want some time together afterwards. They would need some time to talk about things.

He nodded. 'Franklin, Eleanor, we're all rooting for you.'

They climbed out of the van and Smokes drove away. They

walked quickly up the yellow gravel lane. Bees were buzzing and the evening was a little cooler now. The air smelt of violets and new-mown grass. A fat dun-coloured rabbit lolloped out of the hedgerow and into the lane. It paused and sniffed at the air for a few seconds. When it heard Frank and Eleanor coming it froze, then turned quickly and hopped back into the thicket.

The prison gates were flanked by two smug-looking stone eagles on pillars. Frank rang the bell in the white wall. After a moment the gates clicked open. They pushed through and walked up the drive towards the front door.

A thin, nervous guard stepped out into the porch holding a pistol. He seemed to be expecting them and didn't ask to see any identification. He peered around suspiciously as though sure he was being watched, then ushered Frank and Eleanor into the building.

'*Rápido, rápido,*' he hissed.

The guard led them quickly through the long entrance hall. It smelt of candle wax and old leather. The floor was tiled with slabs of black and white marble and there were paintings on the walls, dulled chiaroscuro scenes from the bible and Greek mythology, and modern, abstract arrangements of squares, spirals and triangles, all in thick blocks of primary colour. Heavy velvet curtains hung on the long wall by the stairwell, framing a tall stained glass window which depicted a smouldering volcano. Blue and indigo light spilled from the window down over the staircase. There was a fountain playing in the middle of the hall.

They came to a long narrow corridor and walked briskly down it, almost trotting to keep up with the guard. At the end of the passageway, he led them up a flight of white marble stairs, through a room which contained a grand piano and several cages of squawking exotic birds, through another vast room where all the furniture had been covered with white dust sheets, and then another, full of toppling stacks of old leather-bound books. The place didn't feel like a prison, even though all the rooms had thick black metal bars in the windows.

They came to a cast-iron gate and the guard unlocked it, leading them into another corridor. They passed three old women on their knees polishing the floor. The air smelt musty now, fruity with the redolence of mould and decay. There were cardboard boxes everywhere. There were packing cases, dusty porcelain ornaments and folded curtains. There were silver candelabra, tall lamps with ripped silk shades, tangled music stands and at least two guitars. There were gruesome masks and multicoloured fans on the walls. When they came to a bolted black wooden door, the guard turned to face them, sweating heavily. He put his hand on the bolt.

'*Quince minutos*,' he whispered. '*Y nada más.*'

'Fifteen minutes, Frank,' Eleanor said in a trembling voice.

The guard pulled the bolt and unlocked the door. It opened on to a long room with white brick walls, bare except for an oblong wooden table and four white plastic chairs. There was a painting of President Ortega on the farthest wall. A narrow beam of light danced with specks of dust, before splaying out on the glossy surface of the table.

At the far end of the table a young man was sitting with his back to the doorway. He had on a denim uniform with the word *PRISION* stencilled across the shoulders. He was sitting very still, wearing a set of Walkman headphones over his long dark hair. It was so quiet in the room that they could hear the rhythmic tinny click of the music.

Eleanor stepped forward. 'Johnny?' she said. 'Is that you?'

The guard slammed the door closed. The young man jumped. He stood up very slowly, still facing the wall. He turned and snapped his long hair out of his eyes. He looked very thin and his face was yellow and unshaven. He was wearing handcuffs. He squinted in the dull light. He took a step forward.

'Ma?' he said, uncertainly.

He began to walk across the room towards her, stumbling as he came. His breath was suddenly loud. He knocked into the plastic chairs and sent one tumbling. His eyes were pale.

'Dad?' he called.

Eleanor ran to him, her face streaming with tears. He held his handcuffed hands out towards her. She took them and kissed them. She kissed his face and his hair. She buried her head in his chest and wrapped her arms around his neck.

'Johnny,' she said. 'Oh, thank God.'

Frank walked slowly down the length of the room, feeling his heart thunder. He stepped up to his son and his wife, still locked in a hug, each of them crying now, and he put his arms awkwardly around their shoulders. He kissed them both and held their hands. 'Now,' he murmured, 'we're alright now.' The room seemed to echo with their choking sobs. He held them both very tightly and for some moments nobody said anything at all. He held them and kissed them again, gnawing hard at his lip.

'We're alright now,' he said.

'Dad,' Johnny sniffed, 'Jesus, Dad, how's it going?'

'Are you alright, love?' Eleanor said. 'Have they hurt you?'

He shook his head. 'No, Ma. They haven't.'

'Are you sure? Have they done anything to you? You look sick.'

'No, they haven't. Do you have any fags, Dad? I'm fucking gasping.'

Eleanor stood back from him. They sat down at the table and Frank handed him a cigarette. Johnny's fingers were shaking when he took it. He lit it, threw back his head and sucked at it the way a long-distance runner would suck at the air. Frank lit a cigarette for himself. He reached out and touched his son's hand.

'There's very little time. Do you want to tell us what happened, Johnny?'

'Jesus, Dad, I can't believe you're here. How did you get here?'

'Your friends brought us,' Eleanor said. 'Smokes and the others.'

He coughed on the cigarette smoke. 'What? Smokes brought you up here? And Cherry?'

'Yes,' Eleanor said.

'Are they OK?'

'They're worried sick about you.'

'What happened to you, son?' Frank said.

Johnny took another drag on his cigarette. He looked at his father carefully, then glanced across at his mother, shaking his head in disbelief.

'What happened, Johnny? There isn't much time.'

'I got into some trouble, Dad. I got involved with some people.'

Johnny bent his head until his forehead was touching the heels of his hands. He spoke in a weary voice.

'I needed to get some money. I was stuck for money. I heard these guys were running stuff across the border into Honduras for dollars. Everyone in the town knows about it. It's like a cottage industry around here.'

'Drugs?' Frank said. 'Was it drugs?'

Johnny looked up at his father, chewing his lip. He tried to speak, but then stammered and hung his head.

'God, Johnny,' Eleanor said, half laughing. 'Don't tell me that. Don't tell me you were dealing drugs.'

When he glanced up again his eyes were frightened.

'It was dope, Ma. It was nothing else. I was only delivering.'

'Drugs?' she said.

'Son,' Frank said, 'is it this priest fellow who's in charge?'

Johnny looked up. 'How do you know about him?'

'Never mind, son. Look, did they charge you with something?'

'No, Dad. They found my pockets full of the stuff, but I didn't tell them anything.'

'Good God,' Eleanor said. 'I thought it was only black market things. Drugs, Johnny?'

'I just wanted to do it a few times, Ma. They wouldn't give me my money and I had to do it again. The night of the raid was the last time. I'd made up my mind. But they kept saying they'd do something to me if I stopped. I was really scared.'

He looked at her imploringly, but she turned her head away.

'Son,' Frank said, 'just tell us what happened.'

Johnny sighed. His voice was quieter now, hoarse and strained, and it trembled a little as he spoke.

'I was coming back from the border that night. It's a quiet road in the north. I think it's ten miles north. The people hadn't shown up on the other side. And I was really scared. I was lost and I heard the guns. So I ran. I ran really hard.'

'Take it easy, son,' Frank said.

'I didn't know where I was. I couldn't recognize anything. I came around this corner. Everything was pitch black and I heard this sound. It was pitch black. I thought someone was there and I jumped down into a ditch. I stayed there for a while. I stayed there for an hour. Maybe longer. I was shaking. All I could hear was this one noise. Then I thought it was just a cow or something. I got back up on to the road.'

Johnny's eyes were wide as he spoke. He stared into the middle distance and dragged hard on his cigarette.

'There was a guy lying on the side of the road. He was mumbling, you know, kind of muttering to himself, in German. And he was dying, Dad. He was really messed up. I knelt down beside him, but there was nothing I could do. He started to cry. He kept talking to me in German, but I couldn't understand. And he couldn't seem to hear what I was saying. I tried to speak to him, but he was fucked. He seemed to want me to put something under his head. So I took off my jacket and I lifted his head up in my hands. And he kept crying. He was really sobbing, you know, like a baby. I held his hand for a minute and I talked to him. He asked me where I was from, in English, and I said Ireland, and then he asked me to say a prayer for him.

'I told him I wasn't religious. He said he wasn't either, but he just wanted me to say a prayer because he knew he was dying. He was afraid. So I put my head down close to him and I said the act of contrition into his ear. It was the only thing I could remember. So I said that.'

'Johnny,' Frank said.

'And he died while I was saying the prayer, Dad.'

'Oh, my Jesus.'

'He died. I didn't know what to do. I panicked. I looked through his pockets, you know, trying to find out who he was. Then I found his passport. And then, I don't know, this idea just came into my head. I must have been fucking crazy. I don't know what I was thinking, Dad. I took his passport out and I put my passport and my wallet on him. I thought they'd think I was dead, you see, when they found him.'

Johnny started to laugh, in a weird, high-pitched giggle.

'I thought they'd think he was me. He was so messed up. I thought they'd stop hassling me. I thought they'd fucking leave me alone, you see. You don't know these guys, Dad. They'd do anything to you. They'd . . .'

Frank clenched his hand on his son's arm. 'Alright, son,' he said. 'Alright now. And then they arrested you?'

He nodded. 'Yeah. I've been here since then.'

'But this priest fellow knows you're here?'

Johnny nodded. 'Yeah. He knows. He pays off most of the guards. They're supposed to tell everyone I'm German.'

'Why?'

Johnny shrugged. 'They're supposed to keep things confused. If the *Policía* find out about me, they'll charge me. And that'll be big trouble for the priest.'

'And he's not going to tell them? The police?'

'No, Dad. See, the *Policía* are all party. He can't buy too many of them. But the guards in here are just on the make.'

'Should I go to the police then?'

'No, Dad, fuck, no. I got a message from the priest. Listen. He said he'd get me out in a while, but if I contacted the cops there'd be trouble. He said one word and there'd be big trouble.'

Johnny stood up and walked towards the window. He looked up at the sky, lifting his hands to his mouth and dragging on his cigarette.

'You see, there's this girl, Dad. We had a scene together. He said there'd be trouble for her as well. If I talked.'

'We know that, Johnny. We've met her.'

He turned to him, his eyes bright. 'You met Pilar? Is she alright?'

Frank nodded. 'She's fine, son.'

'No bloody thanks to you,' Eleanor said.

Johnny stared at her. 'OK, Ma,' he said. 'Thanks for the input.'

Eleanor stood up and spoke slowly. 'Do you have any idea what we've been through, Johnny Little? Do you have *any* idea? Does it enter your head for one moment that there's anyone else in the world? You're sitting in here like a bloody lord, letting everyone else go mad with the worry, and you speak to me like that.'

'I needed money, Ma. I hadn't any money.'

'Oh, I see. You needed money. And you've never heard of work before. You're sitting in here without a single bloody word and everyone else is going frantic. We thought you were dead. Do you understand that? *Do* you?'

'Leave it, Eleanor,' Frank said.

'Ma,' said Johnny, 'I'd no choice.'

'And what bloody choice does that poor girl have, out there alone, carrying your child?'

He nodded. 'I didn't know you knew about that.'

'Yes, I do know,' she said. 'Oh, you'd be surprised at some of the things I know about you.'

347

He came back to the table and sat down. 'I tried to get word to her. I bribed one of the guards. Did she not get my letter?'

'Don't you dare talk to me about letters,' Eleanor snapped. 'What letter did *we* get? Cowering in here, afraid of a bloody priest.'

Johnny's face darkened. He lifted his hands and pointed at her. 'Ma,' he said, 'get off my fucking back now, OK?'

'You ran out on that poor girl and you're after putting us through hell. My God, I'm so ashamed of you.'

He hung his head and muttered, 'I don't remember you stopping for air when you fucking ran out on me.'

Eleanor lunged across the table and slapped Johnny hard in the mouth. His head whipped backwards and his long hair fell down into his eyes.

'Eleanor,' Frank shouted.

'You little cur,' she said. 'The day you'll cheek me isn't here yet.'

'Eleanor, stop it.'

Johnny touched his face. He looked up disbelievingly, fresh tears in his eyes.

'Why don't you give me another one, Mother?' he said. 'I see it still gives you a fucking thrill.'

Eleanor froze, then picked up her gloves, turned and walked out of the room. The door slammed. Johnny bent his head forwards and began to cry again. Frank tried to put his arms around his shoulders. He snapped away from him, sobbing.

'Please, Johnny,' Frank said. 'Stop this.'

'Leave me alone. Fucking go with her, why don't you?'

Johnny stood up so suddenly that he knocked over his chair. He walked back towards the window, holding the waist of his baggy trousers. He wiped his eyes and his nose on his sleeve and continued to cry as he stared up at the clouds.

The light in the room was growing dusky. Frank went over and gave him a tissue. Johnny stopped crying. He leant his head against the brick wall and closed his eyes.

'Son,' Frank said quietly, 'your mother's upset. You know how she says things when she's upset. I'll go out now and get her.'

'No,' he snapped. 'I don't want to see her.'

'Don't be too hard, Johnny. You're only starting out in life.

You'll find a bit of understanding is a great thing with people.'

His son shook his head and pulled away. He began to pace up and down the long room, looking around wildly, as though he could knock down the walls with nothing more than an expression. Frank watched him and tried to think of something to say.

'Johnny, please? Look, now, I know she was out of order. But have a bit of understanding?'

'Oh, yeah, understanding, right. I got a great fucking example from you two, didn't I?'

Frank looked at his watch. 'Look, please, there's no time for this, son. I'll just nip out and get your mother.'

Johnny shook his head. 'She can fuck off back to Glenageary for all I care.'

The door opened and the guard came into the room. He tapped on his watch and jerked his thumb towards the door.

'Son,' Frank said, 'look, let me just go after her and we'll say no more about it. Please?'

'No, Dad.'

'*Vámonos*,' the guard snapped.

'Johnny,' Frank sighed, 'I can't believe you're so hard now. It's a sad thing to see in a young person.'

'*Vámonos, hombre. Ahora mismo.*'

Frank put a carton of Marlboros on the table and buttoned his jacket.

'I'm very fond of you, son,' he said. 'You remind me of myself when I was your age.'

'*Vámonos,*' the guard insisted.

Frank put his hand on Johnny's shoulder, just for a moment. He touched his hair lightly, then began to walk towards the door.

'Dad?' Johnny called out.

'What?'

His son was crying again now. 'Get me the fuck out of here, Dad, will you?'

'Yeah,' Frank said. 'Yeah. Don't worry about that.'

He turned and walked slowly from the room.

She was standing in the laneway, crying softly, when she saw him coming. His face was dark with worry and he looked so tired that she almost didn't recognize him. Suddenly he looked very old. He didn't look like Frank Little any more. He came down the darkening lane, limping over the stones, and caught her eye. He smiled with an expression that she recognized. It was a look of helpless and desperate love. It terrified her.

'Are you alright?' he called out.

She turned away from him and began to run. She ran as hard as she could. Her right shoe fell off, but she kept running over the tiny stones, crying out with pain, shaking and breathless. The stones cut into the sole of her foot, but she didn't care. She heard his heavy, flat footsteps as he ran to catch up with her. She heard him calling out her name, but she didn't stop running.

He caught up with her on the edge of the town. He reached out and grabbed her wrist. When she turned he was gasping for breath and his face was deep red.

'Eleanor,' he panted, 'please, love.'

He grabbed her shaking shoulders and she moaned. Her hands clenched up into fists and she dug her fingernails hard into her palms.

'I'm so ashamed of myself,' she cried out. 'I'm such a terrible person. I don't know why I ever got married.'

'Stop it.'

'I've dragged everyone down with me.'

'Please don't run away from me, Eleanor. Please.'

He put his arms around his wife's body. She tried to pull away, but he hugged her hard. And Frank began to cry then. He opened his mouth and wept out loud, his forehead against her shoulder.

'Oh, Jesus, Eleanor,' he sobbed.

'Oh, Frank.'

With his fingers he touched her face. He touched her soft lips and her eyebrows, and then, because it was easy, and because he was not thinking, he pulled her towards him and tried to put his mouth against her lips. He felt her tense up and move away from him.

'Don't, Frank.'

He felt her hand on the back of his head. He felt her fingers run through his hair. 'Don't, love,' she said, softly. And although she made no sound, he could feel her body shaking in the darkness, and he knew that she was crying too.

41

Bendita Seas Entre Todas Las Mujeres

WHEN THEY GOT BACK to the *hospedaje* Eleanor waited out in the street while Frank slipped in the back door and went straight up to Guapo's room. He told Guapo that Johnny was fine, but that Eleanor wanted to go and see Pilar straight away, that she wanted Guapo to take her, while Frank stayed behind to talk to the others. Guapo jumped up, splashed some water on his face and grabbed Claudette's keys. He said he'd drive her up there right now.

'*Está vivo*, Frank,' Guapo said, hugging him. '*Está vivo*.'

Downstairs in the dining room, Frank told the others that Johnny was alright. Lorenzo made the sign of the Cross and Cherry and Smokes flung their arms around each other, jumping up and down for joy. When they starting hugging Frank he said it wasn't time for a celebration. He told them Johnny was in very serious trouble. The smiles froze.

'He was caught running marijuana,' Frank said. 'They haven't charged him yet, but that's only because they don't know for sure who he is.'

Smokes sat down and whistled. 'Fuck me.' He laughed. 'You're pulling my wire, Franklin. Running weed? Jeez Louise, he's put himself in deep shit there.'

'Yeah,' Frank said. 'Thanks. I hadn't figured that out, son.'

'Sorry, Franklin.'

'Well, we'll have to get him out some way. I'll have to get a lawyer for him.'

'Frank,' Smokes said, 'a lawyer's no good. You're gonna have

351

to bankroll someone. Dope peddling is pretty serious around here.'

'But you know they don't take bribes, Smokes,' Cherry said. 'Not since the revolution.'

'That's bollocks anyway,' Frank snapped. 'I gave your man up there a hundred dollars to let me go back tomorrow night. I thought he was going to fucking kiss me.'

Frank stood up and went to the balcony. He could see the prison in the distance, pale yellow in the evening light. It was almost unbearable to think that his son was inside those walls and only a mile away. It filled him with rage.

'There's nothing else for it,' he said. 'I'll have to go back and see our friend in the garage. See if this damn priest can help us out again.'

'Jeez, Frank,' Smokes said, 'José's not gonna like it.'

He turned. 'I'm not asking him to fucking like it, Smokes. I have to get Johnny out of that fucking place. Do you not understand that?'

'Frank,' Cherry said, 'why can't you just call Nuñez?'

He laughed. 'Jesus, kid, you're a howl. I'm supposed to call that penpusher and say, yeah, comrade, I found my son, he's a druggie, please lock him up for ten years?'

Cherry blushed. 'I didn't think of that, Frank.'

'No, kid. You didn't.'

'Now see here,' Lorenzo said. 'Main thing is he's alive. Once he's alive, anything can happen, praise God.'

'Of course,' Smokes sighed. 'But fuck me pink! Johnny Little pushing dope for the Contras? I mean, what a royal asshole.'

'Yeah,' Frank said. 'Well, nobody's perfect, son. If you're looking for angels, you're in the wrong fucking town.'

All night long he could hear Eleanor moving around in the room next door. Once, there was no sound for about half an hour and he was relieved she had gone to sleep. But then he heard her getting out of bed and opening the window. And he could hear her crying then, sobbing quietly on the other side of the wall.

His whole body was aching with shock. He tried hard to make sense of the day, to put things into some kind of shape. He kept attempting to persuade himself that things were easier than they seemed, but he couldn't do it, no matter how hard he tried. He found himself recalling the day Johnny had been born. He remembered that morning clearly, remembered thinking nothing bad could ever happen to him again. He remembered firmly believing that all of the terrible things in his life were over. It still shocked him that he had been so wrong.

When finally he fell asleep he dreamt about the past. He saw the face of his dead father smiling through metal bars, his grandfather's tombstone floating in a blue sea, his brother on stairs of snow, mournfully strumming a guitar.

And he dreamt about walking through a forest with Eleanor. He saw pale light glinting through leaves and he heard her laughter. He ran towards the sound and suddenly the path seemed to melt and the trees burst into globes of flame. He could not find her anywhere.

He woke up shuddering with fear. The pain in the small of his back was worse and there was a dull ache in his arms. For some minutes he was sure that he was having a heart attack. One of the drivers had once had a heart attack and described it to Frank. Apparently, you got a terrible pain in your arms and a heavy feeling across your chest. He lay as still as possible, breathing deeply. He put his arms down by his side and tried to relax. The room seemed very dark and his mouth was dry.

He heard Eleanor walking around again next door. He got up and went out to the passageway. The air was hot and dry. He stood outside her room for a moment, then knocked quietly on her door.

'Eleanor,' he whispered, 'are you alright?'

He knocked again, but there was no answer. He went back into his room and fell asleep.

The next morning Eleanor didn't come down for breakfast. When Cherry appeared she said she'd gone in to see her and that she'd seemed terribly upset. She asked Frank what had happened up at the prison, but he fended off her questions. He told her Johnny was absolutely fine, a little thinner, there was no doubt, but very well considering the circumstances.

'If he's so fine,' Cherry said, 'what's the matter with Eleanor?'

'Love,' Frank sighed, 'it's a difficult time for us all, but he's fine. I just can't go into it more than that.'

Smokes came down, looking bleary, wearing Cherry's red silk dressing gown and a pair of sneakers. He sat at the table and poured out coffee. 'So, Franklin,' he said, 'you gonna go back and see José?'

'Frank should stay here,' Cherry said. 'Eleanor needs him here right now. How about you and me go see him?'

Smokes spluttered. 'Jeez, Cherry, I don't know, babes.'

She shot him a cold glance.

'That *would* be a help,' Frank said. 'I'd like to be here when she gets up. She's just a bit upset about things, you know, the strain of everything.'

Cherry put her hand on his back.

'Eleanor's so damn sensitive,' he said. 'She feels things very deeply.'

'We'll go, Frank,' Cherry told him. 'Don't you worry about it.'

Smokes put his head in his hands. She glared at him again.

'What the hell's the matter with you? Don't be such a goddam baby.'

Frank looked up at her.

'Tell him any money, love,' he said. 'Tell him money's no object. We just want him out. Just say we want him out, full stop, OK?'

Eleanor finally came down at half past one with her face made up and her hair still wet from the shower. Frank stood up when she came into the room, but she didn't look at him. She sat at the table and began to read the newspaper.

He cleared his throat. 'Are you alright, pet?' he asked her.

'I'm grand,' she said. 'Please don't go on, Frank.'

She drank some coffee in silence and refused to eat. She looked very pale and had grey bags under her eyes. He watched her carefully as she drank, but she avoided his glance.

'How was Pilar?' he asked.

'She was alright,' Eleanor said. 'She's very upset that he didn't make an effort to get in touch. And about the drugs business, of course.'

Frank coughed. 'I'm after sending Cherry and Smokes to see this mechanic fellow. See how we can get himself out of that place.'

She nodded. 'Is that the way to do it, Frank?'

'Yes,' he said. 'I think so. If that doesn't work, I don't know. I'll have to try paying off the guards. Or get Nuñez involved.'

She toyed with her teaspoon.

'I'm going up to meet Pilar's mother tonight,' she said. 'Do you want to come with me?'

'Well, I thought I'd wander up and see himself again. I gave your man some dough last night. That soldier.'

She nodded again, then finished her coffee and wiped her mouth with a napkin.

'Well,' she sighed, 'it's like a morgue around here today. I'm going to get to Mass.'

'Sure, I'll go along with you. I could do with the walk.'

'I'm grand by myself, Frank. I'll go alone.'

'Don't be soft,' he said. 'I'll just nip up and get my jacket.'

They walked together into the town without saying a word. The afternoon sky was a clear, bright blue. They crossed the square and went up to the church, but Mass was over for the day. An old woman in black told them to go to the chapel of San Marco, at the other end of the town. They had Masses there in the afternoons.

The tiny church was full of people. Plaster statues of saints and martyrs stood in the alcoves; candles glowed dully against the gold-leaf pulpit. The eyes of a frantic-looking Christ gazed down from above the altar and a group of young people stood around a microphone singing a hymn that Frank thought was a little too jazzy to be affecting.

The young priest strode out up to the altar, slicked back his hair, stretched out his hands and began to pray. Frank listened to the sound of his voice as it rose over the dry mumble of the congregation's responses.

He enjoyed trying to understand the words of the gospel. He recognized *Cristo* and *Padre* and *Amor*, but the homily eluded him completely. Still, he found the ritual of the Mass oddly satisfying. He liked knowing that the Creed would come next, then the presentation of the gifts, the Offertory Rite, the Consecration, the

Responsorial Psalm and the Proclamation of the Faith. He couldn't understand the words, but he enjoyed their rhythm, the shape of what was going on.

The priest held up the host and the altarboy rang the little bell. The congregation bowed their heads. The priset held up the chalice and the congregation bowed their heads again. Light glowed in the stained glass windows. The young people strummed their guitars and the priest tried to join in with the song, looking a little irritated because it went on for too long. There were no surprises to it. It was wonderful.

They stood up for the Our Father. Once again, Frank tried to follow the Spanish words, but somehow he got lost halfway through. The priest bowed his head, praying in silence, then came over to the altar rail, holding out his arms in a gesture of invitation. It was time for Communion.

'Are you going up?' Frank whispered.

She shook her head. 'I broke my fast earlier on.'

'God, what harm is that? Go up and receive, will you.'

'I'm not in the humour, Frank.'

The guitars began to play softly. He watched people move through the aisle towards the altar. A middle-aged woman was pushing a young soldier in a wheelchair. Three girls in white Communion dresses giggled at him. There were lots of old people, dressed completely in black, leaning on each other's arms as they walked. The sound of shuffling feet echoed in the tiny church.

'Would you not come up with me, Eleanor? Sure, if I'm going, you can go.'

She shook her head. 'You go up if you like,' she said. He stood up, expecting her to follow him, but she stayed sitting. He walked up the aisle, waited his turn and knelt down at the brass railing.

The priest had an intense look in his eyes. He held the white host between his middle finger and his thumb.

'*El cuerpo de Cristo.*'

'Amen,' Frank said.

He felt the Communion wafer stick to his palate, its dry taste reminding him of wonder and guilt.

When he got back to his seat, Eleanor was kneeling with her eyes closed and her hands joined together. He tried to pray, but he found that he couldn't. The guitars were still jangling and someone was banging a tambourine. His eyes wandered around the tiny church. He watched the young priest drain the chalice of wine, then rub the inside with a clean white cloth. He remembered his father telling him not to call it wine. Once a priest had blessed it, it wasn't wine any more, it was the blessed blood of the Saviour. He watched the priest put the ciborium back into the tabernacle and lock the silver door. The procedure was meticulous. It was the same the whole world over. There were absolutely no surprises.

He remembered taking Johnny to Mass in Glasthule church one year on the eighth of December, the feast day of the Immaculate Conception. Eleanor had been there too. Johnny had been five years old. The church had been absolutely crammed with people. He had gone up to Communion first, leaving Johnny in Eleanor's arms. Then Eleanor went up and Frank held his son. When she came back from the altar Johnny started to kick and scream because he was so jealous of his father and mother. 'He's locking it all away,' he had roared at the top of his voice. 'He's locking it all away and I didn't get any.' Frank remembered it clearly. It still made him smile.

The priest sat in the throne by the pulpit and put his head in his hands. A scraggy dog wandered up the aisle with a hopeful expression on its face, and some of the children in the congregation laughed. The priest stood up and stalked over to the microphone. He closed his eyes, extended his hands and began to pray:

> *Ave María, llena de gracia*
> *El Señor está contigo*
> *Bendita seas entre todas las mujeres*
> *Y bendita sea la fruta de tu vientre, Jesús*
> *Santa María, madre de Dios*
> *Reza por nosotros pecadores*
> *Ahora, y en la hora de nuestra muerte*
> *Amén.*

When Mass was over Frank took her for a coffee in a little *cantina* down on the pier. She seemed a little brighter now. She was a bit hungry, she said, and he told her that was very good. She ordered ham and eggs and a bottle of orangeade. The food came and she ate it all. He ordered more drinks.

'Well, you know,' he said, 'I enjoyed that Mass in a funny way. It's after getting me thinking.'

'We'll have you converted yet,' she said. 'Sudden prayers make God jump.'

He laughed and shook his head. 'No, that's not what I meant. I remembered something that happened when I was a kid.'

'You've a great memory, Frank. What is it you were thinking of?'

'Oh, well, it's only a small thing. It's stupid really. When I was at the school in Francis Street, there was a brother there. Tommy Devane, his name was. From Caherciveen. He was only twenty, I think. He was an arts student at the time. Well, Tommy was a terrible stickler, you know; he'd biff you as soon as look at you. He gave us an awful lecture one day on being late for Mass. He said, boys, I saw this woman last Sunday, coming in late for Mass, and I was mortified. I was disgusted, boys. Do you think Our Lord was late on Good Friday when he spilled his blood for us? No, boys, he was on time. We were only sinners and he was the son of God, but he was *on time*.'

'They were very hard in those days,' she smiled. 'The nuns were worse.'

'No, no, this is what happened. He went on then, do you see, about geography or whatever it was. Maths, I think. And then, out of the blue, he stops. He looks at us and he goes, that woman I was talking about earlier, boys, I think I was wrong about her. I think I'm after being a bit uncharitable. She could have been looking after a sick person or something. I was wrong to judge her, boys. Who knows what might have been going on in her home life?'

'Really?' Eleanor said.

'Jesus, it was the most amazing thing.'

'Why, Frank?'

'It was just, I don't know, a very surprising thing. It taught us a great lesson about people anyhow.'

She nodded, vaguely, and sipped her coffee. Frank chuckled.

'He had a terrible sex hex, the same poor Tommy. He used to say, boys, there's more people in hell over the fifth commandment than all the other commandments put together. When you looked at it in the catechism it said nearly everything was a sin bar biting your nails. He'd have you thinking you'd roast on the hobs of hell if you looked crossways at a girl.'

'They told us the same about fellows,' Eleanor said. 'Those nuns. They told us to put a telephone directory on a fellow's lap before we sat on it. Such bloody nonsense.'

'In the old days it was gas.' He laughed. 'You'd swear nobody got up to anything, but they were as bad then as they are now.'

'God, yes,' she said. 'Do you remember that poor woman in Stensberg's shop? Her husband put one of the local girls in the family way and then did a flit to England. I often think of her. She used to stand out in the street every day at five o'clock, looking up and down, waiting for him to come back. I don't think he ever did. I'd see her sometimes when I'd be going over to visit your mother. She'd be just staring up over the rooftops, up at the sun, you know. She gave me the willies.'

'Yes,' he said. 'Mad Margaret. God, the last time I saw poor old Mrs Stensberg I had Johnny with me. I took him in there to show him the stained glass windows at the back of the shop. He was only ten, I think, or eleven. He had a little kind of a kiss curl in his hair at the time and she gave him a terrible slagging over it. She told him he looked like Bill Haley, and of course he didn't know who that was.'

'You've such a good memory, Frank.'

'Well, I remember that day clearly. Because, you see, that night he did this picture, you know, of the *Santa María*, Christopher Columbus's ship. And he was acting up, you know, giving lip. No better man, says you. So I put him up to his room. And I gave him a bit of a skelp, I think, on the back of the leg. Well, I felt bad about it then, later on, so I went into the room, you know, to tuck him in. He was curled up in the bed, fast asleep like a little lord. I found the picture of the ship on the floor, and I picked it up for to put it away somewhere. Only when I turned it over there was a matchstick man on the other side, you know. He was after drawing this matchstick man, and a huge knife in his back. A dagger.'

'Oh, my God,' she said. 'Go away.'

'A bloody dagger.' He laughed softly. 'We should have cottoned on that we had a troublemaker there.'

She watched him light a cigarette. She watched the way his big hands moved, brushing ash off the crease of his trousers. He shook his head and flicked the burning match out into the street.

'A dagger, if you don't mind.'

The sky was already darkening. Great sheets of purple and gun-metal grey had appeared and the half-moon was leering down from behind a cloud.

'Are you happy now, Frank?' she said. 'Are you happy with Veronica?'

He thought for a moment and stared into his coffee cup. 'Well, she's a very decent person,' he said. 'I like the company, I suppose.'

Eleanor nodded.

'That's good, Frank. It's not good for you to be alone.'

'Oh, I don't know about that.'

'She must miss you now, with you being away.'

He felt his face redden. 'I'm sure she's delighted to be rid of me.'

'Well,' she said, 'I know she was very good to Johnny. He was lucky now, to have such a thoughtful person in his life.'

He shrugged, feeling the blush move to his neck. 'The best was done for him by everyone,' he said.

'Frank, do you really think we can get him out?'

'God, of course,' he said, trying to sound bright. 'Sure, these people would do anything for a dollar, Eleanor. Don't you be fretting yourself about that.'

'And you don't think we should involve Captain Nuñez?'

He shook his head. 'No, pet. Look, we'll just get him out of that place and we'll take it from there.'

He ordered a beer and another orange juice.

'You know,' he said, 'I don't know exactly how to put it. But I don't mind saying it's been very nice to see you again, Eleanor. To have a little time.'

'Yes, Frank. I know what you mean.'

'And all those things that were said yesterday. I hope you're not too upset now, by anything said in the heat of the moment.'

'No. He was right, I know.'

Frank scoffed. 'He certainly was not right. He was just upset.'

She looked him in the eye and nodded. 'You know he was right, Frank. You're just too kind to tell me so.'

'He was upset, Eleanor.'

Out on the pier children were beginning to play, singing a skipping song and shrieking with laughter.

'Isn't it funny?' she said. 'I mean, the way our lives turn out, Frank? When I was a young girl I never thought I'd grow up to be a drunk who'd walk out on her family.'

He looked at her. 'God, don't be saying that, Eleanor. You had a problem.'

'That's what I was, Frank. A drunk. It's nothing much to be proud of.'

'Well,' he said softly, 'you didn't always get the understanding you needed at home. That's something I'll have to examine my conscience about.'

He felt his heart beginning to thump. He tried to look at her.

'Was there a reason for your problem, love?' he asked. 'Was it me, do you think? I mean, did I let you down some way?'

'Do you mean the booze?' she said. 'That was just in me. It's a disease, Frank.'

He dragged on his cigarette. 'Well, I meant about you and Johnny as well.'

She glanced away from him and said nothing for a few moments. He watched her, the way she moved and ran her fingers through her hair. 'I don't know about reasons,' she said, then. 'It seems so far away from me now. It seems like another life sometimes. Like somebody else's life.'

'Yes,' he said. 'It's neither today nor yesterday.'

'I mean, I do still think about it. Never a day goes by without that. But I don't know what used to come over me in those days. The way I was with him.'

He touched her sleeve. She looked away.

'I went to see a person about it once,' she said, 'when I was in England. He was one of these counsellors, you know?'

'Oh, I see.' He laughed. 'Those characters are gas alright. They have great theories.'

'I found it a help.'

'I know,' he said. 'I don't mean anything bad.'

'I was having the most awful dreams. And then they got worse. After a while, I nearly couldn't sleep at all.'

He nodded. 'About Johnny, were they? These dreams?'

'Yes. About Johnny. About the way I went on with him.' She paused. 'But about other things too.'

'Like what, love?'

She looked up at him, her eyes suddenly filling with tears.

'Tell me.'

She chewed her lip. 'It's very hard, Frank. Putting words on a thing, after all this time.'

'Sure, would you not tell me,' he said, gently.

She shook her head. 'Well, what does it matter now?' she whispered. 'Isn't it all over now?'

'Please,' he said. 'Maybe it would help.'

She put her hand to her eyes.

'I'd help you with anything, Eleanor,' he told her.

She stared up at the roof of the *cantina*, nodding, searching for words. 'Well, then,' she said suddenly, 'one night . . .' She stopped speaking and twined her fingers together, so tightly that her knuckles whitened. 'One night . . .'

He leant towards her. 'One night what, pet?'

She swallowed hard and when she spoke again, her voice shook. 'One night you were out, Frank. Working. It was a while after we had Catherine.'

'Yes.'

'And I was by myself in the house. I was in bed, you see. And she started to cry . . .'

'Go on, love.'

'And she'd been crying all day long, do you see, and she started to cry again.'

Eleanor paused, blinking hard. 'And I was just so tired, Frank,' she blurted. 'I was so tired that I didn't go to her. I'd get so tired in those days. I let her just cry a bit and I went to sleep. I thought she'd be alright, I suppose.'

She looked at him and her eyes moistened. 'But she wasn't alright, Frank.'

He reached out and took her hand, sighing. 'You're not going to go blaming yourself for all that?'

'It was the night before we lost her,' she said, wiping her eyes.

362

'Oh, wasn't it so dreadful, Frank, the way we lost her so soon?'

He kneaded her hand and said nothing.

'It was so terrible,' she said. 'Some things are too hard.'

'I know, love, but wasn't it a virus after all? Isn't that what the doctors said? Sure, it was nobody's fault, pet. I mean, nobody can go for every little cry.'

'So awful,' she sobbed, 'though, heaven knows, it's no excuse for anything. And that's not why I'm saying it. I mean, it happens to plenty of girls and they don't end up like me.'

He stroked the back of her fingers. 'But did I let you down when that happened?' he asked. 'Maybe we had Johnny too soon then. Did we? Do you think we should have waited?'

She gazed into his face for what seemed like a very long time, and then smiled, sadly.

'Oh, Frank,' she said, 'it wasn't that. Of course, I really wanted Johnny.'

'What then, love? Do you know?'

She picked up her glass.

'I don't really,' she said. 'But this counsellor fellow had a few notions about the whole thing. I mean, why I blamed myself so much when we lost her.'

'God, Eleanor, what are you on about?'

She stared into his eyes for a moment, then turned to gaze out at the sea. 'My father always used to say dreadful things to us, Frank. He was such a hard man. He said such awful things. To us especially; the girls, I mean. If we did the smallest little thing he'd tell us we were bad. That he'd never wanted girls. He said God would punish us one day, we were so bad.'

'He didn't say that, did he?'

She nodded. 'He was a very complicated person, Frank. He had his own demons.'

'God, though, what an awful thing to say.'

'He was very unhappy. And he did a lot of harm to the people he loved.' She looked away, blinking hard. 'Like me that way.'

'Eleanor, don't.'

A knot formed in her chin. 'But when we lost her, that was all I could think about. I'd nearly hear him, Frank, saying that to me.' Her voice began to crack. 'You're a bad person, Eleanor Hamilton, you'll get your come-uppance one day.'

'Good Jesus, imagine saying that.'

Tears began to trickle down her face. 'And if it was now, of course, I'd have the strength to cope with it. But then I think I might have believed him. And I think I might have blamed myself some way.'

She looked at him, and shivered. 'Do you know what I mean, Frank?'

'It was nobody's fault, Eleanor,' he said. 'Don't be getting yourself upset.'

'I think I always blamed myself, Frank. I'd have the most awful nightmares. I'd see her poor little face. And I'd hear her calling out to me the way she did that night when I didn't go to her.'

'Stop it now, pet,' he said gently. 'Don't be torturing yourself like that.'

Out on the pier, the children were still singing, chasing each other up and down and throwing stones. Eleanor gazed at them.

'It went on for years,' she said. 'And when I think of the guilt . . . I couldn't ever tell anyone about it.'

He touched her hand again. 'Could you not have told me, no?'

She put her fingers to her face and wiped her tears. 'I thought you'd blame me, Frank.'

'God, Eleanor love, I'd never have done that.'

She held his hand very tightly as she tried not to cry.

'There was this woman,' she said, wincing. 'My grandmother knew her in Galway. She was put away in a home. People used to say she killed her baby. I was so frightened, Frank. I thought if I told anyone the police would come and take me away. Away from you. I thought we wouldn't be a family any more.'

She hung her head. 'And sometimes,' she sobbed, 'and sometimes in the old days, I'd wake up in the night, and I'd feel the warmth of you beside me in the bed. And, Frank, I'd think it was her some way. Because you remember the way we put her sleeping in the bed with us, Frank, when she was only tiny?'

'Jesus, Eleanor,' he said. 'You poor thing.'

'She was so small. Her little hands. Do you remember her poor little hands, Frank?'

'Yes,' he said.

Tears welled in her eyes again and she tried to smile, although her face was twisting up with grief.

'And I couldn't ever tell you, Frank. And I wanted to some-times, but I just didn't understand what was happening to me. I suppose people didn't talk about their feelings in those days.'

'Eleanor.'

She closed her eyes. 'But I felt so low in myself. It made me very unhappy really. And I think I must have taken it out on poor Johnny some way. I loved him so much, but it all got twisted up in my mind. And you know how difficult he could be too, Frank. He'd be fine with you, of course, when you came home, but I was the one who had to mind him during the day. He was like a demon sometimes. He'd do anything for attention.'

'I suppose he picked things up,' Frank said. 'They say an atmos-phere can affect kids.'

'You got daggers in drawings, Frank. I got the dinner thrown across the room at me more than once.'

He was silent.

'He'd go on for hours at me.' She nodded. 'He'd scream and kick up like anything. He'd never stop. And I'm not sure what I was thinking, anyway, but when he got to be the age poor Catherine was when we lost her, I think I just started to go astray.'

Frank sighed. 'But you mustn't blame yourself, love. God, if you'd only spoken to me. You must have thought I was awfully hard.'

'I felt so alone, Frank. I felt so scared in those days. And, you see, I started feeling these awful things. And I'd find myself going mad if he went to school without his lunch. Or if he didn't wear a jumper or something. Things another mother would have laughed about.' She choked back a sob. 'You see, this counsellor fellow told me I must have thought he was going to get sick too. In the back of my mind, do you see? I don't know if that's true or not. For a while I thought it was maybe just what I wanted to hear. To explain everything. But that's what he told me.'

'Good Jesus,' Frank said, 'you must have thought I was an awful creature, Eleanor, all the same, if you were fretting about talking to me.'

'I think I must have been afraid we'd lose him too, Frank. I don't know. And then it went too far. And I don't know what would come over me, but I'd end up hitting the poor mite, for the smallest thing. God forgive me. I loved him more than anything. And how it happened I'll never know.'

'God, pet,' he said. 'I never knew things were so dreadful for you. If you'd only turned to me. Sure, I feel awful now.'

She sobbed suddenly, violently, and looked into his face, trying to speak.

'But I *couldn't* tell you, Frank. Do you not understand that? Do you not, really? I wasn't *able* to.'

Something in her tone of voice terrified him.

'Don't get upset, Eleanor,' he whispered. 'Haven't you told me now?'

She looked away again, her cheeks blotched with mascara, her face distorted and quivering.

'Yes,' she said. 'Only twenty years too late.'

'Don't be saying that, Eleanor. It's not.'

A sudden gust of wind blew into the *cantina*, making the glasses rattle on the shelves. Eleanor raised her napkin to her face. He tried to laugh. 'God, now, you must have thought I was hard as nails, did you?'

'No,' she said. 'Not hard. But I suppose you changed a bit when we got married, Frank. I didn't know what to think about it. You were a bit more open when I first knew you, when we were only kids. When we used to go out dancing.' She looked up at him and smiled through her tears. 'Later on, you were different some way. I always knew your feelings were there, I suppose. But maybe it's different for a woman. Maybe we need to be told things.'

'Surely you don't have to spell every little thing out,' he said. 'I always thought you knew the bond was there.'

She shook her head. 'Sometimes I wasn't sure. I felt like an awful failure to you. I mean, of course you'd want to think the person you married would be a natural mother. That's what any man would want. And you used to make me think I was wrong for you sometimes, Frank, when we'd be fighting. And every time I had to tell Johnny off, I'd feel you were against me. You used to say very unkind things to me. It used to frighten me so much.'

'But people say things in rows,' he said. 'No harm was meant.'

She sobbed. 'You used to say you'd've been better off married to someone else.'

'Jesus, no, Eleanor,' he said softly. 'I wouldn't have.'

'Maybe that's what you still think.'

He took her hand and held it hard. 'No. Please, you're not right about that, Eleanor. If that was ever said, it wasn't meant.'

The tears began to stream down her face again. He reached out and wiped them away with his fingers.

'I've no regrets anyhow,' he said. 'I'd do it all again.'

'Oh, Frank,' she cried, 'I don't know how you can say that. After all the pain we put each other through.'

'Well, I would. God, now, I was mad about you, Eleanor. I don't mind saying it.'

'I used to wonder sometimes,' she said. 'You really made me wonder.'

'But there was an awful lot of love there. Did you not know that?'

'There's no pain on earth like the one love turns into,' she said, 'when you lose it.' She shook her head and tried to smile. 'And there's no loneliness like that. We were like outlaws in a picture, Frank. Running away from everything obvious. And knowing all the time that we'd never make it anywhere. You have to be honest now.'

He stroked the side of her face. 'You're gas,' he said. 'You've a great imagination.'

She laughed and rubbed her eyes. 'I always thought that was worth something.'

'And do you not still?'

She thought for a moment. 'Yes, Frank. I suppose I do. Though I often wonder just what.'

They sat in silence for a moment or two, holding hands. He smiled at her. 'And do you ever go up to the grave, pet?' he asked. 'To Catherine's grave?'

'No, I don't.'

He nodded. 'I go a bit. On the anniversary, you know, or her birthday. Or sometimes I just slip in during the afternoon, if I'm passing in the cab. Sometimes it's nice in the afternoons.'

'Do you, Frank? I never knew.'

'Yes,' he said. 'I find it a comfort sometimes. When she comes into my mind.' He paused. 'And I suppose you'll think I'm a bit touched now, knocking about in graveyards.'

'No,' she said. 'I don't think that.'

He took his hand away from hers and lit a cigarette with trembling fingers. 'I don't know. Maybe you'd like to go up together some time? When we get back home? We could just wander up one of the afternoons and take a few flowers or something. Say a little prayer maybe. Just the two of us together?'

Her eyes flooded with tears. 'Yes,' she said.

He took her hand again. 'Alright. We'll do that, so. That's a date.'

She pushed her hair out of her face. 'That would be lovely, Frank. I'd like that very much.'

'You're a very special person, Eleanor. It's a long time since that was said, I know. But really you're the tops, in my book.'

'God, stop.'

'You are. I must say now, I feel very lucky I ever met you.'

'Go away out of that.' She smiled through her tears. 'You're an awful messer, Frank Little.'

They sat in the little *cantina* for the rest of the afternoon, drinking juice and coffee and talking about Johnny. They agreed that they would try to get him out, then give him enough money to get across the border and into Honduras. If Pilar wanted to join him there, they would give her money too. After that they would have to go back and see Nuñez. They wondered whether or not to tell him they had found Johnny, but they couldn't make up their minds. They decided to talk to Smokes and the others about it, see what they would say.

Then Eleanor said she wanted to go back to the *hospedaje* and take a shower before visiting Pilar's mother. Frank looked at his watch. He nodded and said he'd better be thinking about heading off to the prison. Johnny would be waiting for him. He would want to know if there was any news on getting him out. They called for the bill and paid in dollars. Then, just as they were about to leave, Frank suddenly saw Claudette pull up at the far end of the pier. Lorenzo and Guapo climbed out of the back and Smokes and Cherry appeared from the driver's cab.

'You know who they'll be after,' Frank said. 'You'd better clean yourself up or they'll think we've been having a barney.'

She took a mirror from her bag and looked at her face.

'Oh, God, I look like a panda,' she said, 'with my mascara.'

He handed her a tissue. 'You look fine, pet,' he said. 'You look lovely.'

She wiped her eyes. 'God, you're terrible. I look like the wreck of the Hesperus.'

Cherry came running into the café. She said she'd been looking for them for an hour. They had seen José Ortega and given him Frank's message. He had closed up the garage and left them waiting while he went to find somebody. He'd been gone for hours and when he'd finally come back he'd told them the news.

'Frank,' Cherry said. 'He says the priest can get Johnny out.'

He stood up. 'Game ball,' he said. 'How?'

'Well, that's the thing, Franklin,' Smokes sighed. 'He says it's gonna cost four grand.'

Frank's face fell. 'What?' He laughed. 'You're kidding me. I don't have that kind of dough with me.'

Smokes shrugged. 'S'what the man said, Franklin.'

'But, Christ, Smokes. He must know nobody has that kind of money to throw around. You could buy the whole fucking town for that.'

'I told him money's no object, Franklin. And this is big, man, you know? This ain't parking tickets.'

'Fuck,' Frank said. 'Fuck, fuck, *fuck*.'

'Frank,' Eleanor said.

He shook his head. 'I have to think,' he told her. 'Just do what you were going to do. Go see Pilar and her mother.'

'Would you like me to leave it till later?'

'No,' he said, a little too sharply. 'I mean, just go on up. Just do something normal, Eleanor. That's all I mean, love. That's the best way anyone could help me now.'

42

Two Visits

THE TAXI WAS a battered black Cadillac with ripped leatherette seats and no windscreen. Cherry and Eleanor sat in the back, saying little, fanning their faces with their hands, as the car sped through the dusty streets of Corinto.

They drove through the centre of the town as far as the Calle de la Paz Internacional and then up the steep hill that led away to the east. The landscape was green and lush now and thick-leafed trees shaded the roads. People were working in the fields, digging long trenches and laying pieces of concrete piping into them.

They turned off the road and drove up a mud track until they came to a little red house made of wooden planks and corrugated iron. Pilar was standing outside the house talking to a little boy in a tattered red shirt. When the boy saw the taxi coming he suddenly turned and ran away. The taxi jerked to a stop and the engine cut out. Pilar waved to Eleanor and came over to the car.

Eleanor took two plastic bags out of the passenger seat and handed one of them to Pilar. 'Tell Pilar I was down in the market yesterday,' she said to Cherry. 'I just got a few little things for her mother. I hope she won't be offended.'

Inside the bag was a ripe cheese, some apples, a box of choc-olates and a small bottle of *Flor de Caña* rum.

'It's just the custom in Ireland,' Eleanor explained. 'You don't visit somebody empty-handed.'

'Oh,' Pilar said. 'OK. *Muchas gracias.*'

She handed Pilar another bag. 'And that's just a few little things for you,' she said. 'They're only small things.'

Pilar looked surprised as Cherry explained what Eleanor was

370

saying. The bag contained a pair of jeans, two shirts, stockings and underwear and a sky-blue maternity dress.

Pilar's eyes filled with tears. '*No puedo*,' she said, and she tried to put the bag back into Eleanor's hands. '*No puedo*.'

'Stop that, dear,' Eleanor said. 'Don't be embarrassing me now.'

'She saying *she*'s embarrassed, Eleanor.'

Eleanor laughed and took Pilar's hand. 'You just tell her it's important to feel good when you're expecting. I remember that myself. It's nice to feel confident when you're expecting.'

She squeezed Pilar's fingers. 'Now,' she said, 'it's a very special time for any young woman.'

Cherry spoke quietly to Pilar. Pilar looked away across the fields, then opened the bag again and peered into it. She smiled and looked up at Eleanor.

'OK, *bueno*,' she said. '*Muchas gracias*, Eleanor.'

'We'd better get in now,' Eleanor said. 'We don't want to be keeping your mother waiting after all, or she'll think we're terrible people.'

Pilar's mother was a plump woman with big red hands and a kind face. When she opened the door she started to cry almost immediately. She dried her hands on her apron and held them out to embrace Eleanor and then Cherry. She told them they were very welcome and led them into the front room.

The tiny house was spotlessly clean. There were pictures of the Pope and Augusto Sandino on the walls of the living room and a battered-looking television set in the corner with a wire coat hanger jammed into the top for an aerial. The house seemed to be absolutely full of children. Pilar had five sisters, she explained; each of them had young children and her mother looked after them during the day.

Señora Hernandez brought a cake from the kitchen. They ate slices of it and drank coffee with some of the rum. The rum was delicious, she said, and it was hard to get good rum now, since the revolution. There were always articles about it in the papers. It was a thing people complained about.

All the children crowded into the tiny room, staring shyly at Eleanor, giggling nervously every time she moved or ate a mouthful of cake. They were very beautiful looking, with big sparkling brown eyes and dark faces. A little boy of five or six wandered into the room dressed in dirty Superman pyjamas and sucking his thumb. He gaped at Eleanor as though she was the strangest creature he had ever seen. 'Oh, now aren't you lovely,' she said. 'Aren't you a dote?' She held out her arms to the little boy, but he burst into tears and ran out into the passageway, and then all the other children laughed, and Eleanor laughed too. 'The poor fellow,' she said. 'He thinks I want to run away with him.'

Señora Hernandez said the children meant no harm, but they were just not used to strangers. She stood up and shooed them out of the room. Then she switched off the radio and sat down again, smiling. But the children kept running back in to look at Eleanor until Pilar said finally that she would take them all out for a walk, and her mother said yes, that would be a good idea.

Señora Hernandez said she was very pleased to meet Eleanor. She wanted to know all about Ireland. She had heard that it was very green, full of mountains and lakes, like Nicaragua, and that everyone there was a poet.

'Oh, I don't know about that,' Eleanor said.

Señora Hernandez told her that a man from Ireland had once lived in the town. He was called Sean Boyle, and the place he came from in Ireland was called Boyle too. He used to laugh about that. He had worked for an American rancher in the old days, growing bananas. He was very popular, she said, and he loved singing. He was very handsome too and had many girlfriends. Sometimes the local men were a bit jealous of him, but eventually he married a woman from Condega and went to live with her there. She laughed when she talked about Sean Boyle, the man from Ireland. He would stay up all night singing, she said, if anyone would listen to him. He had a really beautiful voice. And there was nothing Sean Boyle did not know about bananas. He used to go all the way down to Managua to read about bananas in the public library. And he talked about his bananas as though they were his whole life. He had once told her that he would eat ten bananas every morning and not think twice about it. He was a very funny man, she said. He was interesting to talk to.

The *Señora* laughed. Then she said this man had once told her that sometimes it snowed in Ireland. She asked Eleanor if this was true, and Eleanor said yes, it was. '*Ay, qué bonita*,' the *Señora* sighed, and she lifted up her hands as though snow was falling into the room and she could catch it. She had never seen snow in her life, she said, but Sean Boyle had made it sound very beautiful.

Eleanor said Ireland was often cold and rainy, and that sometimes it snowed, but that even on the hottest summer day it was colder than Nicaragua. '*Mucho calor aquí*,' Eleanor said, and the *Señora* laughed and nodded. '*Oh, sí*,' she said. They drank a little more coffee and then the *Señora* asked if Eleanor and Cherry would like to go and sit in the garden. It was cooler out there, she told them, and Eleanor said yes, that sounded lovely, if that would be alright.

The little garden was full of wild purple orchids. They brought chairs and a table out of the house and set them in the shade of the corrugated iron fence. Then they sat down again and drank some lemonade. *Señora* Hernandez wanted to know how Johnny was.

'He's fine,' Eleanor said. 'I mean, he's alright, considering everything.'

The *Señora* flicked the flies away and smiled at Eleanor and Cherry. She gestured towards her own face and then towards Eleanor's.

'She's saying you look like him,' Cherry said.

Eleanor nodded. 'I always thought he was like his father.'

The *Señora* seemed to understand straight away. She said she was very fond of Johnny. He was a very gentle young man, very *simpático*. She said all the children had liked him a lot; he was very good with them and he seemed very happy to be around children, which was unusual for a young man. He seemed happier with children than adults. He used to play baseball with them up in the fields, she said, laughing, and sometimes he used to give them rides on the back of his motorbike.

'Can you ask her about the night of the attack?' Eleanor said.

The *Señora* took a deep breath. The battle had been very bad that night, she said. The Contras had come down from the mountains in huge numbers. Many people had been killed, or kidnapped and taken across the border. When Johnny didn't come home, they thought he had been killed. They didn't know what to do. They waited for a few days, but there was no news. Then they heard that a body had been found in the mountains, the body of a young foreigner. They heard that it had been brought down to

Managua. There was a rumour in the town that the dead man had an Irish passport, but nobody seemed to know for sure. They had been very confused, she said. They hadn't known what was going to happen. Then, last night, Pilar had told her what Eleanor had said, about Johnny being in the jail. But she didn't know why he hadn't tried to contact them. Her daughter was upset about that.

'Protecting himself,' Eleanor said. 'I didn't rear him to run away from things.'

The *Señora* gave her a curious look and shook her head.

'Eleanor,' Cherry said, 'she's saying she can't believe that's right. She says she just doesn't think Johnny was that kind of person. She's been thinking about it, and she figures he must have been protecting Pilar, not himself.'

'My hat.'

'But she says she's heard about this priest guy. He's real bad news, Eleanor. He's been running the town for years. Her husband told her all about him. See, her husband was a big cheese in the revolution, and he used to say one of the reasons he fought in it was to clean the place out of guys like that.'

'Really?' Eleanor said. 'Would the *Señora*'s husband be able to put in a word for my fellow? I mean, I'm not saying anything bad now, but if he has a bit of clout with people?'

Señora Hernandez tried to smile, but a pained expression came over her face.

'Her husband is dead, Eleanor.'

'Oh, no,' Eleanor said. 'Oh, I'm sorry.'

The *Señora* told Eleanor that her husband had been killed by the *Guardia Nacional* back in the time of the General. He was a very political person, she said; he felt things very deeply. He was always talking about his rights and about things that she didn't understand. He was never interested in politics when he was young, she told them, when she first met him. He was very handsome then. People said he looked like a famous actor called Jorge Negrete, who had starred in a passionate film called '*El Rapto*.' And it was true. He was as handsome as Jorge Negrete. But all he cared about then was magic. He wanted to be a magician in a circus. He could do the most wonderful tricks; he could even make birds appear out of thin air. But then he got to know Carlos

Fonseca, the man who founded the Sandinista movement. He went to see him speak at a secret meeting one night in Léon and he started to become interested in politics, then. It was a very unfortunate thing.

They had married at the age of seventeen and it was soon after that that he had got involved with politics. There were often guns in the house, she said; there were many times when she warned him that something terrible would happen. He was always in and out of jail, and sometimes on the run. He was hardly ever at home; he was like a stranger in his own town. In the end, he was arrested one night down on the docks. There was a fight in a *cantina*; that was all she had been told. Some of the *Guardia* had been drunk and there was some stupid fight. She didn't even know what the fight had been about, but he had been taken away and he had never come home to her again after that.

'Oh, dear,' Eleanor said.

It was a terrible time for the family, *Señora* Hernandez said. Nobody knew what to do. She wrote letters to everybody. She wrote a letter to General Somoza, but he never replied. She even tried to see the priest about it, but she had no money, so he refused to help her. Nobody would tell her what had happened to her husband. He had just disappeared, like so many other men. In the end she had spent six months praying. There was a statue of the Virgin Mary in the hills outside Corinto and it was said that if you prayed at this statue your prayer would be granted. She had gone up to the hills many times, to pray for her husband, but he had never come home. Her eyes filled with tears when she said this, and she shook her head, as though she still couldn't understand what had happened. Her husband didn't even have a grave, she said. It was a terrible shame. There was no grave for his family to visit. She pointed to her chest and whispered that his only grave would be in her heart.

Eleanor reached over and took her by the hand. There were no men in the house any more, the *Señora* said. Her three sons had all left the town. One was in Managua, she thought, although he never kept in touch. Another was down in Ecuador, working in an oil well and making good money. Her third son Raul was in El Paso, Texas. He was working nights as a security guard in a factory and training to be a professional boxer. She reached into the pocket of her apron, brought out a tiny photograph and handed it to Eleanor. The photograph showed a handsome teenage boy sitting on a horse, laughing and waving a big cowboy hat in the air. 'Raul,' she said. '*Mi hijo.*'

'*Qué bonito es,*' Eleanor said, and the *Señora* smiled. '*El le parece a su padre. Sí.*'

Señora Hernandez looked at the photograph for a moment, then put it down on the table. She wiped her eyes with the hem of her apron and began to speak again.

'Ireland,' Cherry said. 'She's saying that the ordinary people in Ireland have suffered a lot too. All the bloodshed. And they always had to leave their country, like the people here.'

Eleanor nodded. 'Oh, yes,' she said, 'we've had our fair share.'

Señora Hernandez clicked her tongue. She said something else and Cherry translated.

'All these men and their wars,' she said. 'They start all this trouble and then they leave us at home.'

'Oh, yes,' Eleanor said. 'Men love to fight about nothing.'

Her husband had been tortured, *Señora* Hernandez said. He had told her about it many times. The police had wanted some names, but he had never betrayed his friends, even though the police did some terrible things to him. She couldn't believe that men could think up such dreadful things to do to each other.

Every night when they had finished torturing her husband, they would put him in a cell with a blindfold over his eyes and a chain on his right wrist. Whenever he tried to sit down on the floor of the cell, he felt the chain being lifted up, so that he couldn't lie down and rest. He had been chained up like a poor dog, she said. And then, after a time, he had realized that the chain led through a tiny hole in the wall of his cell, and that there was a man in the next cell also, and that the chain on his own wrist was connected to the other man's wrist. The chain was so short that both men could not lie down at the same time. Her husband had started to shout to the other man. He had started to beg him to stand up, so that he would be able to lie down and sleep. But the other man would never listen.

And then someone had told her husband that the man in the next room was a senior member of the Sandinistas. They said he had been tortured so badly that he was close to death and would die very soon if he didn't get some sleep. So her husband had spent a day and a whole night standing up straight, so that the man in the other room would be able to lie down. So that the man wouldn't die. He was absolutely exhausted, but he didn't want the poor man in the next cell to die. He was that sort of person, she said. He could be generous even in a terrible situation like that.

'Well,' Eleanor said, 'you must have been very proud of him.'

The *Señora* shrugged. Yes, she said, she had been proud at first. But then after his release he had started drinking and going to dances, telling everybody all about his days in prison, about that man in the next cell. He had girlfriends then, she told them. He was nearly forty, but he started going to dances and running around with young women. He liked playing the big hero, and there was a certain kind of woman who went about with a man like that. That story of the man in the next cell, she told them, it got so that she couldn't bear to hear him tell it any more. She began to hate that man in the next cell, as deeply as a person could hate their worst enemy.

'Whatever happened to the man?' Eleanor asked.

The *Señora* said she didn't know. Nobody ever found out about him, who he was or where he was from, even if he had lived or died. Sometimes, she had to confess, she wondered if he had existed at all, but then she doubted that her husband would lie about something like that. But she was often jealous of that man in the next cell, she said, and she laughed guiltily. She was more jealous of him than she was of her husband's girlfriends, because her husband had cared more for him than he had cared for his own family. He would stand up for another man, she said, but he would tell lies to his own wife. He would look his own wife in the face and lie to her.

And then after he had disappeared she had tried to forgive all his lies. Because to tell a lie was natural in the old days, she said. Everybody told lies, all the time. It was considered the normal thing to do. Men told lies to their wives. The government told lies to the people. Children told lies to their parents. Even priests told lies. The whole country was run by lies, she said; it was a terrible place at that time.

'Cherry,' Eleanor said, 'ask her if things are better now.'

The *Señora* shook her head sadly. She looked over her shoulder, as though she expected somebody to be listening, and when she spoke again it was in a whisper. This revolution had brought nothing but heartbreak to her family, she told them, nothing but trouble and bad luck. She said that when the Sandinistas had started everyone had supported them, but now they had turned father against son. Yes, she said, they had taught the people to read, and given them land. But now they were nothing better than criminals who wanted to sell the country to Moscow. They were *ladrones*, she said, they were thieves. Daniel Ortega lived in a huge mansion, she had heard, and he had plenty of money. Tomas Borge had several cars and a house in Miami. The ordinary people had nothing, but the Sandinistas never went hungry. The Pope was against the Sandinistas, she said, and the Pope knew what he was talking about. The Pope had come to Nicaragua and told the people that the Sandinistas were not to be trusted, that they were bad for the Catholic Church and bad for the country.

They heard the children laughing and shouting inside the house. Pilar came out into the garden carrying a chair. She put it down and sat on it, then poured herself a cup of coffee. She said children were nothing but trouble and *Señora* Hernandez looked at her and laughed. She beckoned to her, and Pilar went over and knelt down. *Señora* Hernandez licked her finger and rubbed a greasy stain from her daughter's forehead.

'*Muy Sandinista*,' *Señora* Hernandez said, nudging her. '*Muy revolucionaria. Ella es como su padre.*'

'Oh, I understand.' Eleanor smiled. 'They're all great rebels when they're young. Like my fellow.'

Pilar's face reddened. The *Señora* said something else and Pilar snapped back at her. '*Oh, sí, como su padre,*' the *Señora* said. Pilar stood up and the two women began to argue. Eleanor chuckled. But gradually the argument became more heated. The *Señora* began to shout. Eleanor recognized the word *Comunistas*. Pilar shook her head angrily and her mother folded her arms. She was breathing very heavily now, ignoring her daughter. Eleanor felt uneasy. Pilar went back to her seat, looking upset.

'*Comunistas*,' the *Señora* sniffed.

'But now,' Eleanor said uncertainly, 'aren't there priests in the government, dear, to be fair? That D'Escoto fellow, isn't he a Jesuit after all?'

Señora Hernandez rolled her eyes. '*Oh,*' she scoffed, '*qué pantalones tiene.*'

Cherry giggled. 'What trousers he has,' she explained. 'What a nerve.'

Pilar stood up suddenly, glaring at Cherry. Cherry stopped laughing. Pilar started speaking to her mother again, her eyes flaring with anger. The two women spoke so rapidly that Eleanor couldn't understand anything. Then Pilar began to cry. *Señora* Hernandez wagged a finger at her, nodding her head.

'*Mentirosa,*' she snapped, raising her voice again.

Pilar ran crying into the house and her mother shouted after her, '*El amor es más importante. El lo hizo por el amor.*'

Cherry looked shocked. Eleanor leant over and whispered, 'What's she saying, pet?'

Cherry pushed her hair out of her face. 'She says Johnny got in trouble out of love, Eleanor. She says love is more important than revolution.'

Señora Hernandez shook the crumbs from her apron on to the ground and mumbled to herself. Her daughter shouted something from the house.

'And what's Pilar saying now?'

Cherry turned to look at her. 'She's saying love is fine, but bringing up a kid on your own is tough. She's saying where's the love in that?'

The *Señora* poured another cup of coffee. Her face was purple with anger. She glanced at Eleanor and tried to smile. She said she wanted to talk about snow again.

A nervous-looking guard opened the prison door and led Frank into the hall. He seemed in a very bad mood. He made Frank stand against the wall while he frisked him, patting his armpits, his back and the insides of his legs. When he had finished he stood up and stared at him, as though he expected Frank to say something. His lower lip curled up to his moustache. He pointed at Frank.

'You gonna mess with me today, *gringo*?'

Frank laughed. 'What?'

The guard suddenly reached out and grabbed hold of his collar.

'No joke,' he snapped, eyes bulging. 'You fuck with me today, *gringo*, bad trouble for you. *¿Me entiendes?*'

'OK,' Frank said, 'OK. Take it easy.'

The guard let him go and looked over his shoulder. He appeared to have heard something he didn't like. He turned off the lights in the lobby and put his finger to his lips. They stood in the gloom for a moment and then he beckoned for Frank to follow. He led him quickly through the long corridors and empty rooms until they came to the black wooden door with the enormous key in its lock. He unlocked the door and opened it, motioning for Frank to go in.

'Twenty minutes?' Frank said. 'OK? Is that OK?'

'*Diez*,' the guard said. '*Y nada más.*'

Frank walked into the room and the guard closed the door behind him. The light was dull. Somewhere a mosquito was whining. In the far corner Johnny was sitting on the floor, his hands up over his face. He seemed to be shaking.

'Son?' Frank said. 'It's me.'

Johnny moved his hands and looked up. He was crying. He tried to stand, but fell back flailing against the wall, knocking his head. Frank ran to him. Johnny's cheeks were cut and grazed. A blue-black bruise ran along his right eyeline and the eye was almost closed. His lips were badly swollen; dried blood was encrusted in the corners of his mouth. His shirt was ripped over the pocket. The backs of his hands were covered with tiny jagged cuts.

'Dad,' he wept. 'They hit me.'

'Christ. Who did?'

His voice came thick and distorted. 'The priest's guys. You're not to go to the police, Dad. Sure you won't? He knows I told you about him.'

'Johnny, Christ. I didn't say a word to anyone. I swear to Jesus. Who did this to you? The guards?'

His head fell forward and he touched his neck. 'No. He sent guys in.'

'Jesus.'

'They said you're not to go near the fucking police, Dad. You gotta deal with the priest. Nobody else. That's what they said. They're fucking serious.'

Somewhere outside a man was shouting out orders. Frank could hear the sound of boots crunching up and down on gravel. He put his arm around his son's back and tried to help him to his feet. Johnny flinched and gasped with pain, falling forward into his arms.

'Dad,' he sobbed, 'I'm scared. Get me out, Dad. Can you not get me out?'

Frank manoeuvred him over to a chair and sat him in it. Johnny's head slumped forward again. He grimaced, his eyes screwed shut, trying to stiffen his neck. His tears tracked into the dried blood around his lips, liquefying it. He looked up, trembling.

'Help me, Dad,' he said. 'Please?'

'Johnny, son,' Frank said, 'look, it's going to cost a rake of money. I have to find some way of getting it wired over. I have to get four grand, son. I'll have to go back to Managua in the morning and get a message over to Veronica.'

Johnny lunged out and grabbed his arm.

'No,' he choked. 'Don't leave me here, Dad. Don't leave me by myself. They'll fucking kill me.'

'Well, what'll I do, son? Will I try the police?'

'No, Dad. Please.'

'But . . .'

Johnny's head fell forward again. He slipped out of the chair and to his knees, grunting with pain.

'No,' he whimpered. 'If they find me out they'll lock me up for ten years. Maybe fuck me out of the country. Pilar's gonna be left on her own with the kid.'

Frank grabbed his shoulders and tried to lift him.

'Don't leave me here, Dad. Sure you won't?'

'Alright, son, alright. I'll send someone else down. Give me a chance, Johnny.'

He put his arms around his son's body and lifted him panting back into the chair. The smell of overcooked food was rising up from somewhere below them. The men were still marching up and down outside. Johnny sobbed, violently now, rocking on the seat.

'Dad, please. I'm so scared. You've got to get me out. They'll do me in.'

'Son, look at me. Nothing's going to happen to you, I swear.'

Johnny put his wrists to his head and started to wail. 'Get me out, Dad, please. Get me out. I'm frightened.'

Frank grabbed his hands. 'Trust me, son. Just trust me. I'll get you out of here if I have to tear the fucking place down with my bare hands.'

43

Jailhouse Rock

DOWN ON THE DOCKSIDE, Eleanor, Cherry and the others were sitting in the *cantina* drinking coffee. Guapo pulled a harmonica from his pocket and began to blow softly into it. The light was turning coppery now and the fishing boats were heading out into the sinking sun. Young people were strolling down the pier, linking arms and laughing together. The church bell boomed seven o'clock and the sound echoed weirdly around the high cliffs of the bay.

Suddenly they saw Frank coming back down the pier looking worn and exhausted. He stopped for a moment, looked over his shoulder, then walked on, moving quickly now, with his hands by his sides. He came into the *cantina* and sat down, smiling at Eleanor.

'Well?' Cherry asked. 'How's he doing today?'

'God, never better,' Frank said. 'Johnny's a great survivor. He was asking after everyone.'

Lorenzo went to the bar and ordered him a drink. 'Brother,' he said, 'take a little wine for thy stomach's sake. Saint Paul tells us this.'

Frank laughed. 'OK, you're on. Cheers.'

He sipped his drink and turned to Eleanor.

'Yes, he was asking after you, El. He was in much better form today.'

'Was he, Frank?' she said with a hopeful look. 'And was he alright?'

'Of course he was. Joking away nineteen to the dozen. He was saying he can't wait to see everyone again. And he wished he could come to the gig tonight.'

'Oh, praise God,' Lorenzo said.

'Smokes,' Frank said, 'I was just saying how nobody should be worrying about Johnny. I have it all figured now. You'll have to go down to Managua in the morning and send a wire over to Ireland for some money.'

'Oh, yeah, really?' Smokes said sulkily. 'Can't get his Contra pals to help out, no?'

'Listen, brother,' Lorenzo snapped. 'Are you from this country?'

Smokes peered at him. 'What's that to do with it?'

'Did you fight in our revolution, like Guapo?'

'No,' Smokes said. 'But . . .'

'Then shut the fuck up,' Lorenzo said. 'The brother made a mistake, OK? Let he who is without sin cast the first stone.'

'And you, Lorenzo? Did you ever fight for anything, huh?'

'I lost many friends,' Lorenzo said. 'I lost two cousins and a brother.'

'Oh, right. But you were too busy playing the fucking blues to fight, yeah? Too busy being the poor old blind boy who sold his soul to the devil?'

'For heaven's sake, Smokes,' said Eleanor. 'Sure, how could Lorenzo fight?'

Lorenzo laughed. 'I may be blind, brother. But there ain't none so blind as the man who will not see.'

Smokes turned away. 'Stop that now, fellows,' Frank said. 'Don't be at each other like that.'

'Frank,' Cherry said, 'I was thinking. Maybe we could sell Claudette. And our stuff. We'd get five or six hundred. And I got about three grand in the bank.'

Frank laughed. 'Not at all, pet. That'd take ages anyway. Do you hear that Smokes? Cherry wants to sell the love of your life.'

'Well, I bought her,' she muttered. 'I paid for her.'

He laughed again. 'Smokes, do you hear this terrible woman?'

But Smokes wasn't listening to Frank. He had turned in his seat and was staring out to sea, his arm on the back of the chair.

'Smokes?' Frank said.

Suddenly Smokes jumped up. He walked out of the *cantina* and

384

down to the edge of the pier, shading his eyes and looking out over the bay. Guapo tapped the side of his head. '*Está loco*,' he grinned.

'Now,' Frank said, 'are you all set up for tonight? I hope you're going to give them a good loud show. He might even be able to hear it up there.'

'Sure thing, brother,' Lorenzo said. 'We're gonna rock down the walls of Jericho.'

A minute later, Smokes came back to the table and sat down. He picked up his beer bottle and took a swig from it, looking distracted. He turned to stare at the sinking sun again.

'What is it, love?' Eleanor asked.

'*¿Qué pasa, Marilyn?*' Guapo said.

Smokes stared at them. 'I thought I saw something.' He shrugged. 'I guess I'm just weirding out.'

'Honey,' Cherry said, 'Frank was just saying we play loud tonight and Johnny might be able to hear us.'

'"Jailhouse Rock."' Guapo giggled.

Smokes grinned vaguely. Then he stood up and went back out to the edge of the pier. He squatted down on his hunkers, narrowing his eyes and staring out over the water.

'*Smokes?*' Cherry called, laughing. 'What's with you?'

People began to come out of the cafés. They walked to the edge of the pier. Some of them began to point out to sea. Suddenly three young soldiers ran out from a bar and drew their pistols. The crowd began to shout. Cherry stood up and ran out to Smokes.

'*¡Silencio!*' yelled one of the soldiers. The seagulls screamed and whirled. The waves broke against the pier.

Smokes put his finger to his lips. He was breathing very hard. Rain was starting to fall. Guapo came out of the café, leading Lorenzo by the arm. More soldiers were coming, sprinting down through the streets. A tank rolled quickly on to the end of the pier, swivelling its turret out towards the sea.

'Jesus, babe,' Cherry said. 'What's happening?'

'Didn't you see it?' Smokes breathed. 'There's something moving out there. Just past the rocks.'

'I don't see nothing. Where?'

A low droning sound drifted in over the water. The people on the pier began to shout and scatter. A man's voice shouted out

'¡*La Contra!*' There were screams. The crowd broke. People began to race up the pier and back towards the town. Others came rushing out of the bars, shouting. A siren began to wail.

Smokes stared out towards the horizon. Suddenly he stood and stepped back, as though he'd seen something horrible. 'Fuck,' he yelled. '*Fuck.*' Cherry followed the line of his shaking finger and saw a long line of dark blue speedboats emerging out of the mist.

They saw the first rocket quite clearly. It rose very slowly into the sky, travelling in an arc from the edge of the bay, high into the air, so that it looked as if it would never drop. Then slowly it swivelled around on itself. It came down towards the white rooftops at the northern end of the town and disappeared from view with a dull boom.

Orange and white light flashed over the bay, illuminating the water and the mountains. A low rumbling sound began. It seemed to come from underneath the ground. Another rocket came roaring through the air. Smokes put his hands over his ears. The sky cracked and the ground shook.

From the town came the rattle of heavy artillery fire. Streaks of blue and red tracer flame shot up into the dark sky. Over the radio speakers a calm voice announced '*EMERGENCIA. ATAQUE. EVACUEN. EMERGENCIA. ATAQUE.*'

Another rocket was winding in towards Corinto. It corkscrewed downwards and bashed into the side wall of a tall building, blowing a section of the roof straight up into the air. On the other side of town, a blossoming cloud of white flame and thick black smoke rose into the air over the oil tanks.

'Oh, *fuck,*' Smokes yelled.

Another missile flew in low, leaking sparks. It skimmed against the golden roof of the church in the plaza and bounced back up into the air, whipping around and plunging again. Another rocket whistled in towards the smouldering oil tank. There was a blaze of opal-coloured light. With a sudden roar the tank exploded. A cloud of acrid smoke billowed across the pier. There were more screams. People began to cough and cry. And by the time the cloud had cleared Smokes was nowhere to be seen.

'Honey?' Cherry called uncertainly. 'Where are you?'

Guapo was pointing his finger and roaring. When she turned around to look, Smokes was racing up the pier.

'*Hijo de puta*,' roared Guapo. '*Perro desgraciado. ¡Cobarde!*'

Guapo began to run up the pier after him. Up ahead, Smokes jumped into Claudette. The engine started. Guapo waved his fist and howled. Claudette turned, reversed violently and sped away in the direction of the town.

'*Frank*?' Eleanor screamed.

When he turned she was standing with her hands clasped in front of her body, staring up at the hill. She tried to speak, but no words would come. She pointed. The white jailhouse was burning.

They ran hard up the pier and through the flaming town. Lampposts had toppled across the streets and their naked wires were spitting out blue sparks. They ran into the square. The stage was alight and billowing smoke. Drums and guitars were on fire. On the other side of the plaza the church was beginning to smoulder. They ran across and into the Calle de la Luna. People were running in all directions, running and falling. Some were helping those who fell; others were trampling over them.

They looked back towards the dock. With a deafening gush, another oil tank exploded. Liquid flames shot up into the sky. A fat red fire engine came screaming past them towards the plaza with young men in uniform clinging to the side. All over the town, the houses were blazing now. Melting adobe dribbled from the rooftops. Scorched planks shot out of walls, bursting through the plaster. They turned up a side street. A woman staggered out of her house, spluttering, cradling a huge statue of the Virgin Mary in her arms.

In a narrow gap at the far end of the street, policemen were shouting and beckoning to people. The woman with the statue ran towards them and fell. A policeman rushed over to her and dragged her to her feet, pulling her towards the gap, leaving the statue behind in the mud. A young man tumbled out of another house with a radio in his hands. He made for the gap and the policemen stopped him. One of them pulled a gun and began to search the young man's pockets. Then he looked up and saw Frank and Eleanor. He let the young man go and began to walk slowly towards them.

Cherry turned. 'Frank,' she urged, 'get out of here.'

'No.'

'Francisco,' Guapo hissed. '*¡Fuera, hombre!*'

The policeman began to quicken his pace.

'Run, Frank,' Cherry gasped. 'He's gonna want your permit.'

Lorenzo grabbed Frank's arm. 'You just beat it, brother. You wanna get us in trouble with the man?'

Up ahead the policeman stopped. He was staring down at the statue of the Virgin Mary, nudging it with his foot. Suddenly Cherry took hold of Lorenzo's hand and dragged him into a side street. The policeman looked up and shouted. He turned around and called to his comrades. Guapo shouted at the policeman, then darted into the alley after Cherry and Lorenzo.

Frank and Eleanor turned and ran back into the Calle Morazan. They saw another rocket come down. It swooped out of the sky and slammed into the front wall of an apartment block. They turned left and ran towards the square. Fire seemed to rain from the clouds.

Men and women were smashing windows and jumping through the jagged glass. Flames belched from the buildings all along the street. Streaks of fiery light were arching up from the sea and into the town. Searchlight beams swept across the sky. The sound of gunfire and explosions split the air. Frank and Eleanor ran on towards the Calle Grande.

Suddenly the policeman appeared from around a corner, running towards them with a rifle in his hands. Frank made to turn. The policeman aimed his gun. '*¡Alto!*' he yelled. '*¡Alto, hombre! ¡Manos arriba!*' Frank and Eleanor stopped, panting. They put their hands on their heads.

'*¡Alto!*' the policeman shouted. '*Momentita.*'

Frank stared up the hill towards the prison. Yellow flames were spitting out of the roof now. The policeman approached cautiously, pointing his rifle at them. He grabbed Frank by the wrist.

'*Pasaporte y permiso, yanqui.*'

He pushed Frank up against the wall. A soldier appeared from around the corner. He ran down the street and forced Eleanor to put her hands behind her back. The policeman began to search their pockets. He took out two pairs of handcuffs and blew his whistle. He stuck out his leg and pushed Frank against it, tripping him up and shouting something.

'Eleanor,' Frank murmured, 'what's he saying?'

'Frank,' she said as she sank to her knees, struggling for breath, 'he's saying that if anyone moves they'll be shot.'

44

Broken English

WHEN FRANK WAS TAKEN into the interrogation room at the
police station a sergeant was waiting for him behind a desk. The
Sergeant was a big moon-faced man who smelt of sour sweat and
aftershave. For some minutes he said nothing at all. He just stared,
and then, taking an orange out of his desk, he began to rip off
the skin with his eyes still firmly fixed on Frank.

A soldier came into the room carrying a portable typewriter.
The two men spoke to each other, but Frank couldn't understand
what they were saying. They didn't smile at each other once.
They just kept looking across at him, jerking their thumbs in his
direction and speaking very quietly.

Suddenly the Sergeant stood up. He began to stroll up and
down the room, shouting out questions in broken English. The
soldier tried to keep up with him, his fingers clattering hard
on the noisy typewriter. The Sergeant wanted to know what
Frank and Eleanor were doing in the middle of the war zone
without a permit. He wanted to know who had brought them
into the zone and where they had been going when they were
arrested.

'No entiendo,' Frank said.

The Sergeant turned to the soldier. 'Oh,' he said, raising his
eyebrows. 'No entiendo.' He looked back at Frank.

'No entiendo,' he said, 'drug man.'

'No,' Frank said.

The Sergeant glared at him, then nodded his head towards the
door. The soldier stood up and walked out of the room.

The Sergeant opened his desk and took out a truncheon. He
slapped it against his thigh. He began to walk up and down the

room again, smacking the truncheon against his leather glove.

'*No entiendo*,' he murmured. '*No entiendo*.'

'No,' Frank said, 'I don't understand you.'

'You are a drug man.'

'No, I'm not.'

The Sergeant pointed at him. 'I think you are a drug man.'

Frank tried to laugh. 'No.'

The Sergeant whipped around and smashed his truncheon down hard on his desk. 'For why are you here in Corinto?' he shouted. 'For why?'

'I don't understand.'

He began to shout in Spanish, walking up and down the room and yelling until his face was bright red. He slammed his truncheon on the desk again. He pointed it at Frank and shook his head with fury.

'Why are you here in Corinto?'

'I have nothing to say.'

The Sergeant nodded and put down his truncheon. He took his pistol out of its holster and placed it on the desk.

'Why are you here in Corinto?'

'I'm a tourist,' Frank said, his voice quaking. 'I didn't know I wasn't supposed to be here. I want to call the Irish embassy in Mexico.'

The Sergeant sneered and spat on the floor. '*Tu madre*, drug man.'

He went to the door, opened it and yelled. A young policeman marched into the room.

The policeman pulled Frank to his feet and marched him up the corridor, then down a flight of stairs and into a narrow passageway. There were small cells all the way down the left side, some with open doors. The policeman took him to a cell and pointed.

'No,' Frank said, 'you can't put me in there.'

The policeman smiled. He pointed again.

'No way, son,' Frank said. 'I'm not going in there.'

The policeman lunged at him. He punched Frank hard in the stomach, pushed him into the cell and slammed the door closed.

'*¡A la mierda!*' the policeman yelled.

The cell was completely bare except for one dim light bulb and a steel bucket. Frank lay on the floor for a few moments, breathless with pain, listening to the sound of water dripping. He could hear nothing else. He stood up when he could and went to the door.

'Eleanor?' he called. 'Can you hear me?' His voice seemed to echo, but there was no reply. He shouted her name again. A drunken voice started to sing in a cell further up the passageway, but there was still no answer. A soft buzzing sound came from the light bulb. He wondered about Johnny. Was he alright? Had he got out of the burning jail? Where was he now? He found that he was too exhausted to concentrate. He lay down on the floor and tried to sleep.

Some time later he was woken by the young policeman and told to get dressed. He was taken out of his cell, up the stairs and back to the interrogation room. The Sergeant was sitting at the desk with his head in his hands. The room stank of stale cigarette smoke. The policeman sat Frank down in a chair, then left him alone with the Sergeant.

The Sergeant did not look up. 'For why are you here in Corinto?' He spoke very quietly, putting equal weight on each word.

'*No entiendo.*'

'For why are you here in Corinto?'

'I don't understand.'

'I ask you one more time, *hombre*. You will tell me.'

'I have nothing to say to you. I am an Irish citizen.'

The Sergeant sighed. He took his hands away from his face and pointed at Frank.

'OK,' he said. 'You have very big trouble now.'

He pulled a pack of cigarettes from his breast pocket and lit one, letting the exhaled smoke drift back into his nostrils. He took another long drag and peered at Frank for a while, a weary expression on his face. He shook his head. He held the cigarette upright between his finger and his thumb.

'Now,' he said, 'you will take off your shoes please.'

'What?'

The Sergeant stood up. 'You will please take off your shoes and your stockings.'

Frank bent down and unlaced his shoes, feeling faint and sick with fear, his fingers shaking uncontrollably. He peeled off his socks and tucked them into his shoes. He looked back up at the Sergeant.

'Come here,' the Sergeant said, sounding almost bored. Frank stood up and walked across the room.

'Your hands. Put your hands here.'

Frank held out his hands and closed his eyes. The Sergeant took the cigarette out of his mouth. He held it close to Frank's face.

'For why are you here in Corinto?'

'*No entiendo.*'

The Sergeant nodded. He pulled a pair of handcuffs from his belt and motioned for Frank to put his hands behind his back. He turned him around and hooked the handcuffs on his wrists, then pushed him gently over towards the wall. He kicked his legs apart, so that he almost fell over.

'For why are you here in Corinto?'

'Call Nuñez,' Frank stammered. 'Call Captain Nuñez at the Interior Ministry, and call the Irish embassy in Mexico.'

The Sergeant put his hands on Frank's shoulders and turned him around. He stared into his eyes.

He grasped Frank's shirt collar, manoeuvred him towards the chair and told him to sit down. He went to his desk and lifted the telephone off the hook. He opened a drawer and pulled out a red tie. Then he took his chair and came back, placing it in front of Frank.

'Put your feet,' he said.

'No,' Frank said.

The Sergeant sighed. He lifted Frank's naked feet on to the chair, then knelt down, wrapped the tie around his ankles and knotted it tightly to the chair back. When he had finished he stood up again, cracking his knuckles. He took the cigarette butt out of his mouth and held it in front of Frank's face.

'For why are you here in Corinto?'

'I have nothing to say.'

'For why are you here?'

'I am an Irish citizen.'

The Sergeant bent low. He peered into Frank's face.

'Drug man,' he said. 'You fuck your bastard mother, because I am fucking your father.'

393

Frank turned his eyes away. 'Call Nuñez,' he said.

The Sergeant stood up and stamped his cigarette out on the floor. He went to his desk and wrote something down in a notebook. He picked up his telephone and dialled a number. He turned his back as he spoke, then he slammed the phone down and pointed.

'Big trouble for you now, drug man. Very big trouble for you.'

The Sergeant went out of the room and closed the door. Frank was left alone for what seemed like a long time. After a while he leant his head forwards and tried to sleep.

Some time later two soldiers came into the room. They untied his feet and told him to stand up. They asked him if he knew the Hernandez family, and he said yes. Then they looked at each other, nodded and told him to come with them.

He asked to see Eleanor, but they said that wasn't possible. He asked for his shoes and socks, but again they said no.

They took him out of the room, down a long corridor and into the lobby of the station. To his astonishment, he saw Pilar standing by the counter with an older woman. She called out to him, but when he tried to go over to her the policemen held him back. She said something he didn't understand. The older woman tried to move towards him, but the policemen blocked the way, holding her arms firmly, arguing with her.

Outside, it was raining heavily. Two police cars were waiting in front of the station, their rear doors open. The policemen took Frank to the first car and one of them got in, beckoning to Frank to follow. When he refused, the other policeman grabbed his arms and bundled him into the car. Then he got in himself and closed the door.

They sat in the back of the car for a few minutes. The two policemen laughed and chatted to each other, but he couldn't understand what they were saying. Then the door of the police station opened again, and Eleanor was led out, barefoot and in handcuffs. She was limping heavily and she looked terrified. Pilar and the older woman ran out after her.

Frank called out her name and tried to open the car window. One of the policemen hit him on the arm with his truncheon.

'That's my wife,' he shouted. The policeman hit him again with the butt of the truncheon, then grabbed his inner thigh and pinched hard at his flesh.

'OK,' Frank yelled. 'Jesus, OK.'

He watched as they took her to the second police car and put her in the back. A soldier came out of the station carrying Frank's holdall bag. He walked to the second car and banged on the roof, then came over to the car that Frank was in and jumped into the driver's seat, shaking his wet hair. He looked in his mirror and started up the engine. They pulled slowly out of the police station and the second car followed.

'Where are you taking me?' Frank asked.

The soldier grinned. '*No entiendo,*' he said.

They seemed to be driving out of the town, but he wasn't sure. The cars moved slowly, with their red lights rotating. Panic gripped at his stomach. They were taking him away and there was still no word of Johnny's safety. Was he still in the jail? Had the prisoners been moved? Should he say something to the guards or would that cause more trouble? Where were the police bringing him? He tried to look for landmarks, but he recognized nothing. Then suddenly he saw the little white church with the '*Cristo Viene*' sign over the door. They drove down past the *hospedaje*, then past the garage where José Ortega worked. The cars were still moving very slowly and Frank couldn't gauge where they were heading. He had an odd sensation of driving around in a circle. He recognized nothing for a while, then suddenly he saw the signpost for the Pan-American. They drove down the sliproad for about half a mile and then out on to the highway.

Helicopters were hovering over the long straight road, their searchlights sweeping across the fields. The police cars began to pick up speed. They turned on their sirens. Frank had an idea that they were going south, back towards Managua, but he didn't know. They came to a roadblock. Over on the apron of the highway plain-clothes officers with machine guns were searching a car. Soldiers shone their torches through the windows on to Frank's face. He turned and tried to catch sight of Eleanor behind him. One of the policemen grabbed him by the ears and turned his head around.

They drove on and there were more roadblocks, the same routine every time, a flash of torches in through the windscreen, a wave of a white gloved hand. After a while he asked one of the policemen to tell him the time, but the policeman shook his head and said no. He kept falling asleep and waking up with a terrible sickening shudder, not knowing where he was. Eventually he decided to try to stay awake.

After about an hour he realized that they were definitely travelling south. He felt stupid. If they had been going north they would have been in Honduras by now. That was alright. They were taking them south, back down to Managua.

He wondered how long the drive would take. He tried to recall what Smokes had said about the journey from Corinto to Managua. Was it five hours? Eight hours? Ten? He couldn't remember. It was very hard to stay awake, although he tried to for as long as he could. But the highway was very dark on both sides and there was nothing at all to concentrate on. He saw a signpost for Managua. 180 km. He tried to watch out for the signs then. It would be a good way to stay awake. He saw 170 km, 155 km. He tried to keep his eyes open. 145 km. After the seventh or eighth signpost, he fell into a deep sleep.

When he woke up he felt hot and thirsty. The two policemen were asleep on either side of him. Dawn seemed to be coming and the sky was streaked with blue light. They drove for about another hour and then slowly the yellow haze of the city came into sight.

As they moved through the empty streets of the city, he recognized the *mercado* and the shattered spire of the cathedral. They headed south towards the lake, then turned up along the Calle Julio Buitrago, pulling in eventually at the car park of the Imperial Hotel. Frank was told to stay where he was.

The driver got out of the car and sprinted up the hotel steps. Frank watched while Eleanor was taken out of the second car. He asked to be allowed speak to her, but the two policemen shook their heads again. He managed to wave as they took her up past the taxi rank and into the building. She nodded at him and made a thumbs-up sign.

Ten minutes later the driver came out and got back in the car. Frank was driven down to the Paseo Salvador Allende, to the police station in the Barrio Monseñor Lescano. He recognized the building as they dragged him out of the back seat. He had passed it one night and watched women playing bingo in a little hall across the street. It was only two minutes' walk from Smokes's house.

They took him into the station and he was told to wait while an officer behind the counter filled in a form. Then they led him up two flights of stairs and put him in a cell. He was too tired to argue now. They took off his handcuffs and brought him a cup of bitter coffee. Then they closed the door and locked him in.

The cell was small and built of brick. There was a bunk bed with a folded grey mattress, a wooden chair, a small table and a metal toilet in the corner. He sat on the bed and tried to drink some of the coffee. Compared to Corinto, he thought, this was absolute heaven.

He laughed to himself, remembering a night when the police had come to the house in Glenageary. Some of the neighbours had called them, saying that there was a disturbance going on in Frank Little's house. Frank had come home to find Johnny with bruises on his lips, and he and Eleanor had had a terrible row. She had been drunk and had fallen down the stairs, grazing her face. When the police came, she accused him of beating her, and they took him away. They had been friendly enough, but they had taken him down to Dalkey police station and put him in a cell for the night. They refused to listen to any arguments. It was a terrible night. It was just before Eleanor went to England. But he realized that he would have given a lot to be back in Dalkey police station now, and somehow that made him laugh.

He lay down on the bunk and tried to sleep, but there was so much noise in the building that he couldn't. He could hear men shouting and the sound of the morning traffic starting up on the street outside. He moved his chair to the window and stood on it. All he could see was a line of tall scrawny trees and a slim patch of blue sky. Then, craning his neck, he could just make out the bank of the lake down to the right, and the fires lighting in the windows of the shattered cathedral, where the poorest people in Managua lived. He remembered Smokes showing him the fires on his first night in Managua. The poor people went there at night, to take shelter in the ruins. He wondered about Eleanor. He hoped they had left her in the Imperial Hotel. He hoped she was going to be alright. He wondered about Johnny. What had they done to him? He closed his eyes, a sudden nauseating lightness filling his mind. Had he been burnt? Would he ever see his son again?

A couple of hours later the cell door opened and Captain Nuñez walked in carrying a briefcase. He was wearing jeans and a denim jacket, black sunglasses and the cap from his military uniform. He looked in a very bad mood.

'*Buenos días, Señor* Little,' he snapped. 'I have the great pleasure to see you again.'

Frank stood up. 'You're in trouble, Nuñez. You can't treat me like this.'

Nuñez sat down at the table.

'Where is your son, *Señor*?'

'You know damn well where he is. I want to see my wife. I'm very concerned about her.'

'You cannot be that concerned, *Señor*. You have subjected your wife to a very foolish adventure. Where is your son?'

'He's in the jail in Corinto. I want to see my wife.'

'Your wife has been placed under house arrest at the Imperial Hotel. She will remain there until you decide to cooperate.'

'I want to telephone my consulate.'

'Where is your son, *Señor*? This is very serious.'

Frank said nothing.

'I am asking you where your son is, *Señor*. Do you want to help him or not?'

Frank lit a cigarette. Nuñez shook his head.

'You know perhaps what day it is tomorrow, *Señor*? It is the nineteenth of July. It is the sixth anniversary of our revolution.'

'Big deal,' Frank said.

'Yes,' Nuñez said. 'Yes. We have survived for six years. We will not be undermined now. People like your son disobey our laws, but I warn you firmly that we will not be undermined.'

Nuñez put his briefcase on his lap. He pulled a notebook and a pencil from his pocket.

'*Señor* Little,' he said, 'you and your family are in very serious trouble. I want to help you before it is too late. We are investigating a plot. Drugs are moving through our country, from Costa

Rica, across our northern border and into Honduras. There they are exchanged for guns for the counter-revolutionaries. Certain organizations in other countries are involved.'

Nuñez paused and lit a cigarette.

'We are now aware that your son is involved. You know of course that he escaped from the jail in Corinto during the attack last evening?'

Frank's heart skipped. 'No, I didn't know that.'

'Come, *Señor*? Did you not assist him? You gave him money perhaps? A weapon maybe? You will tell me where he is now, please?'

Frank scoffed. 'You're ridiculous.'

'What are your son's political views?'

'He's one of your lot, isn't he? One of your bloody Trotskyists.'

Nuñez laughed bitterly and wrote something down. 'Political theory is not your strong suit, *Señor*. Tell me about your own ideological views.'

'I work for a living, Captain. I can't afford the luxury.'

'Oh, come!' Nuñez scowled. 'What do you think of our revolution, *Señor*? It is a very simple question.'

'I don't know what I think of it.'

Nuñez wrote in his book again. He pulled on his cigarette, then stubbed it out on the floor.

'*Señor*,' he said, '*Comandante* Borge has authorized me to make an offer. The *Comandante* is prepared to be lenient if your son cooperates. The *Comandante* knows that your son is not a serious criminal. He is very foolish, but he has played only a minor role. He will give us the names of his contacts, and he will find that the Nicaraguan people are very merciful.'

Frank sighed. 'I don't know where he is, Nuñez. I thought he was in the jail.'

'*Bueno*,' Nuñez said, slapping his notebook closed. 'We will see how a spell as our guest here will assist you to see things with more clarity.'

'You can't hold me here. I'm an Irish citizen.'

'We have contacted your consulate in Mexico, *Señor*. Your rights will be fully respected, and so will ours.'

'You can't hold me here. I'll inform your superiors.'

Nuñez suddenly raised his voice. 'I decide what we can do,' he said. 'I decide, sir. *I*. Not you. Your son has broken the law. And you too have broken the law. You might reflect on that.'

He stood up and went to the door of the cell. He knocked hard on the metal and shouted something. Then he turned around.

'Look, *Señor* Little,' he sighed, 'I am a father also. You are in trouble. Why do you not help me to make things better for you? Why do you not tell me where your son is?'

'You're the one in trouble, friend. The police up in Corinto assaulted me.'

Nuñez nodded. 'You must make a complaint. If you have been treated improperly, I assure you that those responsible will be fully disciplined.'

'They threatened to fucking torture me.'

Nuñez tutted and shook his head. 'This is regrettable. But you were very lucky, *Señor*.'

'Lucky?'

'Yes. Before the revolution they would have killed you.'

He snapped his fingers. 'Like that,' he said. 'They would not have even thought about it actually.'

He rapped on the door of the cell again and a soldier came to let him out.

When Frank woke up the cell felt sticky and hot and his head was pounding with pain. He went to the window and pulled back the filthy curtain. He stood on the chair and stared down over the exhausted city. Through the trees he could make out long lines of people moving silently through the streets, carrying red and black banners over their shoulders.

He heard the distant booming of loudspeakers coming from the direction of the square. '*Uno, dos, tres. Uno, dos, tres.*'

He padded over to the door of the cell and tried to open it. Then he knelt down on the floor and began to do some press-ups. His arms ached and he grunted with the effort. He wondered what time it was and how long it would be before Nuñez came back again.

He called the guard and asked for a book. They had no books in English, the guard said. Prisoners were only allowed to read the bible, and that would be in Spanish. Frank told him that would be alright, but when the guard came back he said he hadn't been able to find one.

He lay back down on the bed and thought about Johnny. He wondered if he had made it out of the country, and how long he would last without any money. He hoped he would have the sense just to get a plane ticket to Ireland, if that was possible. Would it be possible though? Could you fly to Ireland from Honduras? Probably not. He might have to go to America. Then he remembered that Johnny had no passport. He had left his passport with the dead German. So even if he could get out of Nicaragua, how would he ever get home to Ireland? If he managed to get up to Mexico, would they give him a passport in the consulate up there? Could he get on a boat maybe? And what about Pilar? What would happen to her now? And what would happen to the child? He closed his eyes and groaned out loud. He couldn't think about these things now. He would have to think about himself and Eleanor.

They brought him some bread rolls and a glass of water. The power was off, the guard explained, so there was no coffee. It was Ronald Reagan's fault. Frank sat on his bed and tried to eat the bread, but it was stale and hard.

About an hour later he thought he heard a familiar voice out in the corridor. He jumped off the bed and went to the door. When it opened, Eleanor was standing there, breathless and excited. The guard stood beside her, watching them carefully.

'Eleanor,' Frank said, 'are you alright?'

'I'm fine, Frank. Are you?'

'You were limping.'

'I just trod on a stone, Frank, that's all. How are you?'

'They're not putting you in here, are they?'

She shook her head and whispered, 'I told them you had a heart condition. I told them you'd drop down dead if you didn't get your pills. I said I wouldn't trust anyone to give them to you.'

She pushed a bottle of tablets into his hands.

'They're just vitamin A,' she said. 'They don't know.'

'But are you alright?'

'I'm fine, Frank. I'm fine. There's no time. How are you? Did you hear Johnny's after getting out of the jail?'

'Yes, yes. They didn't do anything to you? You were limping.'

'No. I just hurt my feet the other night. I'm fine, Frank. Look, I rang the embassy in Mexico.'

'*Señora*,' the guard said. '*Por favor*.'

'Listen,' Frank said, 'ring Billy Spain, will you, in Dublin? He's at the Taoiseach's office. And don't say anything to Nuñez about Johnny.'

'I can't, Frank. They've cut the phone off in my room.'

'Well, fucking try, can't you. Try. You just ring him and tell him I'm a fucking constituent of Garret FitzGerald's, alright?'

'But you're not, Frank.'

'Well, Christ almighty, Eleanor,' he hissed, 'I mean, he won't fucking know that, will he?'

45

Uncle Sam

IT WAS LATE AFTERNOON in Corinto and the breeze swept in from the sea, carrying the smell of jacaranda and cordite along the shattered streets. Some of the houses in the old part of the town were still smouldering. Squads of soldiers were searching the flooded ruins in the hope of finding survivors. Armoured cars and jeeps sped up and down the *avenidas*. The plaza was awash with dirty water, cluttered with scaffolding, piles of brick, roof tiles and shattered, smoking planks. The walls of the town hall were scorched black. A woman wept in the shadow of the church, a framed photograph of a teenage boy in her hands. High over the city, vultures spiralled in the clouds.

In the little *cantina* halfway down the pier, Cherry was sitting at a table with Pilar and wondering what to do. Pilar told her again what had happened. When she had seen the burning jail she had rushed down to the police station with her mother to tell them about Johnny, only to discover that Frank and Eleanor had been arrested and were being taken back down to Managua. She had been ordered to wait. Then, at two in the morning, the police had come back from the jail and explained that thirty prisoners had escaped and that the young man with the German passport was one of them. They had detained her for an hour and asked a lot of questions. She'd had to tell them Johnny's full name and date of birth and give a full description of him. She was sick with worry now. She didn't know where Johnny would go.

All the windows in the *cantina* were broken and the floor was still littered with broken glass. Outside on the pier, people were standing in groups talking about the Contra attack. At least twenty people had been killed; scores had been injured. Some of the fires had burnt for hours. The hospital had been hit. There were rumours that the Americans would send in the marines later that night, that the Contras were advancing on Managua from the south, that Ortega and the rest of the *Dirreción Nacional* were planning to flee to Cuba. There were rumours, too, that the priest had been killed, but nobody knew for sure.

Guapo and Lorenzo came in and sat down, looking exhausted. They hadn't been able to find Smokes or Claudette anywhere. The town was crawling with American pressmen, they said, and the helicopters were still coming in from Managua.

'We're gonna have to get back down there,' Lorenzo sighed. 'Thumb a ride from one of the press guys.'

Guapo agreed. He said they couldn't help Johnny now and they'd have to find Frank and Eleanor. They ordered beers and Cherry told them she had something on her mind. 'And what's that, sister?' Lorenzo said briskly. Cherry cleared her throat.

'Well, hey, guys, we gotta wait and see if Smokes turns up.'

'No, we don't,' Lorenzo said. 'Fuck him.'

'*Coño*,' Guapo muttered. '*Cobarde*.'

'But, guys, there's Pilar too. We can't leave Pilar here.'

Pilar said she'd be fine. She wanted to stay in Corinto, and in any case Johnny might show up at her mother's house. They drank their beers and left the *cantina*, walking up into the town with her. The stench of oil was heavy in the air. There were soldiers and police everywhere, and the streets around the plaza were full of people queuing to see doctors and paramedics. Many of the buildings had been completely destroyed. The cathedral had been badly damaged; the front wall had collapsed in on itself and the steeple had a hole slashed all the way down.

'Hey, Cherry,' a voice called. 'That you?'

Cherry turned to see Hollis Clarke standing on the pavement and peering at her. He took off his hat and came over.

'Cherry,' he laughed, 'what are you doing here? Are you alright?'

'Oh, great, Hollis,' she said. 'Your guys sure had a result last night.'

Clarke looked uncomfortable. 'Yes.' He nodded. 'It looks real bad. Are you OK?'

'You know how many people got killed here last night, man? You gonna tell them that back in fucking Disneyland?'

Clarke's smile froze on his face. He put his hat back on.

'Save that peacenik horseshit for your boyfriend, Cherry.'

A young man came over carrying a television camera on his shoulder. Clarke took a map and a notebook out of his pocket and began to speak to the man in Spanish. He pointed to the map and the cameraman nodded. Clarke laughed and clapped him on the back. The cameraman turned, beckoning to a young soldier who came loping over with a long cigarette hanging out of his mouth. '*Bueno*,' Clarke said, '*nos vamos*.' He turned towards Cherry again.

'I suppose you wanna ride?' he said. 'I'm going back down to the bright lights.'

'No,' Cherry said. 'I'm fine.'

Clarke laughed. 'Listen, Cherry, don't get sore now, but I was out on the *carretera* an hour ago and I saw poor old Claudette. She was burnt out, honey. I mean she's gone to the great big wrecking yard in the sky. Now, I'm not asking you what happened here, I'm just offering you a ride.'

'Have you seen Smokes?'

'Oh, yeah,' Clarke sniggered, 'like, you don't know where he is, right?'

'I don't,' she said. 'Do you?'

He peered at her. 'You don't?'

'Nope.'

'Oh, Christ,' Clarke sighed, and the grin faded from his face.

'Cherry, look, I thought you knew. He was arrested last night out on the *carretera*, just after the raid started. Seems he was doing ninety and they got suspicious, you know – a damn *yanqui* doing ninety towards Managua in the middle of a damn Contra attack. He's in the *Policía*. Apparently, he was clean. He had a *permiso*, but then the dumb fucking sap confessed to bringing *gringos* into the war zone.'

'Fuck,' she said.

'Yeah, right. Fuck. I just went up to the *Policía* to see him, but he asked me not to do anything. He said his damn family would be upset if they heard.'

'You're really not going to?'

Clarke sniggered. 'Jesus, what do you think? Of course I'm going to. I like Smokes, you know. He's a naive son of a bitch, but, hey, I'm into innocence big-time.'

'Oh, God,' she said, 'I better go get him out.'

Clarke stared up at the sky. 'Cherry,' he said, 'now I'm not gonna ask you what's going on here, but I got the feeling you're in big trouble. There's a couple of nice folks ain't been seen around their hotel in Managua for a few days. Eyebrows have been raised here, you know? You go waltzing up to that *Policía* and something tells me you're not gonna be seeing a *Cuba libre* again for a long time.'

'But I can't leave him in jail, Hollis.'

He put his hand on her arm. 'Look, don't be fucking stupid, Cherry. I'm gonna call up his folks soon as I get back to Managua. It's all gonna be kosher, believe me. Don't be a jerk.'

She turned and looked back at the town. Away in the distance a plume of thin white smoke was drifting from the peak of Yalaguina. She thought about Frank and Eleanor. 'Yeah.' She nodded. 'OK, you're right.'

'Believe me,' he said, 'I *am* right. You just get back to Managua and see what's working out. Come on, I'll give you a ride, OK?'

'I dunno,' Cherry said. 'Smokes wouldn't like it.' Clarke sighed and looked down towards the sea.

'Oh, come on,' he muttered. 'One American to another. Let me help you out, OK?'

Cherry hooted with laughter. Clarke shrugged.

'Oh, well, suit yourself.' He turned to walk away.

'I got two friends with me,' she said. 'They ain't Americans.'

'Never mind.' He beamed. 'I'm sure they have their moments.'

Clarke grinned as he shook hands with Guapo and Lorenzo. '*Mucho gusto. Mucho gusto, hombres.*' He clapped Lorenzo on the back and told him he liked his suit.

They kissed Pilar goodbye and told her they'd come back to see her as soon as they found out what had happened. Pilar hugged Cherry hard, then turned back and headed in the direction of the plaza. They walked out of the mangled town, past heaps of shattered masonry, collapsed houses, soaked and charred furniture thrown out into the streets. Guapo led Lorenzo carefully by the arm and the cameraman went ahead.

'Poor old Claudette,' Clarke sniggered. 'I'm really gonna miss seeing her around. I guess Smokes must be *muy triste*.'

'Fuck it, Hollis. You think he's gonna be OK?'

Clarke looked suddenly serious. 'He'll be fine, Cherry. Don't worry. I gave him some dough. I told the goons that Ortega's a personal friend of mine, and if anything happened to dreamboat they'd end up shovelling shit on a state farm.'

'Yeah,' Cherry said. 'Look, thanks, Hollis, OK?'

The grin returned in an instant. 'Hey, *por nada*. I ain't so evil actually, Cherry. I'm a registered Democrat, you know.'

She laughed. 'Oh, get off the fucking stage, man. You musta joined the Democrats because Lincoln was a Republican.'

He shook his head in mock desperation. 'Honey,' he sighed, 'you just don't know who your real friends are. That's your trouble.'

The cameraman stopped and beckoned. They walked on together around the corner. A small black helicopter sat in a field, surrounded by a gang of armed men in blue jeans and baseball caps.

'Well, now,' Clarke said, clapping his hands.

'That's your transport?'

'Yup. I chartered it. Beautiful thing, ain't she?'

Clarke took off his hat and fanned his sweating face.

'Uncle Sam deserves the best,' he said.

46

Nicaragua, Nicaraguita

ON THE MORNING OF Revolution Day, Frank was awakened by
the sound of the church bell down in the *barrio*. He got off his
bunk, stood on his chair and looked out through the cell window,
straining to see something.

The square sounded as if it was absolutely full already. He
could hear people laughing and cheering. Someone was making
a speech, but the microphone was booming and he couldn't catch
the words. He listened for a while and then a man's voice started
to sing.

> *Ay Nicaragua, Nicaraguita*
> *La flor más linda de mi querer*
> *Abonada con la bendita*
> *Nicaraguita, sangre de Diringen*
> *Nicaragua, sois mas dulcita*
> *Y ahora que sois libre*
> *Nicaraguita*
> *Yo te quiero mucho más.*

When the song was over the crowd roared with applause.
  '*¡Patria libre!*' yelled a man's voice.
  '*¡O MORIR!*' the crowd called.
  '*¡Viva el Frente Sandinista!*'
  '*¡VIVA, VIVA, VIVA!*'
  '*¡Viva Nicaragua libre!*'
  '*¡NI SE VENDE, NI SE RENDE!*'
  The sound of Michael Jackson singing 'We Are the World' came

bursting out over the intercom. Frank stood on tiptoe and tried to see over the treetops. Suddenly the cell door slammed open and Nuñez came in.

'*Señor* Little,' he snapped, 'you are doing some sightseeing. But you are very fond of sightseeing of course.'

Frank got down from the chair and sat on the bed.

'*Bueno*,' Nuñez said, 'it is an instructive sight. It is unfortunate that you cannot see it. There are a quarter of a million of our people in the square today.'

'Spare me, Nuñez.'

'Spare yourself, sir. Tell me where your son is.'

'I have nothing to tell you about that.'

Nuñez sat down and pulled out his notebook. 'The *Comandante* has instructed me to say that he will be lenient. Certain facts have come to light now.'

'What facts?'

'Well,' he said, 'shall we say that we understand your son has a close friend, the daughter of a great hero of our revolution.'

'He has lots of close friends.'

'*¡VIVA NICARAGUA LIBRE!*'

Nuñez's eyes narrowed with anger. He pointed. 'I warn you, it is better if you cooperate with me, *Señor*. We do not want to subject the young *compañera* to needless distress at this difficult time. You will tell me all you know of your son's criminal activities.'

'Tough luck, Nuñez. My son's halfway to Mexico by now.'

'*¡VIVA NICARAGUA LIBRE!*' the crowd roared. '*¡NO PAS-ARAN!*'

They started to clap in time. '*¡NO PASARAN! ¡NO PASARAN! ¡NO PASARAN!*' The voices were chanting now, growing louder. Nuñez cocked his head and listened. '*¡NO PASARAN! ¡NO PASARAN!*' He looked back at Frank and nodded. He wrote something down in his book, stood up and knocked on the door of the cell.

'*¡NO PASARAN! ¡NO PASARAN! ¡NO PASARAN!*'

'You leave me no option, sir,' he sighed. 'You will come with me to the court now.'

'I thought it was Revolution Day,' Frank said. 'They'll be closed.'

'No,' Nuñez said without turning. 'Sadly not, *Señor*. There are people like you every day of the week.'

Outside the jail a police car was waiting. Nuñez opened the back door and told Frank to get in. Then he got in himself and the driver took them up the Calle Amanda Espinoza to the Imperial Hotel. Nuñez got out and Frank waited. The driver switched on the radio. It seemed to be broadcasting the demonstration in the plaza. Frank could hear the chant of the crowd over the car speaker. Five minutes later Nuñez came back out with Eleanor. He led her down the steps and told her to get in the car.

'Are you alright?' Frank said. She looked very scared.

'Yes,' she whispered. 'I'm fine.'

They began to drive down through the town in the direction of the lake. Most of the main streets had been closed to traffic, so they had to inch their way through the side streets. All the way down the Calle Williams Romero and the Avenida Bolívar, people were still moving in long lines towards the plaza with placards and banners over their shoulders. The car came to a barricade, and a soldier with a red ribbon around his neck looked through the window. When he saw the Captain he stood to attention and saluted. Then he took off his cap and scratched his head. There was no way through, he said; the crowd was just too big.

The driver turned the car around and drove back up towards the city centre. He turned on to the Paseo Benjamin Zeledon and then took a road that rose up to form a bridge over the Laguna. The roar of the crowd seemed louder now. '*QUEREMOS LA PAZ. QUEREMOS LA PAZ.*' The sound echoed and became distorted. The streets near the western entrance to the plaza were packed with people cheering and waving flags. Over to the east, there were crowds on the roof of the cathedral, looking down into the plaza. Away in the distance three helicopters hovered over the lake.

They drove on through the streets of the city without speaking. Red and black bunting had been strung across the rooftops. There were Nicaraguan flags and cardboard cut-outs of Sandino's sombrero in the windows. Groups of young people were wandering around in fancy dress. Open-air parties were going on in many of the streets and loud music boomed out from steel bands and salsa groups. Children ran alongside the car with red and black balloons. Everywhere people were dancing.

They drove across the *periferico* and pulled up at a stern-looking two-storey building with police cars and jeeps lined up outside. Nuñez got out and told them to wait. After about ten minutes a man in uniform appeared on the steps and called out to the driver. Frank and Eleanor were taken into the building, down a corridor and into a grey room that smelt chalky and had no windows. A moment later Nuñez came in, unbuttoning his jacket. Frank stood up.

'You can't try us without a lawyer, Nuñez.'

'I am not trying you, *Señor*. I am applying for an expulsion order. You will leave our country within seventy-two hours.'

'Well, now,' Frank said, 'I'll be going nowhere until I decide.'

Nuñez nodded. 'We will see what the judge says about that, *Señor*.'

'Captain,' Eleanor said, 'if you're not trying us, what are we doing here?'

'*Señora*, can you tell me anything about your son's criminal activities?'

'Now listen here, Nuñez,' Frank interrupted, 'for God's sake. Look, he got into some trouble and he made a mistake. Now he's out of the country. What harm is done? Can't you just let it be?'

Nuñez stood up. 'I have a surprise for you.'

He went to the door and opened it. Three policemen came in, looking hot and sweaty. Behind them, wearing handcuffs, came Johnny Little.

His face was a mass of blood-flecked bruises. He was limping heavily and his right forearm was bandaged. Eleanor ran to him and wrapped her arms around his chest, trying to hug him. He moved away and sat down stiffly.

'Jesus, son,' Frank said, 'are you alright?'

Johnny nodded but didn't speak.

'But, Johnny!' Eleanor whispered. 'What happened to your face, Johnny?'

He said nothing.

'Now,' Nuñez said, sitting down again, 'I have explained the position to your son. He is unwilling to help us by revealing the names of his contacts, so he has two choices. He can leave the country with you in seventy-two hours, or he can stand trial for aiding the *contrabandistas*.'

'Son,' Frank said, 'are you going to come home?'

He shook his head and spoke in a hoarse voice. 'I can't leave Pilar by herself, Dad.'

'Could you not bring her too?'

Johnny shrugged. 'Her life is here.'

'But, love,' Eleanor said, 'you can make a life anywhere.'

He glared at her. 'Yeah, well, I can't exactly see her in fucking Glenageary, Ma, can you?'

Nuñez sighed. 'I have to tell you that the court will appoint a public advocate to represent your son, should he persist in this foolishness.'

'Well, Johnny?' Frank said. 'What's the story?'

He shrugged. 'I've no choice, Dad.'

'A mistake,' Nuñez said. 'We all have choices, *compa*. We are the sum of our choices, no?'

Johnny pursed his lips and exhaled. The room seemed unbearably hot now. He peered up at Nuñez.

'I can't tell you, Captain,' he said. 'I just can't take the risk.'

Nuñez stepped towards him. 'Just give us a name, *hombre*. Please. I guarantee that nobody will harm you or the *compañera*.'

Johnny shook his head. 'You don't get it, man. He's got people everywhere.'

Nuñez looked at Frank and Eleanor, holding out his hands in a gesture of resignation.

'*Bueno*,' he sighed, '*nos vamos*.'

The soldiers stood Johnny up and led him out of the room.

The courtroom was long and narrow and airless. Metal benches lined the walls. The judge, a middle-aged man with a red face, was sitting behind a squat wooden desk. He was wearing a black gown with a blue and white sash. A Nicaraguan flag hung on the wall behind the desk. Beams of dusty sunlight shone through the dirty windows. There were two tables in front of the desk. A couple of prisoners sat at one, with lawyers and soldiers beside them. There were more lawyers at the other table. There was a wooden witness stand. Cherry was sitting on a bench near the front. When

412

she saw Frank and Eleanor she stood up and ran to them.

A uniformed man turned and hissed at them to be quiet. They all sat down and watched the judge speaking. He hit the desk with his gavel and the two prisoners were led away. The judge stood up and left the court and the lawyers leant across and began to chat to each other. Guapo came into the room with Lorenzo on his arm. They slid into the bench behind Frank and Eleanor.

Five minutes later the judge came back in and sat down behind the desk. He poured a glass of water from a jug, looked up and nodded at his clerk. The clerk shouted, and three soldiers led Johnny in while the clerk read out the indictment. A young woman lawyer came in behind Johnny wearing a black gown and carrying a couple of files. They went to the top of the room and sat down at the table on the right. Nuñez came in with the prosecution lawyer and a man in a civilian suit. They bowed to the judge and sat down at the other table. They whispered to each other and then the prosecution lawyer stood up.

The judge listened while he spoke. The lawyer kept pointing at Johnny and raising his voice. He seemed to be very excited. At one point the judge took off his glasses and peered down at Frank and Eleanor. When the lawyer sat down, Nuñez stood to give his evidence, reading out long sections from his notebook in a strong and efficient voice.

Cherry explained that Johnny was being charged with illegal entry into the war zone and trafficking in marijuana. Nuñez was asking for a custodial sentence. Johnny was pleading guilty to both charges, but he had told his lawyer that he had nothing else to say because he wanted to protect the innocent. His lawyer stood up and spoke to the judge. The judge seemed to be listening very carefully. Then the prosecution lawyer got up again and shouted. The two lawyers began to interrupt one another. The judge held up his hand and they both stopped speaking and sat down, exchanging hostile glances. The judge leant forward and scribbled for some minutes. Then he asked Johnny to stand.

He said he would give the accused the choice of leaving the country permanently or going to jail for a year. Johnny's lawyer leant close and whispered to him. Johnny shook his head firmly. The lawyer stood up and spoke to the judge. The judge nodded and wrote something down. He stared at Frank and Eleanor. He cleared his throat, then asked Frank to stand up. He began to speak in a calm, slow voice that had a slight American accent.

'*Señores*,' he said, '*Comandante* Borge's office has asked me to sign an exclusion order in both your names, which I propose to do. Your son is choosing to stay in our country and be punished. Do you understand?'

'Yes, your honour,' Frank said.

'*Señor*, thank you, but there is no need to address me in that manner. Judge is sufficient.'

'Judge, I just want to say that my son made a mistake and that he was trying to protect the innocent.'

The judge shrugged. 'Protecting the innocent is what our law is for, *Señor*. That is not for your son to decide. He has disobeyed the law. He will go to prison for one year. You understand this? Do you have anything to say about this?'

'I understand, judge.'

'You understand that your son will be imprisoned for a year? That we are showing leniency because of your son's family situation? Also because he surrendered to the authorities.'

'He surrendered?'

The judge looked at the papers on his desk and nodded. 'He escaped from the prison and surrendered to the authorities in Puerto Morazan. This is why the sentence is only one year.'

Frank nodded. 'Thank you, judge.'

'*Señor*, you do realize that your son is refusing to cooperate with our security forces? That he is tying my hands?'

'Your honour, my son is concerned for his family's safety and his own responsibilities.'

The judge paused and looked at his notes again. He peered up and beckoned to Johnny's lawyer. She went to his desk and began to speak to him. The judge shook his head and whispered. After a moment the lawyer came back to the table and sat down.

'There will be the statutory visiting rights,' the judge said. 'Now, do you have anything to say about your own actions, *Señor* Little? You appear to have committed several violations of the civil code. Entering the *zona* without a permit. Resisting arrest.'

'I wanted to find my son, sir. I'm sorry.'

'*Señor*, the law allows me to fine you very heavily for these misdemeanours. Do you understand that?'

'Yes,' Frank said.

'However,' the judge said, 'today is the *Aniversario del Triunfo*. It is a special day for the Nicaraguan people, and so rather than enforce the law to its letter, I would like to invite you on behalf of the people to make a gesture of solidarity. I am thinking about a voluntary contribution of one thousand American dollars to the Hospital Karl Marx. Do you accept my invitation?'

'Yes,' Frank sighed.

The judge leant forward and whispered to his clerk. The clerk nodded and wrote something in his notebook. Then the judge folded his arms and began to speak rapidly, staring down at Frank.

'I hereby grant the exclusion order, in the name of Frank Little and Eleanor Little. You will give an undertaking to leave the jurisdiction within seventy-two hours. You will not return to the jurisdiction for a period of three months. Thereafter you will not return to the jurisdiction without prior notification to the *Ministerio del Interior* in writing. You will surrender your visa to the clerk of the court immediately. You will not approach any embassy, consulate or honorary consulate of the Popular Republic of Nicaragua for the purpose of obtaining a visa for a period of three months.'

He took off his glasses.

'Do you understand me, sir?' Frank nodded. The judge sighed and hit the table with his gavel. Everyone stood up and bowed as he left the room.

The soldiers put Johnny's handcuffs back on and began to lead him down through the court. He seemed to be trembling, and limping more heavily now. His eyes swept over the benches and he nodded at his friends, trying to smile. 'Courage, brother,' Lorenzo called. As they approached the entrance door at the back of the room, the guards in the doorway moved aside. Suddenly Johnny stopped. His shoulders slumped.

Out in the passageway, Pilar was standing under a long narrow window. The bars in the frame cast a cruciform shadow across her body. She turned and the light caught the side of her face. She and Johnny stared at each other. He stepped forward and whispered her name. The guards put their hands on his shoulders and led him quickly away down the corridor.

47

Anything Is Possible

THE NEXT AFTERNOON, while Eleanor was at Mass, Cherry
came over to the Imperial Hotel. She bumped into Frank in the
lobby and he offered to buy her lunch. They ate cold meat and
limp salad and listened to the band playing country songs. Cherry
said she was going back home to America.

A letter had come while she was away to say her mother wasn't
at all well now. The cancer was spreading into her lungs and she
hadn't got very long left. Cherry wanted to see her while there
was still time. And she'd had enough of Nicaragua anyway. There
wasn't much left here now that Lorenzo and Guapo were breaking
up the Desperados. Guapo was going back to Ocotal to kick
around for a while with some girl he'd met up there and Lorenzo
was moving home to Bluefields. She was going to miss them,
she said. Things weren't going to be the same without Lorenzo
and Guapo.

After lunch they went to sit by the pool. When he told her he
was still worried about Johnny, she said she thought he'd be alright
in the jail in Managua. At least people could visit him there. And
he was a long way from the priest. Guapo had gone to see him
the night before, and he'd said Johnny couldn't believe Frank and
Eleanor had come all this way to find him. He just couldn't believe
it. He'd been crying about it, Guapo had told her.

'Yes, well,' Frank said, 'that gentleman is like his bloody
mother. He cries too easily. Any news on your fellow today?'

'Yeah. His dad is coming down next week to bail him out.'

'His dad? I thought Smokes's old man was dead?'

Cherry scoffed and shook her head. 'No way, Frank. I suppose
he fed you all the card-shark stories too, huh?'

'Are they not true, no?'

She took a sip of her *Cuba libre*. 'Frank, his father is George Bush's local campaign manager and he publishes encyclopedias in Portland, Oregon. He's, like, a multi-millionaire.'

'Good Jesus,' Frank said. 'Well, I hope you're after the offspring for his money.'

'Yeah, really,' Cherry said. 'His dad cut him off without a nickel ten years ago. See, he got arrested in Los Angeles one time for passing a bad cheque in a liquor store. Bounced all the way home to Daddy.'

Frank sighed. 'Sacred Heart of Christ, Cherry, what the blazes are you doing with that fellow?'

She shrugged and pushed her hair out of her eyes. 'I dunno. He's not a bad person, Frank. I guess I thought he needed me.'

'A good foot in the arse is what he needs.'

She laughed softly. 'Well, you're the one talks about stayers, babe. I guess I'm a stayer. I'm like you. Ain't that funny?'

'Fucking hysterical,' he said. 'We've both got "Welcome" embroidered on our backs.'

She smiled. The sun washed down over the white stones. She reached out and hugged him.

'Oh, Frank,' she said, 'I'm really gonna miss you when you go.'

The pale pink room was hot and full of flies and the light from the high windows was dim. A wall of steel bars bisected the space. Bored-looking guards with truncheons in their belts strolled up and down on both sides of the grill setting out plastic chairs. On the prisoners' side were three pool tables, a long steel food counter and a basketball hoop high on the back wall. A bell rang. Some prisoners came in and sat down at the bars. There was no sign of Johnny. Frank sat and waited. He watched one of the prisoners strumming a guitar. On the other side of the bars a young black woman in a red dress was singing to him. He hated this room. It smelt of sweat. He wondered where his son was. He felt tense and sick. Eventually Johnny came in and sat down. He was wearing a blue tracksuit and had his long hair in a ponytail.

'Christ, where were you, son?'

'Sorry, Dad. The lawyer was here. She's trying to get me more visits.'

'Oh, right.' He paused. 'Well, how is it?'

'It's jail, Dad. How do you think? How's the Imper?'

'Oh, grand. I'm just down the way from your mother.'

'Lucky you.'

'Yeah. Look, I tried to get that stuff for you. The soap and the toilet paper. Guapo said he'd bring them up tomorrow. He's taking us out to the airport.'

Johnny nodded and turned to stare across at the prisoner who was playing the guitar.

'So, you're alright anyhow?'

'Yeah, Dad.'

'And you still have your balls?'

He smiled reluctantly. 'They're not like that since the revolution.'

'I'm joking, you gobshite. Did you have your chat with Pilar?'

'Yeah, yeah. She's coming again tomorrow.'

'She's a lovely bit of stuff now, I must say. She must be getting between you and your sleep.'

'We're having a kid, Dad. It makes a difference.'

'Must be great to be young and in love.'

Johnny shrugged and looked down the row of visitors. 'I never said anything about that.'

'You know, son, I was just thinking. Do you remember a time I took you into Mushatt's shop, down in Francis Street?'

Johnny rolled his eyes. 'No, Dad. I don't remember that.'

'Ah, you do. Old Mrs Mushatt was there. She was mad about you. She always told me you'd end up with a rare beauty, but I never knew how right she was.'

'Yeah. Look, is Ma alright?'

'I suppose so. She's not in here after all.'

Johnny sniggered. 'She'd love to be in here. There's nothing she likes better than being the fucking martyr.'

Frank laughed. 'You're right. She'd be driving them all mad with her talk.'

'Yeah. Give us a fag, Dad, will you?'

Frank patted his pockets and pulled out a pack of cigarettes. A guard came over and took it from him, peering into it. Then he dropped it through the bars, and Johnny lit one.

'How's Arsenal doing, Dad?'

Frank shrugged. 'I don't know.'

'Is Stephen Roche riding the Tour de France this year?'

'Jesus, son, you're a gas. I've more on my mind than that.'

Johnny tore a piece of card from the cigarette box and began to clean his fingernails.

'You know, Johnny,' Frank said, 'your mother isn't a bad person. We were very fond of each other when we were younger.'

'Yeah, yeah, Dad. Your good times. I heard.'

'We were the best of pals, your mother and me. There was a lot of feeling there.'

'I know.'

'And you were the best thing that ever happened. You were the gravy, son. God, when you came along, we thought we had it made.'

Johnny looked at him. 'I know, Dad. Don't go on about it.'

'I'm not going on, Johnny. I'm just telling you. In case they take you out at dawn and fucking behead you.'

His son peered at him. 'Yeah, well, you always said I'd a neck like a jockey's bollocks, Dad. So I'd like to see them fucking try.'

The bell jangled on the wall. Johnny looked up at it.

'Five minutes,' he said.

'Listen, son, don't get rattled now, but your mother's outside. She'd love to see you before we go. Just to say so long.'

Johnny shook his head. 'No, Dad.'

'Son, look, please? Do me one favour. She'll be bending my ear all the way back to fucking Shannon if you don't.'

Johnny looked down the row at the young woman in the red dress. She was still singing to the prisoner. Some of the guards were eyeing her, nudging each other and laughing.

'Please, son? Do your old fellow a favour? I mean, it's a fucking long flight back to County Clare.'

Johnny nodded his head briskly towards the door. 'Go on.'

Frank turned and spoke to the nearest guard. The guard went to the metal door and unlocked it. Johnny folded his arms. Eleanor came in wearing a white dress and a straw hat, a *malinche* flower in her buttonhole. She walked towards them, looking distractedly

419

around the room. She came to the bars and sat down beside Frank.

'Now,' Frank said. 'Sure, this is great. Here we all are.'

'Hello, Johnny,' Eleanor said. 'I just wanted to say hello.'

'Hello, Mother.'

'Are they feeding you?' she asked. 'Do you have things to do?'

'Yeah, Ma. It's practically Disneyland.'

'Do you know,' Frank said, 'apparently fruit is a great thing. You know, for a balanced diet.'

Eleanor reached into her handbag and pulled out a tissue.

'And I was just saying to him, Eleanor, that Pilar is a lovely-looking girl. I was saying how old Mrs Mushatt always said he'd end up with a beauty queen.'

The bell jangled again. Eleanor put the tissue to her eyes and began to cry.

'Well, then,' Frank said gently, 'I suppose that's starter's orders. We'd want to be making a move.'

She wiped her face. He buttoned his jacket and put his hand on her shoulder.

'Come on, pet,' he said. 'It's time to go now.'

She stood up, gnawing her lip. Frank took her hand and squeezed it.

'Everything will be fine,' he said. 'I bet you anything we'll all be laughing about this together soon.'

'Take care, love,' she whispered, 'won't you?'

He didn't look at her.

'You know, Johnny,' Frank said, 'your mother would love to see the nipper. I mean, when the time is right.'

'I'm sure she would.'

'Well, God, naturally she would, son. Eleanor just wants to be a glamorous granny.'

'I'm sure she does.'

'Of course she does,' Frank said. 'First grandchild and all that. Sure, that'd be nice for all concerned.'

Johnny exhaled a mouthful of smoke. 'You both know where he'll be.'

Eleanor stepped forward. Her face contorted with tears.

'Do you think that would be alright, Johnny? For me to see the baby when it comes?'

He looked up at the ceiling. The bell jangled again. All the other prisoners stood up.

'I suppose anything is possible,' he said.

The guard came over and told them to leave. Eleanor reached out and pushed her hand through the bars, taking hold of her son's fingers. She held them for a moment and he looked at her. She touched the side of his bruised face. Tears welled up in his eyes. He nodded.

'You better split,' he told her. 'You'll get me in trouble.'

'*Por favor, Señores.*'

'So long then, old son,' Frank said. 'Don't forget now, keep the faith.'

'Yeah. Look, I better go, Dad.'

Frank reached through the bars, feeling tears pricking his own eyes now. 'Keep the old flag flying, scout. We'll miss you.'

Johnny stared down at his father's hand. He nodded, turned around and walked back towards the metal gates.

48

The Wild Colonial Boy

ON THE LAST NIGHT they had dinner with Guapo, Cherry and Lorenzo. They went down to the Bar Casablanca afterwards and ordered *Cuba libres*.

The bar closed at two o'clock, but the manager said they could sit in the lobby and have some more drinks. A few people came out and sat around in the fat armchairs, and after a while some of them started to sing. An American journalist with a beautiful bass voice sang 'Joe Hill'. Someone else sang 'The Wabash Cannon-ball'. Guapo tried to chat up a very attractive woman from Wales, who was over in Nicaragua to help lay telephone wires.

Frank watched Eleanor, who was sitting in the corner with Cherry. She looked very tired, he thought, but still as beautiful as ever. He listened to the singing. He sat with Lorenzo and Guapo and a couple of other people whose names he didn't even know. There was a lot of drinking, and a lot of arguing, and then more people started to sing. Cherry stood up on a table and sang 'The Tennessee Waltz'. At about four o'clock he saw Eleanor slip quietly up the stairs towards the lifts.

Another tray of drinks came out from the bar. But there was no more singing now. People were huddled in close-knit groups, talking very quietly together. The barmen came out and began to play poker for dollars. Guapo went down on his knees and whispered to the Welsh woman, kissing her hand until she stood up and told him to get lost and staggered off to her room. After a while the manager bustled out into the lobby and started to turn on the lights. Everybody groaned, but he said it was nearly dawn now. It really was time for bed.

Frank kissed Cherry goodnight. He shook hands with Lorenzo

and Guapo and he watched from the lobby as the three of them tottered arm in arm down the road towards the Barrio Monseñor Lescano. He watched for a long time, waiting until he was sure they had gone from sight. Then he slipped out of the front doors of the Imperial Hotel and walked down the hill into the battered city.

The morning was cool and very quiet. He walked all the way down to the edge of the lake, enjoying the silence and the stillness of the sweet-smelling air. He picked up a flat stone and tried to skim it across the grey water. He found himself thinking about his father.

He remembered being in Glendalough with his mother and his father. It was one day in the summer after the war had ended. It was a hot summer day, so very bright that you would not think the sun had ever gone down the night before. They had walked all the way around the lake and someone had told a story about Saint Kevin. A woman had once fallen in love with Saint Kevin, and he had thrown her into the Glendalough lake, and someone had written a song about it. It was a bottomless lake, people said. It went down all the way to hell. If you fell into that lake, you would have no chance at all.

On the way back home they had stopped at a small café in Roundwood for tea and sandwiches. A little band had been playing patriotic songs, he remembered. People had been dancing to the music. It was the 1940s. People were still patriotic in Ireland then. Everyone knew someone who had fought for Ireland in the old days. It was long before the North. It was still an innocent time, a time when it was alright to believe in something called Ireland. The band played 'Kevin Barry' and 'The Rising of the Moon' and 'Bold Robert Emmet, the Darling of Erin', and when they started into 'The Wild Colonial Boy', his father and mother got up to dance.

They waltzed around the little room, laughing in each other's arms. And his father had been so smooth and deft in his movements. He had never seen his father move like that before. It was astonishing to Frank. He had never seen his father look more manly, or his mother more elegant. And after the dance was over, his father had wrapped his arm around his mother's waist and kissed her hard on the mouth, and all the children had laughed out loud. It was the first and last time he had ever seen his parents dance. He could remember the pleasure of it so clearly that it hurt.

He remembered sitting on the bus back to the city, watching the yellow lights glisten in the distance over Dublin Bay. The world had seemed to be bursting with possibility. He remembered thinking about his father and mother in each other's arms, kissing, and feeling breathless with joy at what he had seen. And then his mother had held his hand in the bus and told him they would be home soon. He remembered the love in her voice. *Hold my hand, Frank. We'll be home soon*. He had never felt more safe. It was the first summer after the war. It was the summer he met Eleanor Hamilton, the summer his father lost his job. It was the time when everything in his life began to change.

He walked back up to the Imperial Hotel as the sun began to redden the sky behind him.

When he went up to his room, Eleanor was lying on the bed beside his, fast asleep, a copy of the bible face down and open across her thigh. He tried to be as quiet as possible, but she mumbled, seeming to sense his presence. She sat up with a start and looked around.

'Oh, Frank,' she said, 'I'm sorry.'

'Shush, love. You're alright.'

'I fancied a fag. I came in to filch one and I got reading. I must have dropped off.'

'Stay where you are,' he whispered. 'There's two beds.'

'Oh, no. I'll slip next door.'

'Don't be soft. You're grand there.'

She lay back down and put her hands to her head.

'What time is it?' she asked hoarsely. 'I was getting worried.'

'I only went for a saunter. That shower of bowsies had me drunk as a lord.'

'They're good kids, Frank.'

He sat on the other bed and opened the collar of his shirt. His neck felt sunburnt and raw as he reached down to slip off his shoes.

'We said we'd write to each other,' she yawned. 'Cherry and me.'

'Good.'

'And Lorenzo and Guapo are coming over later. Lorenzo is dying to see you again before we go.'

'Oh, there was a message about that, Eleanor. That embassy fellow's after arranging the tickets. It's Aeroflot, Mr Little, he says to me.'

'Good, Frank.'

'I don't know what's so fucking good about it. The tax I pay, I was expecting fucking Concorde.'

'God,' she said, 'weren't they in great voice last night? I thought we'd all be put out.'

'There's nothing like singing.'

'Would you not take your shoes off, Frank? If you're going to lie on that good bed.'

'My shoes are off, Eleanor. Are you blind?'

He lay flat on his back and folded his arms across his chest. Outside the birds were beginning to chirp and whistle.

'Frank,' she said, 'you wouldn't be able to sing to me, would you? I'd love to hear one of the old songs.'

'God, you're a panic. At this hour of the morning?'

'Please, Frank?'

He coughed. 'Sure, I've no voice any more. I couldn't think of a song anyhow.'

'You could so, if you tried. Any old come-all-ye.'

He put his hands over his eyes, feeling the start of a hangover. His temples throbbed and he could not concentrate.

'Well, now.' He laughed. 'On your own head be it.'

'Go on, Frank.'

He took a deep breath and sat up, leaning his hands back on the pillows. Pale sunlight slanted through the curtain. He tried to keep his voice very quiet as he began slowly to sing to her.

> O believe me if all those endearing young charms
> Which I gaze on so fondly today
> Were to change by tomorrow and fleet in my arms
> Like fairy gifts fading away
> Thou wouldst still be adored
> As this moment thou art
> Let thy loveliness fade as it will
> All around the dear ruin each wish of my heart . . .

He stopped, feeling hot tears in his eyes. He whispered to her that he couldn't remember any more of the words, but she did not answer him.

He walked into the bathroom and went to the toilet. He filled the sink with hot water and shaved. When he came back out she was curled up on her side, sucking her thumbnail. She had fallen asleep again. He walked over to the bed and moved a few strands of hair from her face. He took a blanket from his own bed and put it gently over her sleeping body. She mumbled something, but she did not wake up.

He touched her hair again. 'Oh, Eleanor Hamilton,' he whispered.

He looked at his sleeping wife. The rain was starting to fall now and he listened to the sound it made on the roof of the Imperial Hotel. He went to the window and opened it wide, peering down through the heavy curtains.

Blue smoke and the smell of cooking food were rising up from the Ciudad Sandino. Down by the lake the fires were already burning in the windows of the ruined cathedral. Far in the distance, a soft grey mist obscured the peak of Momotombo.

He walked very quietly from the room and closed the door behind him, leaving her asleep in the dull pink light. He went down to the lobby and woke up the cashier. He got a pile of *córdoba* coins and rang Veronica in Dublin.

They talked about Aeroflot. They talked about love. They talked about how much he was looking forward to coming home.

When his money ran out, he sat in the lobby and waited for the dining room to open. He was very tired now and nothing at all seemed to be moving in the Imperial Hotel. There was silence, except for the sound of the rain. He felt like the last man in the world. He closed his eyes and waited, listening to the sound of the rain.

Joseph O'Connor

Cowboys and Indians

All alone, with only his electric guitar and his overactive ego for company, Eddie Virago, proud owner of the last mohican haircut in Dublin, leaves his home town to find fame in the wild world of the London rock scene. A bewildering array of acid-house ravers, saloon-bar revolutionaries, music biz wideboys and media primadonnas all seem oh-so-anxious to help Eddie on his way . . .

'Eddie Virago is the best fictitious Irish immigrant to arrive over here since Edna O'Brien sent *The Country Girls* to London over twenty-five years ago. With *Cowboys and Indians*, Joseph O'Connor emerges as the most immediate voice to come out of Ireland in years'   *Mirabella*

'This is an impressive debut: a good story, well told, great characters, with sardonic, very knowing digs at youthful pretension . . . clever, wry and often hilarious'   *Time Out*

'Well-written, tremendously confident . . . O'Connor has managed the almost impossible: he has created a thoroughly unlikeable hero whom the reader, while detesting, actually worries about. An excellent debut'   *Irish Independent*

'Very funny . . . full of sharp, tightly-focused realism . . . This is an immensely readable and entertaining book, full of truth about the world we live in, without a dull moment'   *Sunday Independent*

'*Cowboys and Indians* has characters that leap out at you like figures in a pop-up book. Joseph O'Connor's first novel suggests he's bound for fame'   *Observer*

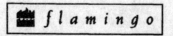 *flamingo*

Joseph O'Connor

True Believers

'First, the good news: Eddie Virago's back. The hero of Joseph O'Connor's widely acclaimed novel *Cowboys and Indians* features in the first of thirteen stories that make up *True Believers*, and he makes a tasty entrée. Now for the great news: there's plenty more where Eddie came from.'   *The Times*

Opening with the story that won the *Sunday Tribune* Hennessy First Fiction Award, *True Believers* projects the reader into a world of characters stunning in their variety. Here are sad-hearted priests, old friends, young lovers, rockers and rebels. Here are runaway husbands and runaway wives. Here are jokers and fanatics, punks and poets, thinkers and drinkers, chancers and killers. Here are the true believers, all clinging to some kind of faith in a mutable and dangerous world.

'With an acute ear for speech patterns and a nice line in self-irony, O'Connor has a gift for fixing a person or place in a phrase. The laureate of the rising Irish generation, he combines the demotic wit of Roddy Doyle, the social concern of Dermot Bolger and the structural guile of Colm Tóibín. A significant writer of a very contemporary kind.'   *Irish Times*

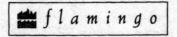

flamingo

Kate O'Riordan

Involved

'A striking debut by an original and strong writer.'

DERMOT BOLGER

When Kitty Fitzgerald falls for Danny O'Neill it seems nothing could spoil their perfect relationship. Not even their very different backgrounds. But the carefree Danny Kitty knows in Dublin is not the person she finds when they both travel North to meet his family.

The O'Neills – Ma, the formidable matriarch, her daughter Monica, and the disturbed and menacing eldest son Eamon – are bound by blood and history to a past they can never forget. As time goes on long-kept secrets rise to the surface and Kitty finds herself locked into a bitter struggle for the possession of Danny's soul. . .

A superb debut, *Involved* is an extraordinarily powerful novel about love and obsession, the intricate pull of family and blood, and the dangerous arrogance of those who seek to loosen the ties that bind.

'A truthfully imagined and gracefully tense first novel from a terrific storyteller.'

JOSEPH O'CONNOR

ISBN 0 00 654761 3

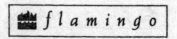

Brian Moore

No Other Life

'Brian Moore is a brilliant narrator. *No Other Life* is comprehensive, delicate and mysterious.'   Kate Kellaway, *Observer*

When Father Paul Michel, a missionary on the desperately poor Caribbean island of Ganae, rescues a little black boy, Jeannot, from abject poverty, he has little idea of the dramatic and perilous events the future holds in store. Jeannot becomes a revolutionary Catholic priest and is subsequently elected president of a land previously accustomed only to despair and dictatorship. A brilliant messianic orator, Jeannot bravely urges his black brethren to rise against the forces determined to topple him. But is he a saint or a rabble-rouser? Even Father Paul can no longer be sure of his protégé's true motives . . .

'In this explosive book Moore brings a world pulsatingly to life, with vivid descriptive writing and a series of beautifully accurate vignettes.'   Anthony Curtis, *Financial Times*

'Poised, bracing and moving . . . if pleasure indeed corrupts the soul, then this very novel is a twenty-four carat sin.'
                    Tom Adair, *Independent*

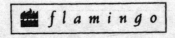

Brian Moore

The Statement

'Unputdownable is the only word to describe Brian Moore's masterly opus. It is utterly riveting.'

MARK PORTER, *Sunday Express*

Pierre Brossard is on the run. For his life. From a determined squad of unknown hit-men. From his former 'friends'. From his past. Condemned to death *in absentia* by French courts for crimes against humanity during the war, he has been in hiding for over forty years. Now, perhaps, justice will be done.

'Once you have opened its first page you won't be able to stop reading. A superbly plotted story with a brilliant twist.'

A. N. WILSON, *Evening Standard*

'*The Statement* blends conscience and guilt with fast-moving storytelling. Brian Moore is a man of profound human insight as well as a master storyteller . . . the most subtle, most readable, least pushy of guides.'

ANTHONY THWAITE, *Sunday Telegraph*

'A thriller in which crises of conscience are as tense as the escalating manhunt . . . *The Statement* has a tightly controlled pace, its plots converging against the clock. There are false denouements and cunningly concealed clues. Brian Moore unseats the conventional conclusion of his plot with something much more strange and disturbing . . . it contains a relevation so mysterious that it resonates far beyond the pages of the book.' LAURA CUMMING, *Guardian*

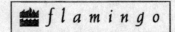 *flamingo*